PARTLY SUNNY

By

TERRY LEE

Featherstone Creations

Cover: Christina Keats
Editor: Maxine Bringenberg
Publisher: Featherstone Creations

Dedication

To Taylor, Jackson and Joshua who remind
me _every_ time I see them what love looks like…

A special thanks and hug to Renie, my beta reader (Beta-Gram☺),
who helped so much not only throughout the entire story of
Partly Sunny,
but also, after a four-hour stint at Starbucks, assisted
in creating Ms. Viola's backstory.

And to Maxine Bringenberg, my editor,
for laughing and crying at all the right times in my stories…

Chapter 1

The dark room flickered with the shadows from the muted television screen. A thread of light wormed its way through a slit in the blackout drapes. Darcy lay face down on a bed, her head dangled over the side.

One eyelid inched open and slammed back shut. Her mind plummeted down a black hole, and her body felt nailed to the bed. *Where am I?*

I haven't a clue. Her inner voice, the voice of reason and often sarcasm, obviously had plunged down the same black slippery slope.

With effort, she forced her eyelid up again. Carpet. Rose-colored carpet and painted red water snake Jimmy Choos. The color clash churned her stomach like a cement mixer ready to explode. The shoes she claimed…the carpet…no way. She'd never go with…what color was that anyway? Her mother, stuck in the eighties, would call it mauve, which she knew for a fact because everything, e-v-e-r-y-t-h-i-n-g in her mother's house had been power-washed with country blue and this, this…color.

With more strength than she knew she had, she heaved her weighted body over to her backside, which sent firebombs shooting behind her eyes. She pressed fingers into her eye sockets to stop the ricocheting pinballs. She needed to preserve brain cells.

Her head felt like a Mr. Potato Head on a tooth pick when she lifted it to pan the room. This wasn't home. She'd *die* for these high dollar furnishings. Must be a hotel room. A nice one. Darcy's eyes fixed on the plasma TV mounted on the wall. She pawed around on the bed till her hand located the remote, then aimed it toward the screen.

"Watching out for you, News 3 Today, Las Vegas."

"Ah, Las Vegas." She blew out air. The panic vibrating through her body subsided. She hadn't been drugged or kidnapped, and her parents wouldn't need to send a fat wad of money for her release: which was a good thing, because they didn't have money. Not fat wads, anyway.

Oh yeah, Becca's wedding. Tonight at the Bellagio.

The clock radio beside the bed beamed 9:59 a.m., and the message light on the phone was blinking. She dropped the remote and hoisted herself into an upright position, steadied her bobble head, and pushed play.

"In case you're wondering, Lisa and I got you up to the room last night." Miranda's brass-filled voice could direct traffic. "The door key thing is on the dresser by the TV, and I've got your cell phone. What's with you and tequila anyway?"

The mention of tequila stirred some of Darcy's remaining comatose brain cells. Miranda yelled at what Darcy could only imagine to be some innocent guy admiring Miranda's curves. "Don't forget Boop, 11:00 at the pool," she said, and ended the call.

Darcy closed her eyes and forced air into her lungs. "Poor guy." She shook her head ever so slightly. "She's such a bitch." Rethinking the disjointed message, Darcy propped her hand under her chin to add reinforcement to her head.

You should have known a lethal dose of something had glued your tongue to the roof of your mouth.

Her peripheral vision spotted a bottle of Evian beside the clock radio. She snatched the water and chugged. A split-second later she bolted off the bed, barely reaching the toilet before the water came back up.

Sinking to her knees, Darcy grabbed a washcloth.

That went well.

She stayed on the icy marbled floor for a few minutes to insure, as much as possible, that there would be no more heaving. She didn't need that nonsense today.

She showered, did a half-assed job of blow-drying her hair, then threw on khaki capris and a black tank. After digging through her suitcase, she slipped her feet into a pair of Jack Rogers Navajo sandals. A glance in the mirror suggested her hair needed some help. She twisted the almost-dry wad and secured it to the back of her head with a large clip, then grabbed her key card, Gucci shades, and fake Coach purse and shuffled down the hallway to the elevator.

***

Becca, her smartest and richest friend, would exchange vows with fiancé Brian at the Bellagio. Darcy and Miranda had booked a room across the street at Bally's. Leaving the coolness of the lobby, the dry heat of September smacked Darcy across the face. She was used to heat, for Christ's sake—she lived in Houston—but this wasn't the humid dog days heat that clung to the body like a wet blanket. This was serious. The high and dry Las Vegas fieriness shot at her from all directions, pinging her skin like darts.

Danger, Will Robinson.

She touched her head to make sure it was still attached.

Her watch read 11:15. She forced one foot in front of the other, used the handrail for support, and inched her way across the arched walkway over South Las Vegas Boulevard. The royal compound, The Bellagio, loomed ahead.

"Okay, I can do this." Her voice sounded hoarse and far away. Brunch, pedicures, manicures, hair, make-up, and then…oh God, say it's so…a nap.

She found her friends at a small poolside table near the cabana Becca had reserved for brunch. The women sipped mimosas, their boisterous babble drawing stares from several of the other cabana occupants.

Spotting Darcy, Miranda held up a fluted glass. "Mimosa, Boop?" Miranda nicknamed everyone, and Darcy was Betty Boop. The "Betty" had died off sometime after middle school, but "Boop" stuck.

The women's chatter silenced and they exchanged quick looks.

"No mimosa." Darcy sank into the chair next to Miranda and thunked her head on the table.

Miranda winced. "That's gotta hurt."

"Is there an air conditioned hole I can crawl into?" Darcy asked.

"What in the hell happened last night?" Lisa signaled the cabana waiter. "Bloody Mary, please."

Although face down, she could see Lisa directing the Bloody Mary her way. The waiter nodded and made his exit. "That's *my* question," Darcy said. She desperately needed something starchy to soak up the alcohol before she could even think about a Bloody Mary.

"I knew we should have gotten her out of there sooner." Becca swiveled around in her pool chair, her turquoise dangle earrings swaying.

"What do you remember?" Miranda asked.

"Eating at Margaritaville." Darcy raised her head. "Then what?" Her stomach knocked around in her midsection. She wondered if she needed to puke again. "Anyone got any crackers?"

Lisa handed over a toasted bagel in a napkin. "Here." Darcy reached across the table, too squeamish to do anything but nod a thanks.

"The party was great till you switched to Top Shelf margaritas," Miranda said. "Didn't seem to sit well with your Cheeseburger in Paradise." Miranda exaggerated a thumbs down. "You went downhill fast, girlfriend." A grin twitched at the corner of her mouth.

"Why did ya'll let me do that?" Darcy ran a hand over her stomach.

"Drink too much?" Becca asked.

"She didn't just drink too much, she was shit-faced." Miranda rubbed her chin. "So I guess you haven't noticed the tattoo."

Darcy rubbed her eyes underneath her shades until the target word registered in her brain. "I got a trash stamp?" Her voice sounded like a foghorn aimed at her ears.

The frantic question hung in the air for a short moment before the other three women's contained smiles erupted into laughter. Darcy covered her ears, her head threatening to explode all over the table.

"I'm thinking this is *Hangover 2* material." Miranda took a slug of her mimosa. "Hold your bladder a minute Boop, we all got one."

"Yeah, see mine?" Lisa lowered the edge of her capris, exposing a small ladybug on her hipbone.

Darcy's mind freeze-framed. Her eyes panned around the table and stopped at Becca. "Seriously? You got a ladybug tattoo?"

"Of course not." Becca sipped her mimosa. "A heart."

"This is *not* happening." Darcy ground her teeth. She peeled down the waistband on her capris and found what she hoped she wouldn't...a colorful green lizard with a curly tail etched on her hip. The reptile had escaped notice during her hurried shower.

"Ah shit."

"Izzy will love it, don't you think?" Miranda teased.

You're dead meat.

"Izzy will flippin' kill me!"

Didn't I just say that?

Darcy held a decent job selling designer eyewear and had family and friends who loved her, but no Prince Charming. She wanted a Prince Charming. Hell, she wanted the whole damn fairytale, although her dream/scheme to become Mrs. Charming held three major flaws.

One: She wanted what everyone else had. (ie. Lisa's stability, Becca's money and IQ, Miranda's looks, wardrobe, and Midtown loft).

Two: She had convinced herself she'd never find Mr. Charming without the above-mentioned MIA life factors.

Three: Izzy, her grandmother. As much as Darcy coveted the fairy-tale life, Izzy was hell-bent on making it happen. "I want you married before I kick the bucket," Izzy had said. "It's my last dying wish." She'd heard her grandmother's last dying wish for years, and it irritated the hell out of her. Izzy would turn eighty in October and was as healthy as a horse, and not dying anytime soon.

"You're awful, Miranda." Becca blotted pouty lips after applying fresh gloss.

Miranda finished off her mimosa and directed her gaze at Darcy. "Oh, lighten up, hootchie-mama. Your little guy ought to wear off in a couple of weeks. And besides, you're thirty. Time to cut Grandma loose."

"I've tried. She won't go away."

Darcy massaged her temples while the other three women exchanged "oh, really" looks.

"Okay, maybe I haven't." Darcy needed food, a bed, and a different topic…pretty much in that order. "You swear this thing is temporary?"

"How many times has she called?" Miranda caught the eye of a nice-looking guy climbing out of the pool.

"Get off my ass, Miranda," Darcy snapped.

Miranda shrugged and raised her eyebrows. "Fine with me."

The women turned to see what had captured Miranda's attention. Lisa rolled her eyes. "Don't you think of anything besides men?"

"Tried. Didn't work." Miranda's open-for-business sign flashed across her face. The guy nodded and gave her a smile. "Hey Becca, what are the stalking laws in Nevada?"

"Depends. For a person being stalked or a stalker?" The sarcasm sailed right past the bride-to-be, also the resident lawyer of the group.

"Not sure yet." Miranda sported her all too familiar tigress smile and stood up. "But I'll let you know."

Becca scribbled her name on the bill and jumped to her feet. "Oh, no you don't. We're on a schedule. Time to go."

Darcy watched the inviting lounge in the cabana slip into the distance. The group hustled her away for their day of beauty at the Bellagio spa.

Oh joy….

***

With cotton wedged between her toes after her pedicure, Darcy waited for the hair stylist. A rolling service tray draped with a linen tablecloth sat at her side. She peeked under the silver dome to find the club sandwich she had ordered. "I want to be rich. You know, have this kind of stuff every day." Darcy thought how posh it would be to have lunch presented to her daily on a tray with a mini vase of fresh-cut flowers.

"Does Izzy know this pre-requisite? Could narrow her search." Miranda's tray held a hip-expansion order of cheese fries. She struggled to open her personal-sized bottle of catsup. "Stubborn little sucker."

"How can you eat crap like that and not gain weight?" Being in the air-conditioning for a while had revived Darcy enough to whine. "That's so unfair."

"Oh, get off it," Miranda replied. "I hear this shit from you at least once a week. It's getting old."

Darcy switched subjects. "Becca is so stinking rich. I can't imagine how much all this is costing her parents." She routinely hosted her own pity-party when comparing the Russell's family wealth against her yo-yo checking account and sham of an apartment. The place was a hellhole, but the address legitimately allowed her to say she lived in Houston's Uptown Galleria area.

Except for her designer shoe collection, everything in her life was a knock-off. Granted, she had tons of Gucci demo shades, but few of her own. Her clothes she bought at Stein Mart, high end resale shops, Ross, or Marshalls. Her jewelry and occasional handbags came from Harwin, a designer knock-off district in southwest Houston. She could swing with Bag, Borrow, or Steal once in a while to tout a designer purse, but she could *not* bring herself to join Shoe Dazzle. The policy stated that you either bought the shoes they shipped to you or returned them. How could she *ever* be expected to return a pair of designer shoes her feet had already developed a relationship with? Nah, her shoes had to be the real thing and on her terms, which meant Macy's, Saks, Neiman Marcus, or Zappos. Designer shoes, her obsession, needed to be kept low key in the presence of her family, who constantly hounded her about the extravagant lifestyle her feet had established.

By 7:30 Saturday evening, Darcy's hair had been curled and glued on top of her head, her makeup applied with an airbrush, and her body stuffed into a tight size eight strapless bridesmaid's dress the color of a pumpkin. She managed the trip down the aisle of the Bellagio's South Chapel without a mishap, to witness Becca cross the line drawn in the sand and join the ranks of "no longer single." Lisa had crossed over back in college, only the pregnancy preceded the wedding. Rob had followed Lisa to Texas State in the spring semester of their sophomore year, and nature eventually took its course. She now had two precious boys, and proudly wore the crown of "Mother Teresa," as ordained by Miranda.

***

The next day, Becca and her new husband jetted off to Hawaii, while Darcy and Miranda took seats on their non-stop flight back to Houston. The wedding had been perfect…Becca, perfect…reception dinner at The Fix, perfect.

Blah, blah, blah. Another single woman bites the dust.

"Do you have any Tylenol?" The late dinner and the boatloads of champagne toasts had left Darcy with a headache. She had returned to Bally's at 1:30, 3:30 Houston time, but had no idea when Miranda came in and didn't ask. She just hoped the flight home would be smooth.

"I've got Vicodin."

"God, Miranda." Darcy rubbed her forehead, already knowing work the next day would be hell. "Is that all you have?"

"I work for a drug company, not CVS." Hangovers weren't Miranda's problem.

"Forget it." Darcy thumbed through the current *In Touch Weekly* she'd bought at the airport.

"You know, you get a real stick up your ass when you're sober."

Rolling her eyes, Darcy pulled the magazine closer to her face and wished she was home.

"Hey, did you see the guy up there with the blond hair?"

Darcy slammed the magazine into her lap. "Do you ever stop? How many did you meet this weekend?" She clawed the bottom of her fake Louis Vuitton for crumbles of a pain-reliever.

Miranda's fingers popped up one at a time. "Just two. No, three...four, if you count the bellhop on the way out this morning. He comes to Texas every year for 'Austin City Limits.' We might hook up next weekend."

"You're a slut." Darcy swallowed half an Advil dry.

"And you're a prude." Miranda eyed herself in her compact mirror and touched up her lipstick. "At least I have dates."

"That's low," Darcy said. "Even for you."

"I know."

"Damn it, Miranda." Darcy shook her head and once again picked up her magazine. She wondered if the best part of their friendship had taken a nosedive for good this time.

"I'm trying to make a point." Miranda exaggerated the "t" in point like she was spitting it across the isle of the plane. "You bitch all the time about not having dates, but you never do anything about it."

"Drop it," Darcy said, knowing Miranda's next move. She wasn't wrong.

"If you'd just try the Internet, at least you'd go out once in a while."

The all too familiar knot formed in Darcy's stomach. An old high school letter jacket secretly hung in the back of her closet as a reminder of how she viewed herself...and dating. Miranda had brought the Internet dating issue up a dozen times, but Darcy always kept quiet about her high school secret. And besides, she hated the idea of advertising herself.

"I told you—"

"I know what you've told me." Miranda minced no words. "And it sucks. It's stupid."

"Don't call me stupid," Darcy fired.

"I'm not calling you stupid, I'm saying what you're doing is stupid," Miranda said. "Big difference."

"Is not." Darcy wished she could wiggle her nose and be in her apartment.

"Whatever." Miranda placed ear buds in her ears, pushed her chair back, and hit play on her Nano.

Neither spoke for the duration of the trip.

***

While she waited at the baggage terminal, Darcy yawned and turned on her cell phone. Two messages. Wow. It had been a while since she'd had two.

The first was from her grandmother. "Details. I want details," Izzy said. Darcy rolled her eyes.

The second wasn't any better. "I've told you not to keep your TV on that Animal Planet station when you leave town. Those shows upset poor Ike. I'm leaving you a note on your door. Don't do it again!" Darcy's apartment manager barked orders in exclamation marks.

Welcome home!

Two messages and both from females who qualified for the senior citizen discount at IHOP. Darcy blew out air and deleted both voice mails. She glanced across the terminal and found Miranda smiling, cell phone to ear, flipping her hair back…a clear indication of the caller's gender.

Luggage retrieved, she and Miranda exchanged a stilted hug and parted ways, Miranda in her BMW convertible, Darcy in her Mazda CX-7, the SUV she'd convinced herself mimicked the small Lexus SUV she wanted but couldn't afford. Relieved to be at her less-than-lush apartment and away from Miranda, Darcy tore off the Animal Planet note taped to the front door and dragged her luggage over the threshold. Stash, her part Jack Russell terrier, part whatever rescue dog, barked once, rolled over on his back, and pawed the air, making a goofy "aug-aug-aug" sound.

"I've warned you about messing with the TV," Darcy said. "We're in trouble again." She casually stepped around what looked like a dog having a seizure. "What have you done with Mel?"

Mel—a pudgy, orange tabby with an I-don't-give-a-shit temperament—had appeared on Darcy's balcony two years earlier and refused to leave. A visit to the vet and $175 later, Mel became family...one more weakness to add to Darcy's list; taking in strays. She couldn't help it. Besides identifying with them, they never criticized or talked back, and were almost always glad to see her.

Her eyes panned the small living area. No Mel. She figured she'd find him in his super-secret hiding space under her bed. She called it the "cat house," and scolded Stash when he tried to squeeze his wiry body down around the boxes under her bed. "It's a cat house, you crazy dog. Go build your own clubhouse."

Darcy pushed the unlit message button on her recorder just for the hell of it.

"You have no new messages."

Too tired to hunt down Mel, who couldn't care less that his master had returned, Darcy rummaged through the refrigerator for food. Nothing. "Grocery store" had not been crossed off her to-do list before the Vegas trip. She found a few stale Goldfish in the pantry and stuffed them in her mouth. The note on the counter caught her eye.

Done. Need more cat litter, and you have no food. Later, Me

Andrea had more free time than anyone on the planet. Taking care of her animals while Darcy was in Vegas made her younger sister at least responsible for something.

"Send her away to college," Darcy begged her parents. "The child needs to grow up." But Andie, the baby of the family, had her own plan. She'd live off her parents, post every move or emotion on Twitter or Facebook, shop obsessively with Mom and Dad's credit cards, and maybe take a course or two at Houston Community College if time permitted.

Darcy grabbed a Diet Coke from the refrigerator to wash down the Goldfish stuck in her throat and to clear the way for dinner: extra-butter microwave popcorn. Retrieving the remote from the bookshelf of unread self-help books, she pointed it at the decrepit

TV she desperately wanted to replace. She scanned the on-screen cable guide and clicked to *Extreme Makeover*. Back in her pity-party mood, Darcy needed a reality check. *Extreme Makeover* usually did the trick.

She reached beside her and powered on her laptop, then checked emails and Facebook. Most of her friends were married with children or somewhere in the process. A newly posted Facebook picture showed a friend's little chunky-monkey in a high chair, pureed sweet potatoes smeared across his face. Several shots of the Vegas wedding had already appeared on Becca's wall.

She tapped her chin with her fingers and stared at the screen. Edging the cursor up to the top, her fingers moved across the keyboard and Googled "top online dating services." She pushed enter and shot Stash a don't-you-say-a-word glare.

Three quick knocks echoed from the door. "Darcy?"

"Geez," she whispered, clicked back to Facebook, and slid the laptop off to the side. She grabbed the bag of greasy popcorn and exchanged looks with Stash.

Another series of knocks. "Darcy? Can I speak with you for a moment?"

"Swell. Just what I need," she muttered, recognizing her weird downstairs neighbor. She calculated whether she could get away without answering the door, sighed, and yelled, "It's open."

Lawrence entered the apartment. "I've been waiting all weekend for your return." He grabbed his chest. "Oh good God, what are you eating?"

"Microwave popcorn…extra butter. Want some?" Darcy licked her fingers.

"I certainly do not and neither do you." Lawrence snatched the almost empty bag away from Darcy, and with two fingers dumped it in the kitchen trashcan like a chunk of bad cheese.

"Hey! That's dinner."

"I cannot stand by and watch you poison yourself. Didn't you see the article in the New York Times last week?"

"No, I didn't see the New York Times." *Not last week, not ever.*

"USA Today?"

"Nope."

"Washington Post?"

"What is your point, Lawrence?"

"I read that four of the nation's largest microwave popcorn manufacturers are frantically working to remove diacetyl from their product."

"What the hell is that?"

"A chemical in the butter flavoring. They believe it causes lung ailments."

Darcy raised an eyebrow and gave him something between a grimace and a smile. "You threw my dinner away for that?"

Lawrence lived in the apartment directly below hers. His IQ placed him in a small but elite class of snobbish intellects. He was the youngest son of an extremely wealthy and well-known family in River Oaks, and he was broke. Having squandered his trust fund allotment on fine dining, exquisite Russian antiques, and charity events, his finances were in shambles and his next advance was still two years away, leaving little to no wiggle room. According to his CPA, his next dining experience could be at the Salvation Army if his current spending habits didn't change. His tastes scream Beamer, but his bank account had him tooling around in a Ford Fiesta.

"Could I interest you in a meal out?" Lawrence washed and dried his hands after the popcorn disposal.

With him?

Darcy's dance card was pretty darn empty, but Lawrence? Uh…no. "I don't think so."

His eyes closed. "I can almost taste the crab cakes at Pesce's. Their Chardonnay cream sauce is to die for. Unfortunately, all I can manage is splitting a seafood salad at Captain Benny's. I'll spring for the crackers."

"I said no," Darcy voiced, harsher than she intended.

"Well, alright then." Lawrence dug his fists into his pockets and stared at the carpet.

Damn, she'd hurt his feelings. Actually, she found Lawrence likeable in a weird and annoying sort of way. Besides sounding like a walking menu, Lawrence appeared closer to normal than most of the people she'd been with for the last couple of days, which spoke volumes for her Vegas trip.

"Order in?" Lawrence asked.

He's not leaving.

"Stay and watch *Extreme Makeover*. We'll order pizza." Geez, she'd just invited her weird neighbor to stay for the evening.

18

"You mean from one of those places where delivery people drive banged up cars with little signs stuck out their window?"

"You know, you could insult a lot of hard working people with that kind of talk. And they're not always banged up…but yeah, that's what I'm talking about."

Lawrence folded his arms across his narrow chest. "I couldn't possibly do that."

"Besides being a snob, why couldn't you possibly do that?" Sarcasm made Darcy feel better.

"Because…because I never have."

She blinked hard and forced herself not to shake her head in disbelief. "Well, grab a chair. You're in for a treat."

Lawrence gnawed on his inner lip, assessed the situation, and took a seat in the armless chair next to the couch. Stash pounced over and sat at Lawrence's feet, giving him a steady glare. "Good dog. Does he bite?"

Darcy shifted her attention back to *Extreme Makeover* and dialed for dinner. "Darcy Daniels. One large thick crust, all the way. Delivery please," was all she said to the pizza place that rang her doorbell at least once a week.

"I must tell you, I don't do pepperoni…or dogs either, for that matter." Lawrence tried to cross his legs, but Stash growled and denied the gesture.

"Then leave."

"I'll stay, thanks," Lawrence quickly replied, and offered Stash a clenched-teeth smile.

By the end of the show, Lawrence had blown into three tissues and declared *Extreme Makeover* the most emotional show he'd seen since *Dr. Zhivago*. Darcy's response was a belch, which produced a shocked expression across Lawrence's face.

"Sorry. I guess you're not used to that kind of behavior." She wiped a napkin across her mouth. "You ought to try it sometime though."

Lawrence's stare melted. He shook his head and let out what could have been a laugh. "I'm learning all sorts of things tonight, aren't I? This pizza is excellent, by the way."

Darcy squinted her eyes and studied the man dressed in brown brushed-tweed slacks, a white-red-brown striped Ralph Lauren shirt, and Italian-woven calfskin Cole Haans. Although she didn't know Lawrence well, she knew he considered this to be his casual look.

"Do you have a nickname? Something less formal, maybe?"

Lawrence moved his chin around like a tie was too tight around his neck. "My full name is Lawrence Milton Ousted." His eyes dropped to his hands. "My parents never liked me."

He isn't going to start bawling, is he?

"Oh, c'mon." He looked like a pitiful little kid whose hamster had just died.

"My father is William Frederick Ousted, III. My older brother is William Frederick, IV. When I came along, they stuck me with Lawrence Milton after my uncle on my mother's side. I never liked him."

Darcy scrounged around in her brain for words of comfort, but found none.

"I wanted a number. I always wanted a number." Lawrence's gaze clouded over, his eyes fixed on the television screen. "In first grade I told my teacher my name was Lawrence Milton Ousted, I. She sent a note home to my parents."

Darcy maintained a serious look, despite a nagging grin. "Soooo, what did you want to talk to me about?"

Lawrence snapped out of his Eeyore persona, his look moving from desolate to disturbed on the emotions chart. "Oh, that's right." He straightened in his armless chair. "I had a most unsettling weekend." He stood, pulled a neatly folded piece of paper from his back pocket, and handed it to Darcy. "This was on my mailbox." Worry lines pleated his forehead. "I've been agonizing over it all weekend. These people scare me. There's one on your mailbox also."

Darcy took the flyer and gave it a once over. "Shit."

"Not exactly the word I would use, but close."

She read the flyer out loud:

> Fountain Oaks First Annual Fall Get-Together
> Next Saturday, 4:00 PM
> Fountain Oaks Courtyard
> (bring a dish—I expect everyone to attend)
> Viola Middleton, Apartment Manager
> ($50 off next month's rent for attending)

"Are you going?" Lawrence's eyes trailed after her like a faithful dog. "I don't think I can make it. Unless you go, that is. Then maybe I could rearrange my schedule. Please say you'll go."

So, she expects everyone to attend, does she?

Next Saturday. One week to come up with an excuse. "Yeah, pretty sure I'm going to be busy."

"Did you read the fine print?" Lawrence pointed to the bottom of the flyer.

Darcy narrowed her eyes to bring the tiny letters into focus. "Fifty dollars off next month's rent for going to this stupid thing? She's bribing us?" Double shit.

You're screwed.

"Ah, so you *are* going." Lawrence sighed. "Thank goodness. I couldn't decide if fifty dollars was worth not having to face that woman. Well, that's settled. By the way, how was Las Vegas? I forgot to ask."

Darcy stood and waved Lawrence out the door. "I'll tell you about it next Saturday. Long day." Fake yawn. "I'm beat. Bye."

"Have a good evening," she heard through the door.

Shooting Stash a look, she said, "You're so lucky you don't have neighbors." She clicked off previews of the next family to get a home makeover and glanced back to the non-blinking answering machine. She contemplated further online dating research, but instead grabbed the recent *In Touch* magazine and headed to the bedroom.

Terry Lee

Chapter 2

Darcy's cell phone blared at 7:00 A.M. She rolled over and smacked the snooze button, knocking the alarm clock to the floor, but the noise continued. She grabbed her cell phone and squinted at the caller ID.

"Shit." Before her feet hit the ground, she realized any hope of a calm Monday had just flushed down the toilet.

"I need you in Richmond today," a female voice said. "I'm firing Crystal. She hasn't met her quota in three months. Optic Visions called late Friday afternoon. They want to place an order." Short pause. "You need to be there at nine-thirty sharp. We cannot lose that account. Understood?"

"Vanessa, my appointments are all in The Woodlands today."

The gap in the conversation lengthened. Darcy squeezed one eye closed. No one talked back to Vanessa Hargrove.

Crystal did....

"Is there a problem?"

Darcy silently snarled. "I'll take care of it."

"Good." The call ended.

"What a bitch." Darcy rolled out of bed, quickly showered, and brushed her teeth while blow-drying her hair. Richmond wasn't her territory.

You'd better get a commission on this.

Vanessa often "forgot" her account reps' territories; or maybe she just didn't give a flying rat's ass.

Thirty minutes later, Darcy sat at a red light, waiting to join the parking lot on the 610 Loop. Her fingers drummed the steering wheel. The Galleria, *the* place to live, sucked traffic-wise. She glanced down to ensure her white button-down shirt was buttoned correctly and peeked at her J Crew suede platform heels. When putting on the anchor grey shoes, she had thought they matched the tweed pencil skirt. Now, in broad daylight, she wasn't sure.

Vanessa Hargrove, Senior Account Executive for Gucci and boss extraordinaire from hell, called at 9:33 a.m. to make sure Darcy had arrived in Richmond and again around noon. "Did you get the order?" The boss from hell barked.

"They made me wait over an—"

"Did you or did you *not* get the order?"

"I did."

"And?"

"They only ordered eight frames." Darcy still felt the heat on her face from the sucky order.

"Eight?"

"*Only* eight."

"Very well then." Click.

Darcy tossed her phone over to the passenger seat. Eighty would have been a decent order, not a flippin' eight. She gripped the steering wheel. She'd had to reschedule two morning appointments and drive twenty-five miles south to Richmond for eight lousy pair of glasses. What a waste of time. The drive north to The Woodlands would take more than an hour if there were no delays. She could head straight up Highway 59, but the chance of hitting a traffic snag was high, considering the lunch hour and the bottleneck near downtown. The clock on the dash read 12:15. Darcy veered onto the Sam Houston Beltway. Mileage wise, the Beltway tallied up more miles than Highway 59 to The Woodlands, but traffic moved better. Toll roads usually—

"Ah, damn it!" Darcy yanked open the small pocket compartment on the dash and scraped out a handful of loose change. She hadn't given the EZ Tag store her new account number after losing her debit card last month. The letter on her kitchen counter explained her EZ tag would become inactive as of September 15, last Wednesday, if arrangements had not been made for current automatic withdrawal. Arrangements had not been made. Damn. She'd have to stop at three booths now, not to mention the toll fee. She opened her clenched fist and counted six quarters, four dimes, a couple of nickels, and some pennies. Her 1:30 in The Woodlands were not going to be happy campers.

***

"I'm sorry I'm so late," she repeated all afternoon. None of her clients cared about her butt-head boss or her pit stop at Valero's for cash back on a Diet Coke to pay toll fees. The workday over, Darcy pulled in front of her parents' house just as the low-fuel light blinked.

"Great." She rested her head on the steering wheel and closed her eyes. Her stomach rumbled like a herd of early shoppers on Black Friday. She hadn't had time for breakfast or lunch, and payday, four days away, didn't sit well with the remaining forty-two dollars and change in her checking account. And now she needed gas.

Darcy's maternal grandmother met her at the front door. "How'd it go? Meet anyone interesting?"

"Can I come in first?"

Izzy backed up a few paces, her hands perched somewhere around where her hips should be. Shorter and rounder than Darcy, she waddled instead of walked. Bad knees, she'd say.

"Because if you didn't, Mildred's nephew's roommate's cousin knows of a guy that might work. We're waiting to hear if he's gay. That could knock him down a notch." The list of marital candidates for Darcy lengthened every Friday after Izzy's standing hair appointment.

"Izzy, if he's gay, he's out. Off the list." Darcy rolled her eyes. "What's for dinner?"

"Spaghetti," Izzy said, heading to her bedroom. "In thirty minutes." Izzy planned her days around *The Price Is Right*, *Millionaire, Judge Judy,* and, of course, *Wheel of Fortune,* which should be on now. She'd moved into Darcy's old bedroom five years earlier after Darcy's grandfather died of a heart attack.

"Easy out," her dad had said. "The old guy just needed some peace and quiet."

Darcy sighed and moved through the family room, and found her mother in the kitchen. She dropped her phony Coach purse on the table.

"How was the wedding? Are those new?" Nina Daniels moved to the sink and washed her hands, her eyes fixed on Darcy's suede platform heels.

Darcy stuck her head in the refrigerator and backed out with a cheese stick. *Crap.* The Payless generic black heels she lugged around in the back of her SUV were for exactly this sort of situation.

"The wedding? Beautiful," Darcy answered.

Nina eyed the expensive shoes. "How much did those cost?"

"Mom," Darcy whined. "You're on my side, remember? Anyway, I think they were on sale."

On sale? Yeah, right.

"I need to give Andie a check. Where is she?"

"At the library." Nina removed garlic bread from the oven.

Doing what?

Darcy slipped off her shoes and pushed them behind her dad's recliner in the living room. Her sister studying? At the library? What a joke.

"Those new?" Izzy pointed to the stashed platforms.

"*Wheel of Fortune* can't be over," Darcy said.

"Don't change the subject. Are those real or not?"

"Not." The lies kept piling up.

"Whatever. Tell me about Vegas." Izzy shuffled to the kitchen table and lowered her rounded torso into a chair. "Is he rich? Does he call his grandmother?" Izzy wore black pants, black SAS lace-up shoes, and a blouse splashed with assorted colors. The splashes changed daily, but everything else remained the same.

"I didn't meet *him,* but Miranda met four guys."

"Miranda's a hussy." Izzy poured a glass of wine.

"No she isn't," Darcy argued. Again, another lie. Hussy sounded mild compared to the word she'd recently used to describe Miranda. They hadn't spoken since their heated exchange on the plane.

"You'll never find a decent man hanging around that one, I tell ya. Listen to your grandmother. I know what I'm talking about."

Darcy raised her eyes to the ceiling and realized she should have gone straight home. Starvation, however, had its own motivation.

"Andrea ran into your nasty apartment manager on Saturday," Nina said. "She told your sister to turn off the TV."

"I know. I got a note *and* a voicemail." Darcy figured Ms. Viola to be way overdue for her distemper shots.

"You tell me if that woman bothers you," Izzy said. "I know how to deal with people like that."

"How?" Darcy asked. "Put a contract out on her?"

"I could, you know." Izzy drained her wine glass and reached for a refill. "My friend Marge...the one who cheats on Poker Wednesday? She saw an ad in the newspaper. Said, 'I'll do anything. Call me'."

Nina's mouth dropped.

"Izzy, that's an ad for a prostitute, not a hired gun. Marge is reading *The Press*, not *The Chronicle*." Darcy wondered at the safety level of leaving Izzy to her own devices. Wednesday nickel-dime poker games, TV shows, and hair appointments seemed harmless. However, *The Houston Press* spelled d-a-n-g-e-r in blinking neon letters for her grandmother's generation.

Darcy stood, the decision to skip dinner reached, when her dad entered through the back door and dropped his brief case. Her clean get-away botched by mere seconds, she sat down.

"Hey Darce. How's everybody? Where's Andie?" Stephen Daniels walked into the kitchen and poured himself some wine.

"At the library." Darcy and Izzy's timing sounded rehearsed.

Her dad's arm froze, the wine glass halfway to his mouth. He blinked hard, shook his head, and took a long swig. He turned to Darcy.

"What's up kiddo? Bank balance below sea level again?" Her dad winked and sent her a smile while her mother set plates of spaghetti on the table. Darcy's money management struggles were not front-page news.

Any lingering joy from the jab at her sister disappeared. "That's cold."

"I know," her dad said.

"Then why keep bringing it up?" Darcy asked.

"Because it keeps happening." He took a bite of spaghetti.

"Actually, I came to give Andie a check for feeding the animals." She felt her dad's eyes burn into her.

"And?" His arched eyebrows mingled with the lines on his forehead.

Darcy slid around in her chair. "And what?"

"I feel a stipulation in there somewhere."

Darcy smoothed an imaginary wrinkle from her white button-down blouse and examined an invisible piece of lint on her sleeve. "She can't cash it till Friday."

"There it is." Darcy's dad chased the last bite of spaghetti around the plate, drained his wine glass, and moved to the recliner in the family room.

Darcy mentally clicked the heels of her ruby-red slippers three times and silently repeated, *there's no place like home...there's no place like home.*

"What else is going on?" Nina, the peacemaker of the family, asked.

Too exhausted to bitch about Vanessa, which she did often, or her Richmond-Woodlands day, Darcy chose option number three.

"My apartment manager is having a pot-luck thing this Saturday. I have to bring a dish."

"Something's wrong with that woman," Izzy said. "Don't eat anything she brings, you hear? Better yet, I'd skip it."

"I can't. It's worth fifty dollars off next month's rent." Darcy added.

"Humph. Why don't I go with you and check her out? It'll give me a chance to meet your neighbors. You might be overlooking someone I can put on the list."

"I don't need a chaperone, Izzy. Besides, the men living there aren't my type."

"Type? You have a type?" Izzy dug into her pocket and retrieved a small notebook. She flipped to a clean page. "This could help. Go ahead."

There's no place like home...there's no place like home.

"Gee, I've got to go." She handed the check to her mother and lowered her voice. "Not till Friday. Promise?"

Retrieving her shoes from behind her dad's recliner, she hoisted her purse to her shoulder. She blew the family a kiss, backed out of the house, and shut the door on Nina offering her seven-layered dip for next Saturday. Darcy slid into the driver's seat of her SUV and thunked her head on the steering wheel.

"Crap. My life is crap." She bought designer shoes she couldn't afford and lived in a run-down sham of an apartment—only to say she lived in the Galleria area—and had a dating headhunter for a grandmother. She loved life...she just hated hers. Ignoring the blinking low-fuel light, Darcy sighed and pulled away from the curb. Monday had finally ended.

***

Topping the stairs at Fountain Oaks, shoes in hand, she spotted Lawrence sitting in a chair outside her apartment, an open book lying on his lap and a less than half-full cordial glass in his hand. She'd misjudged Monday. The day had a few more drops of blood to squeeze out of her.

Where's your fire escape? You need one.

"You're late." Lawrence held the liqueur glass in a Nathan Lane pose.

"And you're not my mother." Key in hand, Darcy made her way into the apartment and scooted the door closed with her bare foot. Lawrence followed her in, book tucked under his arm, the cordial empty.

Stash thundered into the living room, dragging his leash between his teeth. He braked, dropped the leash, and sniffed Lawrence's pant leg.

"Grab the leash or you're gonna have to dry-clean those slacks."

"Oh, good God!" Lawrence fumbled to secure the leash onto Stash's collar. "Now what?"

"Out. Both of you!" Darcy pointed toward the door.

Lawrence and Stash raced out. She thought she heard whimpering when the two clattered down the stairs.

Dog or man?

Grabbing a doggie poop bag, she joined Lawrence and Stash in the courtyard of the small complex.

"Number one checked off the list. Can we go inside now?"

"Why were you sitting outside my door?" Darcy grabbed the leash.

"I tried the door but it was locked," Lawrence said.

"You'd better be kidding. Look, I've had a shitty day," she snarled. "I need for you to go away." Darcy walked Stash to the edge of the property, Lawrence tagging behind, carefully stepping around anything that might have to be cleaned off his loafers. Light pooled on the courtyard from the street light.

"This is disgusting." Lawrence stopped to examine a row of lifeless shrubs. "Total urban decay. Something must be done about this deplorable situation," he said. "I'll call my lawyer."

"Be my guest."

"Never mind." Lawrence studied the ground. "My lawyer won't take my calls anyway. Seems he's developed an aversion to clients who don't pay."

Darcy rounded the top of the stairs and stopped. Lawrence plowed into her backside.

"Go *away*," she said through clenched teeth.

"Hear me out. I need to discuss dress code for the soiree on Saturday." Lawrence followed her into the apartment. She turned to close the door and smacked right into him.

"I mean it, go. And it's not a soiree."

Whatever the hell that is.

"I understand. Really, I do." Lawrence grabbed his book off the corner of the couch. "About the dress code, and then I'll be off."

"Casual." Darcy pushed Lawrence out the door.

He wiggled back in a step to snatch his empty cordial. "How casual?"

"Very." Slam. She waited until she heard his door close downstairs before slipping back out to give Stash a few more minutes. She walked the dog around the perimeter of the property, ready for the routine sniffing to end and the serious dog business to begin.

The motion-detector light over the carport blinked on, one of the few working exterior lights on the premises. Darcy stopped and yanked Stash back into the darkness. Someone stood near her car. She hauled her cell phone out of her pocket and punched 911. Her finger hovering over *talk,* she paused. A man in camouflage pants and a drab, brown t-shirt stood in the carport, a water hose hung over his shoulder…Fletcher, the maintenance man.

What's he doing to my car?

Not convinced a 911 call was unnecessary, Darcy quietly flipped her phone shut, but kept it in her hand. Her heart slowed to a reasonable pound. Snatching the leash loop out of Darcy's hand, Stash charged the man in Army fatigues. She took off for the carport after the dog.

Fletcher, the Bill Murray *Caddy Shack* clone, spotted the dog. He dropped the water hose and opened his arms. "C'mere boy."

Stash flew into the man's embrace, the leash trailing behind. Darcy closed the gap to the carport in time to see her ferocious guard dog lick every inch of the man's face.

"You're a good dog," Fletcher said in the funny way people talk to animals and babies. "Yes you are."

"What are you doing?" She realized she'd never seen Fletcher smile.

"I like dogs." Fletcher scratched behind Stash's ears, handed the dog back to Darcy, and hoisted the water hose back up on his shoulder.

"Is something wrong with my car?"

"No."

Get to the point…what the hell are you doing?

"Then, what are you doing?" Sometimes her alter ego needed to work on her tact.

"2100 security check." Fletcher spoke to the ground. He raised his head and Darcy noticed his eyes, a hazel greenish-brown, matched his fatigues. "Security patrol. West end of the compound. 2100 hours." His voice rolled out in one long monotone.

"Right." She nodded and did a 180.

"Saturday?"

Darcy turned. "Excuse me?"

"4:00."

Nodding again, she headed up the stairs. Once inside her apartment, she locked, unlocked, and relocked the deadbolt on her door. "Bizarre. Don't these people have a life?" she asked Stash, then added, "Don't even say it." How desperate had she sunk to put up with these misfits for next Saturday's fifty dollar bribe?

What was Dad's term? Below sea level?

Terry Lee

Chapter 3

Saturday morning Darcy woke to sun streaming through her bedroom window. She reached for the remote and turned to the "Local Weather On the 8's." Not a cloud in the whole state.

Where is the hurricane fairy when you need her?

She rolled out of bed, stretched, and pulled back the window shade. Two card tables pushed together sat in the center of the courtyard with three chairs lined up on each side. Six chairs, six tenants. Maybe Izzy *should* come…they could play musical chairs. After throwing on her running clothes, she spent an hour at Memorial Park pretending to exercise. At the store, she picked up needed ingredients, mainly Velveeta and a can of Rotel, for the queso she'd make that afternoon. Cooking had never been her strong suit, but queso and a bag of chips she could handle.

The clock beamed a quarter till four. She glanced out the window. The only new additions to the courtyard were plastic red-checkered tablecloths, an ice chest, and a trash can. Giving the cheese-beer-Rotel concoction another nuke in the microwave, she headed to the bedroom.

Struggling into black stretch slim-fit pants, Darcy pulled on a white v-neck linen tunic and dug around in her closet for her French Sole black ballet flats. She re-applied makeup, slipped on a knock-off Av Max long scale chain necklace, added tiered linear drop earrings, and skimmed her demo cases for a pair of over-sized rounded black sunglasses with gold Gucci hardware on the sides. Being an eyewear rep in the Houston area meant demo cases filled the corners of her apartment and the back of her SUV. She glanced in the mirror and sighed. "Casual" took a lot of work.

Three fifty-nine…one last glance out the window. No one. Okay, she'd be the first to arrive and the first to leave. Darcy poured the warm cheese into a casserole dish, slapped a piece of foil on top, grabbed the bag of chips, and headed out the door. By the time she reached the courtyard, four of the six chairs were filled. She squeezed one eye shut and realized she'd never seen all the Fountain Oaks misfits—uh, tenants—at the same time.

What the hell kind of Twilight Zone reunion is this?

Lawrence sat in the chair farthest from Ms. Viola. A foil-covered plate sat in his lap. Darcy blinked hard at his outfit. Khaki dress slacks, fancy loafers, and a hideous blue and yellow Hawaiian shirt spattered with bright red cockatoos. She raised her eyebrows. "New?"

"It's my new very casual look. Do you like it?"

What could be said about a shirt resembling Jimmy Buffett on crack? She sat down and watched him remove the foil from the paper plate. Yellowed limp asparagus wrapped in what could be packaged lunchmeat lay across the plate.

"What *is* that?"

"Asparagus appetizers," Lawrence said. "My favorite as a child."

Darcy struggled with her gag reflex.

"I found canned asparagus for two dollars and forty-six cents. And the Buddig ham? This entire plate cost less than five dollars."

"Really." Canned asparagus reminded Darcy why she had despised the vegetable as a child. "And…how much for the shirt?"

"Six bucks. I found it on a clearance rack at Walmart. I think I've turned a corner on my money crunch situation."

Darcy gave Lawrence a "yeah, right" look, positioned the queso and chips on the table, and returned to her seat.

She surveyed the group. Mr. Will, an ancient-looking man dressed in a plaid shirt, wrinkled khaki pants, Gilligan fishing hat, horn-rimmed glasses, and a professor bowtie, sat next to Ms. Viola. Ms. Viola sported faded black tennis shoes, a yellow t-shirt, and rolled-up mid-calf overalls with a fringed straw hat plunked on her head. Ike, the ancient sand-colored cocker spaniel, flattened out on the small space of grass between the two older people. Fletcher, on the other side of Will, held two cans of Vienna sausages, a bag of pork rinds, and a half loaf of white bread.

Lawrence leaned toward Darcy. "Who's missing?"

After a quick mental head count, she whispered, "Sister Mary Alice."

"We have a nun living here?" Lawrence asked.

"She's our neighbor."

"That's impossible. My upstairs neighbor is noisy."

"That's me, you goof-ball. I'm your upstairs neighbor." She'd run into the elderly woman on a few occasions at the mailboxes. Strained smiles and exchanged hellos covered their conversations, which could be said for any of the tenants at Fountain Oaks. Six strangers…better yet, six very strange people.

Fountain Oaks consisted of two washed out sand-colored brick buildings lined face to face, separated by a strip of brown grass posing as a courtyard. Each building held four two-bedroom apartments—two up, two down—with a vacancy in each. A frayed yellow "For Lease" banner with barely legible red letters had hung from Darcy's balcony for the past year. Darcy, Lawrence, and Sister Alice lived in the building facing east; Ms. Viola, Mr. Will, and Fletcher occupied the west building.

Ms. Viola stood and cleared her graveled voice loud enough to disperse a crowd, or in this case, gather attention. Her wrinkled arms, propped up on one of the tables, seemed to keep her upright.

"I guess you're wondering why you're here today."

"She can't raise our rent, can she?" Lawrence whispered to Darcy.

Raise the rent?

"Shhh," she hissed, then felt her stomach knot. The only reason she had moved into this dump was because of the location and the ridiculously low dollar rent. Fountain Oaks had to have been built when God was a child, but over the years the Galleria area had risen to legendary status. She could legitimately say she lived in Uptown, merely a stone's throw from the most prestigious, upscale shopping arena in Houston. *Everyone* knew the relevance of living in the Galleria area.

"Despite the small print on the flyer, which I assume is why you've even bothered to attend, I'm glad you're here," Ms. Viola said. Darcy and Lawrence's eyes dropped to the dead grass. Busted. Will and Fletcher wore "out to lunch" looks.

"We're a community here at Fountain Oaks, and I think it's time we get to know each other, so fix a plate and let's talk." Ms. Viola removed covers from the dishes on the card tables. "Fletcher, bring your food here," she ordered.

That's it? There's got to be more.

Fletcher dumped his offering on the table. Mr. Will leaned forward. "I didn't know we were supposed to bring food. I'll be right back." The old man wrestled his ancient frame out of his chair.

"Will, sit!" Ms. Viola commanded. "You brought the Jell-O salad."

"I did?" Will lifted his fishing hat, scratched his head, and eased back into his chair. "Huh, what do ya know?"

Ms. Viola unveiled smoky sausages in a dark, almost black barbeque sauce, the lime green Jell-O salad, and a bag of Fig Newtons. She glanced past Fletcher's menagerie of food and opened the sack of chips for Darcy's hot cheese dip.

"Who brought this?" Ms. Viola pointed to the nasty plate of lifeless asparagus. No one answered. "I *said,* who brought this?" Fletcher's hand raised and pointed stiff-armed at Lawrence, who leaned sideways to hide behind Darcy.

Ms. Viola swung around. "You're responsible for this?"

Lawrence swallowed hard. "Yes."

"And you're sure it's edible?" Ms. Viola asked.

"Yes." Lawrence's words shook like they'd been run over a washboard.

"Fine. You eat the first one." Ms. Viola extended the plate toward Lawrence.

The small crowd waited.

"No thank you," Lawrence said.

"I figured as much." Ms. Viola dumped the paper plate in the nearby trash can. "Well, don't just sit there. We haven't got all day. Eat!"

The tenants, on their feet, walked around the table and eyed their options. Darcy had hit pay dirt with the queso. The gooey melted cheese dip looked safe and was the first serving bowl to empty.

"Are those Vera Wang?" Ms. Viola pointed to Darcy's French Sole ballet flats.

Darcy halted, the surprise unmistakable on her face. "Yes," she stammered, "they are."

36

"I thought so. I see you in the mornings when you leave for work." Ms. Viola chewed on a tortilla chip. "You're fond of Jimmy Choos, aren't you?"

How in the hell does this crusty old lady know about designer shoes?

A long moment passed before Darcy found her voice.

"I love Jimmy Choos. You know designer shoes?"

And why is she watching you? Creepy….

"I do." Ms. Viola's voice screeched like fingernails on a chalkboard.

"But how…?" Darcy mentally smacked her forehead, the implication clear. Her ass was grass.

Rut-roh….

"How could an old broad like me know anything about fashion?" Ms. Viola's cheeks flushed, her eyes narrowed. She pointed a crooked finger at Darcy. "Listen here, missy. I've been a lot of things in my life…dumb isn't one of them."

All eyes cut to the space between Ms. Viola and Darcy with open-mouthed shock. Darcy's heart knocked around her chest like an oversized pinball.

That didn't go well at all. You want me to go get Izzy?

Ms. Viola relaxed in her chair, crossed her legs, cleared her throat, and plastered a fake smile on her face. "What I meant to say is there are a lot of things you don't know about me. Or any of you, for that matter." The old woman pulled the straw hat down to her lap. "And I think it's time we get to know each other. We're a community here. So get some food and sit down." She pointed to the ice chest beside her. "Drinks are over here."

The Fountain Oaks tenants did as they were told and then returned to their chairs.

"I'll go first." She blew what Darcy could only imagine to be hot air. "My name is Viola Middleton. I turned eighty on July 4. I've been a widow for the last twenty-three years. I don't have children because I don't like them, although I do tolerate my nephew. I'm an old woman, I'm set in my ways, and I wear funny looking clothes. My dogs have always been named after presidents. I don't know why, so don't ask me. I eat KFC on Tuesdays, and I never touch that raw fish shit. I volunteer for Meals on Wheels on Thursdays. Who's next?"

Darcy forced her hand in the air. "So…how do you know about designer shoes?"

"Not that it's any of your business," Ms. Viola spat back. She adjusted herself in the chair. "I apologize. That wasn't nice."

That had to burn like vinegar coming out of her mouth.

"In my younger days, I managed the shoe department downtown at Sakowitz. I also studied fashion design." Ms. Viola gave a quick nod, putting an end to any further explanation. She furrowed her eyebrows at Darcy. "You're next."

Darcy lifted her eyes to the sky and raced through a quick background check. She pushed her shades up on her head and decided to hold back on her love for wine in a box, fudge brownie nut ice cream, and tacos from Jack-in-the-Box. She'd skip her personal views on politics and religion, especially how she hated rude people, which was certain to cause a backlash with her apartment manager.

"I'm Darcy Daniels and I'm thirty years old. I sell designer eyewear in the Houston area. My parents live out off Highway 6, and I have a younger brother, Alex, who works for Microsoft. My little sister, Andrea, goes to Houston Community College." Darcy paused. "Is that enough?" She doubted the group cared that her ears stuck out, her lips were too pouty, her freckles tended to run together in the summer, and she'd never fit into size four jeans.

Ms. Viola repositioned her uncomfortable glare. "What about your animals?"

Darcy flinched, *The Animal Planet* thing still fresh in her mind. "Stash is my dog, and I have a cat named Mel."

"And you like expensive clothes, shoes, accessories, etc.," Ms. Viola stated.

"I uh…well, yeah, sort of."

"Sort of, she says. Who's next?" Ms. Viola peered around the group.

Lawrence and Fletcher exchanged looks. Will stared straight ahead.

Ms. Viola nudged the man at her side. "Will?"

"Huh?" He acted like he'd been interrupted from an important mental news bulletin.

"Tell the folks about yourself," Viola said.

"What do you want me to say?" Mr. Will panned the group like he'd suddenly realized people were sitting around him.

Ms. Viola's rolled her eyes. "I ran into Will three years ago at the VFW. Friday Bingo Night. He's been a widower for ten years. His daughters want to put him in a nursing home." Ms. Viola shot Will a look. "He's fine, just getting old, that's all. I keep an eye on him. For his daughters, that is."

Will broke away from his personal news station and gave Ms. Viola a smile before turning to the other tenants. "Do you like my tie?"

"Yes. Uh-huh. Very nice," said the peanut gallery.

"I'm not over-dressed, am I?"

The three younger people shook their heads.

"Will, do you want to add anything?" Ms. Viola asked.

"I like to fish. Do you fish, boy?" Will had directed his question to Lawrence, who choked on a little black sausage.

"Let the boy tell us about himself first," Ms. Viola suggested.

"Huh? Alright, go ahead boy," Mr. Will said. "Tell us something."

Lawrence got past the clogged Lit'le Smoky after several slaps on the back from Darcy. "My name is Lawrence Ousted." He pursed his lips and studied the slimy Jell-O salad on his plate. "I'm thirty-five. My parents live in River Oaks and I have an older brother. I have a PhD in social and behavioral science from Yale, and I work contract for several hospitals in the area."

"You're a shrink." Ms. Viola's lips sneered upward.

"No, just a psychologist; no prescription pad here." A weak smile pressed across his face.

"Is that your Ford Fiesta out there, boy?" Will raised a bony finger toward the carport.

"Yes," Lawrence muttered.

A long—really long—moment passed. "Nice car," Will replied.

Lawrence leaned over to Darcy, maintaining eye contact with the group. "Is he talking about *my* car?"

"Shut up," Darcy hissed.

Will scrunched up his nose to peer at Lawrence through his horn rims. "You like to fish, Larry?"

Ms. Viola cut Will off. "What about you, Fletcher? Tell the folks here about yourself."

Fletcher scooped up Jell-O salad with a chip and stuffed it into his mouth. A flush crept up his neck and worked its way across his face. His deadpan eyes pleaded with Ms. Viola for a pardon.

One side of Ms. Viola's mouth screwed upward. "Fletcher Vance, our maintenance man, has worked and lived here for the past five years." Ms. Viola's words spewed forth like darts. "He was injured in Desert Storm back in the early '90s, and he has that head trauma thing."

"Traumatic brain injury?" Lawrence asked.

"Yeah, whatever," Ms. Viola said. "His mother and I were friends."

All eyes turned to Fletcher, which caused him to squirm and stare at the ground.

"I like animals." His voice sounded flat. "And I have a plant named Judith."

Eyebrows rose.

"You have a plant named Judith?" Lawrence asked.

Fletcher nodded.

"You fish, boy?" Will asked.

"That's enough Will." Ms. Viola brought herself to her feet and gathered the Fig Newton's and the dishes she had brought. "Take fifty dollars off next month's rent." The cranky old woman tugged at Will's shirtsleeve. "C'mon Will, walk me home."

Darcy stood. "Excuse me?"

Ms. Viola whipped around.

"I was wondering who we file a complaint to?" Darcy asked.

Viola's reserve of charm mustered for the afternoon had run dry. "What the hell about?"

Darcy swallowed hard. "The landscaping." Darcy stepped toward the old woman. Lawrence hovered behind her.

Ms. Viola's eyes narrowed. "What about it?"

"It's dead," she said. Lawrence stood so close behind her his breath tickled the back of her neck. "I thought we could write a petition to the owner…or management company."

"Oh you think so, do you?" Ms. Viola spat, stepping forward.

All eyes rotated to Darcy. She felt foolish to think this crazy woman's icy exterior had thawed even an inch. Ms. Viola dumped the dishes and bag of Fig Newton's into Will's arms, put her head down, and marched directly toward Darcy.

40

"You've done it now," Lawrence whispered from behind. "I've got your back, though."

"Thanks a lot," Darcy muttered, and braced herself the best she could for battle.

The woman halted barely two feet from Darcy, her hands clamped at her waist.

"I apologize, again." Ms. Viola seemed to study Darcy's face. "You're not a bad person, and I say things I don't always mean; although I do know a petition isn't going to help."

"But why?" Darcy asked.

"I just know, that's all. It's not open for discussion." Ms. Viola did an about-face and returned to where she had left Will, dirty dishes and Fig Newtons in hand.

Darcy grabbed her empty container and headed to her apartment.

"That was close." Lawrence said, close behind her. Darcy kept walking. "Can we talk?"

"What is it Larry?"

"I'm not amused."

"Why?" Darcy teased. "I think you've made a new friend. Maybe he'll adopt you."

"I find that extremely unlikely and quite terrifying, to be perfectly honest." Lawrence followed Darcy up the stairs.

Geez, he can't take a hint, can he?

Darcy stood her ground outside her closed apartment door. Lawrence was an okay guy, but like a dog no one wanted. And yes, she had a soft heart for strays, but she was way over her quota.

"I think we should process for a moment."

Darcy winced. "Process? Is that psycho-babble?"

"Yes, it is." He plunged forward. "I found parts of the soiree quite disturbing."

"Which parts?"

"All of it, actually," Lawrence said. "Do you realize we live among a conglomerate of potentially hazardous misfits?"

"And you say that because we're normal, right?" Darcy snorted under her breath, and gave up her attempt to make Lawrence leave. She opened the door to her phone ringing and Stash chasing Mel around the coffee table.

"Good lord!" Lawrence ranted. "It's not any safer up here."

"Halt!" Darcy screamed. Both animals skidded to a stop, turned to regard their owner, and took off again. She shrugged and reached the phone just as her own voice finished the recorded message.

"Hey Boop." Miranda's voice was unmistakable, even without the Boop. No surprise, music and laughter filled the background. "Come out tonight. I'm celebrating, and you know you can't stay mad at me. We're at Sammie's. Give me a call."

Darcy glanced at the clock in the kitchen—five forty-five. Going out meant she might actually meet someone new; a ray of hope, considering her current dry spell. She had several guys she dated on her very small Rolodex, but nothing ever stuck...no sparks, no nothing.

Maybe you should go out.

Sammie's, an upscale jazz bar in Midtown, meant she'd have to come up with a hot outfit fast.

Push yourself, do something different.

"A friend, I take it?" Lawrence asked.

"My best friend."

"And she calls you Boop?"

"Yep. Ever since middle school."

"I see." Lawrence moved to the bar and sat down. "Doesn't make Larry sound so bad."

"Hang around Miranda for a while and you'll get a name too," Darcy smirked. "And you're right, Larry might be an upgrade."

"How so?"

"She's only seen Ms. Viola once. Now she calls her the Wicked Witch of the West."

Lawrence grabbed a paper towel to work off a water ring on the counter top. "But that's appropriate."

"And Sister Mary Alice is the Nun Hun."

"She sounds like an interesting person," Lawrence said. "How did you become best friends?"

Darcy searched the ceiling of her apartment for an answer. "I have absolutely no idea." She kicked off her shoes and pulled a box of wine from the refrigerator. "I guess we're sort of like *The Banger Sisters.* You know, totally opposite personalities. I'm Susan Sarandon and she's the crazy Goldie Hawn...the one everybody likes. Wine?" Darcy pulled a couple of stemmed glasses from a cabinet.

Lawrence's gaze fixed on the box with a spout.

"Let me guess." Darcy stood on the kitchen side of the bar, her hand on her hip. "You've never had wine from a box."

"Uh, no."

Darcy spent most of her time inventing ways to cut corners. Wine in a box was an early discovery when she had found that a box of Chardonnay lasted her a week…two if she was good. And if she drank cheap wine out of a nice stemmed glass, she couldn't tell the difference.

Actually, that's a total lie. Cheap wine in a Solo cup suits you just as well.

Her wine palette didn't match her persona, but she had gotten good at faking it when she had to. "Now that you're buying shirts from Walmart and entertaining with canned asparagus, you're ready for boxed wine." Darcy filled two glasses and handed one to Lawrence. She held up her glass. "Cheers."

Lawrence touched his stemmed glass to Darcy's, then swirled the wine around a couple of times before taking a tentative sip. He held the liquid in his mouth, swishing it from side to side.

"Oh, good lord. Swallow!"

Lawrence closed his eyes and followed the order, his head cocked oddly to one side. Darcy watched with curiosity. His eyes opened slowly; he looked like he'd just ingested one of his putrid asparagus spears. He attempted a smile. "I think I could get used to this."

She knew he was lying. "Stick with it," Darcy said. "It gets easier." She stood in the kitchen, knowing she needed to decide about that night. Going out would be good for her; however, several drawbacks popped into her mind:

She and Miranda lived in parallel universes. Miranda, besides being a human firecracker, lived in a high-priced loft in Midtown. Unless you actually *lived* in Midtown, which Darcy did not, you had to fight for a parking spot, not to mention a hefty bar tab charged to her already high balance credit card, and hanging out with a noisy crowd till dawn.

At five forty-five—still daylight—the "celebration" sounded like it was in full swing, and Darcy knew it would not peak until way after midnight.

No way in hell could she throw on something that remotely resembled "hot."

She bit the inside of her lip and scratched her neck. Decision made. "Okay, I'm getting hungry. Want to go grab a burger? Do you have plans?"

Why do you keep asking him to share a meal? I mean, how desperate are you? Forget I asked that.

"Well, let me think. No, no plans," came the immediate answer. "What did you have in mind?"

"I'm thinking Roznovsky's."

"What's Roznovsky's?" Lawrence finished his first-ever glass of boxed wine, which Darcy refilled.

"You really haven't been around much, have you?"

He raised his nose, "snob" smeared across his face. "That depends on what you mean by 'being around'."

"Around...like, outside of River Oaks."

"I remind you, I am a Yale graduate."

"So?"

"So, I've been around Connecticut."

"Does Connecticut have good burgers?"

"I wouldn't know."

"My point." Darcy said. "I'll call Miranda with an excuse." She picked up the cordless phone, dialed Miranda's number, and crossed her fingers. "Don't answer. Don't answer." Darcy's face relaxed when the recorded voice kicked on.

"Hey, got your message," Darcy began, and then downshifted into a clothes-pinned nasal voice. "Think I'm coming down with a cold. Gonna get in bed with a book," she said. "Talk to you later." She clicked off the phone, shoved her feet back into her French Sole flats, and grabbed her purse. "I'm driving, but we're not going anywhere till you change that shirt."

"Why?" Lawrence glanced down. "I'm growing quite fond of it."

"Trust me on this one," Darcy said. "Roznovsky's is casual but...uh, no."

"If you insist," Lawrence said.

"I do."

***

44

Darcy eased into one of the front parking spaces at Roznovsky's, a local favorite hangout known for their homemade chili and cheeseburgers.

"This looks like it used to be a gas station," Lawrence said.

Mischief tugged at Darcy's mouth. "Another first for you, I'm sure. C'mon."

Over cheeseburgers, chili cheese fries, and long necks, they discussed careers, parents, non-existent love lives, and their Fountain Oaks neighbors. Darcy returned to the table with two new bottles of beer.

Lawrence sat, arms folded across his chest. Eyebrows sewn together, he studied the television mounted on the wall. "See that?" He nodded at the television. "A crime scene. That could very well be Fountain Oaks. I tell you, I have an uneasy feeling about that maintenance man."

"Fletcher?" Darcy took a healthy swig of ice cold beer. "He's harmless. Odd…but harmless."

"He has a plant named Judith."

"So?"

"But that's not normal."

"We've been through this Larry." Darcy wadded up the thin paper wrapped around her cheeseburger and tossed it into the plastic basket. "None of us are normal. We're a bunch of misfits living in the same complex. I think we're safe, just pathetic."

A smile hung at the corner of Lawrence's mouth. "Did you see Ms. Viola's outfit?"

"Right out of *Hee-Haw*?"

"Exactly." Lawrence tore off several sheets from the paper towel roll on the table, cleaned their eating surface, and neatly stacked the plastic baskets. He then pulled a handkerchief from his back pocket and used it as a makeshift koozie around his beer bottle.

Darcy rolled her eyes and mentally added OCD to Lawrence's character traits. "You don't get out much, do you?"

Like you do.

"Not much. My social calendar has a plethora of open slots these days."

"Do me a favor," Darcy began. "Unless you want me to start calling you Webster, stop talking like a human dictionary. And no more Hawaiian shirts from Walmart, okay? You need to go to Harwin."

"I hate to keep asking these maniacal…I mean crazy…questions, but what is Harwin?" Finished with his beer, Lawrence laid his handkerchief out on the table to dry.

She studied the odd man for a moment, then shrugged. "It's hard to describe." She finished her own beer and grabbed her purse. "Just promise, no more knock-off Buffett shirts from Walmart. And tell me you know Jimmy Buffett."

"I'm not a complete moron, I'll have you know. I knew about *Hee-Haw*, didn't I?" Lawrence stood, pushed his chair under the table, and refolded his handkerchief.

"You don't have a clue about Jimmy Buffett, do you?"

"Not even close."

The neon clock on her dash read nine o'clock. Darcy doubted Miranda's party had reached full-blown status yet, even with the early mid-afternoon start. She glanced at the passenger seat and realized the night hadn't been too terribly awful. Lawrence had turned out to be a good listener, even if it was his profession.

"I have to admit, I'm still frightened by Ms. Viola," Lawrence broke into Darcy's silent conversation. "I thought you were toast when you brought up the complaint letter."

"Yeah, that was weird how she charged me and then backed down." Darcy couldn't get a handle on Ms. Viola's mood swings. "The woman even smiled."

"I'm not sure I'd categorize that as a smile," Lawrence said. "However, it seemed to be a somewhat honest effort."

Darcy mentally shook her head at Lawrence's attempt at casual conversation. But what the hell, she didn't have to eat alone…which reminded her. "Hey, thanks for paying. I should've chipped in though. I'm the one who kept ordering the beers."

"That's okay," Lawrence said. "I owe you for the pizza last weekend, and I'm already ahead fifty dollars on next month's rent."

Darcy climbed the stairs to her apartment and wondered what bizarre events she'd missed at Sammie's.

Chapter 4

She rubbed a thumbnail across her bottom lip and lifted a window slat of the mini blinds. Fletcher moved methodically about the courtyard area, disassembling the tables and chairs.

"Well, that's done." Viola made her way to the small private photo gallery to the right of the media screen and ran fingers over the pictures, lives that once were, each permanently imprinted in her psyche. Pulling the frayed straw hat from her head, she moved to one of the recliners in the living area and eased down into the soft leather chair, rethinking the afternoon, which hadn't turned out so badly after all. At least the pretense of bringing the tenants together wasn't a total lie, not to mention a few others she had told. A sense of community, her one saving grace all these years, was always a good thing. Right? And besides, one day they *could* be helpful to each other…one day. But more important, her plan had worked. A somewhat civil exchange of words had been held with the young female tenant she'd been observing. It had been so long since she'd attempted a pleasant conversation with anyone, she'd almost forgotten the parameters. For almost a year she'd honed in on Darcy's designer clothes and shoes. She had guessed her to be around thirty. Bingo.

Viola reached over to the modern side table between the recliners and lifted the lid of the smooth rectangle cedar box resting on the smoked glass top. Her hand slipped inside, and as her fingers felt the soft velvet lining, they closed around the object she longed to touch…her ritual. She carefully removed the chain from the box and settled it in her lap. Without hesitation, her fingers ran across the name and ID number on the tags. When her thoughts were skewed, as they had been for so long, this ritual helped her feel centered. She

47

sometimes found herself holding the dog tags without any recollection of retrieving it from the cedar box.

Leaning her head back, she closed her eyes. Her life hadn't turned out the way she'd thought it would. Did anyone's? Twenty-three sounded better than forty. Forty years as a widow sounded pathetic.

"I know you're listening, Robert, and if you hadn't died on me we could have gotten through this."

She often talked to her deceased husband. Sometimes she thought he answered, or at least offered a comment...nothing distinguishable, but it didn't stop her conversations. She'd been mad at him for years for dying, though how could you blame a person who died from a broken heart? Yes, he'd had heart problems, but he never got over the loss of their son. Viet Nam had been a horrible war. So many died. Michael, *their* Michael, had been among the numbers in 1970 listed as MIA, then confirmed dead. Four months later, Rob died from a massive heart attack. As mad as she'd been at him all those years, she knew his heart just couldn't handle the grief.

With the dog tags held to her heart, her thoughts moved on to her maternal grandmother. Nona had taught her things her mother didn't have the slightest inclination to, like cooking, crocheting...being kind to others. She'd always wanted to be like her grandma.

Her mother's fourth marriage had come with a boatload of money. After the ridiculously elaborate ceremony, the whole crew, Nona included, had moved into a fancy-shmancy house in West University, an elite and extremely old money area of Houston that came equipped with a staff of housekeepers, gardeners, and cooks. Until that time, Nona had never had much more than a pot to pee in, but she'd always seemed happy. Going from nothing to having everything imaginable never changed Nona's tender and loving disposition. Viola never understood, but found her grandma's outlook on life comforting.

Viola and her older sister had been primed for the Junior League of Houston, according to her mother's new stature in society. At first, Viola thought she'd love all the glitz and glimmer, but quickly found it pretentious. She'd often sneak away from a "function" and spend time with Nona, quietly reading a book while Nona wrote in her journal. Her lack of enthusiasm and participation in debutante activities soon led to her name being dropped from the list of potentials for the Junior League. No big deal to Viola, although her mother and stepfather were far from pleased, which left her older sister the shiny (but far from the brightest) bulb in the tanning bed.

She could have said she liked being alone all those years after losing both Michael and Robert within a four-month span, but who'd believe that rubbish? She'd lived at Fountain Oaks for twenty-three years. If it hadn't been for her nephew, she figured she'd still be living in that same old house, surrounded by nothing but long forgotten days of a life she once had.

Not having any children had been a lie, of course: just her usual tactic to avoid painful questions. But she didn't lie about having a nephew. Timothy was a good boy...man, she should say. No one called a sixty-year-old man a boy. She more than tolerated him; she loved that man, always had, just like he was her own. It was Timothy's mother, her older sister, she detested...her older sister *and* Timothy's twin sister. Both females were cut from the same shallow, la-de-dah mold. How her sister had managed to produce two totally opposite human beings still muddled her mind.

Timothy had convinced her to move to Fountain Oaks, which had probably been the right thing to do; however, it did little to improve her disposition. She managed the small apartment complex over the years, dressed like a bag lady most of the time, and didn't care what anyone else thought...except Timothy. Michael and Timothy had not only been cousins, but best friends. They'd enlisted together, and were both sent to Vietnam after basic training. Remembering the crack in Timothy's voice when he presented the flag to her and Robert at Michael's military funeral caused her to wince.

Tim had a good family, the kind portrayed on a Hallmark Christmas special. He and his wife, Georgia, had two sons, and included Viola in all family gatherings. The ones her sister and niece attended, she'd opted out of. The day after, as always, Timothy would show up with the kids and plates of food, and lies about how much she had been missed. He meant well, he just lacked the mean streak she had perfected. She guessed she owed her nephew and his family her life, what was left of it.

Following her great nephews in their Little League games brought her immense pleasure. She'd show up with her lawn chair, umbrella, and can of Dr. Pepper every Saturday. Sadly for the boys, but lucky for her, their grandmother never felt the urge or understood the importance of playing the grandma role. The boys, Lucas and Clayton, were now grown and twinkles in Viola's eyes. Lucas had become an attorney…Clayton, a CPA.

A picture of Darcy flashed once again across her mental vision. The little chick-a-dee wanted to file a complaint about the landscaping. After all these years, she paid about as much attention to the upkeep of Fountain Oaks as she did to her wardrobe. But maybe Darcy had a point. She'd have to chew on that one for a bit.

Viola knew her outlook on life, from the outside and sometimes on the inside, sucked. She wasn't a total bitch, although she had no problem with the tenants thinking she was. She had mentioned her working with Meals on Wheels, but left out her involvement with the VA. For many years she'd belonged to the Volunteer Transportation Program, getting vets to their doctors' appointments and back home. As she grew older and didn't trust driving around other people, especially vets who had enough problems of their own, she switched to the VA Holiday Gift Distribution. She'd even persuaded Lucas and Clayton to join the VA Advocacy Program. On many occasions she'd drop by the hospital to visit the many men, and often women, in wheelchairs sitting around the lobby of the hospital. Viola often wondered why they sat there, day after day. To view the outside world, a society where they once belonged? Hoping someone, such as herself, might stop for a few minutes? After leaving the VA, she always struggled with the clash of emotions. Yes, she'd done her due-diligence by volunteering her time, but…she could get in her car and leave. So many couldn't.

Returning the dog tags to their home in the cedar box, she pushed herself out of the recliner and put the teakettle on the stove. She rubbed her eyes and thought about the tenants. She had known for many years about Fletcher and his disability. She'd delivered meals to his mother until she died. Without hesitation, Viola had invited Fletcher to move into Fountain Oaks, and had put him to work around the property doing odd jobs.

Then she'd persuaded Will's daughters to let him rent an apartment. She'd seen the inside of nursing homes, and Will wasn't there yet. His memory wavered, but then again, that was what happened in the eighth decade of a person's life. Sister Mary Alice had lived at Fountain Oaks longer than Viola had. Way into her retirement years, the nun still volunteered at St. Joseph's Hospital and Houston Hospice down in the Medical Center.

Lawrence feared her, no doubt. She rather liked that, and guessed that made her a bully in a way, like getting a kick out of scaring small children. This she wasn't particularly proud of, but he was just so easy. And besides, he was an adult…he didn't *have* to act like a child. *Spoiled brat*, she thought, but hey, he paid rent.

And then there was Ms. Darcy Daniels. The young woman seemed to have a good job, nice clothes…she obviously had money, so why live at Fountain Oaks? Something about Darcy had always intrigued her, and after today, she'd confirmed her suspicions. She'd nailed this one dead on. Darcy Daniels replicated the image of herself at that age.

Viola didn't burn food often, but this time she'd forgotten about the flame under the barbeque sauce until it had turned a nice black color. At first she had been tempted to pitch the batch she'd made for the party and start over, but at the last minute gave it a "what the hell" and shrugged off the urge. She dumped the remaining Lit'l Smokies down the disposal and scraped petrified barbeque sauce from the serving bowl. In the past, her humanitarian acts had targeted people with obvious needs. Darcy's weren't overt, yet for some reason, she felt a desire, a strong one, to help this woman. She needed to get to know Darcy better. But how? Pulling a Fig Newton from the package on the counter, her hand stalled mid-air on its way to her mouth.

"I know what I'll do." Having lost interest in sitting with a cup of tea, she turned off the fire under the teakettle, preheated the oven, and lined up items from the pantry and refrigerator.

Chapter 5

Darcy slept deeply and dreamlessly for a change. She might have rolled right into Monday except for the banging on the front door. Her bedside clock read eight forty-five...in the morning. She muscled past sleeping animals, squinted through the peephole, growled, and flung open the door.

"Liar." Miranda pushed through with a sack of something smelling darn good in her hand. "I knew you weren't sick."

In a black spandex dress which barely covered her behind, Miranda walked past her in black fish net stockings and sparkly stilettos. Hints of mascara smudges lined her eyes. Other than her hair looking like it had been styled by a stun gun, she looked pretty good for someone who hadn't been to bed yet. Maybe Darcy assumed too much.

"What do you mean 'liar'?" She headed for the sack Miranda placed on the leather ottoman coffee table.

"I taught you that whiny-ass fake voice." Miranda kicked off her shoes and threw herself onto the couch.

"Oh yeah, I forgot." Darcy poked through the bag of food and pulled out breakfast burritos and two large Styrofoam cups of coffee.

"How'd the pow-wow go yesterday?" Miranda accepted a coffee.

Thinking for a moment, Darcy said, "Not too bad, considering I almost got decked by the Wicked Witch."

"Did she bring her broom?"

"Not unless it was up her ass," Darcy said between bites. "I wanted to write a letter about the landscaping. It pissed her off."

"Which reminds me...Radar's downstairs watering dead shrubs."

"His name is Fletcher," Darcy added.

53

Miranda shrugged. "Whatever. Fletch is watering dried-up dead plants."

"He's our maintenance man, and we're soooo proud." Stash walked over and gave Darcy the it's-that-time look. She pulled herself to her feet and grabbed the leash. "C'mon."

Stash and Miranda raised their eyebrows. Miranda spoke first. "Who are you talking to?"

"Both of you." Stash pulled the two women onto the dried grass in the courtyard before he started to empty his tank. Darcy shielded her eyes from the morning sun. Her vision cleared and sure enough, Fletcher stood watering a bed of way-past-gone shrubs. She lowered her hand in a half wave. The maintenance man stared with his usual "nobody's home" face, although this time the look was probably geared more toward Miranda, sporting her sprayed on dress and fishnet stockings. Darcy hardly thought it could be her long t-shirt and baggy-assed sweat pants. People, men in particular, gawking at Miranda wasn't exactly a news flash.

"How ya doing?" Miranda yelled. She lowered her voice. "Is he always in costume?"

Fletcher raised his index and middle finger in a "peace" salute back to Miranda.

"Always," Darcy answered. "Found out yesterday he has a metal plate in his head or something from Desert Storm. He used to scare me, but now I think he's pretty harmless."

The three made their way back upstairs. "Wonder what station he's tuned in to?" Miranda asked.

"He has a plant named Judith." Darcy couldn't hide a smile.

"Your neighbors are weird," Miranda said. "Tell me about the Wicked Witch of the West."

"I can't figure her out," Darcy shouted from her bedroom. She emerged a few minutes later wearing grey Capri yoga pants and a pink and grey-striped fitted top, a step up from the sweat pants and over-sized t-shirt. She wadded her hair into a knot on the back of her head and secured it with a large clip. "One minute she's Attila the Hun, and the next she's a commentator on the red carpet." Darcy returned to the couch. "Yesterday she noticed I wore my Vera Wang flats. *And* she said she sees me leave in the mornings."

"She's *stalking* you?"

Darcy shrugged. "I doubt it. Anyone looking out their front window can see what goes on around here."

"But it doesn't explain how she knows about your shoe fetish."

Normally, Darcy would consider the fetish remark an insult, but Miranda got away with that kind of talk.

"She used to be the manager of the shoe department at Sakowitz when she was younger," Darcy said.

"*The* Sakowitz? No way." Miranda stood and padded to the kitchen.

"She names her pets after presidents."

"You'd better keep your eyes and ears open," Miranda said between gulps of bottled water. "Sounds like one of those people you hear about on TV. A little weird, never bothers anyone, and then "blam"…blasts through the post office with an automatic weapon."

Both women jumped at the bang on the front door. They locked eyes. Miranda moved her finger to her lips and tiptoed to the peephole.

"Who is it?" Darcy whispered, and crossed her fingers it wasn't Lawrence.

"I don't know; my x-ray vision isn't working at the moment."

"I know you're in there. I hear voices."

There was no mistaking Ms. Viola's growl. Darcy pushed Miranda away. She shot her friend a "please behave" look, and opened the door to find the old woman with a plate in one hand and a leash attached to her arthritic cocker spaniel in the other.

Ms. Viola shoved the plate forward. "Here." She wore baggy rolled-up jeans, what looked to be a man's shirt, and a waxy rehearsed smile. An Astros cap helmeted down her hair.

"What is this?" Darcy asked.

"Cookies."

"Cookies?"

"Chocolate chip."

"Chocolate chip?"

"Were you a parrot in a former life?" Ms. Viola asked.

She could feel Miranda's eyes taking in the scene and prayed her friend would keep her trap shut.

Don't give in to panic. Get a grip. Think like…a grown-up.

"No, of course not. I'm…just surprised to see you." Darcy hoped her voice sounded normal, although she knew it chirped more like PeeWee Herman. "Come in?"

Ms. Viola's gaze swerved past her and spotted Miranda, who looked like a hooker just in from a profitable night.

"No, I see you're busy," Ms. Viola said. "Here." The scary-looking apartment manager shoved the plate into Darcy's chest before she turned and yanked on the dog's leash. "C'mon Ike."

"But why the cookies?" Darcy immediately realized the stupidity of her words.

Ms. Viola whirled around. "I thought it would be a nice thing to do," she said, and made her way down the steps. "You can bring the plate back this afternoon."

Darcy closed the door and leaned against it. "The Wicked Witch has left the building."

"And Toto has crossed over to the dark side. Damn, I hate it when that happens," Miranda said. "Did she call that dog Ike?"

"I told you she names her dogs after presidents." Darcy moved to the bar and removed the plastic wrap from the plate.

Scooting onto a barstool, Miranda asked, "You're not going to eat those are you?" She picked one up for a closer examination. "Hey, I know someone who can analyze these."

Darcy snatched it out of her hand and tossed it back on the plate.

Miranda brushed residual crumbs from her hands. "Maybe they're laced with anthrax."

"What's weird is, she volunteers for Meals on Wheels," Darcy said. "Fletcher's mother was a friend of hers, and he moved in here right after she died. *And* she keeps an eye on Mr. Will."

"Who's Mr. Will?"

Darcy smiled and leaned toward her friend. "Remember Norman Thayer from *On Golden Pond?* A clone. Even wears a bowtie."

Miranda slid her eyes toward Darcy. "For real?"

"Yep."

"You know, I came over to chew your ass out for not coming to Sammie's, but now I see why you hang out here." Miranda smirked. "You've got Radar, the Wicked Witch of the West, Nun Hun, and Norman Thayer."

"Which reminds me, you haven't met Lawrence."

56

Miranda's eyebrows rose. "There's more?"

"He's thirty-five and comes from old money. Has a PhD from Yale."

"A shrink?"

"Noooo, pharmaceutical person," Darcy smirked. "You need a medical license for that, remember?"

"Oh yeah, I should know that." Miranda finished her bottle of water. "What the hell is he doing living here?"

"He's broke till his next trust fund money is freed up, and his parents won't let him move back home." Laughter flickered behind Darcy's eyes. "I took him to Roznovsky's last night."

Miranda jerked her head back as if she'd caught a whiff of dead fish. "You're dating him?"

"Of course not," Darcy defended.

Are you sure?

Was it a date? Oh God, she'd sunk to an all-time low. No! Not a date. Definitely not a date.

Whatever....

"Good. If he'd already seen your little green lizard, I was going to smack you over the head."

"No need," Darcy said. "I do that pretty well all by myself. And by the way, who are you to talk?"

Throwing the remark aside, Miranda glanced at her watch and stood, pushing down her spandex dress to a respectable street level. "Should've come last night. Plenty of single guys. So when do I get to meet Dr. Seuss?"

Darcy smiled. "I told him you'd give him a name."

"It'll have to do till I meet him." Miranda winked and smiled. Darcy's crazy best friend grabbed her shoes, blew a smoochy air kiss, and left. She and Miranda often had their little cat fights, but they never lasted long.

She watched Mel jump onto the bar and sniff the cookies. "She just blows in and lights up a room, doesn't she?" Darcy smoothed her hand down Mel's back. "Let's hold off on these." She slid the plate out of Mel's reach, resealed the plastic, and scratched under the cat's chin. "You're a good judge of character. What do you think about Ms. Viola?" The Garfield cat rotated his head in a circular motion, enjoying the attention. "Wanna come when I take the plate back this afternoon?" Mel bounded off the bar, which sent Stash in a full-throttle charge toward the orange tabby.

"Chicken." She mentally ran through her to-do list for the day. She glanced at the clock and picked up the phone, dialing her parents' number.

Stop. What are you doing? Going to your parents' house every Sunday is getting you nowhere.

Change of plans. She drove to the grocery store and forced herself to spend fifty dollars—the money she'd be saving on rent—on groceries, which was the mature thing to do. She hated having to be mature. Being a grown-up sucked. She balanced out the mature gesture by hanging around until noon so she could pack a box of wine in her cart.

Dumb Blue Law.

She slid her mock expensive SUV into her assigned slot under the Fountain Oaks carport and loaded her arms with groceries. Using her backside to close the car door, she spotted Lawrence sitting behind the wheel of his Ford Fiesta. She walked around to the driver's side.

"What are you doing?" she asked.

"Hiding."

"From who?"

"Mr. Will."

"Why?"

"He wants me to go fishing."

Darcy smiled. "You're serious."

"Very," Lawrence said. "Why else would I camp out in this, this…vehicle."

"Been here long?" The grocery bags pulled on her arm muscles.

"One, two hours, maybe."

"You're exaggerating. Get out and make yourself useful." Darcy readjusted the load in her arms. Lawrence grabbed the remaining two grocery bags and box of wine from Darcy's car, peeked around the corner into the courtyard, and zipped up the stairs.

"Drop them anywhere," she yelled. "Be out in a minute." Darcy closed her bedroom door and changed into running clothes. Five minutes later she emerged from her bedroom. "Stop!"

Lawrence froze, his cheeks full, the remaining half of a chocolate chip cookie in his hand. "What?" he garbled.

"Ms. Viola brought those over this morning."

Lawrence, fluid in his movement, walked around the bar to the kitchen and spit the chewed cookie into the garbage can. "Milk? Baking soda? Vinegar? Any of those will neutralize poison."

"I've got milk, but it doesn't pour well." Boxed wine made the grocery list, not milk.

"If I should begin to die, my insurance card is in my wallet," Lawrence said. "If the hospital refuses to take it, call my father. Surely he'll pay if I'm dying."

"How'd it taste?" Darcy picked up a cookie.

"Actually, quite good." He wiped his mouth with a paper towel. "Odd that Ms. Viola brought you cookies."

"Odd being the key word. Seems to be a requirement to live here." Darcy noticed Lawrence's shirt and slacks were less than flashy…no ridiculous cockatoo shirt this time. She figured he had purposely dressed to fly under Mr. Will's radar. "Tell me about Mr. Will."

"First, you must tell me about these cookies."

Darcy took a seat on a barstool. This was the second day in a row she was hanging out with Dr. Seuss. "There's not much to tell. She knocked on the door about ten this morning and handed me the cookies."

"What did she say exactly?"

Darcy rummaged around in the recall section of her brain for a moment. "She said, 'Cookies. Chocolate chip.' I was so shocked to see her I couldn't do much except repeat everything she said, which seemed to piss her off."

"Of course," Lawrence agreed. "Then what?"

"I made the mistake of asking why she brought me cookies, which I guess was rude."

"Yes, but understandable." Lawrence sat up in his seat. "She didn't hit you, did she?"

"No, she didn't hit me," Darcy started. "She said she thought it would be a nice thing to do."

"What? Not hit you?"

"No, bring cookies."

Lawrence rubbed his chin. "Very interesting."

"What are you thinking?"

"Schizophrenia." Lawrence had his PhD cap on.

"Oh pu-lease."

"Or possibly MPD."

"What the hell is that?"

"Multiple personality disorder. Did you see *Sybil?*"

"Is that where Sally Field was like a gazillion different people?" Darcy rubbed the goose bumps forming on her arms.

"Yes, exactly."

"That show scared the crap out of me." Darcy shook her head to rid her mind of the images. "Get a grip, Lawrence. She's just a kooky old lady. She's looking after Mr. Will, *and* Fletcher, *and* she volunteers for Meals on Wheels. She can't be all bad."

Lawrence rolled his eyes around toward the ceiling as if making a calculated conclusion. "I hope you're right. Did she say anything else?"

"Just that I could bring her plate back this afternoon."

"To her apartment? Are you going alone? Do you need me to accompany you?"

"No, I don't need you to accompany me." Darcy noticed Lawrence's immediate relief. She didn't look forward to returning the plate to Ms. Viola, but she wasn't scared...or so she kept telling herself. "Okay, your turn. Tell me about Mr. Will."

"Well, let's see." Lawrence crossed his legs and leaned back against the barstool. "It was around eight thirty this morning and I was about to rinse off my cucumber mask when he knocked on the door."

"You answered the door with cucumber smeared on your face?"

"I'll have you know it's the highest quality organic mask CVS had on clearance. It cleanses the pores as it rejuvenates. It must stay on for exactly thirty minutes to reap all the benefits."

"You answered the door with cucumber on your face," she reiterated. If nothing else, Lawrence provided her with a boatload of hilarious mental images.

"It's my one splurge, and I still had eight minutes to go." Lawrence's chin lifted, feigning indignation.

Darcy tried to swallow her smirk. "Sorry."

"I don't think you are."

She realized she'd gone a bit far this time. She scrunched her eyes shut and tried a more serious look. "Okay. I apologize. I didn't mean to hurt your feelings."

"Very well. I accept your apology."

"Thank you." Darcy realized Miranda type comments didn't work as well for her as they did for Miranda. "So what did Mr. Will say?"

"I believe his exact words were, 'Larry, you wanna go fishin' this mornin'?"

"What did he say about your kabookie make-up?" The line slipped out before she could snatch it back.

Lawrence raised an eyebrow.

"I was just *asking*," Darcy said. "You've got to admit it probably looked pretty shocking to someone like Mr. Will."

"Actually, I don't think he noticed. He said he had misplaced his glasses."

Good thing, otherwise the old man could have keeled over.

"So, what excuse did you give him?"

"I thanked him profusely, and then informed him I still had to give myself a manicure." Lawrence readjusted his position on the barstool.

This got another burst of laughter out of Darcy. "I bet that went over big."

"I'm sure I don't know what you're talking about." A wrinkle creased his brow.

"Oh, c'mon. You didn't really expect him to buy that, did you?"

"It wasn't a lie. See?" Lawrence held out both hands.

She nodded a couple of times, not trusting her voice.

"Sunday is my personal maintenance day." Luckily, his feathers didn't seem ruffled by Darcy's last faux pas. "I have to do these things myself since I'm, well…."

"Broke."

"Yes, exactly," Lawrence said. "I haven't become comfortable with the word yet."

"Why were you sitting in the car?" Darcy found the conversation boring.

Then stop asking him questions, moron.

She decided as soon as Lawrence left she'd drop the plate off on her way to Memorial Park. That way she'd have an excuse not to stay long. Jogging would be optional, as usual.

"…And that's why you found me sequestered in my vehicle."

She wasn't about to ask him to repeat the story, yet followed with another stupid question. "So what else is on your personal maintenance agenda today?"

"Ironing."

"Of course." Darcy had an idea. She stood up and whistled. "C'mon Stash, let's go do your doggy-do."

"Well, I've stayed long enough." Lawrence jumped to his feet. "Those clothes aren't going to iron themselves, now are they? I'll see myself out."

Worked like a charm. Remember that one.

Just as the front door closed Stash came thundering in from the bedroom, tongue out and wide-eyed. He tried to apply his brakes but skidded on the old wooden floor and plowed into the barstool. Darcy reached down and rubbed his head. "Good dog." Stash smiled his goofy grin and then trotted over to nudge the leash that hung on the doorknob. "You've got this thing down," Darcy said. "Next, I'll teach you how to walk yourself." She snapped on the leash and let Stash pull her out into the dank hallway and down the stairs. Stepping out into the afternoon sunlight, she glanced in the direction of Ms. Viola's apartment just in time to see the curtains fall back together.

Growl, guess there's no way you're getting around the plate-returning thing.

She walked Stash around the perimeter of the property, and after he emptied his tank, she herded him up the stairs, resisting the urge to snatch yet another glimpse toward the other building. Back in her apartment, she laced up her Nikes on the slim chance she actually made it to Memorial Park, ran a brush through her hair, and applied strawberry lip-gloss. Mel sat on the counter and supervised as the cookies were transferred to a plastic container and Ms. Viola's plate was rinsed off.

"If I don't come back, dial 911." She glanced one last time in the mirror next to the front door and decided her natural look would have to do. And it wouldn't hurt to actually get to Memorial Park. Her running clothes were snug, not to mention her jeans. She grabbed the plate and forced herself out the door before she changed her mind.

It's just a plate. She's the apartment manager who brought you cookies. So what? Get a grip Daniels. You're not in fourth grade.

The lecture continued while she mentally cracked her knuckles and made her way across the courtyard. She stood in front of Ms. Viola's door, sucked in air, and knocked.

"There you are." Ms. Viola, minus the Astros cap, wore an apron over her man's shirt and baggy jeans, Ike at her side. "Back up," she barked to the dog, and pulled the door open enough for Darcy to enter.

"I can't stay," Darcy began. "I just wanted to return your plate."

The faded blue-grey eyes left an ice burn on Darcy's face. Ms. Viola took the plate extended to her. "I said, come in."

"Okay." She *so* felt like she'd just walked into the principal's office. Darcy entered the apartment while Ike ambled over to his bed and did a belly flop.

Ms. Viola pointed toward one side of the living area. "Sit. I've got to finish something in the kitchen."

Darcy moved to an old but quite expensive-looking couch along one wall and shifted her weight from one foot to the other. Something wonderful simmered in the kitchen and filled the apartment with a familiar aroma, which zapped her back to her childhood. She lowered herself onto the couch, her hands grazing the soft texture of sky-blue knapped velvet. Intricate doilies from another century draped the back of the once popular-styled couch.

Surveying the room, she realized she didn't know what she'd expected, but this wasn't it. An imaginary line seemed to run down the middle of the living room, clearly defining two distinct eras: modern and ancient. A deep mahogany-colored trestle coffee table with a glass top had been positioned in front of the couch, with a round heavy crystal candy dish perched on top. Through the diamond-patterned lid, Darcy could see that M&Ms filled the canister. A vintage Tiffany floor lamp, complete with crystal prisms hanging from the domed shade, provided light for the antiquated side of the room.

At the end of the living area stood an enormous plasma flat-screen mounted on a sturdy walnut sofa table with two storage cabinets beneath. The wall to the right of the oversized television held a montage of frames with mostly sepia-toned pictures. She switched to the contemporary side of the imaginary line in the sand. Two expensive ergonomic recliners in blue leather lined the opposite wall, perfectly positioned for optimum viewing of the high-tech media device. A small square table with smoked glass separated the Swedish-designed chairs. Weird.

I know, right?

She'd be more comfortable on the modern side of the room, but resisted the urge to move from where she had been commanded to sit.

How fast can you get out of here?

"Would you like some tea?"

Darcy's heart bounced to the ceiling and back at Ms. Viola's gravelly voice from the kitchen. Ike raised his head for a moment but didn't get up. Fighting the urge to bolt for the door, she gulped. "I'm fine, thank you."

"I'm making some anyway."

"Fine," Darcy whispered under her breath.

"I'll be just a few more minutes."

"Take your time. I'll be here," Darcy yelled back.

Can we leave?

She forced her hands to un-ball. She wanted to look casual. Lean back? Sit up straight?

Don't look at me, I don't have a clue.

She got to her feet and walked around, tempting Ms. Viola to send her back to her assigned seat. The breakfast area held a small modern Ikea-looking kitchen table with four matching high-back chairs. An antique oak sideboard backed up against the breakfast room wall with at least half a dozen stacks of woven squares of yarn in random colors on top. Darcy recognized the squares to be crocheted, due to Izzy's persistence to teach her the skill as a young girl. She had fought her grandmother at every turn, but had learned the stitches regardless.

"What are you doing?"

Darcy grabbed her chest to ensure her heart didn't pop out right there on the Ikea table. She turned to find Ms. Viola and Ike barely three feet away. The old woman held a silver tray topped with an ornate porcelain teapot, china teacups and saucers, silver creamer, sugar bowl, and spoons. The apron had disappeared.

This is just so weird.

"I said, what are you doing?"

"I'm…I just…I mean…." No one was going to believe she had been invited to a tea party with the Wicked Witch of the West. Darcy took a step away from the crocheted squares.

Hell, say something.

"Can I take that for you?"

The old woman eyed Darcy up and down. "No." She walked into the living room and deposited the tray on the coffee table. "Come sit. I'll get the cookies."

Darcy followed orders and returned to her seat on the couch. Cookies. Humph.

Let her take one first.

But what if she takes the one that's not poisoned?

Too obvious to kill you off in this apartment. Too incriminating.

That's right…besides, Miranda and Lawrence know about the cookies.

Oh yeah, and Lawrence ate one this afternoon and as far as we know he hasn't di—

"Here." Ms. Viola held out a fresh plate of cookies.

An awkward pause passed before Darcy blinked, picked a cookie, and shoved it into her mouth. Lawrence had been right…they were delicious.

Ms. Viola set the plate on the tray and poured two cups of tea. She handed one to Darcy and took a seat beside her on the couch.

How uncomfortable is this?

Darcy could feel her fake smile melt off her face like a Popsicle on a hot sidewalk. She willed the smile back into place.

"I appreciate you coming by this afternoon." Ms. Viola had set her cup and saucer down on the coffee table, her arms stiff, her hands cupped over her knees. "I don't have many visitors."

And she wonders why?

Darcy raced through her list of small-talk topics.

She sold designer eyewear to most of the optometrists in Houston. Surely she could fabricate some semblance of a conversation with this old lady.

"I see you crochet."

Ice-breaker. Good.

"Yes."

"I used to crochet. Some."

"Did you?" The words came out as a statement that required no follow up.

Darcy pushed on. "Izzy—that's my grandmother—taught me a long time ago."

"Really." Another flat statement.

Realizing the conversation had passed uncomfortable about two minutes ago, she balanced the saucer on her lap and shot a look around the room. "I like your television."

Ms. Viola nodded a couple of times. "I'll remember that."

"What?"

Did she say she'd remember that?

"Nothing." Ms. Viola reached for her tea and took a sip. Another long span of time passed before Ms. Viola cleared her throat. "You were uncomfortable when I said I see you in the mornings, weren't you?"

"No. Of course not."

Why are you lying?

"Yes you were. I saw the look on your face, kinda like the one you're wearing now."

"Well, maybe a little," Darcy said. "I just never thought anyone would be...you know, watching me."

The deep-lined face studied Darcy for a long moment. Her eyes narrowed. "You like expensive things, don't you?"

"Shoes. I like expensive shoes." Such a lie. Expensive shoes were just the only thing she bought. She'd buy everything expensive if she could afford it.

"I used to like expensive things too. Got over that a long time ago." Ms. Viola seemed to have tuned into a mental oldies station that replayed snippets of her past. Her eyes sort of glazed over and wandered up toward the ceiling.

That doesn't explain the fancy-shmancy leather recliners and to-die-for flat screen.

She glanced at Ms. Viola and found softness had crept onto the woman's face, diminishing some of the creases. "I should be going." Darcy set her cup and saucer on the serving tray.

"Please...don't go." Something close to a plea mingled through Ms. Viola's response. The tone seemed to shock both of them. "I mean...." The old woman appeared to search for words. "It's been nice visiting with you. You should stay awhile longer."

She's got to be kidding…the woman can't stand you.

But then…the cookies. "I'm heading out to run at Memorial Park." The excuse line.

Ms. Viola batted her hand in the air. "Exercise is over-rated. Never indulged in it myself."

Something kept Darcy in her seat. She hadn't been prepared for Ms. Viola actually wanting her to stay. "Well…." Darcy bit her lip, "I guess I could miss just this once."

Ms. Viola gave her a total-bullshit raised eyebrow.

Oh yeah. The old lady's got your number. You're SO busted.

She sank back into the cushions of the velvet couch and decided not to make the hole she'd dug any deeper.

"About crocheting," Ms. Viola began. "Do you know what those squares are for?"

***

Almost two hours later, Darcy still sat visiting with Ms. Viola. She'd tasted the pot of pinto beans and ground meat simmering on the stove, the wonderful aroma she'd recognized earlier. It had been one of her favorite meals as a little girl when she visited Izzy and her Papa Harry.

She learned Ms. Viola's likes and dislikes of TV shows, movies, and actors. She found out the crocheted squares were to be sewn together to make blankets. Ms. Viola even brought out her laptop and pulled up the Warm-Up America website that sponsored the making of blankets for those in need.

Darcy not only received a lecture on the hazards of pollution to the water systems, the importance of solar energy, and saving the planet by recycling, but also a first-hand look at the old woman's system of dividing plastic, aluminum, glass, and paper. Did Darcy know a used Diet Coke can could be recycled and back on the grocery shelf in as little as sixty days? Or, that same aluminum can dumped in a landfill would still be there in a hundred years? She also learned not to ever again get Ms. Viola started about plastic bottles…and she had thought the aluminum lecture was bad. Although way too much information for one sitting, Darcy decided the visit hadn't been too bad. Enjoyable, even. She glanced at her watch and sucked in air. Six thirty? How could that be?

Ms. Viola had taken the laptop back to the bedroom. Darcy really needed to leave. She had clothes to fold and put away, paperwork, *Extreme Home Make-Over,* and *Desperate Housewives,* not to mention Stash probably crossing his legs by now. She glanced again at her watch and tapped her foot. Still no sign of the old woman.

"Hello? Ms. Viola?" The floor plan similar to hers, Darcy edged her way down the short hallway and froze. Ms. Viola leaned against one of the bedroom doors, her fists clutched to her chest, her eyes squeezed shut. The pain on the woman's face was unmistakable.

"Ms Viola!" Darcy bolted to the woman's side. "What is it? What?"

Ms. Viola's breathing appeared short and jagged. "Next to...my...bed," she gasped. "Little...bottle."

"I can't...leave you!" Darcy's disjointed breathing matched Ms. Viola's.

"Go...." The word was barely audible.

Darcy snapped out of her helpless panic mode, bolted to the bedside table closest to the door, and found nothing but a pair of horn-rimmed glasses.

"Oh no. No, no, no!" Her panic escalated. "Where is it?" She raised her eyes and scanned the room. A second table stood on the far side of the bed, where a miniature bottle sat. She tucked in her arms and hurled herself across the bed, landed on her feet, and grabbed the small brown vial.

Ms. Viola hadn't moved, and her eyes were still shut. Darcy fumbled with the bottle top, spilling the tiny white pills on the floor. She dropped to her knees and picked up a handful.

"Here!"

Ms. Viola forced her eyes open and slipped one of the tiny pills Darcy offered into her mouth.

"Now what?"

A moment passed. "Can you help me to the living room?" The voice sounded shallow, but somewhat steady.

With an arm wrapped around the frail body, Darcy inched the woman back down the hall.

"The recliner please." Ms. Viola's tone was hushed. Darcy lowered the woman into the soft leather chair. Her face resembled the color of a winter sky on a cloudy day. "Could you get me a sip of water?"

Darcy had to lean in close to hear Ms. Viola's words, then returned with the water and lifted the glass to the woman's lips. She pulled up a nearby footstool and sat next to the recliner. A good five or six minutes passed before Ms. Viola opened her eyes and focused on Darcy's drawn face.

"You look like shit." The words fell out of Ms. Viola's mouth more as an observation than an insult.

Darcy shook her head to clear her thoughts.

The old woman almost croaks and says you look like shit?

She thought about firing back an appropriate response, but her mother had taught her better. "What happened?"

The cloudy gray tint slowly left Ms. Viola's face and her eyes began to clear. "I'm fine. It was nothing." She hauled herself up to a sitting position. "What were we talking about?"

The remark brought Darcy to her feet. She crossed her arms and stood statue-still for a few beats before coherent words began to form in her scrambled brain. "Excuse me, but you just scared the crap out of me. Nothing? You call that nothing?" Darcy's heart still banged unusually loudly in her chest. Forget Memorial Park, she'd had her cardio workout for the day.

"Yes, I said it was nothing." Ms. Viola's surly disposition had reappeared, yet physically she looked shaken and small.

"Have you seen a doctor?"

"Yes." Ms. Viola checked her watch. "It's getting late. You should go."

Darcy didn't budge. "What medicine did I give you?"

"None of your business," Ms. Viola snapped, and then tightened her lips. "I mean," the woman started, tried to paste her waxy smile on her face, but failed. Her hands dropped in her lap. "Oh hell, I don't know what I mean." Her eyes fixated on some unidentified spot above the over-sized television. "Just go."

Although too tired to get totally irate, Darcy did manage to muster some half-assed annoyance. For a while she thought they were actually getting along.

Stupid, huh?

She gathered the scattered pills in the hallway and stooped to rub the top of Ike's head before letting herself out of the apartment.

Before going to bed that night Darcy wrote her letter of complaint concerning the landscaping at Fountain Oaks and addressed the envelope to F.O.A.M., the management company on the receiving end of her rental checks.

Chapter 6

Darcy woke before her alarm, which had become the norm since her visit with Ms. Viola. For the last four nights she had battled her thoughts and the covers. She couldn't decide if anger or worry kept her awake.

It was Thursday morning and she had a full day of appointments. Hauling herself out of bed, she did her usual shower thing and threw on sweat pants and a t-shirt while coffee brewed. Stash sat at attention close to the front door with a goofier than usual look on his face. She yanked the towel off her head, ran her fingers through the tangled mass, and anchored her hands on her hips.

"Let's go."

The morning dawned hazy and muggy. Autumn in Houston could not really be considered a true autumn…more of an extended summer, which made her realize sweats had been a stupid choice. Walking into the courtyard, the humidity crinkled the hairs around her face, signaling that she'd have some serious repair work to do before leaving for work. She glanced in the direction of Ms. Viola's apartment, her usual routine the past four mornings, and found no curtain movement. Stash pulled her through the walkway to the front of the complex where she spotted Ike, the lazy cocker spaniel…and Fletcher. The two non-canines locked eyes. Fletcher raised his hand in a quick wave and then disappeared with the dog around the corner of the building.

Why is Fletcher walking Ike?

Her lungs heaved in and out, eyes locked on the ground in front of her. After Stash did his business, Darcy followed Fletcher's path around the side of the building. Nothing. Retracing her steps, she walked back to the courtyard just as Lawrence emerged from his apartment, dressed in a charcoal grey pinstriped suit, white starched shirt, and steel blue-grey tie; definitely his preppy look.

"Did you see Fletcher and Ms. Viola's dog just now?" Darcy reined in the leash so Stash couldn't spoil Lawrence's pinstriped attire.

"No, I didn't."

"Have you *ever* seen Fletcher walking Ms. Viola's dog?"

He paused for half a beat. "Yes. I believe I have. One day this week. Why?"

Darcy shrugged and shook her head. "I don't know. Just wondering," not ready to discuss the events of Sunday evening concerning Ms. Viola...not with Lawrence...not yet. "Where are you going, dressed so phoo-phoo? It's early."

"I'm speaking at the HBS Breakfast Club." Lawrence straightened his tie and patted his breast pocket.

"What's HBS?"

"Harvard Business School."

"Ew," Darcy said. "I thought you went to Yale."

"I did. However, I have quite an excellent reputation in the city, and they have a breakfast alumni meeting once a month." Lawrence dug into his pants pockets.

"What are you doing?" she asked. Stash pulled her toward the stairs.

"I seem to have misplaced...here it is." Lawrence pulled a plastic Tic-Tac container from his left pocket. His eyebrows bobbed up and down. "Fresh breath is a must."

What a nerd.

"So, do your Harvard buddies know where you hang your hat these days?"

"Of course not. Have you gone mad?"

"Yeah, well, that's a possibility."

"I have to go...mustn't be late, you know." The nerdy Yale grad disappeared around the corner to the carport.

"Well, isn't he fun," she said to Stash, and then yelled "see ya" to the empty walkway. She reached the top of the stairs and halted, which yanked Stash to a stop in front of her. An envelope had been taped to her front door.

How'd that get there?

Scoping out the landing and finding nothing besides the usual debris and cobwebs, she tore off the envelope, scooted through the door, and dropped the deadbolt in place. The sinister penmanship contained four words:

Nitroglycerin. I apologize.
-Viola

"Nitroglycerin?" Where had she heard that word? She entered the apartment and glared at the beaming clock on the microwave. As predicted, the morning humidity caused her to spend longer than usual to straighten the waves and creases out of her hair, which would make her late, again. Luckily, she had set her clothes and shoes out the night before. She threw on the black Craig Taylor shirtdress she had found at Marshall's for a steal, and clamped on the pewter scales bracelet that could almost pass for the one she'd spotted at Neiman's. Her shoes: grey Kenneth Cole baby-calf pumps, with three-inch heels and pointed toes. She released a quick sigh when she slipped her feet into the well made, and of course expensive shoes. In Darcy's book, there were times when a person absolutely had to cut corners. Shoes were not on that list.

Several times throughout the day the nitroglycerin word ran through her tangled web of thoughts. It wasn't a word she'd heard often, yet it played a part in some wedge of her vocabulary from some point in time. She bet that her grandmother would know. Climbing back into her SUV after her last appointment, her cell phone buzzed. She glanced at the caller ID. "Speak of the devil."

"I've run it through all my sources and the old geezer checks out."

"Hi Izzy." She found it amusing that her grandmother referred to Ms. Viola as an old geezer when they were so close to the same age.

"Hi darlin'," Izzy responded. "Did you hear what I said?"

"Every word."

"Still, stay away from her."

"I think she's harmless, Izzy." Provoking her grandmother, she added, "In fact, she seems like a nice person."

"Humph," Izzy puffed. "I seriously doubt that."

"Hey, what's nitroglycerin?" Darcy knew the question would start another inquiry, but she had to know.

"Why?"

Here we go.

She thought a minute. "Just heard it today," which wasn't a lie. She *had* said the word out loud. "Where have I heard it before?"

"Darlin'," Izzy said. "Nitroglycerin is the medicine we kept on hand for your grandfather's heart."

Something inside Darcy cracked. She could almost feel the snap, the wall separating reality and disbelief.

"It's for angina," Izzy explained. "That and making dynamite."

"What's that?"

"It blows things up. Bam. Blewey. Kaput. Gone."

She squeezed the steering wheel with her free hand and gritted her teeth...a much safer option than a serious eye-roll in Houston traffic. "Izzy, I know what dynamite is."

Your fault for starting the conversation.

"What's angina?"

"Heart pain," Izzy said. "What's wrong with your heart?"

"Nothing. My heart's fine," although it did feel heavy at the moment. She heard a beep.

Thank God.

"Izzy, I have another call coming in. Talk to you later." Darcy clicked over to the other line.

"I'm having a party." Miranda's voice splintered through the phone like darts through a pellet gun.

"So what else is new?" Darcy held the phone several inches away, her new resource for preventing hearing loss when talking to Miranda. She veered off the freeway at the Westheimer exit and hit the brakes. Tail lights...all she could see ahead were red tail lights. Traffic, a bitch in rush hour around the Galleria, wasn't exactly a news flash.

"Halloween, you dufus. Save the date. And you have to wear a costume."

"Aren't we a little old for dress-up?" Darcy did a mental calendar check. "And isn't Halloween on a weeknight this year?"

"You have to wear a costume." Miranda's volume escalated. "What's wrong? Won't Granny will let you come out and play?"

"Very funny," Darcy spurted, and then a thought dawned. "You know Halloween is Izzy's birthday. We might—"

"Don't even go there, Boop," Miranda said. "Halloween is on Monday. The party is the Saturday before. No excuses. And if you don't have a date, bring Dr. Seuss. I gotta get a handle on this guy."

Darcy blew out air. Nothing less than a death certificate was going to get her out of this one. "Alright. Saturday, the twenty-ninth. Got it."

Traffic remained sluggish, but at least her vehicle actually moved, although walking would definitely have been faster. Her SUV edged toward the light at the busy intersection while the word "nitroglycerin" danced across her mental radar screen. "It's for heart pain," Izzy had said.

After careful navigation into her narrow Fountain Oaks assigned space, she grabbed the envelope containing the complaint letter she'd been carrying around for the past four days from the passenger seat. With only slight hesitation, Darcy by-passed her stairwell and crossed the courtyard. The sun had taken refuge behind Ms. Viola's building, dropping the temperature a hair below the eighty-degree mark. The tinted pink clouds and smoky haze of approaching autumn settled around her. In front of Ms. Viola's door, she wrestled with the decision over whether to deliver the letter she'd hammered out in anger. She raised her hand to knock but never made contact. The door swung open, causing Darcy to rock backwards.

Ms. Viola stood and eyed Darcy from the feet up. "Kenneth Cole?"

"Uh…." The envelope and her arm both suspended in mid-air, her mind was a flurry of nitroglycerin tablets, heart pain, her grandfather, and the woman standing in front of her.

"Your black sling backs look better with that dress," Ms. Viola said, one hand clamped on her hip, the other rubbing her chin.

"Dior or Marc Jacobs?" Darcy asked.

"Jacobs."

Darcy froze, her eyes locked with Ms. Viola's. *What the hell?* Weird seemed to be an understatement. She resumed her original dialogue, "Uh…," and forced her arm to move the letter closer to Ms. Viola.

The woman snatched the envelope and held it up to the last bit of daylight. "What's this? You paying rent early?"

"Uh…." Darcy, a college graduate, struggled to handle anything more than a handful of stupid uhs. "I mean." Her brain farts weren't any better. She blew out hard and let the words tumble out. "It's the letter to the owner about the landscaping." She closed her eyes and braced herself in case a body punch came her way.

"Oh," Ms. Viola said. "Whatever."

Darcy forced her eyes open in time to see the envelope land on the table by the door.

"Come in," the woman ordered.

"I'm not staying." Darcy set her tone to calm and spoke in a strong, assertive voice.

Ms. Viola's face registered something between shock and disappointment. "I guess I deserved that." She bit the inside of her cheek and studied Darcy's face. "You get my note?"

"Yes." Darcy planted her Kenneth Cole's squarely in front of Ms. Viola and crossed her arms. "What's wrong with your heart?"

"Nothing."

"You're taking nitroglycerin." Darcy returned the woman's glare. Her stance gave her strength, although it did nothing for the knocking around of her heart.

"So?"

"So, why are you being so nasty about this?" Darcy dropped her arms and paced back and forth in front of the open door; her calm, assertive tone had left the building. "One minute you seem nice, and the next you bite my head off. You don't even know what it took for me to bring that stupid plate back. And then I ended up staying, for crying out loud. We even had a nice talk. I thought we bonded…sort of. And then you had that attack thing."

Ms. Viola grabbed Darcy's arm. "Stop. You're losing valuable tread on those shoes."

She yanked her arm free. "What is with you? Do you like me? Do you not like me? What?" The pitiful whine in her voice added to her annoyance.

Viola's eyes seemed to search the area around Darcy before she blew out a heavy sigh. "Come in for a minute."

Darcy paused.

"Please?" An obviously uncomfortable word for the old woman to spit out.

Darcy stepped past Ms. Viola and took a seat on one of the modern recliners. *Wheel of Fortune* blared on the flat screen. Ike, sprawled on his bed, raised his eyes at Darcy, but maintained his lounging position.

Ms. Viola sat in the empty matching chair and crossed her legs. She grabbed the remote, muted Pat Sajak, and then brushed imaginary pieces of lint from her faded work shirt. The silence filled the apartment like a smoke bomb. After a lapse that felt like an hour, Ms. Viola spoke. "I apologize." She leaned an elbow on the arm of the recliner and rubbed her hand across her mouth. "I seem to be doing a lot of that lately."

Darcy felt the urge to blurt, "Apologizing wouldn't be necessary if you weren't such a bitch most of the time," but decided to hold her tongue.

"I should thank you for your concern."

A serious eyebrow arch rolled across Darcy's forehead, which she aimed at the old woman.

"Very well." Ms. Viola cleared her throat. "Thank you for your concern."

"You're welcome." Okay, maybe standing up to the Wicked Witch wasn't such a bad idea. "Now, tell me what's wrong with your heart."

"I have water on the stove for tea." Ms Viola hauled herself up from the recliner.

"Sit." It was the tone Darcy usually reserved for Stash or Mel, but it seemed appropriate…she hoped.

Ms. Viola shot Darcy a look of something like surprised resignation. The bitchiness seemed to slip from her eyes. She lowered herself back onto the recliner. "I don't usually allow people to talk to me like that, you know."

"I don't know why," Darcy began. "*You* talk to people like that all the time." She was so proud of herself for her quick retort she forgot to be ashamed. Her mother would have killed her for speaking to an older person like that. Izzy, on the other hand, would have cheered from the bleachers. She stopped patting herself on the back long enough to catch Ms. Viola's glare. An idea hit. "Okay, why don't we try something new?"

"Like what?"

"How about we try being nice to each other?" Darcy shifted in her seat. "Could we do that?"

"Very well, we can try."

Surprised at how readily the woman had agreed, she pushed a bit farther. "So, what's wrong with your heart?"

Ms. Viola sat silent for a moment. She turned slightly and looked around the room. "It's getting old, that's all. Sometimes it goes thunk, thunk, instead of beep, beep."

"And the thunk, thunk hurts?"

"Sometimes." Her eyes narrowed. "It's hell getting old. If it wasn't for this damn body I'd live forever."

Darcy exhaled. They were actually talking again. She couldn't understand why she felt relieved, but she did.

"You like *Wheel of Fortune?*" Ms. Viola picked up the remote and aimed it at the flat screen.

"Not done." Darcy had held up a hand to silence Ms. Viola. "Give me a minute here."

Viola lowered the remote.

"What does your doctor say?"

The remaining outside light faded, darkening the room except for the flicker from the *Wheel*. "He says to take the nitroglycerin when the angina flares up. That's about it."

Darcy doubted that was the extent of the doctor's advice. She studied the old woman, who seemed to have shrunk into the recliner. Ms. Viola looked tired. "Can I ask you a question?"

Ms. Viola blinked a few times and then nodded. "Go ahead."

"Why the cookies?" Maybe the mystery could finally be solved. At least she'd have something to tell Izzy and Lawrence.

Propping an elbow on the arm of the recliner, the woman rested her chin in her hand. "You intrigue me."

Wide-eyed, Darcy asked, "I do?" Not at all an answer she expected.

"You remind me of myself when I was your age."

Darcy had a brief moment of panic when the words began to sink in. Her self-esteem, always questionable, felt in serious jeopardy. Like Ms. Viola? Her mind fast-forwarded, seeing herself as an old lady wearing overalls and straw hats, and collecting empty Country Crock containers. She mentally shuddered.

"My turn to ask a question," Ms. Viola said. "Are you happy?"

The words, once again, caught Darcy off-guard. Her mind replayed the crappy apartment complex she lived in and her pretend-to-be-a-Lexus SUV before honing in on her closet, filled with occasional designer seconds from Marshalls and Harwin…all knock-offs. Next the mental video panned to the shoeboxes. The real thing. Except the real thing was the *one* thing she couldn't afford. Sadly, this part of the docudrama didn't even touch on the lack of a meaningful relationship, the letter jacket hiding in her closet, or the green-eyed monster of wanting what others had…which was everything.

"I'm happy."

Liar. You hate your life, and at the moment you hate her for bringing this sad state of affairs front and center.

Ms. Viola's eyes said she knew Darcy was lying. "Well, if that's true, I'm glad." The old woman yanked her shirt down as if to knock out some of the wrinkles. "I just didn't want you to make the same mistakes I did." She pulled herself out of the recliner, signaling the end of the conversation.

"I can walk Ike for you sometimes."

"That's kind of you." Ms. Viola patted Darcy's shoulder and led her to the door. "Fletcher's been helping me out, but I'll remember that."

Darcy let herself into her apartment and was almost knocked over by Stash. Good grief, she'd forgotten about the dog and the fact his bladder was probably about to blow. She grabbed the leash, hooked it on the dog's collar, and barely made it back to the courtyard before Stash squatted, which was his girly way of relieving himself when in a hurry.

She raised her eyes and inspected the courtyard with the ugly brown grass, spiky weeds, and dead shrubs. A patch of brown in front of Fletcher's apartment, sectioned off with yellow caution tape, was filled with dirty water matching the dirty grass. Charming. She lived in a cesspool. It mirrored her life, perfectly. Which was all so very sad.

Back on the couch, Darcy comforted herself with a glass of wine, a bowl of Goldfish, the latest *US Weekly*, her iPhone, and the remote. She took a large swig of wine and flipped through the guide on the television. She needed a distraction. *Grey's Anatomy* would be on in thirty minutes. Good. Everyone's life sucked on *Grey's*.

Nothing like an uplifting weekly series about a bunch of doctors having way more problems than the patients. She glanced at *US Weekly*. Gag. Another young female starlet, drunk and disorderly. She opened her iPhone and entered Miranda's party in her calendar. What kind of costume would a thirty-year-old single female wear?

She scrolled over to November. Not much there except Thanksgiving, which signaled two events: black Friday, the best shopping day of the year, and the annual Turkey Day rivalry between Texas A&M and the University of Texas. A house divided. Her dad had graduated from Aggieland, but Texas State, being so close to Austin, registered her as a Longhorn. She'd like to say she and her dad were honorable adversaries on game day, but she'd be lying…just the nature of the beast between the two universities' traditional showdown. However, after this year the father-daughter-angst would be put to rest when A&M moved to the SEC. There would be more peace in the house around Thanksgiving, or else they'd find some other fence to rival over.

December. Her lips puckered. The dreaded month. On the fourteenth she'd turn thirty-one. Thirty had been bad enough, but thirty-one tipped the scale toward forty. She shoved a handful of Goldfish into her mouth, several falling to the ground. Stash sat at her feet waiting for the fallen treasures, always a strong possibility when Darcy was in a pissy-I-could-care-less mood. Hell, it was pretty much a sure thing on her best day.

That's because you're a klutz.

She slouched down between the cushions with one hand deep into the Goldfish bag and her wine in the other. In spite of the pity party she had plunged into, she couldn't keep thoughts of Ms. Viola away. The old woman seemed to be reaching out by giving "nice" a try. Obvious to the casual observer, the word wasn't part of the woman's daily repertoire, but she did seem to be making an effort.

"She said she liked me," she said to Stash while he downed a few fallen Goldfish. "How weird is that? The Wicked Witch likes me." She flipped to a *Sex in the City* rerun, upped the volume, took another swig of wine, and almost sprayed it on the ottoman coffee table when someone knocked on the door.

Uh, let's think, think, think…who could it be?

"It's open Larry."

Lawrence entered. "I must ask that you stop calling me by that horrible name." He dropped onto the couch next to Darcy.

"Why? What's wrong with Larry?" Darcy asked. "Mr. Will doesn't think it's horrible."

"He's also fond of plaid shirts, bow ties, and fishing vests," Lawrence said. "Do you mind if I join you? It's not a good idea to drink alone."

"Sure. Grab the box. Help yourself," Darcy said. "If I didn't drink alone, I'd hardly ever drink."

"My point exactly."

She rolled her eyes, not really needing a sermon right now. "I take it back. If you're going to lecture me, go home. If not, shut up and sit down."

"Tou-chy," he said. "I'll stop if you promise never to call me Larry again."

Darcy mentally balanced the wager. "Fine."

Retrieving the box of wine and a glass from the kitchen, he returned to his section of the couch and held the glass up to the light.

"It's clean, you dufus." It sucked she was spending so much time lately with her snobby OCD neighbor.

"I'm looking to see what kind of crystal this might be." Lawrence turned the glass upside down.

"Ikea. Six for five dollars." She *so* wanted to give him a head thunking.

"You must be joking."

"I never joke about Ikea," Darcy said.

"Delightful." Lawrence filled his glass. "You must take me there sometime."

Delightful? Who talks like that?

Which reminded Darcy: "How did your speech with the elitists of Houston go this morning?"

"Very well, thank you." Lawrence took a sip of wine, swirled it around in his mouth, eyed the ceiling for a moment, and swallowed. "Although they are all Harvard alums, I'm quite well received among that group."

Darcy turned her voice to pretentious and responded, "Well, of course you are."

Lawrence sat up and turned. "You're mocking me, aren't you? Bad day, I take it?"

Deflated, she realized at the moment Lawrence was her immediate friend. The sarcasm, although usually entertaining and self-soothing, wasn't called for this evening. "Sorry. I've been pretty bitchy lately."

The two sunk back into the couch cushions and watched a woman cheerfully relay that side effects from a certain medication included blurred vision, vomiting, increased risk of stroke, and in rare instances...death. *"Contact your physician immediately if any of these occur."*

She raised her glass in a toast to the commercial. "Makes you want to run right out and take a whole bottle of that stuff, doesn't it?"

Lawrence rolled his head sideways. "You really are having a bad day, aren't you?"

She wanted to scream "ya think?" but stopped. If she didn't start censoring her words before they flew out of her mouth, she'd be sitting by herself eating Goldfish until she was...Ms. Viola's age. She settled for a lame smile.

Lawrence picked up the remote and muted the television. "I've been meaning to ask you," he said, refilling Darcy's wine glass. "How was our lovely apartment manager last Sunday when you returned her plate?"

"Okay, I guess." She didn't have her editing hat handy at the moment so she spilled the entire visit, ending with her recent confrontation with the old woman about the nitroglycerin.

Lawrence stared off into commercial land, his face thoughtful. "That's quite shocking."

Darcy's eyebrows raised just a smidge. "Which part?"

"About her having a heart."

Something started to rumble deep inside Darcy. The unfamiliar feeling inched upward, past her chest, and spewed out in spurts of a hawking noise...Darcy's belly laugh. She crossed her arms over her stomach to try to squelch the spasm but it didn't work. Nothing did. Shooting a glance at Lawrence she caught a flicker of a giggle behind his eyes. He snickered a few times before letting loose with a high-pitched squeak that sounded like a wounded bird, which only made Darcy laugh more. She fell over on the couch, losing her breath as gulps of snorts and howling took up air space in her lungs. The more she tried to regain her composure, the more impossible it became. Lawrence slipped down onto the floor on all fours and hunched his knees up under him.

Darcy snapped out of her deliria and put her hand on Lawrence's back. "Hey, are you okay?"

A strange hiccup noise escaped from Lawrence. "Heegh. Heegh. Heegh." Tears rolled down his face. He stayed hunched over "heegh, heegh, heegh-ing" which sent Darcy back into waves of her own out-of-control hysterics.

A few moments passed before the seizures subsided and they were able to reclaim their spots on the couch. "My gosh." Darcy swiped at her face. "I haven't had a belly laugh in ages." She couldn't remember the last time she had let loose like that, and it felt *so* good.

"Is that what it's called?"

Darcy thought Lawrence was making another joke until she saw his dead serious expression.

"Yeah. You've never had a belly laugh before?"

"I don't think so. And if I did, I doubt it was called a belly laugh."

Darcy shook her head, the giggles not far away. She reached out and gave Lawrence a friendly punch on his upper arm. "Oh, c'mon. Your family laughed sometimes, didn't they?"

He rubbed the site of the punch. "I suppose so, although it wasn't so much a family affair." His voice toned down to solemn. "Actually, I believe I was the source of much of the laughter."

"Huh," was all Darcy could think to say. And she thought *her* family was dysfunctional. The somber mood brought her thoughts back to Ms. Viola. "I think I'm starting to like our apartment manager," Darcy said. "I gave her my landscape letter tonight and she didn't throw it back. I take that as a good sign." Stash had meandered around the ottoman coffee table and rested his chin on Darcy's knee. She rubbed his head. "She even patted me on the back when I left."

Lawrence's face registered genuine shock. "Really?"

Darcy realized she had missed the first ten minutes of *Grey's*. She aimed the remote at the ancient television and neither of them spoke until the next commercial.

"I pretend I'm Meredith and McDreamy can't keep his hands off of me," Darcy said.

"So do I."

It took a minute for his words to sink in. She turned to her neighbor with arched eyebrows.

"What? You have to admit he *is* a very handsome man."

"Do you…like men? I mean…I never thought to ask," Darcy said, but oh, this could explain so much.

"No. I. Do. Not."

"Hey, it's okay if you do. I mean—"

"Well, thank you," Lawrence said. "But I prefer women. I'm almost 90% sure of it. I just feel if I had hair like Patrick Dempsey I would be more attractive."

Darcy pressed her lips together and nodded. "I agree."

Lawrence paused with his wine glass midway to his mouth and eyed Darcy.

"Oh. I didn't mean you aren't attractive. I meant…." Oh hell. "We should all have that kind of hair. It's gorgeous, don't you think?" This wasn't going well at all.

Lawrence resumed movement of the wine glass to his mouth. "Yes," he replied.

Quick subject change before she insulted him again. She cleared her throat. "About Ms. Viola."

"Yes. So, you think it could be serious?"

"Well, yeah," Darcy said. "You should have seen her when she had that attack. She was in some serious pain. Scared the shit out of me."

"I'm sure it did." Lawrence finished his second glass of wine and stood. "And I think it is admirable of you to befriend the manager of our decaying abode." He walked to the kitchen and found Mel in the sink. He shuddered, dumped the cat onto the floor, and rinsed out his wine glass. "I, on the other hand, prefer to keep my distance from her. You do understand the sanitation risks of allowing your cat to wallow in your kitchen sink, I take it?"

"Yeah, I'm sure it's right up there with him drinking out of the toilet." Darcy easily switched back to sarcasm…so much easier. Could Ms. Viola have been this much of a smart-ass when she was thirty? Shudder.

Lawrence straightened and shot a glance at his watch. "Well, well. Look at the time. I must be off." Before he closed the door he turned to Darcy. "And for the record, I have nothing against the name Larry. It's a perfectly acceptable name. Just not for me." And he was gone.

"Must have been the crack about the toilet," Darcy said to Stash. She purposely hadn't said anything to Lawrence about Miranda's party. She needed a date. And she didn't need for it to be Lawrence…unless all else failed.

Terry Lee

Chapter 7

The list of available men for Darcy to date could be written in large print on one side of a business card. Four guys…a blip compared with Miranda's Rolodex.

She had met Derrick while running at Memorial Park. Her "running" more closely resembled a distressed plopping of one foot after the other, which prompted him to stop her one day and ask if she needed assistance. Darcy hadn't been able to drop the pained expression from her face while exercising, which obviously caused some concern for on-lookers. How people could look relaxed, much less happy, while feeling their lungs were going to explode any moment muddled her brain. There was nothing fun about running. Her sole purpose lay in being able to button her jeans and keep eating tacos from Jack in the Box. That, and the double fudge brownie nut ice cream she ate with a spoon right out of the carton. Tacky, but true. Punching in his number, she debated whether she really wanted him to answer. Decision made…she hung up when the call went straight to voice mail.

Brian, a voice talent at a production company in Sugar Land, had sandy-brown hair and warm puppy dog eyes. He occasionally called with tickets he had landed for a concert or sports event. They'd been out about four times over the last year. Nothing had evolved past some really fun nights out and a couple of really great good-night kisses. He didn't seem to be interested in anything more, and Darcy wondered why. *She* wasn't, but why wasn't he? Guys never pursued her the way they did Miranda. She gave Brian a call. He seemed glad to hear from her, but already had plans for next Saturday night.

Bummer.

Next on the list was Matt...tall, dark and handsome; the George Clooney of optometrists, and he knew it. In her line of work she knew a good many eye doctors. Most were male and married, but a few took pride in being the "uncatchable catch." Matt, thirty-eight and a confirmed bachelor, had as many women in his file as Miranda had guys. Go figure. Some things in life just weren't fair, and this was one of them.

The only time Matt called, Darcy figured, was when his first ten choices couldn't get out of previous engagements. Once he had taken her to Tony's, an over-the-top expensive restaurant, where prices actually printed on the menu would be too gauche. If you had to ask, you shouldn't be there. Another time they had driven down to Clear Lake and sailed on a friend's yacht for a sunset dinner with a bunch of people who talked about nothing normal, which made her think of Lawrence. Asking Matt to a Halloween party, in costume no less, would not work. Besides, Matt found himself too pretty, and on this, she had to agree. Even her most expensive Jimmy Choos couldn't hold a candle to his perfectly tanned skin and never-a-strand-out-of-place gorgeous head of hair. He had turned prematurely gray, which added a sense of debonair to his alluring playboy looks. Definitely metro sexual. Nope, not Matt.

The last person on her short list would be Justin, the guy she had dated her last semester in high school. They had gone to prom, dated occasionally during the summer, but parted ways when Darcy went off to Texas State and Justin decided college was not his "thing." He took a job at a sanitation company down by the ship channel where he met Jennifer, who—oh, surprise—immediately became pregnant. They got married exactly three weeks before Ellie, their daughter, made her appearance, and the marriage lasted until their daughter turned two. Since that time Justin, lucky duck, had been at the right place at the right time and purchased half ownership of the sanitation company. Two years later he bought out his partner and was currently a millionaire twice over.

Even owns his own jet, for crying out loud.

Justin called occasionally when he was hosting a party cruise to the Caribbean or flying a dozen or so of his closest friends out to the Venetian in Las Vegas. High-roller. Justin was the one done-with-relationship from which she'd managed to salvage a friendship. He'd probably die young, but with a smile on his face. He lived life in the fast lane, smoked like a barbeque pit at rodeo time, and drank his daily caloric intake. Occasionally, she thought about the closet she could have had with Justin, but that was about where the daydreaming stopped. No, as wild as Miranda's party would surely be would still be a drag for Justin. So much for her dating options for the Halloween party. Crap. She *so* needed a life.

***

The following Saturday Darcy arrived at Miranda's loft a little after nine. She had waited until the sun had gone down…way down. By the grace of everything that was good, she lucked out and squeezed her SUV into the only remaining parking spot on the street; close enough for a quick get-away if necessary.

She swung both legs around and slipped out of the vehicle, which took considerable effort wearing the hot pink strapless dress that was clinging to her like a tattoo. Her thick light brown and often frizzy hair had been shoved under a platinum shoulder-length wig that had already started to itch. The diamonds on her wrist, ears, and around her neck, of course, were fake, fake, and fake. However, the silver Monolo Blagniks were real, and really, really expensive. On her shoulder hung a knock-off Nancy Gonzalez metallic silver crocodile satchel. To complete her Paris Hilton ensemble, she had borrowed a miniature Chihuahua from Izzy's hairdresser's gay nephew, whose roommate (also gay) had a cousin (gay again) who owned the dog. Pierre wore a rhinestone collar around his pencil-thin little neck…the perfect accessory. She raced to Miranda's front door as fast as her sewn-together knees could get her there and waited for Lawrence to catch up.

"I have an itch," he said.

Darcy rotated her head to the right. "So do I, but keep your hands off your body," she instructed. Miranda opened the door in a skin-tight black cat outfit that looked like it had been applied with a spray gun, complete with fishnet hose and unusually high black stilettos. Her long dark hair cascaded down around her shoulders, her eyes covered by a sleek black mask. Catwoman.

Well, of course.

"Hey Boop…I mean Paris." Miranda's voice boomed louder than usual. "I didn't know if you'd be able to clear your calendar." Her eyes danced with mischief behind her mask. She swung her gaze sideward and gave Lawrence a quick once-over. "And who do we have here?"

He stood beside Darcy clothed in furry chaps, western boots from God-knows-where, a western shirt with the proverbial snaps up the front—complete with vest—and a bandana tied around his neck. A ten-gallon hat sat low enough on his head to flatten his ears out Yoda-like, and a pencil-thin mustache had been glued to his upper lip. The ensemble from hell.

Miranda's eyebrows arched high above her seductive black mask. "Roy Rogers or Howdy Doody?"

"Be nice." Darcy grabbed Lawrence's plaid arm and pushed past Miranda. "He scares easily." Lawrence had the same stupid look on his face most men did when they first laid eyes on Miranda, causing her to revisit Lawrence's heterosexual percentage. But then again, even gay guys gawked at Miranda. "I think he's Doc Holliday," Darcy yelled back over the music, and then turned to her strange friend in the ridiculous outfit. "Tell me you're not Howdy Doody." Lawrence's shell-shocked look spoke volumes. Swell evening…Darcy could already tell.

"What'll it be, cowboy?" Lisa and Rob, the evening bartenders, sported Mike and Carol Brady outfits. Mike, an architect and father of the Brady Bunch crew, sported a burnt orange polyester leisure suit and a close permed curly wig. Carol's ensemble complimented Mike's. She wore a yellow polyester pantsuit with a wide-collared orange and yellow flowered blouse and bell-bottoms. Her sandy-blonde hair had been tucked under a mullet-shag wig…the ideal outfit for mothering in the seventies. "Hey Paris, your usual tonight?"

Darcy gazed around. Miranda's loft had little jack-o-lantern lights strung around the ceiling, black lights beaming up at floor level, and cobwebs strung across the furniture. "What's the specialty, Carol?"

"Mike's the chief bottle-washer here," Lisa said.

"Blood-red pomegranate martinis," Mike replied.

"Charming," Darcy said. "I'll start with that."

Lawrence held up a finger and forced two words to fall from his mouth. "Me too."

Darcy grabbed her drink and handed another plastic martini glass to Lawrence. "What's wrong with you? Your chaps too tight"

"Beautiful."

Darcy rearranged Pierre under her arm and mentally crossed her fingers that the damn dog wouldn't pee in her Nancy Gonzalez satchel. She tucked back a strand of white hair that had fallen forward. "Thank you *dawling*."

"No." Lawrence's pointed finger followed Miranda breezing across the room. "Her. She's a goddess."

"Yep, that's pretty much what they all say." Darcy took a swig of her bloody martini. She could easily hate Miranda if she wasn't her best friend. Not that she cared that Lawrence had fallen into the well-known feline trap, but…geez. "I'm going to mingle. You gonna be okay, cowboy?" He nodded, though his eyes never left Miranda.

Darcy eased herself away from the furry chaps and moved through the crowd, passing a Geico Caveman, Dracula, and Dorothy and Toto. All three dress-ups and Toto caused Pierre to yap. Standing next to the tall windows overlooking the Houston skyline, she spotted Snow White and Prince Charming.

"I win," Darcy said. "Hi Joe."

"Win what?" Becca asked.

"Catwoman and I bet on who you two would be." Darcy smiled. "I won." Which was probably a first.

"What'd she guess?" Becca asked.

"Statue of Liberty and Donald Trump."

"Oh puleese," Becca moaned. "I'd never spray myself with silver paint."

"Yeah, that would be more of a Tin Man thing." Darcy took a sip of her bloody drink. "I think Miranda had more the toga, crown, and torch look in mind."

Becca pressed her ruby red lips together. "Tacky. What was your choice?" Snow tugged at her coal-black wig.

"Some nice Mr. and Mrs. Charming married couple. Like I said…I won." Darcy swirled the drink around in the stemmed glass, trying to avoid slamming down the martini.

"Who's your cowboy?" Joe asked.

"Doc Holliday lives in my apartment complex," Darcy answered. "His name is Lawrence, and he's not my cowboy." Darcy grinned at the couple, who looked like they'd just stepped out of a Walt Disney backdrop. She smiled back at the handsome couple and made her way back to the Bradys tending bar.

"Have you met Miranda's Captain Kirk?" Lisa took Darcy's empty glass.

"She has a Captain Kirk?" Darcy held up a hand when Rob started to refill her glass.

"Her date. Internet," Lisa said. "He's her main squeeze."

Darcy's eyes squinted. Her brain mulled the words *Internet* and *date*. "And she already has him dressed up as a Trekky?" She curled down one end of her mouth. "I wonder what other hoops he's jumping through."

Carol Brady shot a look at her husband. "Don't even go there," she warned.

"The word contortionist keeps coming to mind," Rob said, which produced an elbow to the ribs from Lisa.

Paris, Carol, and Mike Brady watched Catwoman across the open loft space of highly polished wood floors, her tail and Doc Holliday trailing closely behind.

"What's wrong with him?" Rob asked.

"First time he's met Miranda," Darcy said.

Mike and Carol both gave knowing nods. "Happens to the best of them," Carol said.

"Best my ass. It happens to all of them." The green-eyed monster had slipped into Darcy's red drink. "Just look at her. And she eats cheeseburgers and chili fries, for God's sake."

Becca and Joe joined the threesome at the bar. "So what's new with you?" Becca asked. "I've hardly seen you since Vegas."

Darcy swayed back and forth to *Rehab* by Amy Winehouse, which was blaring throughout the loft. "Same old, same old. Working my ass off to make my monthly quota."

"Which is?" Becca asked.

"$100,000."

"Wow, that's a lot of specs," Becca said. "Is that Gucci's quota or your own personal creation of hell?"

She debated on another martini, struggled with the issue for half a minute, then relinquished and took the offered drink from Rob. "Mine." Her competition? Darcy Daniels. Reaching her personal quota her first year at Gucci had been a double-edged sword. She received the high salesman award for her district, a huge honor. Determined to hold on to the status and recognition, she set her quota a tad higher each year. $100,000 in monthly sales translated to around a thousand pairs of eyewear to sell every thirty days, which put her in the million dollar plus annual sales category. She was darn good at what she did. She only wished her salary had as many zeros.

Halfway through the evening, she slipped out to allow Pierre to do his thing and ran into Miranda on her re-entry to the loft.

"Hey Boop, did you meet Captain Kirk before he left?"

"The Enterprise taking off sooner than expected?"

"Actually, he has another party," Miranda said. "We're meeting up later."

Darcy glanced at the rhinestone watch clamped to her wrist…twelve forty-five. "Later?" Her eyebrows arched up around her hairline. "You are one crazy Catwoman."

"That I am."

The evening couldn't end fast enough. Darcy's platinum wig itched and she had tired of trying to keep the strapless dress in place. Of course, Miranda still looked perfect…exactly the way she had over four hours ago.

"Hey, I talked to Dr. Seuss for a bit. Not very talkative, is he?"

Darcy mentally replayed the numerous times his jabbering nonsense had forced her to push him out of her apartment. "Ah, actually he's usually an intellectual motor-mouth, although tonight it seems Catwoman got his tongue."

"I don't think I've ever seen a Doc Holliday like that before." Miranda brushed right past Darcy's sarcasm.

"He went a little overboard," Darcy said. "I think he was shooting for the Val Kilmer look." She winked at her crazy best friend. "He missed."

Miranda smoothed her hands down her sprayed-on feline outfit. "Want to see him purr?"

"Do me a favor and leave him alone," Darcy said. "I don't think his heart can take it."

"If you insist, Boop," Miranda said, and disappeared into the crowd.

"Hey!" Darcy yelled at Catwoman's backside. "I've been meaning to ask. Why don't you have a nickname?"

She turned. "I do, you've just never asked."

The words hung in the air a long couple of seconds. "Well?"

A seductive smile eased onto Miranda face. She batted her long eyelashes a few times. "Madonna."

The remains of the evening progressed without much ado. She met Batman, aka Sam, who asked for her number. *Sure, why not.* His name, along with the others, could still fit on a business card. Mingling through the hard-core partygoers, she found Lawrence in a somewhat sitting position on Miranda's couch; eyes closed, his hand clamped around an empty martini glass nestled into one leg of his furry chaps. Not even a gentle face slap moved Lawrence to any semblance of wakefulness. Batman offered to carry Doc Holliday to the car. She had little choice, since the Geico man had returned to his cave and the Bradys and Charmings were home in their respective "happily ever after" abodes.

Darcy had painfully learned her lesson with martinis. One: okay. Two flashed the branded b-r-a-k-e n-o-w sign across her brain, which signaled the time to switch to bottled water. Lawrence either hadn't had the same sort of martini nightmare or he'd forgotten how to count. Worse things had happened to guys who fell into the Miranda web.

Boy, he is going to regret this in the morning.

She resisted the urge to pull out her iPhone to video Batman swinging the lifeless Doc Holliday over his shoulder. Lawrence looked like a little boy who had fallen asleep at a kiddie convention and had to be hauled out by a super hero.

After giving Pierre one more outing, she eased into the driver's seat and pulled off the itchy wig. Bone tired, she closed her eyes for a brief moment, having no idea how to get Lawrence from her car to his apartment. Doc had lost half his pencil-thin moustache sometime during the evening, and a blood red martini stain down one side of the furry chaps could easily pass for a gunshot wound at the O.K. Corral.

Pulling into the apartment complex, she glanced at the clock on the dash...two twenty. She sat for a moment and weighed the outcome of leaving Lawrence in the car for the rest of the night. Bad idea. Two reasons flashed across her mind. No, three.

Lawrence might wake up and become violently ill (which would surely happen).

Besides leaving a permanent stain in her car, she couldn't handle pomegranate puke.

Fletcher might perform one of his late security checks, see the fake gunshot wound, and call 911, leaving her to explain how

Howdy Doody, with half a moustache, had sustained a pomegranate blood martini wound.

Nope, leaving him in the car wouldn't work. She looked at the disarrayed Doc and remembered him to be a couple of inches taller than her and not much heavier. She reverted to her college mentality, when things like this were done on a regular basis. Granted, Miranda usually got *her* inside back in those days, but occasionally Darcy would get a turn at being the more sober of the two.

She kicked off her Monolos and pulled Lawrence from the SUV, surprised at how light Doc actually seemed. With more dragging than carrying, the two moved forward, plopping one foot in front of the other, until they reached his apartment. She smashed his intoxicated frame up against the doorframe to search under the furry chaps for his keys. This story was *not* going to be repeated. No way. Ne-ver.

As she opened the door, they both spilled forward. Luckily for her Lawrence cushioned her fall, which she hoped didn't break his nose. Glancing around, Darcy immediately noticed the sparse furnishings. No wonder he ended up at her place all the time. Doc was total dead weight, but she was able to drag him over to a small couch, rest his head on one arm, and drape his legs, chaps still in place, over the other end. Lowering her head to his chest, she heard the faint thump-thump of his heart, reassuring her he was drunk and not dead from alcohol poisoning. She scooted a chair from the modest dinette set over to the couch and placed his cordless phone on it. In the kitchen, she found a small wastebasket to place beside him for what was surely to come. There. Mission complete.

Darcy retrieved the stilettos and crate holding the sleeping Chihuahua from the SUV. She had no clue how her animals would react to having an uninvited Pierre for a sleep over. And as Rhett had said to Scarlett, "Frankly my dear, I don't give a damn." Which was the God's awful truth…she had passed exhausted hours ago.

Stash woke Darcy sometime mid-morning, anxious to get outside. He was way too enthusiastic for the morning hours after one of Miranda's parties. But then he hadn't had to spend his Saturday night dressed up in a ridiculous costume, drinking blood-red martinis. Rolling over on her side, she forced her eyes to focus on the clock. Geez…eleven-fifteen. She threw on clothes, hooked Stash to his leash, grabbed Pierre's crate, and headed down the stairs.

Reaching the courtyard, she opened the tiny crate door. A stiff-legged Pierre muddled out onto the grass, stretching first his back and then his front mouse-thin legs. Stash sniffed the small dog in all the places dogs do before pulling Darcy over to a dead shrub to lift his leg. There was no sign of life from Lawrence's door, and no sneaking a peek through the curtains on Ms. Viola's side of the courtyard.

Pretty dead around here. Damn. Bad choice of words.

After showering, she headed back out the door. She had exactly one hour to return Pierre to his rightful owner before he turned into an itty-bitty pumpkin. She stopped in front of Lawrence's door, knocked softly, and waited a few minutes before knocking again. The sound of movement from inside the apartment caused her to breathe in relief, but it took several more minutes for the door to actually open. Doc Holliday stood before her in all his finery, half of the pencil-thin moustache still MIA. The pallor and thin bead of sweat on Lawrence's forehead only added to the portrayal of Doc Holliday…a truly sick man.

"Hi cowboy," Darcy said. "How's it going?"

"I'm ready to die now," Lawrence said. "But first I have a few questions." He moved aside so Darcy could enter.

She pulled a chair from the small dinette and placed the crate down beside her. "Fire away."

"Don't tease me, woman." Lawrence, looking way more fragile than usual, eased himself into the chair next to Darcy and tried to cross his legs. The furry chaps said no way. He settled for the head in hands position.

"Want me to shoot you now?" Darcy asked.

Blood-shot eyes peered out between his bony fingers.

The man, obviously in agony, zapped Darcy back to some of her own nightmarish drinking escapades. "Sorry. Can I get you anything?"

Lawrence barely shook his head. "How did I get home?"

"Me," Darcy said. "I sort of drug you across the parking lot."

"Where is the rest of my moustache?"

Darcy shrugged. "That I don't know."

"I see." Lawrence dropped one arm heavily onto his furry chaps. "One more thing."

"What?"

"Did I make a fool of myself last night?"

Another easy opener. But no, she'd cut Doc some slack. "No more than anyone else," she lied. She had a feeling the Sunday ritual of a cucumber facial wasn't going to happen today. She stood. "I've got to return this silly dog, but I'll bring you something to make you feel better."

"What on earth could that possibly be?"

Darcy smiled. "Whataburger, my hangover remedy."

Lawrence covered his mouth. As expected, he didn't look anywhere near ready to face food.

"Trust me." Darcy headed to the door.

"You know," Lawrence said. "I had the strangest dream."

"What?"

Lawrence eyed the ceiling as if replaying the scene. "It had something to do with the Caped Crusader."

Darcy sucked in air. "Sounds like a good dream." She let herself out of the apartment before blowing out what surely would have been a true classic remark.

***

She returned Pierre to Izzy's hairdresser's nephew, who promised to get the mousy dog with the rhinestone collar to his roommate's cousin. Back at Lawrence's door within an hour and a half, she balanced two orange-striped bags and a flimsy cardboard drink holder containing two large orange-striped Styrofoam cups.

Lawrence had showered and changed into his comfy-knock-around-on-Sunday khaki slacks, polo shirt, and Cole Haans; however, he hadn't been able to wash away the spider lines from the whites of his eyes. His hair, still wet, had been slicked down in its usual style. A thin red streak etched across half of his upper lip.

"Now, there's the Lawrence I'm used to." Darcy pushed her way in and dropped the bags of food on the small dinette table. He closed the door and without a word took a seat.

She pushed a cheeseburger, fries, and drink in front of him. "Here, eat."

His face resembled a chiseled rock. "Are you sure about this?"

"Absolutely. Trust me." Darcy stuffed a handful of French fries in her mouth and unwrapped her cheeseburger.

Lawrence followed suit, only in slo-mo and with a single French fry versus a handful. One fry led to another, and before too many

97

minutes had passed he launched into his cheeseburger like Tom Hanks after his *Castaway* rescue. "You know," Lawrence said, his mouth full. "I think this really works. I actually don't feel like I'm dying."

"It's miracle food," Darcy said between bites.

"How in the world did you discover this?" Lawrence carefully wiped the corner of his mouth.

Darcy shrugged and took a long draw from her Diet Coke. "I don't know. Just kind of came with the college education." She sat back in her chair. "They don't teach that kind of stuff at Yale, do they?"

"Don't start." Lawrence folded the thin paper from his cheeseburger until he had created a small Origami triangle.

Her eyebrows shot upward.

Weird.

"What?" he asked.

Deciding to let yet another opportunity pass, she changed the subject and pointed to his face. "Why is half your upper lip so red?"

He raised a finger and touched the raw spot. "I had some difficulty removing the remaining half of my moustache."

"Ouch." She gazed around the almost bare apartment. "What did you do with the costume?"

"I thought about burning it, but I can't afford to," Lawrence said. "It's resting in the bedroom." His eyes brightened. "By the way, I found the other half of my moustache. It had stuck to one of my chaps." Lawrence, looking smug, sat back and crossed his legs. "Should save me two dollars, which I'm sure will be applied to the cost of removing the martini stain."

Darcy squeezed her lips tight and nodded. The mental vow not to throw sarcasm Lawrence's way was not easy. But not today. After all, he had agreed to go with her to Miranda's party. She glanced at her watch and hoped she could keep her promise. "So, you finally got to meet Miranda." Diversion, her only hope.

"Good lord. The woman is a goddess."

"She's Catwoman."

"None the less, a goddess."

"Yeah, well, whatever." Darcy wadded her orange-striped sack and headed for the door, giving herself a thumbs-up for all the oh-so-easy comments she could have forked over.

Chapter 8

Monday turned out to be hazy and somewhat muggy. It was also Halloween…and Izzy's birthday. Darcy swung by and picked up her grandmother for their annual celebratory lunch. Izzy waddled out dressed in her usual black slacks, black SAS shoes, and flashy blouse. Today the flashes were psychedelic orange jack-o-lanterns.

"Do you like my new blouse?" Izzy asked.

"Sure, but orange isn't one of your colors, is it?" Izzy still purchased clothes according to her seasonal color wheel of the early eighties.

"I know. I couldn't help myself." Izzy fastened the seatbelt across her round frame. "Your mother took me to a craft show last Saturday. Four blouses for fifty dollars. I got one for Halloween, Christmas, Easter, and the Fourth of July. And look…." She leaned toward Darcy's side of the car, exposing miniature skeletons dangling from her ears. "I'm accessorized."

"Dar-ling." Darcy did a mental eye roll and backed out of the driveway.

"I thought you'd like them. I know how you are about accessories." Izzy wore an I-know-something-you-don't smile. "So I got you something for your birthday."

The mental eye rolling turned into mental headthunking. "Izzy, don't spend your money on things like that for me. Besides, my birthday isn't for months."

And besides, you'll never wear them.

"Don't be ridiculous," Izzy said. "I can buy my favorite grandchild a gift if I want to. About six weeks, and it'll be here before you know it."

"Thanks for reminding me."

See? No way you were gonna slip past this birthday.

And even though she and her grandmother had a close relationship, Darcy knew for a fact she played the favorite card with all her grandchildren.

There were two standing traditions on Izzy's birthday. One: lunch with her "oldest" favorite grandchild at La Madeline's. Two: dinner out with the whole family. The unusual twist to the dinner out thing was Izzy's insistence on paying. "It's my birthday, and I get to do what I want," she always said. "So there."

The lunch tradition at La Madeline's had started Darcy's first year out of college. When Darcy was little, Izzy used to take each one of the grandchildren out for a special lunch. Now Darcy wanted to do the same for her grandmother, though she often had to wrestle Izzy for the check. The only variance in the tradition came down to the dessert Izzy insisted they order and split. Darcy's tray held a bowl of the French bakery's well known tomato-basil soup, a small Caesar's salad, and mango iced tea. Izzy chose the Quiche Lorraine, fresh fruit salad, and coffee. Their dessert choice for the occasion—drum roll please—tiramisu.

Darcy finished off her lunch and took her first bite of the ladyfinger delicacy.

"Met anyone interesting lately?"

"I can't believe we almost made it through lunch this time." Darcy eased the savory first bite into her mouth. "Thought you were slipping."

"Oh horse feathers," Izzy said. "Answer my question."

Darcy sighed, so tired of discussing her non-existent love life with her overly involved grandmother, but thought she'd throw her a crumb. "I met Batman last Saturday at Miranda's party. He asked for my number."

Izzy stopped, fork frozen midway between mouth and plate. She eyed Darcy briefly before resuming movement of the tiramisu to her mouth. "Batman. Really dear, can't you find a normal person?"

Aside from the irritation, Darcy couldn't help but chuckle. "Izzy, it was a Halloween party. His name is Sam." And quickly added, "And no, he hasn't called yet."

"Call him."

"That doesn't sound like you," Darcy said. "What's wrong, aren't you feeling well?

"Nothing's wrong with me." Her grandmother paused. "Well, except for my knees. And possibly my eyes. I really need to go back to the eye...." her voice trailed off for a split second before picking up momentum. "Hey, what's the name of that eye doctor you see? I could have my eyes checked and put in a good word for you."

"Matt."

"Matt what?"

"I'm not telling you."

"Why not?"

"Because you might really make an appointment with him." Darcy finished off her half of the tiramisu and pushed the plate toward Izzy.

"But he's available."

"He's too high maintenance." Darcy immediately regretted her words.

"Oh, and you're not, Ms. Jimmy Kung Foo."

Darcy forgot to hide her eye roll. "Jimmy Choo, Izzy."

"Whatever, he's still available."

"Izzy, listen," Darcy began. "Matt is a pretty boy. You wouldn't like him for a grandson-in-law, or whatever he'd be called."

"So he's pretty. Big deal." Izzy paused. "Wait a minute. Does that mean he's gay?"

"No Izzy. Not at all. He's a player."

"What does he play?"

"Women," Darcy said. "Lots of them. All the time."

Izzy nodded, which rocked the little skeletons hanging from her ears. "I see." She reached into her purse, pulled out a small notebook, and made a note on a page.

"What are you writing?"

"Still available." Izzy studied her list. "He loses half a point for being a player."

"Please stop." This was such a disturbing conversation on so many levels...time to switch subjects. "So, where are we going tonight?"

Izzy looked at her granddaughter as if she'd grown spiked pink and purple hair. "Where do you think? Christie's, of course." Christie's, a long-standing seafood restaurant in Houston, had been a time-honored tradition with the Daniels. The original South Main location had closed in 1979 and the restaurant had moved to its new, and still current, location on Westheimer.

Dinner that night proved chaotic, as were most events when the entire crew gathered. Reservations were for 7:00 p.m. Darcy arrived early due to strategically planning her last appointment for the day near Christie's. She was sitting at the bar enjoying her first glass of wine when her parents, Izzy, and Andie showed up. Her grandmother still wore her Halloween ensemble, although she had traded her skeleton earrings for sparkly jack-o-lanterns. Andie, with an obvious affection tonight for Goth-like black eye-liner, touted a tight blue-jean skirt and a light-weight button down white shirt, no doubt from Aeropostole, which would have resembled something close to proper except for the neon-green bra she wore underneath. What were her parents thinking? Darcy's eyebrows shot up an inch, which either her parents ignored or didn't care to comment on. Izzy responded with her own wiggled eyebrows, which translated into "I know. And she used to be *such* a pretty child."

Shortly after being seated, Alex and Anna arrived. Both her brother and his girlfriend looked like they had just walked away from an Abercrombie & Fitch photo-op. Drinks had been served and orders were placed, which consisted of fried shrimp platters, another family tradition at Christie's. All was well until Anna ordered. She spoke the unthinkable words that shocked everyone at the table, with the exception of Alex. "I'll have the Greek salad with grilled chicken. And water with lemon please."

Chicken? There was no *chicken* at Christies. Darcy grabbed the menu she hadn't bothered with earlier, and sure enough found grilled chicken printed right there in front of God and everybody. And only water? On Izzy's birthday? Very un-Daniels like.

"She's allergic to shell fish," Alex explained. "And alcohol."

Everyone except Darcy nodded and resumed their small chatter, munching on crackers and pats of frozen butter from little saucers around the table.

"Wow. Allergic to seafood *and* alcohol? That is so sad." Crumbs spewed from Darcy's mouth.

Nina shot Darcy a look to take care of the comment, with enough left over for the cracker crumbs she spewed.

"Sorry." She stuffed another cracker in her mouth to shut herself up.

"Oh, that's okay," Anna said. "It won't kill me or anything. I just swell up like a toad."

Just as she captured the mental picture of her brother's prim and proper girlfriend exploding into a blowfish, Alex raised Anna's left hand. "I guess this is as good a time as any." Alex blew out some air. "We did it. We're engaged."

All eyes turned to the brilliant glare spawning from Anna's ring finger. Cheers, congratulations, hugs, and tears flowed forth from the Daniels clan. Darcy gave her brother and his fiancée hugs.

Yet another leapfrog move for the prodigal son.

This announcement could only mean one thing. Izzy's MO would be dropkicked into overdrive. Darcy wasn't wrong.

Everyone settled back down at their places as six fried shrimp platters plus one lonely grilled chicken Caesar salad were delivered to the table. Izzy grabbed a spoon and clinked it against her martini glass. Every year on her birthday Izzy had one (and only one) Grey Goose martini before switching over to her favorite, Killian's Irish Red beer.

"I have an announcement to make myself." Mischief danced behind Izzy's eyes, causing Darcy's antenna to reach alert status. She had no idea about the announcement, but felt pretty sure about two things, according to the sinking feeling in her stomach. One: it had something to do with Darcy. Two: she wasn't going to like it.

"What is it, Mother?" Nina asked. Darcy's dad grumbled something, followed by an immediate "ouch" after Nina kicked him under the table.

Izzy, loving to be the center of attention with tonight being no exception, reminded Darcy of the trickster crazy Cheshire cat in *Alice in Wonderland.*

Darcy glanced around for their waiter. She needed more wine…a lot of it. Something bad was brewing, like watching two trains minutes before they collided.

"Well, go ahead Mother. We're all waiting," Nina said.

Izzy eyed her audience before spilling out the dreaded words. "Darcy has a new beau. Maybe we'll have a double wedding!"

As expected, all eyes switched to Darcy, who spoke rather rapidly to the nearest waitress she could grab, knowing fairly well Christie's couldn't possibly have enough wine to drown out this evening.

Nina rose to give her daughter a hug, which sent Darcy's hands flying upward. Nina halted. Darcy caught her dad's expression, which looked like a puppy who had just been whacked on the nose with a newspaper. Izzy's birthday dinners were a concession for him. Alex's announcement…predictable. Darcy's…not at all. Stephen Daniels looked like he'd had all the "good news" he could take, even before he swallowed his first fried shrimp.

"No, no, and no." Darcy stared at Izzy, not wanting to publicly slam her grandma on her birthday. Tomorrow, however…fair game. "I don't have a boyfriend. I just met someone at Miranda's party last Saturday. Izzy, you're so funny." Darcy *so* wanted to be somewhere else. Anywhere a genie in a lamp could zap her to would be perfectly fine. How many times could a woman say, "I don't have a boyfriend" without sounding totally pathetic? Luckily, her words had turned everyone's attention, with the exception of Izzy, back to their food.

"Not to worry. He'll call, thear." Izzy's speech indicated the Grey Goose had kicked in. "I know thez thingths."

Great. Her grandma was plastered. Darcy shot Izzy a look she hoped would squelch any further boyfriend comments and then accepted her third glass of wine from the waitress.

"I'll have my Killian's now," Izzy shouted much louder than necessary. The waitress looked at Nina, who gave a quick no shake and then a yes nod, which Darcy knew translated to *no* on the beer and *yes* to the birthday dessert ritual.

Darcy glanced around the table, grateful that no one ever paid much attention to Izzy. Alex and Anna swooned in their own happiness, her dad focused on his food, and Nina looked like Nina always did when her family got together, content…somewhat. Andie's glow came from her neon green bra, and Izzy, in Grey Goose land, managed to put on her "oh, I'm so surprised" smile when the waitress placed the sparkler-topped slice of cheesecake in front of her. The entire wait staff sang the traditional "Happy Birthday," which resulted in a round of applause from the others in the restaurant. As also was tradition, Izzy stood and took a bow. Darcy's grandmother loved attention.

Her dad made the obligatory wrestle for the check, which everyone knew to be a waste of time, and Darcy made it back to her parking space at Fountain Oaks by 9:00. She sat in her acceptable-to-everyone-but-her SUV and thunked her head on the steering wheel. She felt her life had sunk to a new low, closing in on her like one of Miranda's spandex outfits.

"I need a sign," she told God. "I need to know you're watching over me and not just having a good laugh at my expense." Said out-loud, her words sounded even more ridiculous than they had flitting around in her brain. She slipped her Ferragamo-clad feet out the car door, grabbed her fake Michael Kors hobo bag, and made her way up to her apartment. At the top of the stairs she glanced toward her door and slammed to a halt.

You asked for a sign....

Once again, she found Lawrence sitting in a chair outside her apartment.

You ought to burn that chair.

Darcy felt like a kindergartener after a really bad day. All she wanted was to go home and have some milk and cookies...but alone.

"Trick or treat?" Lawrence handed Darcy a bright orange piece of paper.

"What's this?"

"I'd say it's our Halloween treat," Lawrence said. "Either that or an answer to your dilemma."

Which one? The list is long.

"Be more specific."

"You know. The one about where to go on Thanksgiving?"

"I don't have a dilemma about Thanksgiving."

"You do now."

"What do you mean?" Along with feeling annoyed, she now added confused.

"I'd read it to you, but frankly, I haven't the heart."

"Since when?"

"What's wrong? Get ice cubes in your trick or treat bag tonight?"

"Alright. I deserved that one." Darcy dug around in her over-sized bag for her key. She unlocked the door and was all but mowed over by Stash bouncing past the two of them, sliding around at the end of the hall, and bounding down the stairs.

"What in the world?" The orange piece of paper was still stuck in his hand.

"A dog with a full tank is my guess," Darcy said. "Either that or there's a monster bigger than him in my apartment."

Darcy and Lawrence moved inside. Before she could even throw her bag down on the counter, Stash had made it back upstairs, and without so much as an apology for the ambush headed for his water bowl.

"And he would be a latch-key dog if he could work the lock?"

Despite her crummy evening and God's weird sense of humor, Darcy felt a smile creep onto her face. "Not bad," she said and laughed, which felt surprisingly good. "What's with the orange paper?"

"Want to get some wine first?" Lawrence asked.

"That bad?"

"Let me think. Yes." Lawrence made his way toward the kitchen. "Was that no to the wine?"

"I'm over my quota." The taste in her mouth reminded her of the gulping she'd done at Christie's. From her vantage point on the couch, Darcy could see Lawrence helping himself to the boxed beverage in her refrigerator.

"Do you mind?" he said.

"Does it matter?" Was on the tip of her tongue, but instead of releasing the words, she shook her head and drew her legs up under her. Lawrence took a sip of wine, which Darcy noticed no longer caused him to grimace. He set the glass on the ottoman coffee table and opened the orange paper.

"We're invited to accompany our loving apartment manager on Thanksgiving Day to feed the hungry at the George R. Brown."

Darcy could feel her nose wrinkle. She knew Lawrence waited for a response so she searched her insides from head to toe, but couldn't find anything to rant about. "Okay," Darcy said. "That's not so bad."

Lawrence's next swig of wine obviously went down the wrong pipe, which sent him into a spewing and coughing spell. After blotting up the spillage down the front of his shirt and across the ottoman, Lawrence shot a look at his neighbor. "Did I mention there is no rental incentive reward program to this offer?"

"I'll talk to Ms. Viola and see what's up," Darcy said. She had learned there was a lot more to their apartment manager than what appeared on the surface. Although Ms. Viola played a mean old witch, Miranda's term that usually fit well, something about the elderly woman puzzled Darcy…something she hadn't been able to quite grasp.

Lawrence sat for a long moment and stared at the dark television screen in front of them. "This is not at all the reaction I expected from you." He downed the last sip from his glass. "I think you should go to bed immediately. You're obviously not yourself tonight. I'll check on you first thing in the morning to see how you are feeling."

She appreciated his point of view. He was right…she would have also expected more of an outburst from herself. But she didn't feel sick. She felt…well, she didn't know how she felt.

"I'm not sick." Darcy glanced over his head to the clock on the microwave. "I'm just tired." She got to her feet. Walking Lawrence to the door seemed to be the quickest and most pain-free way of getting him to leave. "Today's my grandmother's eightieth birthday. She likes to celebrate…all day."

"I've never met your grandmother…or any of your family members for that matter." Lawrence reached the door.

"I know." How could she explain Izzy's dating Rolodex, or her little sister who wore neon under garments? Actually, he'd probably get along just fine with Alex. Her mother would smile politely and her dad would give him a quick once over look and assess that Lawrence would not be the kind of guy he could take—or want to take—to a sports bar.

"I haven't met your parents either." Darcy couldn't think for the life of her why she had to add that little tidbit to the mix.

Lawrence's lowered his head and looked deflated. "They're not normal."

"I don't think there is such a thing," Darcy said. "I mean, when you look up 'normal' in the dictionary, you won't find my family either."

"Thank you for that," Lawrence said, and made his exit.

Darcy shrugged, ran her fingers through her hair, and closed the door. She padded over to the answering machine and pushed the button that wasn't blinking just for the hell of it.

"You have no new messages."

She turned out the lights and headed for bed.

***

November had always been Darcy's favorite month. October, so-so, but once the calendar dipped into November, the cool mornings and subtle color changes of the trees left no doubt that summer had taken its leave. Good riddance. Finally, she could bring out her pseudo-designer fall and winter clothes.

Saturday morning Darcy opened the living room window to take advantage of the decent outside temperature and noticed Fletcher walking Ike. It wasn't the first time this week she'd seen this, or the second. She tapped her finger on her chin and decided she needed to pay Ms. Viola a visit sometime over the weekend.

She sat cross-legged on her couch sipping her second cup of flavored coffee. A new shipment should have arrived at Harwin during the past week, so by 10:00 she'd be on the road. And Lawrence wanted to tag along. She couldn't even roll her eyes on this one. She'd invited him. Why was Lawrence the person she seemed to be hanging out with lately? Lisa had her family, Becca had her new husband, and Miranda had gone MIA. She hadn't heard from her best friend since the party. Miranda led a busy, fun-filled life, but she always kept in touch.

Probably tied up with Captain Kirk.

Darcy's mind flipped back to Rob's contortion remark. She nodded, agreeing his comment could be a strong possibility. Oh well. The day with Lawrence would be bearable because she had a date that night…a real date. Sam had called…and no, Izzy didn't know. They were going out to dinner. She blew out air. Thank goodness…it had been a while.

Darcy showered, threw on the $29.99 Lucky jeans she had found at Marshall's, a white t-shirt, and a graffiti print hoodie sweatshirt jacket. She pulled her black Delman flats out of their box in her closet and switched to her Coach (she wished) purse. Maybe she could find something to wear on her date. Or at least, a new…well, something.

Lawrence stood at the bottom of the stairs, rubbing his chin with his thumb and index finger, his eyebrows pulled together.

"What's up?" Darcy asked.

"Something is strange out there."

She glanced at her watch. Timing was everything after a new shipment arrival on Harwin. "C'mon, let's go. Tell me about it in the car."

Lawrence stood his ground and pointed to the far end of the courtyard. "The plants are living, and I smell manure."

Darcy shot a glance over her shoulder in the direction Lawrence was pointing and stopped so quickly her purse almost flew off her shoulder. "What the hell?" The response seemed a little harsh, but total shock often produced her profanity vocabulary. They crossed the courtyard to the site of the former dead shrub cemetery.

"They've resurrected," Lawrence said.

"Yeah, right." Darcy rolled her eyes in Lawrence's direction. "In a parallel universe, where the sky is purple and we both have a love life."

"But they're alive." Lawrence's eyes glued to the scene in front of him.

"That's because they're new." Darcy's mind spun like tires on ice, examining the variegated green and gold very healthy and very newly planted shrubs. "And look at these little guys." She stooped to examine two rows of flowering plants at the front of the bed in different shades of yellow, gold, and rust. The old dried dirt had been weeded, turned, and mixed with rich planting soil and mulch. The bed itself had been raised. Very professional looking, and definitely un-Fountain Oaks-like.

"And look!" Lawrence had turned to view their own building. The beds there had also been worked and raised. Shrubs in buckets and bedding plants in their flats stood nearby waiting to be put in the ground.

"I don't believe it," Darcy said.

Lawrence used his hand to cover his nose. "Why does it smell like manure?"

"Because mulch has manure in it," Darcy said. "Haven't you ever smelled fresh mulch before?"

"Let me think. No," Lawrence replied. "Because of my allergies I was not allowed outside when the gardener was...." Lawrence swirled his free hand around in a small circle, his index finger pointing at the fresh mulch. "Messing with that."

"Wow," Darcy said. "A gardener."

"Don't start."

"Let's go." Darcy turned her back on the freshly planted flowerbed.

"It must have been your letter," Lawrence said, catching up with her. "You're my hero."

"Humph." Although she'd had the same thought...about the letter, not the hero thing.

"Is that a good or bad 'humph'?"

"I haven't decided." Darcy backed out of the parking lot and headed for the freeway. Landscaping could wait...Harwin couldn't.

Three hours later they sat at Roznovsky's, indulging in their second beer and Lawrence's newfound comfort food— cheeseburgers. The first beer had slid down entirely too easily after a morning at Harwin, which made way for round two, and surely an afternoon beer nap.

"It's astonishing." Lawrence leaned back in his chair and wiped his mouth with a paper towel. "I've never seen anything like it. All these years I've been indulging in Rolexes and Armani suits, when I could have been pandering my desires on exceptionally good quality knock-offs."

Darcy finished off her burger and rested her elbows on the table. "Snob."

"Quite right." Lawrence reached for a remaining French fry. "However, that was in my other life. I'm now a reformed snob."

Raising her adult beverage, Darcy tipped it in his direction. "Welcome to the real world."

"And I owe it all to you." Lawrence reached for his wallet. "Let's see. You've introduced me to boxed wine, which I've grown quite fond of. Pizza." He held out his hands, palms up. "This place. Not to mention Miranda, and a whole new highly affordable shopping district."

"I'd say my work here is done." Darcy stood. "The bill's paid...you can leave the tip."

"Very well then." Lawrence downed the last of his beer and dropped a five- dollar bill on the table.

At home, Darcy spent the next couple of hours snoozing softly on her sofa. By 6:00 she had showered, done her hair and make-up thing in what she hoped looked classy, and donned her carefully orchestrated outfit. The plan called for her to meet Sam at 13 Celsius, an upscale and well-known wine bar in Midtown, Miranda's stomping grounds. From there they would head to Osaka Japanese

Restaurant, and then downtown to a dance club. Sam seemed to be going all out, and Darcy wanted to fit in.

She stood in front of her full-length mirror and chewed on her fingernail. She wore a Karen Kane metallic cowl neck top with matching cardigan, black wide-waistband pants, Michael Kors metallic two-tone open-toed shoes, and textured hoop earrings. The top and cardigan she had stumbled on while foraging through an overcrowded rack at Marshall's. The earrings she'd found at Stein Mart. She turned and viewed her profile. Three and a quarter inch heels. She couldn't remember Sam's height, but figured anyone who could sling Doc Holliday over his shoulder ought to be able to handle her in three inch plus heels. The Michael Kors matched her top and cardigan perfectly. Of course, she had paid full price for these beauties at Nordstrom's, but for once the shoes were under $200. Her approach to putting together an outfit fell under the category entitled "unusual." She started with the shoes...always the shoes. Then she'd work her way up to piece together an outfit.

Today's Harwin excursion had landed her a fake Dooney & Burke black drawstring shopper bag. Perfect. Well, almost. The topstitching didn't match the thread color of the seams, and the little protective feet studs on the bottom were silver. Anyone in their right mind knew all metal trim on a D&B to be brass, not silver. She could handle the little studs on the bottom of the purse...she only hoped the topstitching wasn't too noticeable. She shot one last critical once-over in the mirror, shrugged, grabbed her not-quite Dooney & Burke, and headed out the door to her not-quite-Lexus SUV.

The evening progressed relatively well. Sam, a guy with a nice job and good manners, turned out to be a little formal...or maybe he just went a tad overboard trying to impress her. All in all, however, he scored in the nice category. 13 Celsius was cool, no pun intended. All the wines were stored in a real wine cellar at the optimum temperature—13 Celsius. The building, a 1920s Mediterranean-style structure, had been modeled after the cozy wine bars in Europe. Not that she'd ever been to Europe, but she had done some Google research on the place.

Osaka's had been excellent. She chose sushi because sushi was cool, but could have been just as happy—happier, actually—with a double order of the fried soft shelled crab listed as an appetizer. They never made it to the dance club downtown, which suited

Darcy. It had been a long time since she'd engaged in conversation with a nice-looking man for any length of time, which wasn't meant to be a slam toward her intellectual neighbor. Lawrence just wasn't what she'd consider to be her type.

And what is your type? Izzy still wants to know.

She hoped Sam would call again. She really did, although halfway through the evening her new outfit started to feel uncomfortable and her feet hurt...a big no-no for expensive shoes. As much as she enjoyed the conversation and being taken out for a nice and quite expensive evening, she felt much more at ease back at the apartment in her sweats, white fuzzy socks, and soft fat-lady shirt. What was wrong with her?

She snuggled into the cushions of her couch, opened the bag of microwave popcorn, and watched another *Sex in the City* rerun. Stash sat at her feet, waiting patiently for his sloppy seconds. Mel, curled up in a ball, snoozed beside her. "What do you think?" she asked her most-of-the-time loveable mutt. "Have I lost it?"

Stash squirmed, wagged his tail, and let out an excited yelp.

"Use your words." Darcy reached into the bag and hurled a piece of popcorn across the room. Stash retrieved it after one bounce and raced back to resume his position at her feet. Dressing up in expensive shoes and marked-down (way, way down) designer clothes used to be the one thing that made her feel...well, special.

"I used to live for that kind of crap," she said to the dog. "A nice guy asks me out. I get all dressed up, and I'm looking forward to this?" She glanced down at Stash, who had rolled over onto his back, all four legs in the air, nothing at all moving except the wiper blade motion of his tail, which Darcy referred to as the dead-dog position. She finished the popcorn and stood. "And do you know what I have to look forward to tomorrow?" she asked her goofy pet in his crash position. "Visiting Ms. Viola. How's that for an exciting Sunday?"

***

Darcy rolled over and looked at the clock...eight forty-five. Glancing out through the half-opened mini blinds, she saw a deep, clear blue sky...Norman Rockwell blue. She stretched, threw the covers back, then pulled them back up, allowing her mind to examine her plans for the day. Running would be great at Memorial Park this morning. Then she could head over to her parents for a quick meal and pick up a few things at the store before making the stop at Ms. Viola's. The woman's Thanksgiving plans for her tenants, although still weeks away, had piqued Darcy's curiosity about the George R. Brown event.

After taking care of the animals and downing a breakfast of yogurt and a multivitamin, she threw on running clothes and headed out the door. At the bottom of the stairwell, she glanced to her right and saw the completed flowerbed along the wall of her building, as pristine and colorful as the bed she and Lawrence had discovered the previous day. With keys in hand she headed for the carport, but at the last minute did a 180 toward Ms. Viola's apartment, moving the visit to the top of the list.

A hand knocked on the door…she was somewhat surprised to find it was hers. She waited for what felt like a day before she heard movement inside the apartment. There was absolutely no way she could have prepared herself for what awaited her.

"What do you want?" It wasn't said in a mean way, just a simple question…probably the first one that popped into Mr. Will's head. He stood before Darcy in striped long-legged pajamas, mostly covered by a well-worn blue terrycloth bathrobe. What hair he still had looked like it had been blow-dried in a wind tunnel. He squinted, his glasses nowhere in sight.

"Who is it, Will?" Ms. Viola's strained voice came from somewhere inside the apartment.

"I dunno." Mr. Will squinted harder.

"Oh hell, Will. Let whoever it is in and go get your glasses," Ms. Viola said.

Will backed up two steps and pulled the door with him. Darcy crossed the threshold, her mind struggling to put thoughts and words together. Ms. Viola sat in one of the expensive leather recliners, looking shriveled and tired. Darcy forced one foot ahead of the other until she stood in front of the velvet couch with dainty doilies. Her eyes met Ms. Viola's. She edged backwards until she felt the couch touch the back of her legs, then lowered herself into what she hoped to be a sitting position.

Ms. Viola also wore a terrycloth robe over a long nightgown. Her feet were shoved into frayed house shoes that looked like they'd been Ike's chew toy. Darcy heard Mr. Will rummaging around somewhere toward the back of the apartment.

"A little early for a social call, isn't it?" Ms. Viola shot right past pleasantries, which wasn't unusual.

Darcy nodded and pushed hair away from her face, her brain in freeze-frame until the dots started to connect. Pajamas. Bathrobes. Glasses.

Glasses?

Glasses on the bedside table the day Ms. Viola had her attack.

Mr. Will's glasses?

The next set of images took Darcy's mind on a road trip she immediately regretted. *Reverse! Reverse! Full-throttle reverse!*

Holy shit....

"Well?" Ms. Viola either didn't care what Darcy's dot-to-dot mind had discovered, didn't feel well enough to comment, or was concerned about the stricken look on Darcy's face. "You're staring at me," Ms. Viola said.

"Yes." She tried to shake the shock from her face and search her hard drive for the reason she sat on the velvet couch in the first place.

You're a grownup. C'mon, you can handle this.

This pep talk didn't work. The silence felt about as comfortable as an unwanted passenger in a smart car.

"Can I help you?" Ms. Viola asked.

Words slowly worked their way to the surface. Darcy cleared her throat. "I'm sorry...I...I didn't...but then...and so...." Words were surfacing, they just weren't forming coherent thoughts.

The old woman ran her hand across her wrinkled forehead, rubbed her nose, and lifted her chin. "Well. Now you know," Ms. Viola said as Mr. Will emerged from what Darcy now knew to be the bedroom. The horn-rimmed glasses sat cock-eyed across his face. He had dressed in his usual plaid shirt, rumpled khakis, and fishing hat. He shuffled into the living room and wrinkled his nose to help push the glasses up on his nose.

He eyed Darcy. "Oh." As if he finally figured out the mystery guest. "Is Larry around?"

"I...he...there's a...." Darcy mind could only think about Lawrence's Sunday morning cucumber mask ritual, only today Mr. Will would be wearing his glasses.

"I need to teach that boy to fish." Mr. Will swiped the ancient fishing hat off his head, bent down, and landed a kiss on top of Ms. Viola's head. "See you at dinner."

"You're not driving, William." Ms. Viola's voice sounded much stronger than she looked.

"I know. I know." Mr. Will waved a hand and pulled open the apartment door. "That's the boy's chore."

Darcy watched the door close. She had not bargained for this latest news flash and wished she had stuck with going to Memorial Park. Dragging her ass around the running path would have been less painful. Her gaze wandered around the room. "Where's Ike?"

"Fletcher has him today." Ms. Viola's faded blue eyes squinted and settled back on Darcy. "Fletcher can use the company and Ike needs the exercise. But you didn't come here to ask about my dog, now did you?"

The words the old woman spoke were the same, but with an absence of malice. Actually, Darcy thought she even caught a glimpse of a smile around the edge of Ms. Viola's face. Her mind cleared a bit and she remembered her original intent of knocking on the door this morning. "No. You're right, I didn't. I came to find out about Thanksgiving. I got the flyer."

"Good." Ms. Viola leaned forward in her blue leather chair. "Will you come?"

Darcy wiggled on the couch. She wanted information: Ms. Viola wanted a commitment. "Well, can you tell me more about it?"

The wrinkled old woman studied Darcy's face and then settled back into the fine leather recliner. When she spoke, her words came out not in exclamation marks but more like a bold font. More dots began to connect in Darcy's already over-stimulated brain. The cynicism in Ms. Viola's voice had disappeared, which made way for yet another surprise. Passion…Ms. Viola had a big heart and she cared, cared about a lot of things. She explained how volunteering for Meals on Wheels had led her to participate in the citywide Thanksgiving Day Feast at the George R. Brown Convention Center, which fed anyone who needed or wanted a meal. Last year the program had served turkey and dressing to over thirty thousand people.

Darcy's mind was trying to calculate how many turkeys fed thirty thousand people when the silence in the room signaled that

Ms. Viola had stopped talking. "What? I'm sorry," Darcy said. "What did you say?"

"What do you usually do for Thanksgiving?"

"When I was little, I spent the day with my grandparents." Darcy explained that her dad graduating from A&M in the Class of '71 translated into her parents usually being in College Station or Austin on Thanksgiving for the Turkey Day game.

Ms. Viola nodded. The annual rivalry was not exactly a news flash for people living in Texas.

Darcy relayed how each year Izzy would take her and her two younger siblings downtown for the big parade. They'd have their Thanksgiving meal at L&C Cafeteria, and then Izzy would treat them to a movie, which gave Darcy's grandfather the best Thanksgiving ever—the chance to watch football all day long...alone.

Now, Thanksgiving meals were held at her parent's house. Darcy's dad and Alex spent most of their time glued to the television, while the women planned for the most important day of the year: Black Friday, the prime shopping day. It was the best shot Darcy had to land a designer something or another from an actual upscale, for-real department store, which now, all of a sudden, sounded extremely lame. She finished her narrative and studied Ms. Viola's face. "What time?"

The almost smile, once again, broke across the old woman's face. She reached over and patted Darcy's knee.

Chapter 9

Darcy left Ms. Viola's apartment in a daze...so much so, she completely forgot about the trek to Memorial Park, which came as no great surprise since her reasons to attempt jogging in the first place boiled down to a short and sweet list. A chance to meet a George Clooney clone (her Prince Charming), to zip up her jeans while in a vertical position, and...well, something else she couldn't remember at the moment due to the mind-bolt she'd received at Ms. Viola's. Besides the holy-shit scenario of two old people rolling around in the sack, she now had the Thanksgiving invitation to consider. She knew the old woman had to be ill...very ill. Ms. Viola had looked more like hammered shit than usual.

The Wicked Witch of the West had pushed aside her costume. Darcy just couldn't figure out why. Wasn't there a nice witch in the Wizard of Oz? Overall, Darcy considered herself to be a considerate person. She took good care of her animals, held doors open for elderly people, and took her grandmother to lunch every year on her birthday. Hell, she even gathered wayward grocery carts on a regular basis and returned them to their little assigned parking lot depository. But lately the *me, me,* and *me* sort of girl seemed to have taken center stage. And Ms. Viola's temperament, up until recently, had led Darcy to believe that the old woman was also a member of the *Me Club.*

She pulled to the curb and studied the front of her parents' house. For twenty-five years the shutters around the windows had been painted blue...country blue. The once small trees now provided shade for much of the yard, and the shrubs were mature and neatly trimmed. Darcy had begged her mother to change the color of the shutters, maybe to something earth tone, or even black...anything different. "Blue," her mother had said. "It has to be blue."

Izzy shocked her back to reality as Darcy, lost in thought, made her way to the front door.

"Did you have a date last night?"

"Yes Izzy, I did."

"I knew it! Batman, right?"

Darcy deflated an inch or two. "Please don't call him that. His name is Sam."

"Yeah, well, okay." Izzy looked as excited as if she had just scored a triple word on Scrabble. "So where did he take you? Some place nice? I bet you looked gorgeous. What did you wear?"

Not in the mood for Izzy's investigative reporting, she knew she had to throw something out for her grandmother to chew on. She mentally cracked her knuckles. "We went to 13 Celsius in Midtown, then Osaka's Japanese Restaurant. I wore a fabulous Karen Kane outfit and Michael Kors shoes. He was *very* impressed with my choice of clothing. Twice I was mistaken for a celebrity. We hit it off wonderfully. We both had sushi, and I'm meeting him at Jared's this week. Any meatloaf left?"

There had been few times in Darcy's life (if any) when she managed to say exactly the right thing at the right time to bring her grandmother up speechless. She usually picked her fights, and ended up losing most of them. However, she'd nailed this one dead center. Breezing past an open-mouthed Izzy, she found her mother in the kitchen talking to Andie, who was nose-deep in an *In Touch* magazine.

No doubt researching a topic for her next English paper.

Her mother would have fared better talking to the blue-tinted fruit painted on the lattice kitchen wallpaper.

"Oh, hi sweetie." Nina left her podium and gave Darcy a quick hug. "How's my Toodle Bug?"

"Mom, I thought we'd talked…." Darcy felt her voice drift off into a land far far away. Nina had nicknamed her first child Toodle Bug. No one knew why, not even Nina. Darcy had lived with this highly irritating animated name her whole life. And for some unknown reason she had suddenly misplaced the need to correct her mother for the millionth time.

"I'm fine, Mom," Darcy answered instead. "How are things here?"

"We're good." Nina returned to the counter where she had recipes spread around. "Andrea and I were deciding on dressings to make this year. Weren't we sweetie?"

Andie pried her eyes away from her research project, shot a look in Darcy's direction, smiled, and tucked her head back into whatever current scandal held her attention.

"Your father likes the crawfish dressing, and, let's see…you like the one with the sausage, jalapeños, and pecans, right?"

"Mom, let's make it simple this year," Darcy said. "Just make a dressing and that'll be it. Dressing—no 's' at the end. If Dad likes the crawfish kind, do that one."

"I don't like fish in my dressing." Andie spoke as if she read the words straight from the magazine.

"And I guess I need to think about Anna and her allergies." Nina pinched her lips together, then sorted through some more recipes.

Izzy waddled into the kitchen sucking on a Jolly Rancher. "Darcy's engaged, did she tell you?"

"What?" Nina froze, her hand mid-air, holding one of the recipe cards. "Did you say engaged?" Even Andie's nose lifted out of *In Touch*.

Touché Izzy.

"Nooo. I'm not engaged." She shot Izzy a "gee, thanks" look. "I had a date, that's all. We had a good time. I hope he calls again. There."

"Was it that Batman person?" Nina gathered the recipe cards and stacked them on the counter.

Darcy tossed another look toward her grandmother, but Izzy had her hand buried deep in the jar of Jolly Ranchers. "His name is Sam. S-A-M. He wore a Batman costume when I met him at Miranda's party." Nina gave an understanding nod, Andie shrugged and turned back to her magazine. Her hand still in the candy jar, Izzy smiled. How apropos.

"Where's Dad?"

"In the backyard raking leaves," Nina said. "His favorite chore." Stephen Daniels hated yard work as much as Darcy hated running out of wine. His idea of getting the job done entailed mowing the grass in a zigzag golf course pattern, then heading to the house for a beer. If Nina nagged enough, she could get him back out to trim and sweep. Her dad's strategy: yard work when his wife left the premises. Her mom's strategy: run interference with the above stated plan. Sometimes she succeeded.

"I'll go say hi." Darcy made her way to the backyard. Five small pyramids of leaves stood strategically piled around the yard. Her dad was currently working on the sixth. As a little girl she'd raked leaves into a floor plan design for her imaginary house. Most little girls had dollhouses; she only wanted leaves, a rake, and the floor plans in her head. After careful maneuvering the thin rows into her maze of a house, she'd sit in her leaf-lined room and read her library book. Yes, a real library book. And yes, she knew how weird that all sounded.

"Hey!" Nothing. "Dad, yo!" she yelled to his backside, and then noticed his ear buds, obviously blocking out anything except whatever piped through the wires. Without warning, her dad dropped his yard tool, shoved both fists in the air, and let out a very clear "YEESSS! It's about damn time!"

Darcy returned to the house. "Dad listening to the Texans' game?"

"I imagine. It's the only way he can get the leaves raked." The recipe cards out of sight, Nina pulled meatloaf from the refrigerator. Nina, Darcy, and Izzy sat around the kitchen table picking at the leftovers. Andie couldn't be bothered.

"By the way," Darcy said. "What time is the big meal on Thanksgiving?"

"It's usually about one," Nina said, "but we're moving it to later. Anna's family has dinner right at noon, so she and Alex won't be here until around four."

"Good," Darcy said in her most nonchalant tone. "I'll come over about then."

"Batman taking you to the parade?" Izzy asked.

Not knowing if there was water in the pool, Darcy dove in head first. "Actually, I'm going to volunteer for the Thanksgiving Day Feast at the GRB."

One set of eyes lifted from *In Touch,* while two sets of eyebrows shot up somewhere way above the water line. Izzy popped another Jolly Rancher into her mouth and pushed the hard candy to one side of her mouth. "You, my granddaughter, are going to serve food."

Grammatically, that last sentence should have ended in a question mark, which would easily have given her a chance for a rebuttal. However, Izzy had strategically formed the words into a declarative statement. Her mother's eyes fixated on Darcy, sort of trance-like.

"I'm not cooking if that's what you're worried about," Darcy said, and hoped that was the truth. "But yeah, I think I want to volunteer." Silence. "Mom." Darcy snapped her fingers in front of her mother's face.

Nina shook her head and returned from her mental road trip. She smiled, which produced soft wrinkle lines at the corner of her eyes. "I think that's wonderful." She stood and reached for the meatloaf platter, when suddenly the smile dropped from her face like water off a duck's back. "You're not in trouble are you? I mean…is this like community service?" She shot Izzy a look, who in turn hiked her shoulders almost up to her ears to signal her own bewilderment.

Darcy's mouth gawked open. "Mother, aren't you confusing me with your other child? I'm the good one," she said, forgetting Andrea sat beside her.

You have to be the good one, don't you? Alex doesn't count, which leaves…surely you rank higher than that neon-glowing-bra-wearing-almost-old-enough-to-drink sister who has the emotional development of a tween. In-sulting.

"I'm sorry, sweetie," Nina said. "How rude. I think it's a wonderful thing to do. I was just surprised, that's all. Isn't that right, Mother?" Darcy and Nina turned their gaze toward Izzy, who didn't wear anything near a gracious look. Mothers' character assessments of their own children were usually tainted by a healthy dose of blind love, and grandmothers, traditionally speaking, were the softest people on the planet. Izzy, however, wrote her own rules.

"Surprised isn't the word I'd use." Izzy pushed the candy jar toward the center of the table. "There's more to this. Believe me, I know these things."

"Then what?" Darcy huffed. "Tell me. What do you think I'm not telling you?"

"I don't know yet." Izzy used her arms as props and raised her round body to a standing position. "But what I *do* know is volunteering is not your scene."

Darcy crossed her arms over her stomach. "My scene? You've been watching too much TV, Izzy. And besides, I don't know what 'my scene' is."

Stephen Daniels burst through the back door, eyes down, ear buds still in place. He marched straight to the refrigerator, and in one continuous move pulled out a beer, twisted off the top, and slammed down half the bottle. Only after lowering the brew did he notice his oldest daughter at the table. He pulled the ear buds free. "Hey Darce, when did you get here?"

"Our little Darcy is volunteering to serve Thanksgiving dinner at the George R. Brown this year," Izzy said after retrieving the Sunday paper from the family room.

Darcy's dad slugged down the rest of the beer, tossed the bottle in the trash, and put his hands on his hips. "Community service?"

"No!" Darcy blew out air. "Is it so far removed for any of you to think I could do something unselfish?" She felt nine years old all over again.

Her dad shifted his gaze, moved to her side, and gave her a quick hug. "Of course not, honey." A lull hung in the room like a swag lamp. Stephen Daniels shoved his hands together. "Well, I'd better get back to work," and re-positioned his ear buds.

Izzy waited until the back door closed. "Okay. What gives?" she asked, sifting through the Houston Chronicle.

Drumming her fingers on the table, Darcy had to decide whether to remain vague about Thanksgiving or come clean. Maybe coming clean would stop the inquisition. "Okay, here's the deal," Darcy said. "Ms. Viola used to help feed the elderly on Thanksgiving, and now she volunteers for the Thanksgiving Day Feast. She sent out a flyer asking all the tenants to join her."

"How much off rent?" Izzy asked.

"Nothing."

"And this is something you'd like to do?" Izzy didn't seem convinced.

She couldn't argue with her grandmother's skepticism. Volunteering had never been on her radar for normal behavior. But, what the hell...Ms. Viola had grown on her. The verdict was still out on how she felt about the old woman shacking up with Mr. Will (bad visual), but underneath all that crusty bark, the woman had a soft side. And it had been a long time since Darcy had stepped out of her small box existence. She nodded her head. "Yeah, I think so."

Izzy continued to scan the Sunday paper.

"What are you looking for?" Darcy asked.

"Your horoscope. I need to check something. I don't remember reading anything this morning about Sagittarians going through a personality change. They're generally…you know…temperamental, impatient, restless people." Her gaze found Darcy's. "Not volunteers."

Maybe the horoscope could explain her recent attitude toward doing something, well…unselfish. Certainly Sags had *some* positive traits.

"Ah, here it is." Izzy folded the paper to the daily horoscope listing. "Doesn't say a word about doing things for others." She sat back in her chair. "I need to have your chart done."

"I can't believe you're saying that, Izzy." Darcy looked equal parts irritated and injured. "You know, most people say I'm just like you."

There, that ought to shut her up.

Izzy tilted her head. "You're a lot of things, darling. Being charitable isn't one of them. And you don't see me volunteering to serve the masses dried up turkey, do you?" Izzy paused. "When's the old lady's birthday?"

Okay. Round two. She offered her grandmother the most innocent look she could put her hands on. "July 4th is what she told me."

"Ah, Cancer." Izzy ran her finger down the horoscopes. "That's a tricky sign. Compassionate, but can have a short fuse. Intimidating. Let's see—"

"She turned eighty this year." Darcy felt the ba-zinga pleasure button pull at the corners of her mouth. "That makes her your age, Izzy."

Izzy's finger came to a dead stop somewhere on the newsprint. She lifted her eyes. Nina sat idly by like a spectator following a tennis ball volley back and forth across the net. The yellow bouncy thing had landed in Izzy's court.

"Whatever," Izzy huffed, and breathed what could only be described as dragon-temperature hot air. She flipped the paper over and found the crossword puzzle.

Darcy, busy doing her mental victory lap, locked eyes with her mother and was given a look Nina rarely exercised, which immediately zapped Darcy back to feeling nine years old. Again. If Darcy still had her old room, she'd slither from the table and put herself in time-out. Being an adult didn't allow her the luxury of escape. She bit her lower lip instead. "That wasn't nice. I'm sorry Izzy," she said. "Did I hurt your feelings?"

The silence became as noticeable as a Buick parked in the kitchen. Andie had left the room, leaving the three women at the table, two of whom watched the third work her magic on a crossword puzzle.

Izzy finally broke the ice, her eyes glued to the newspaper. "What's a five letter word for smart-ass."

Darcy and Nina pulled back.

"Ah, yes," Izzy said. "D-A-R-C-Y."

"Hey, no fair," Darcy huffed. "I said I'm sorry. I even asked if I hurt your feelings."

Her grandmother scratched in a few more letters and dropped her pencil. "No, you did not hurt my feelings. What do you think, I'm made of cream cheese or something?" She picked up her pencil again. "Missy, I'll take you on any day."

Darcy pouted and gave her mother the "I tried" look. Nina's response, a slight raise of the eyebrows, which translated into "it doesn't matter, you were out of line, but at least you apologized look."

Being a grown up is such a bitch, isn't it?

Nina cleared her throat and threw out a subject change. "Mother, is Gloria making her tamales again this year? If so, I'll take two dozen. We'll have them as appetizers."

Darcy *loved* Gloria's homemade tamales. "I'll take a dozen. Chicken. No, mixed." Gloria was a wonderful older Hispanic woman who worked at Izzy's beauty shop…a loving, truly gentle woman…the kind of stuff traditional grandmothers were made of. Plus, she made excellent tamales. "Make that two dozen."

Izzy slowly raised her eyes. "I'll see what I can do. No promises though."

What's a five-letter word to describe a crabby old grandmother? Ah, yes. B-I-T-C-H.

Wrinkling her nose, Darcy ran fingers through her hair. She bet Grandma Gloria didn't have a bitchy bone in her body.

***

Thanksgiving morning at 9:00 sharp, the Fountain Oaks residents gathered in the parking lot with the exception of Sister

Alice, who had her own volunteer agenda. Ms. Viola, Fletcher, and Lawrence squeezed into the backseat of Darcy's SUV. Mr. Will rode shotgun.

Ms. Viola had suggested Darcy cast aside her high-dollar look for the event and wear something sensible; a totally different mind-set for Darcy, but one she surprisingly accomplished with little effort. However, Ms. Viola had gone the other way. Instead of overalls and a straw hat, the older woman turned out in a nice Alfred Dunner slacks and blouse outfit, and informed the SUV occupants they would have the ten-to-two shift. Darcy wondered if Ms. Viola would be up to working four hours on her feet, and even ventured to ask the question, to which she received a one-word answer. "Yes."

Mr. Will sported his regular attire, except the rumpled khakis were neatly pressed and the bowtie sat at the correct angle in front of his Adam's apple. He still wore his fishing hat; however, Ms. Viola announced the dang thing would not be entering the GRB. Darcy assumed she referred to the fishing hat. Even Fletcher's fatigues seemed to be clean and the dirt smudges on his face were gone, which dispelled Darcy's notion about their permanence.

You've got yourself quite a group there.

Lawrence, at the last moment, had agreed to join the volunteer group (like he had so many other options) in exchange for some Fountain Oaks gossip Darcy dangled for bribery. During the four-hour stint at the GRB, Lawrence learned about Ms. Viola and Mr. Will's carnal knowledge living situation. If a chair had not been behind him, Darcy would have had to scrape Lawrence off the floor. The only other time she remembered Lawrence at a loss for words was after being caught in the Miranda web at the Halloween party.

Once he regained his speech he said, "I'll never be able to look at them the same way again."

Ditto.

Earlier she had helped him decide on his attire for the day, which didn't take long. With the exception of the Hawaiian shirt, everything else in his closet had come from A&F or Brooks Brothers. She decided on casual (as casual as Lawrence got) khaki slacks and a shirt that didn't scream designer. She even dug out a worn pair of Cole Haans.

Ms. Viola had stressed the importance of community to Darcy, which meant coming together as a collective whole. Volunteering did not mean well-to-do (or the pseudo-well-to-do, in Darcy's case) showing up to help those less fortunate. "It's people helping people. Period. Paragraph."

The four-hour shift flew by. She and Lawrence spent the first hour and a half helping set up tables and chairs. The last part of the shift they served food. Mr. Will had parked himself in a chair, and had been assigned the duty of dinner-roll-hander-outer. Darcy smiled, watching Ms. Viola shoo Fletcher out of the food line after he'd already filled his plate twice.

People of all shapes, sizes, and colors attended the event...quite a diverse group except for one commonality; smiles. Ms. Viola seemed to be some sort of official greeter. She'd walk around tables and stop from time to time to shake a hand or sit for a minute and talk. Most of the GRB volunteers seemed to not only know the Fountain Oaks apartment manager, but actually like her, a facet of Ms. Viola that Darcy hadn't been able to quite understand. But she did know one thing. Somewhere behind that crusty exterior grouchy façade was a really nice person.

At exactly two o'clock the crew piled into the SUV and headed back to Fountain Oaks. There'd be just enough time for Darcy to take Stash for a quick spin in the courtyard before zipping over to her parents' house. Her first volunteer effort had her feeling exceptionally gracious, and before she knew it, she had invited the entire group to her parents' house for dinner. Lawrence quickly accepted. Fletcher smiled, nodded, and then shook his head, which Darcy took as a no. Ms. Viola voiced her thanks but said she needed to rest. Mr. Will wrinkled his nose, pointed a bony finger toward Ms. Viola, and said, "I'm with her."

"Oh. My. God." Was the first thing out of Lawrence's mouth once he and Darcy were back in the SUV. "It's true."

"Ms. Viola and Mr. Will? Of course it's true," Darcy said. "You think I'd make that crap up?"

"I wouldn't have thought so, but...I just, I just can't—"

"Then don't," Darcy warned. "The visual isn't good."

With the exception of a quick run-down on her zoo of a family, the rest of the trip to her parents' remained void of conversation. Lawrence's thoughts were who knew where, and Darcy, once again, spent time wrestling with her almost non-existent love life, which became blaringly obvious with Lawrence in the passenger seat. Even

Ms. Viola and Mr. Will were in a relationship. *That* realization slammed a shudder through her.

She pulled in front of her parents' house.

This ought to be interesting.

After mentally shushing her inner voice, she had to wonder which would be more shocking, her family meeting Lawrence or vice versa. She could conceive of no way to prepare her family for meeting Lawrence, so she didn't. Izzy must have had her "grandma radar" turned off, because they were not met by the official greeter at the front door. The minute Darcy walked into the entryway, her memory bank zapped back to all the Thanksgiving Days of her teenage years. The television blared, and the smells from the kitchen snuggled around her like an electric blanket.

Nina and Izzy rotated around the kitchen like a well-oiled machine, both women talking, but neither listening. Andie sat at the kitchen table diligently researching department store ads from the day's Chronicle special edition. Nina worked over the stove, stirring whole cranberries and orange juice, while Izzy pulled her famous chocolate pecan pie from the oven. A pan of non-crawfish dressing, Nina's version of green bean casserole, and a sweet potato dish lined the counter, ready to be shoved into the oven. Homemade yeast rolls stood nearby, waiting their turn.

"Guess who's coming to dinner?" Darcy pulled Lawrence up beside her. Both older women jumped at the sound of her voice. Andie raised her eyes without bothering to raise her head.

Nina spoke first. "Sam, I'm Nina, Darcy's mother," she said, wiping her hands on a kitchen towel. "And this is Darcy's grandmother, Izzy." Nina came over to give her daughter a hug. "Hi sweetie."

"Mom, this is Lawrence, my neighbor," Darcy said. "Not Sam." She pointed to Andie at the table. "And that's Andrea, my baby sister." Her sister showed her teeth in a smile and did a quick hand-wave.

Lawrence turned to Darcy and mouthed, "Sam?"

"Batman," Darcy whispered, to which Lawrence nodded, no doubt conjuring up very bad memories of chaps, pencil thin moustaches, and blood-red martinis.

Izzy closed the oven door after loading the racks with the casseroles. "So, you're Lawrence." Izzy wore a blouse decorated with cornucopias overflowing with autumn-colored gourds and Indian corn. Little rhinestone turkeys dangled from her ears.

"Yes," Lawrence said. "And I must say, Darcy has told me quite a lot about you." Nina and Izzy's eyes zeroed in on Darcy, Nina's round, Izzy's slits.

"All good!" Lawrence added, and rocked back on his heels. "Yes sirree. All good things."

Darcy gave Lawrence a "nice save" glance, while Izzy's look read more like "yeah right." Nina maintained the deer-in-the-headlights expression she often chose to wear.

"So nice of you to join us today," Nina said. "Darcy, take Lawrence out back to meet your dad."

"Has he dunked the turkey yet?" Darcy asked.

Nina glanced at the clock on the oven. "Should be any time now."

"C'mon." Darcy pulled on Lawrence's sleeve. "You've got to see this."

"Your father dunks turkeys? I don't believe I've ever seen that."

Darcy grinned. "Yeah, I'd say probably not."

On the patio the propane burner sat fired up, ready for action, a long-stemmed thermometer clipped to the side of the huge pot of near-boiling peanut oil. Darcy's dad had an over-sized injector needle stuck halfway into the breast of the turkey, which rested on a small outdoor table.

"Dad," Darcy said.

"Hold up a minute," Stephen yelled, slipping the large bird down around the vertical pole of the frying rack. He then connected an over-sized hook onto the slot at the top of the rack holding the fourteen-pound turkey. Strain mashed into Stephen's face when he heaved the big bird up over the pot of peanut oil and slowly lowered poor Tom down into the sizzling liquid. The strained expression switched to satisfaction. He looked up to see he had an audience. "Gonna be a good one," Stephen said. "Who've you got here?"

"Always is," Darcy said, and gave her dad a hug. "Dad, this is Lawrence, my neighbor."

With only a slight hesitation, which Darcy expected, her dad offered his hand. "Stephen Daniels."

"Hello sir. Lawrence Ousted." The two shook hands. "Darcy invited me over for dinner. I hope you don't mind."

"Not at all," Stephen said. "You…don't watch football, do you Lawrence?"

"Ah…no, I don't."

"Didn't think so." Stephen gathered his injector supplies and headed back into the house. "But you're still welcome."

"Thank you," Lawrence replied before Stephen disappeared inside. He and Darcy turned towards Tom to watch his ugly bubbling oil fate.

"I think that went well," Lawrence said.

She resisted shaking her head and pulled Lawrence back through the door into the house.

***

"I thank you again for allowing me to join you today," Lawrence said once everyone had settled in around the formal table in the dining room, the least used room of the house. With the exception of Easter, Thanksgiving, and Christmas, the room rarely saw traffic. But with this being one of the three annual events, it was seeing the full-shebang of a formal meal, complete with linen tablecloth, napkins, and lit tapered candles. An additional place setting and chair had been added for Lawrence. Alex and Anna had finally arrived, not looking exactly eager to chow down their second big feast of the day.

"Lawrence, we're happy you could join us," Nina said. "Are your parents out of town?"

Lawrence shot Darcy a pitiful "bail me out" basset hound look. The silence grew bigger than the room. All eyes turned toward Lawrence.

"Actually, his parents are out of town. They'll be having their Thanksgiving meal this weekend though," Darcy said, coming out with a bald-faced lie. "Isn't that right, Lawrence?"

Lawrence only nodded. Darcy couldn't quite read the look on his face, but if she had to guess, she figured water works could spill at any moment. Time to switch channels. "Anyone want to hear about our day?"

"Yes," Izzy piped up. "I'm interested to hear how my granddaughter fared in foreign waters."

Nina shot Izzy an "Oh, Mother" expression, while Alex and Anna looked perplexed. Stephen kept his head down, carving Tom.

"Izzy, what are you talking about?" Alex asked.

"It's no big deal," Darcy offered before Izzy could add some other smart-aleck remark. "Ms. Viola, our apartment manager, asked us to volunteer at the Thanksgiving Feast at the GRB. So we did."

Alex raised his eyebrows and paused, but managed to say, "Way to go."

"Thank you," Darcy offered, eyeing the rest of the family. "I'm glad I did it. In fact, I just might make it an annual event." Silence tiptoed around the table, which Darcy took as a good thing.

"Yes, it was quite enjoyable," Lawrence added. "I've never done anything like that before. However, I have to say I felt rather humbled by the whole experience. Almost magnanimous."

"Magnanimous," Izzy repeated. "Now that's a word I haven't heard around this table before."

"Izzy," Darcy started. "Lawrence thinks we're a semi-normal family. Don't burst his bubble. We haven't eaten yet."

"What? I can't speak?" Izzy retorted.

"More wine anyone?" Nina stood and grabbed a bottle from the sideboard. "Lawrence, you look like you could use a refill." She topped off his nearly full glass.

"Don't stop there." Stephen held up his own stemmed glass. "We might need something stronger before *this* meal is over."

Darcy sat back in her chair and smiled. Her family. Normally, she'd be checking her watch, gauging when she could make her get-away. Today, however, she smiled. She really had enjoyed herself, and for the first time in a very long time, she actually felt she had done something worthwhile. Just for the day, she wasn't going to let anyone take that away from her; not even her crazy—and in their own way loving—family.

Chapter 10

Thanksgiving and Black Friday out of the way signaled one thing to Darcy; that her birthday loomed on the horizon. She had dreaded her thirtieth, as all good southern women did, but at least thirty held significance…a milestone of sorts, a true coming of age. Turning thirty-one just sucked. Maybe she'd take a trip to New York, get some Christmas shopping done, and be G-O-N-E for the big event. Nah, turning thirty-one *and* being alone in a strange town didn't sound like that hot of an idea. Oh well.

At the end of the day, Darcy covered her mouth to stop a yawn and pulled into her parking spot at Fountain Oaks. Monday was definitely not her favorite day, especially a Monday after a long holiday weekend. She grabbed her briefcase, stepped out of her SUV, and came to a halt. In the middle of her yawn she must have missed the rows of newly planted shrubbery on both sides of the wide driveway. Healthy red-tipped photinas lined up in the same turned and raised flowerbed fashion as in the courtyard. Even the hazardous dead tree that had loomed over the carport for the last two years had been removed. Damn. She must have written one hell of a complaint letter.

After paying due-diligence to Fountain Oaks's newest landscape addition, she stopped at the short row of mailboxes and pulled out circulars and a few bills from her locked slot. Dumping the weekly grocery inserts into the trash receptacle, her eye caught a fluorescent orange piece of paper taped to the mailbox wall.

Oh geez, what now?

ATTENTION
FOUNTAIN OAKS TENANTS
Exterior painting of the premises
Wednesday, November 30th

Painting *and* landscaping?

She flipped on the light in her apartment, dropped purse and keys on the bar, and pushed the blinking light on her answering machine. "You have one new message." She hit play.

"Darcy, this is Becca," the message began. "I haven't seen you in ages, and I just had an idea. Let's have a girl's weekend at my parents' bay house for your birthday. Don't say no...I've already talked to Lisa, and left Miranda a message. Bye."

Darcy chewed on the inside of her lip and rubbed the tip of her nose. The Four-of-a-Kind, Miranda's nickname for their group, hadn't been together since Vegas. Miranda's party didn't really count. The idea might work. Becca's parents had a fantastic bay house on Tiki Island, just on the inland side of the causeway before crossing over to Galveston. A weekend with her three closest friends might actually take the sting out of her dreaded birthday. She'd give it some thought, although Becca made it sound like the decision had been made.

In her bedroom, she kicked off her DKNY Annabelle ankle boots like an old pair of tennis shoes. Slipping out of her work clothes, she pulled on sweats and shoved her feet into worn house shoes. She planned to do laundry, having purposely waited past the weekend, hoping to find the dilapidated washer and dryer available. The facilities at Fountain Oaks were pre-laundry room vintage, and the present management company felt no compulsion to add amenities.

She hauled the laundry basket under one arm, hooked the leash to Stash's collar, and grabbed a handful of quarters. In the courtyard, she ran into Fletcher. The maintenance man had not only retrieved the water-hose-on-the-shoulder look, but had reapplied the smudges on his face. For a fleeting envious moment, Darcy wondered how it would be to wear a uniform every day and not to wrestle with wardrobe choices...ever.

"Hey, are you responsible for the new flowerbeds around here?" she asked.

Fletcher appeared to weigh Darcy's words, as if she had spoken a foreign language, he didn't understand the question, or he had forgotten who she was. His eyes seemed like dark holes boring into pools of nothingness. Seconds away from doing the hand-wave in front of his eyes to see if life resided somewhere within, she jumped when Fletcher reengaged by spotting Stash.

His solemn facade broke into a half smile. "I like dogs," he said. "Can I walk him?"

"Sure. I'm just going to wash some clothes." Darcy stared at the unusual man. "Fletcher?"

He dropped the water hose to the ground and took the leash from Darcy. "Yeah?" His eyes never left Stash.

"Did you plant all the new flowers and shrubs?" Darcy readjusted the laundry basket on her hip.

Fletcher squatted down to Stash's level and rubbed the dog's ears. "Yeah." His voice was a total monotone.

"Does Ms. Viola—?"

"Yeah."

"Fletcher?" Darcy sat the basket on the ground and knelt down beside the man, the water hose, and her dog.

"Yeah?"

"Will you look at me?" Darcy felt like she tiptoed through a mental mind field.

Fletcher continued to rub Stash's ears and remained silent, which left Darcy, once again, wondering how much he comprehended. His eyes moved from Stash, to the ground, upward towards the sky, before settling on her face.

She smiled and placed a hand on Fletcher's wrist. "It's all starting to look great. Just great, Fletcher."

"Yeah."

If not for the hint of a smile across his face, she'd swear *Rain Man* had asked to walk her dog. She pulled herself back up and grabbed the laundry basket. "I'm going to take this to the laundry room. Be right back." She headed down the walkway toward the washer and dryer area.

"Ms. Darcy?"

Darcy stopped and turned. "Did you say something?"

"Yeah." Fletcher still stood rooted where she had left him. Stash, at his feet, cocked his head to one side.

133

"What is it?"

What seemed like a very long moment passed before Fletcher spoke. A corner of his mouth pulled upward. "You'll like it."

"Like what?" Darcy scrunched her eyebrows together.

Fletcher shrugged and tugged on Stash's leash. "C'mon boy."

She stood for another glacial moment and watched the man in fatigues and combat boots walk her dog around the courtyard. She didn't feel afraid around him anymore. In fact, he seemed to have a rather kind heart...especially toward animals.

The laundry room stood on the far end of the courtyard behind a lattice partition. At one time, she supposed, the partition had been positioned to...well, to hide the laundry room. Now it didn't seem to matter much. The small laundry room building looked as washed out as everything else on the property. She fumbled with the loose doorknob, using her weight and the filled laundry basket to shove open the door, and flicked the light switch.

The unexpected brightness caused her to drop the basket and shade her eyes. She felt like she had walked onto a car dealership showroom floor. A sea of shiny red stretched across the length of the back wall. Blinking hard a couple of times to clear her head and adjust her eyes to the glare, she focused on the wall of red.

It is a showroom!

Four brand-new and extremely red front-loading shiny machines stood at attention before her...two washers, two dryers. The walls had been freshly painted, and the damp, stained cement floor had been covered with an indoor-outdoor carpet. A table for folding clothes had been positioned against the adjacent wall.

How long she stood rooted in place, gawking at the red shine and the refurbished laundry room, she had no idea. She did, however, feel she'd stepped through a *Chronicles of Narnia* wardrobe into another dimension...definitely not a Fountain Oaks dimension. Her eyes refocused, which broke the trance. She retrieved the laundry basket and edged toward the machines. This had moved beyond weird...flowerbeds, painting, plus a whole string of top of the line washers and dryers?

She easily fit her clothes into one of the over-sized washers and pulled out quarters from her pocket, but could not find a coin slot on any of the machines. She pushed a few buttons and the washer started to fill. Surely this was some kind of joke. Darcy scanned the laundry room for hidden cameras and found nothing out of the ordinary…except everything.

Back in the courtyard, with arms hanging at her sides and mouth gawking open, Darcy walked the distance to where Fletcher had connected his shoulder-harnessed water hose to one of the outdoor faucets. Stash sat by his side. The evening air felt clear and cool, though at the moment Darcy hardly noticed. Weather-wise, nothing too exceptional happened in November in Houston, except a comfortable temperature drop at night that usually lasted until the middle of the following morning.

She raised an arm toward the laundry room. "What," Darcy began, "is that?"

Fletcher rubbed a grubby hand across his already smudged face before he answered. "Washers and dryers."

Like the blind leading the blind….

She needed to get a grip. "I mean, why?" Which wasn't exactly what she'd call a grip.

Fletcher shrugged. The half-smile slipped off his face.

"Did you paint the laundry room?" Darcy asked.

He nodded.

"And the carpet?"

"Didn't paint that." Fletcher looked as confused as Darcy felt.

She shook her head…hard. "I mean…did you put in the new carpet?"

Seeming to understand the question, Fletcher's eyes cleared a bit. He nodded again.

Zeroing in on the smudged face and empty eyes, she said, "You did a good job."

Fletcher found his half smile again. "I like your dog."

"Yeah, he seems to like you too." She took the leash out of Fletcher's hand and smiled.

"Bye." Fletcher raised his hand in a brief wave and walked away.

Darcy glanced back down at the water hose lying at her feet. "Hey, aren't you going to water the flowerbeds?"

Fletcher didn't break stride or even turn around. "Not at night."

"Not at night," Darcy repeated, realizing she'd just had the longest conversation *ever* with the maintenance man. And the exchange made sense, in a simple sort of way. Fletcher spoke when he had something to say, which didn't seem to happen often.

Wonder if he talks to his plant, Judith?

Aside from the shock of actually talking with Fletcher, something bigger crowded her brain. Something brewed...something weird. She needed to plan another visit to Ms. Viola.

By the end of the week, her birthday dilemma had been resolved. Thursday, December 13, would be the token family dinner at Christy's. Then Friday morning, the girls would "play hooky" and head to Tiki Island for a long weekend. Everyone had confirmed except Miranda, who was a holdout. Darcy had called three or four times, leaving tacky Miranda sound-alike messages. Obviously, she lacked the forceful, blunt, Madonna-tone that brought people to attention—and often to their knees—asking what they could do for her. Unfortunately, Miranda knew Darcy was no Madonna, and Darcy knew she was no Miranda.

Lisa had talked to Darcy and Becca. Becca had talked to Lisa and Darcy. Darcy had talked to Lisa and Becca. No one had talked to Miranda. Where in the hell was Madonna?

***

The week had been unsettling. November had come to a close, and Darcy had fallen short on her Gucci monthly quota. Optometrists were cutting back on their inventory, and Darcy seemed to have misplaced her persuasion chip, her ace in the hole. Lately, pounding the pavement to obtain the top rep position in her region had lost its luster. She actually found herself spending more time getting to know her customers than talking them into buying stock they didn't need. Totally uncharted territory for her...weird, but not unsettling.

After changing into her sweats, she filled a wine glass from her boxed chardonnay and parted the slats of the mini blinds in the living room. New floodlights had replaced the burned out bulbs, which greatly added to the improved look of the courtyard. The entire exterior of the complex had been splashed with fresh paint, upgrading the apartment's aesthetics. Everything looked quiet in the courtyard...and very bright.

Friday night and once again, she had no plans. She toyed with the idea of washing more clothes. With fancy new washers and dryers, the laundry room could be her new Friday night date. Izzy would give her grief about that one, but what the hell. Darcy gathered up what clothes she could find to wash, stuffed them into her laundry basket, threw in her new *US Weekly,* and managed to juggle the basket and glass of wine out the door.

Coolness hit her cheeks when she entered the courtyard. The first serious cold front of the season supposedly would hit sometime over the weekend, which she found exciting. Exciting because living in the southern part of Texas meant most of the year was warm, if not downright hot. Maybe when she turned Izzy's age she'd appreciate the warm weather. Her grandma had a sweater handy twenty-four seven, no matter what month. But for Darcy, the first cold front of the season meant she could pull out her pseudo fall-winterish clothes, which looked practically new, not getting much wear-time. With any luck, winter in Houston lasted about three months. So her winter wardrobe barely had a chance to cycle through before being packed back up and exchanged for the clothes she wore the other nine months of the year.

The courtyard stood empty, but she could see through the lattice partition that the laundry room light was on. Careful not to spill her wine, Darcy slowly pushed her way into the laundry room and found Lawrence standing in front of the new machines, his own laundry basket held out in front of him. He turned when Darcy entered.

"I'm not sure where I am," Lawrence said. "This isn't our laundry room."

Darcy smiled and let her basket slide down her leg to the floor. She took a sip of wine. "Cool, isn't it?"

"What is it?"

Darcy pursed her lips and smiled. "C,mon, it's fun. I'll show you." She set her stemmed glass on the laundry table and attempted to take Lawrence's basket from him.

"Stop that." Lawrence kept a tight grip on his dirty clothes.

"Don't want me to see your Underoos?" Darcy asked. "I have a brother, you know."

"I realize that." Lawrence still clutched his laundry basket. "But, still…."

"Whatever." She released her hold, which rocked him backward on his heels.

After he filled one of the new bright washing machines, Darcy instructed him on the mechanics of the wash cycle before hoisting herself up on the laundry table. Lawrence stood next to her, rubbing his chin.

"Something's not right," he said, watching his clothes circle round and round. "This is all highly suspicious."

"Do ya think?" Darcy took a swig of her wine.

He wheeled around. "Maybe there is a new owner. No wait...maybe the property is up for sale." Lawrence started chewing on a fingernail.

She slapped his hand away from his mouth. "That's the first unsanitary thing I've ever seen you do. Stop that."

"But if the property is sold, rent is surely going to skyrocket. I won't be able to live here." Lawrence's eyes rounded with panic.

"Slow down Larry," Darcy said. "You're jumping the gun a bit."

Lawrence either ignored the name he despised or felt too upset to notice. "But what other explanation is there? This place almost looks—"

The door to the laundry room slammed open. "Go ahead, finish that sentence." Ms. Viola pushed her way in, Ike trailing behind her. She wore a bulky off-white sweater pulled over her frail body and signature overalls. Black All-Star tennis shoes completed her outfit. The lines in her face seemed more creased than usual, her pallor non-descript, almost opaque.

Darcy jumped off the laundry table at the sight of the apartment manager. Lawrence slipped behind Darcy. "Ms. Viola, you scared us," Darcy said.

"Good. Now finish the sentence, young man." Viola pointed a half-straight finger at Lawrence. "What were you saying about how things are looking around here?"

Darcy took a step to the side and glanced at Lawrence, who looked like he'd just been caught stealing a piece of bubble gum from the 7-Eleven. His Adam's apple protruded like he'd swallowed a golf ball. He sucked in air and raised his eyes upward, as if hoping Scotty would beam him up.

Ms. Viola followed Lawrence's lead to the freshly painted ceiling. "I don't see anything up there. For an educated man you sure don't use many words." She looked directly at Darcy. "What's wrong with him?"

Darcy put an arm around Lawrence's shoulders. "He's fine. For some reason he just gets a little intimidated by you, though I can't imagine why."

The old woman's faded eyes squinted at Darcy's sarcasm. Lawrence continued to choke on his golf ball.

"He does speak though," Ms. Viola said, as if Lawrence had turned into an inanimate object. "He was talking when I walked in, wasn't he?"

Darcy squeezed Lawrence's shoulders. "C'mon. Tell Ms. Viola what you were going to say."

Lawrence's eyes studied Darcy's face for a long moment before they shifted to the apartment manager. He cleared his throat and forced a fake smile. "I was saying how nice everything looked." Darcy knew that wasn't even close to what Lawrence had to say, but at least he got something out.

"What are you doing out here tonight?" Darcy decided to cut Lawrence some slack and change the subject.

"I was walking Ike and saw the light on," Ms. Viola answered. "Fletcher is running an errand for me, so I'm making a security check."

Darcy had no doubt Ms. Viola would be able to scare off an intruder, frail or not. Lawrence stood beside Darcy, shaking in his Underoos.

"I like the laundry room." Lawrence said. He must have rounded up all his grown-up courage to actually speak to Ms. Viola without being prompted.

Both women swung their gaze to Lawrence. Darcy sucked in her lips, trying not to break a smile, thinking how much his words sounded like Fletcher.

Ms. Viola eyebrows shot up into her forehead. "Good," she said. The crooked line across her mouth sort of resembled a smile. "Walk me home."

"Huh?" Lawrence stared at the old woman with a deer-in-the-headlights expression. Darcy looked puzzled.

"I said, walk me home," Ms. Viola repeated.

Lawrence stepped forward, as cowardly as if he were approaching a firing squad. All he needed was a hood to hide from the killers.

Ms. Viola raised a crooked finger. "Not you. You."

Lawrence stepped back in line, relief washing across his pale face. Darcy shoved her empty wine glass toward Lawrence, took Ms. Viola's elbow, and led her out of the laundry room.

"What's wrong with that boy?" Ms. Viola pulled her sweater closer to her small frame.

"Nothing."

Sure about that?

"Why are you so hard on him?"

"I don't know," Ms. Viola started. "But I have thought about it." She paused briefly. "He's a wuss. Weak. An easy target. Probably a mama's boy."

"I wouldn't call him a mama's boy," Darcy said, although she couldn't dispute the other remarks. "I don't think either one of his parents are very nice to him."

"An outcast, huh? Makes him perfect for here, doesn't it?" Ms. Viola patted Darcy's hand, which still hooked through the old woman's elbow. "I guess I could try to be nice to the boy."

Darcy smiled. "That would be good. I don't think he has a lot of friends." Darcy had to slow her pace for Ms. Viola. A good stiff wind would carry the old woman into the next county. She couldn't weigh more than ninety pounds these days.

"Will seems to think he's okay," Ms. Viola said, more to herself. "I'll try," she reiterated. "No promises though."

Darcy couldn't help but smile. It seemed that, against Ms. Viola's better judgment, she had become a softie. Her "mean old lady" exterior appeared harder and harder to keep in check. The mention of Mr. Will reminded Darcy she hadn't heard a word from Lawrence about the fishing trip.

"He's just worried his rent will go up with all the improvements around here." Darcy paused for a split second. "It won't, will it?"

The floodlights in the courtyard still beamed, illuminating the newly landscaped courtyard. Darcy hardly recognized the grounds as being Fountain Oaks, which she considered a plus.

Ms. Viola slowed her already snail's pace. "It is looking better, isn't it?"

Darcy could tell, once again, that she and Ms. Viola were slipping into what could be considered a normal conversation, which felt so much easier than the banter that usually took place between them.

"It's looking great." Darcy secured her grip on Ms. Viola's elbow. "Actually, I wanted to come tell you exactly that." They came to a stop at Ms. Viola's door.

"I'd invite you in, but Will is…," Ms. Viola started, then slightly shook her head. "Well, there's no telling what he's doing."

"Not a problem," Darcy quickly added, while unwanted images of Mr. Will in—well, maybe nothing—crept in. She let go of Ms. Viola's elbow and took a step back, glad she had gotten the old lady safely from point A to point B. "Are you feeling okay?"

Ms. Viola shot Darcy one of the squinty-eyed mean-old-lady looks. "Why do you keep asking me that?"

Darcy remained steady, no longer shocked or spooked by Ms. Viola's hot and cold temperament. "I don't know. I guess I care, that's all."

"Oh." Ms. Viola reached for the door that would and could lead to Mr. Will, doing who-knows-what. "Can you come back this weekend? We need to talk."

Scenes of childhood flashed before Darcy at the tone of Ms. Viola's voice. How easily she could be reduced to a child in her own mind.

"Sure," Darcy replied, and turned to head to her apartment. She stopped and whirled back around. "What about the rent? Is it going up?"

"Phhth," Ms. Viola's hand shooed Darcy away like a mosquito. She entered her apartment and closed the door behind her, leaving Darcy alone in the courtyard.

Scrunching up her nose, she scratched her neck and headed to her apartment. Rounding the top of the stairs, as she could have predicted, she found Lawrence sitting by her apartment, holding her empty wine glass. "What's *wrong* with you?" she asked, repeating Ms. Viola's question.

"You'll have to be more specific. The list is rather long."

Darcy smiled. Lawrence was one (and she emphasized one) of the strangest animals on the planet, but his intellectual sense of humor she found comical.

Because seriously, who talks like that?

"You act like a bumbling idiot around Ms. Viola," Darcy said. "You're this walking Wikipedia, and the minute she says anything to you, your IQ reverts to Sponge Bob."

"Thank you for adding to my humiliation." Lawrence handed over the glass. "Although I do believe I've had a breakthrough."

"Oh yeah, Einstein? What is it?"

"She reminds me of my mother." Lawrence stared at the new indoor-outdoor carpet that had recently replaced the uglier-than-dirt orange outside Darcy's apartment. "My mother talks to me like that."

His words left a strange impression on Darcy. It almost— almost—made her appreciate her own dysfunctional family again. Her parents and grandma were weird, but Lawrence's sounded just plain mean. Even Ms. Viola was stripping away her harsh exterior, revealing a much kinder persona. For the first time Darcy got a true glimpse into the history of this snobbish Yale grad, who seemed to have had it all as a child...or so she had once thought.

He lifted his eyes, and Darcy saw the face of a very sad little boy who only wanted approval from his parents. She smiled as normally as possible and chose to stay silent, fighting the urge to pat him on the head.

"I realize that's why I act like a blubbering idiot around Ms. Viola. I learned rather early to dodge conversations with my parents as much as possible. Most anything I had to say seemed to have a rather negative effect on them. I knew I'd never be able to stand up to them. I make the Cowardly Lion look like The Terminator."

A part of Darcy's heart, which hadn't seen the light of day in a long time, opened. "C'mon. Let's go finish our laundry."

Lawrence followed Darcy down the stairs like a faithful puppy. "And by the way, if you must give me a nickname I highly prefer Einstein to Larry."

Hitting the bottom step, Darcy remembered. "Hey, that reminds me. You never said anything about your fishing trip with Mr. Will."

"That's because I don't want to talk about it."

"Why? I think Mr. Will likes you."

"Yes he does." Lawrence slipped back into his intellectual dialect.

Darcy raised her eyebrows and threw a "Well?" look his way.

Lawrence moved his neck around as if trying to dodge a bullet he knew he couldn't. "I now have my own fishing vest, and one of those distasteful Gilligan hats."

Chapter 11

Darcy forced her eyes open to check the time…eight thirty. She rolled till her feet hit the ground and shuffled to the kitchen to brew coffee. Saturday, her favorite day of the week. Sunday lost points for being the day before Monday. She reached her arms straight up and then dropped them towards the floor, stretching out the backs of her legs. With arms and head down around her knees, she caught an upside down glimpse of Stash patiently sitting by the door.

She checked her attire and decided her long boxer PJ shorts and tank top might suffice for a quick trip to the courtyard. She connected Stash to the leash, opened the front door, and was hit with a whoosh of not just cool but cold air. Her kneejerk reaction recoiled her back into the apartment, yanking Stash off his feet like a puppet on a string. The confused look on the dog's face needed no explanation.

"Sorry bud." Darcy picked up her pet and checked around his collar for signs of whiplash. Convinced she hadn't done any permanent damage, she set him back down and scooted to the bedroom. Minutes later she returned in a sweatshirt, the heaviest yoga pants she could find, and thick bulky socks.

"Let's try again." Apparently not totally convinced his owner could be trusted, Stash kept his seat even after Darcy opened the door.

"Okay, I said I was sorry." The warmer clothes were an improvement, but the rush of cold air still made her shiver. "Move it!" Darcy commanded, which sprang Stash into action. They made the trip downstairs and back up to the apartment in record time. Even Stash seemed to be affected by the temperature change.

It happened like this every year. After spending so many months enduring hot, humid temperatures, the first for-real cold front always took some getting used to. Although welcome, Darcy's internal thermostat didn't immediately adjust. She unleashed the dog and made her way to the coffee pot. Sitting at the bar, she sipped the steaming liquid and made a to-do list for the weekend, which had only three items: Miranda, Ms. Viola, and winter clothes. She had a feeling the first two were not going to be easily accomplished.

True to her nature, after downing a bowl of Cheerios and a multi-vitamin, she decided to tackle the third and least challenging item on her list. Entering the smaller-than-a-walk-in-closet second bedroom, she scrounged around until she found two large storage containers and lugged them to her room. Next, she flipped through her hanging clothes, quickly passing over the letter jacket, and pulled out anything sleeveless, short-sleeved, or lightweight. These she stacked on her bed to make way for the winter slacks, skirts, blouses, vests, and accessories crammed into the cracker-box closet in the spare room.

After hauling several armloads back and forth from bedroom to bedroom, she emptied the chest of drawers of shorts, tank tops, t-shirts, and lightweight PJs. The first container held sweaters, sweaters, and yes, more sweaters, from Armani to Eileen Fisher to Ralph Lauren. All seconds, which meant they were flawed in some way, but each had their own designer label firmly intact. The next storage box held her cozy, yet very un-sexy, flannel pajama bottoms, long-sleeved t-shirts, and warmer running outfits. I *will* start exercising again, she promised herself for the umpteenth time.

With the exchange of clothes from summer to winter finished, she had only one more chore to complete...the shoes. With the exception of a few choice flats that could work year-round, she pulled boxes of sandals, spring and summer flats, open-toed shoes, and slings out of the closet and stacked them randomly in piles on her bed; Sergio Rossi, Fendi, Prada, Michael Kors, Dolce and Gabbana, Gucci, Dior. She had transformed her bed into a miniature skyline of famous shoe designers. Eying the embarrassing number of expensive shoeboxes reminded her to be thankful she lived alone. This could be embarrassing, and didn't even cover the more expensive winter stock.

From the other room she hauled box after box of ankle and knee boots, closed-toe pumps, and casual (but designer, of course) shoes. She opened the UGG box and hugged the sheepskin boots to her chest. Nothing. Hmm...interesting. She pushed around a couple of boxes until she found her Burberrys that had cost way more than a car payment. She eased them from the box and pressed the Italian suede to her face, inhaling deeply. Again, nothing. She shrugged and returned the boots to the box, rubbing her hand under her nose. Her closet used to be her haven. She'd sit for hours just to engulf her senses with the smell of leather and suede, which equated wealth, the promise of success, and certainly Prince Charming. Strange. Her own personal adrenaline rush had taken a hike.

The designer shoebox exchange had been completed painlessly, except that the size of the winter shoe and boot boxes completely engulfed any remaining space in her closet. Leaning against the closet door, she caught sight of Mel sprawled out on the bed like the fat cat he was, his greenish-hazel eyes focused on her.

"Don't say a word." Mel's response...a yawn.

She ambled back to the kitchen and emptied the remaining coffee into her mug. After stirring in sweetener and some flavored creamer, she landed back on the barstool, scratched off item number three, and grabbed the cordless phone. As had happened for the past couple of weeks, Miranda's phone went to voice mail. Darcy waited for her best friend's harsh voice to finish its command to leave a message.

"Okay. I've called for a couple of weeks and I haven't heard back from you." Darcy used her most serious voice. "Call me. I'm worried." She clicked off and stared at the phone she still held in her hand. Something was wrong in River City...she could feel it. Miranda didn't dodge phone calls.

Yeah, that's your MO, not Madonna's!

Darcy combed her hair back in a slick ponytail, brushed her teeth, and threw on some make-up. She tossed aside her grubby sweats and pulled out a pair of warmer—and yes, more fashionable, although not designer—exercise clothes from her chest of drawers. Swiping some lipstick across her mouth, she grabbed her cell phone, keys, and purse, instructed the animal kingdom to behave, and headed out the door.

The drive from Fountain Oaks to Midtown only took ten minutes. The closer Darcy got to the high-class loft area just outside of downtown Houston, the more the area reminded her of New York City. Sidewalk cafés and coffee houses filled many of the ground floors of the high-rise lofts. Hoards of trendy residents filled the tables. It was where *the* people lived, and where Darcy had always *wanted* to live. She circled the area around Miranda's building before finding an open metered parking space a block away.

Walking up the parking garage ramp of Miranda's building, she checked her best friend's assigned spot. There sat the shiny BMW convertible Darcy had always coveted. It didn't necessarily mean Miranda was home, but it was a start. Taking the elevator to the fifth floor, she stood outside the door to Miranda's loft, pulled out her cell phone, and punched in Miranda's landline. After five long rings, Darcy heard Miranda's raspy voice recording kick in through the cell phone and the loft front door. She waited for the beep.

"I told you, I'm worried. You won't return my calls," Darcy said. "So open up, I'm at the front door." Darcy tried to make her voice sound as parental as she could, which wasn't one of her strong suits. She snapped her phone shut and put her ear to the door. She heard the television…a sign of life. The unlatching of the dead bolt caused Darcy to jump. She crossed her arms and tried to look stern as the heavy door edged open.

Darcy peeked around the half-opened door and spotted Miranda padding back to the couch…at least she *thought* it was Miranda. Her long dark hair had been tied in a messy ponytail at an angle sort of toward the top of her head, and she wore a full-length silk kimono, the sash pulled tight around her waist. Miranda eased herself back down on the expensive leather couch into the cozy nest of pillows and blankets she had built for herself. Darcy dropped her purse on the adjacent matching couch and took a seat.

"Hi," Miranda said, her eyes fixated on the television screen, her voice more throaty than usual. Dark half-moon rings circled her eyes.

Darcy stared for a moment. "Hi."

"What's up?" Miranda grabbed the remote and silenced the Home Shopping Network.

This whole scene switched Darcy's fake worry to reality. She glanced around, alarmed at the state of disarray. The pristine showroom model loft now held a clutter of Seven-Up cans and plastic empty Sunny D containers, along with magazines and newspapers littering the wooden floors. An empty cracker box stood upright on the coffee table, and a small trashcan filled with wadded up tissues sat at Miranda's feet. With the exception of the expensive furnishings, the clutter could pass for Darcy's apartment, or what she imagined the inside of her head looked like. But not Miranda's. *This* was not Miranda.

What's up?

"What's up?" Darcy asked. "I've been worried about you. What's going on?"

Miranda pulled a blanket around her shoulders and laid her head on the pillow beside her. "I've got a bug or something."

"Do you have a fever? Have you been to the doctor?"

Miranda sighed. "No. And no."

"So, how long have you been sick?"

"Awhile."

"Have you…been to work?" Darcy struggled to wrap her brain around seeing Miranda so lifeless.

"Some."

Some?

Miranda had been sick for a while. She'd said she didn't have a fever, and she hadn't been to the doctor.

"Do you want me to call someone? Your mom?"

"No! Do *not* call my mother." Miranda's voice blared stone cold.

Darcy knew Miranda and her mother weren't particularly close, but still, she *was* her mother.

"Miranda, you're scaring me." Darcy scooted over to sit beside the bundled up Miranda lump.

"I'm just tired, Boop." Miranda closed her eyes. "I can't seem to catch up on my sleep."

"Have you eaten anything?" Darcy could tell Miranda had lost weight. The perfectly slim physique Darcy would have given a good pair of shoes for now looked more like a stick figure.

"Not much."

"I bet you have mono." Nurse Nancy made a calculated, quick diagnosis with the tiredness, no fever, and lack of appetite. "I bet that's—"

"That's not it, Boop."

"But how do you know?" Darcy asked. "You haven't been to…"

"I'm pregnant."

The clouds slowly parted around Darcy's mind as the words seeped in. She sat perfectly still, forcing her lungs to breathe in and out, her eyes locked on the lump of blankets beside her. "Pregnant?"

"Pregnant."

"For real?" Darcy said, reverting to one of their middle school colloquialisms.

"Four EPTs for real. Yeah…I thought the first plus sign didn't look right, so I took three more."

"But how?" Darcy felt confused. Things like this didn't happen to Miranda.

"The sex was pre-meditated. Not the pregnancy. The usual way, Boop."

A half-smile tugged at Darcy's lips. A hint of the old Miranda had surfaced somewhere in that lifeless body.

"You *do* remember sex, don't you?" Miranda had sat up and pressed the heels of her hands into her eyes.

Darcy moved closer and put her arm around Miranda's thin shoulders. "Didn't we learn about that in health class?"

Miranda pulled her hands away and stared at the muted television. "Yep. That was it."

Darcy bit her lower lip. Miranda pregnant. "How long have you known?"

Miranda flung herself back against the leather couch. "I don't know."

"I've tried to get in touch with you for weeks."

Miranda hugged her pillow.

"Why didn't you call?"

"Mostly because morning sickness is kicking my ass," Miranda said. "Except it's not just in the morning, it's flippin' all day long. I can't keep anything down except crackers, Seven-Up, and Sunny D."

Darcy glanced around the loft and nodded. "So you haven't been to the doctor yet?"

"Nope."

"Is…Captain Kirk the father?"

"Yep."

"Does he know?"

Miranda gave out a throaty smirk. "Oh yeah. He knows."

Darcy winced at Miranda's tone.

"He's not convinced he's the father."

"And…you're positive he is?"

Miranda attempted a smile. "Boop, I may have had a lot of men, but I have them one at a time."

"You've always been able to do that."

"Do what?"

"Stay friends. You're the kind of girl who has amicable break-ups and mountains of friends. That's always worried me a bit…seems unnatural." Darcy had spent a lot of time wondering what it would be like to be in Miranda's shoes. But for once, her own felt just fine. "Do you know what you're going to do?"

"Children have never been on my radar. I don't have a psycho grandmother like Izzy, whose job in life is to remind me my eggs won't be fertile forever."

"Thanks for the reminder."

The back of Miranda's thin hand rubbed her cheek. "I've been here before."

So had Darcy, but only a scare back in high school…a scare no one ever knew about, except for the guy whose letter jacket hung hidden at the back of her closet. She forced her attention back to Miranda. "I know."

Darcy well remembered their second year at Texas State when Miranda had an abortion. She dropped out for the rest of the semester and jetted off to Europe for a couple of months, compliments of the sperm donor. She returned tan, beautiful, and as wild as ever. The abortion discussion had been dropped…permanently.

"I don't think I can go through that again." Miranda raised dark, sunken eyes.

"What are you going to do?"

Miranda twirled a thick wad of tangled hair around her finger, her lips pursed. "Well, from what I recall, pregnancy can usually lead to an infant."

"Adoption?"

"Yeah, I thought about that too. But hell, Boop, I'm not a teenager anymore."

Darcy braced herself for the last conceivable option. "You want to keep it?" Nothing on the planet could have shocked her more.

"I think so."

Darcy swallowed hard...real hard. Wow. Miranda with a baby. She tightened her grip around her friend's shoulder. "Well, let's talk about this." Darcy rarely found herself in the position to be the rational mind.

"You think I'm crazy, don't you?"

Touching her head to the side of Miranda's, she thought for a moment before she spoke. "I don't think you're crazy." She felt a small shudder and didn't have a clue whose body shook. "I just think we need to discuss this. You've got to be absolutely sure this is what you want before you're in the delivery room at five centimeters."

"Before *we're* in the delivery room," Miranda whispered.

"We who?"

Miranda bumped her head against Darcy's. "You and me."

"Whoa." Darcy pulled away, creating distance between them. "Me?" Her brain pixilated. "But I don't...I'm not...and I never—"

"Yeah well, me neither." Miranda dropped her head into her hands. "I've just been going over and over this whole shitty situation. I'm not like Lisa...I don't know how to be a mom."

"Oh stop," Darcy said. "That sounds like something I'd say. And if there's any chance you're going to keep this baby, we need to stop referring to him or her as a shitty situation."

Miranda lifted her head. "Wow, Boop, that was good."

I agree. You even surprise me sometimes!

She'd never felt so grown-up, even if flying by the seat of her pants. "And look at Madonna; she's a great mom."

"Hmm." Miranda rubbed fingers over her chin. "She is, isn't she?"

"Yeah, and you will be too," Darcy said with more confidence than she knew she had. "You may have to have one of those swear jars, but we'll figure this out together."

"What's a swear jar?"

"Every time Madonna slips in front of her kids with some profanity, she has to put money in the swear jar."

"How in the hell do you know that?"

Darcy lifted her chin, unwilling to admit that everything she read in *US Weekly* ranked right up there at the top of the rubbish heap. "I know things." Giving Miranda the best reassuring smile she could muster, she stood and gathered some of the immediate trash lying around. "So, you've told your mom, I take it?"

Miranda sucked in some air and scrunched her eyes closed. "Yeah, that's a phone call I regret making."

"What?" Darcy turned back towards the couch. "What did she say?"

"Don't get me started." Miranda pulled herself out of the nest of blankets and pillows. "Except the Cliff Notes version is she's not thrilled about being a 'granny'."

Miranda's mother, currently working her way out of marriage number four, had probably financed the remodel of her plastic surgeon's River Oaks mansion with all her nips and tucks. Darcy, once again, said a quiet "thank you" for her own dysfunctional family. They may have freaked out if Darcy had turned up pregnant, but she knew without a doubt they'd be there for her. She'd have to eat some crow and listen to Izzy's speeches about keeping her knees together, but yeah, she'd bet money on their support.

Getting a verbal commitment Miranda would answer her phone, Darcy returned home an hour later, a box of Captain Kirk's "gifts" in the back of her SUV.

"Get rid of it," Miranda had said. "Seriously, take it away."

Her mind in a heavy stupor, she turned the key and smiled at Stash banging his tail against the door, doing his funny dance. She sighed. Her pets almost always seemed happy when she arrived home. Even Mel made his way to the living room to see about all the commotion, no doubt from his super-sneaky hiding spot under her bed. The lazy Garfield cat stretched, yawned, and tried to look attentive.

After spending some playful time with the animals, she made her way to the kitchen, passing the to-do list on the bar. She put a line through Miranda's name and wrote W-O-W out to the side. Only one item remained, but she'd had quite enough excitement for one day, thank you very much. Ms. Viola would be a Sunday chore.

***

At 10:00 Sunday morning, Darcy stood outside Ms. Viola's door. With any luck, fingers crossed, both elderly people had changed out of their PJ's. A half smile pulled at the corner of her mouth, and she shook her head. Several months ago she would have rather stuck needles in her eyes than visit her apartment manager.

Blowing a strand of hair out of her face, she knocked and took a step back. From behind the door she heard Ms. Viola yelling at Ike. *Please let Mr. Will be dressed.*

The door opened and Ms. Viola had what Darcy considered a smile on her lips. A thin squiggly line smudged across the lower half of Ms. Viola's face looked like it had been drawn on with a red pencil. Fairly convinced the odd gesture was meant to be a smile, Darcy offered one back. She raised her hand in a quick wave. "Hi."

"How do you take your coffee?" Ms. Viola asked as if she had been expecting the knock.

Darcy bounced her head from side to side. "Sweetener…cream, I guess."

Smell that? Something is actually being baked…in an oven. And it smells wonderful. Why don't you ever do that?

"Fine. Go sit down." Ms. Viola pointed toward the breakfast area and headed to the small kitchen.

"Can I help?"

Ms. Viola stopped and looked at Darcy like she had two heads, then shrugged. "Okay."

She followed the old woman into the kitchen. Muffins cooled on a rack near the oven. "Smells good."

"Uh-hm." Ms. Viola pulled two small plates from a cabinet and filled the coffee mugs. "If you like them, I'll give you the recipe." She handed Darcy her coffee. "Here, do what you need to for this."

She doctored her coffee and found Ms. Viola sitting in one of the Ikea high-back chairs at the kitchen table. A pencil and the crossword puzzle from the morning paper sat in front of her.

"Come sit." Ms. Viola broke off a piece of muffin. "The coffee's decaf." The old woman's lip twisted up in a snarl. "I hate decaf. Sissy coffee if you ask me."

Darcy took the seat across from Ms. Viola. "Then why drink it?"

The woman closely examined Darcy's face. "Because Missy, I like coffee with my muffins." She took a sip from her mug. "And the doctor says no caffeine." She gave her thin red pencil smile. "I'm being good."

So how's that working for you?

Luckily she had enough snap this morning to keep her sarcasm from spilling past her lips; however, her alter ego had no intention of keeping quiet. "I think that's a good idea."

"Humph." Ms. Viola reached for a small lined pad of paper from the oak sideboard, flipped to a clean page, and started to write.

"What's that?"

"Muffin recipe."

"You don't have to look it up or anything?" Lots of things occupied space in Darcy's head. Recipes weren't one of them.

"Nah." She tapped a crooked finger against the side of her head. "Got it all up here." Ms. Viola scribbled on the pad and then shoved the piece of paper across the table. "This might come in handy one day."

Okay, like that's going to happen.

She pulled apart the muffin and took a bite. Delicious…really delicious. Well, maybe…one day.

"I want you to do something for me." Ms. Viola had turned back a page and tapped the list with her pencil. "Well, actually, a couple of things."

"Okay," Darcy muffled, polishing off her muffin.

"Remember the crocheted squares I had stacked over there?" Ms. Viola casually flipped her finger towards the sideboard. Darcy nodded.

"Well, I've sewn them together, and I need you to get half of the blankets out to Katy for me. Can you do that?"

"Sure. I've got several clients—"

"Here's the woman's name and email address." Ms. Viola tore another sheet of paper out of the notepad. "She's the contact person for Warm Up America here in town."

"No problem."

"The other half goes down to the VA Hospital." Ms. Viola rubbed her eyes. "I can't remember the address. You know, the hospital that's down off Holcombe on the other side of the Medical Center?"

"Yeah, okay. I'm sure I can find it." Darcy remained still, her hands in her lap. The conversation had taken a congenial-personal turn. Then the other shoe dropped.

"Now about the rent increase."

Darcy's eyes rounded just about the time her stomach dropped.

This can't possibly be good news....

Ms. Viola leaned her bent spine against the high back. "So what do you think of the improvements?"

Good lord, what could she say? Admitting to how much better everything looked (which it did) would be giving a seal of approval for a rent increase. Her checking account was already struggling for air. She chewed on the inside of her lip and decided to roll the dice.

"The complex is looking really...nice." Darcy nodded up and down like a bobble head.

"So about the rent increase." Ms. Viola watched Darcy carefully. "I've been informed...." She paused.

Darcy, her teeth clenched, leaned forward, teetering on the edge of her chair.

Is she purposely dragging this out?

"It won't be necessary."

Darcy's mouth dropped open. Flapping it back shut, she squinted at the old woman. "What do you mean?"

"I don't see how that statement requires an explanation."

Darcy's hands slapped her cheeks. "They really said that? No rent increase?"

"Yes, they really said that. No rent increase...but I still need you to help me with something."

Here it comes.

The "No...but" always meant there was a catch. If the shoe had dropped earlier, it had come from Payless. No doubt this one carried a designer label.

"So, will you help me?" Ms. Viola asked.

"How? Do what?" She cleared her throat. "I mean, what can I do?"

Ms. Viola circled an item on the list with her pencil. "We have two apartments vacant. We need tenants. Can you place an ad in the paper for me?"

Darcy weighed the designer shoe.

That's not so bad.

"I can do that."

"And another thing." Ms. Viola broke a small piece off another muffin. "Will you do a walk-through of the vacant apartments and help Fletcher with a list for repairs?" She popped the bit of muffin into her mouth and took a sip from her coffee cup. "Fletcher does much better with a list. Otherwise, he'll just walk around with that garden hose on his shoulder all day. Can you do that?"

An hour later Darcy gathered up six afghans, details for the classified ad, and the muffin recipe. Making her way to the door, Ms. Viola stuffed another piece of paper in her hand. "What's this?"

Her voice dropped so low Darcy had to lean down to hear. "My chocolate chip cookie recipe."

"Why are we whispering?"

"Because I've never given it to anyone before," Ms. Viola said. "I've told you about my sister, the bitch from hell? She's tried to get her hands on this for years. It's our grandmother's recipe…and she gave it to me. Me!" Ms. Viola scratched out a laugh; at least Darcy thought it was a laugh, though it sounded strange…but not unpleasant. The gesture actually turned the deep creases in Ms. Viola's face upward for a change.

"Uh, no." Darcy rearranged the afghans and paperwork. "You've never talked about your sister."

Ms. Viola swatted air. "A story for another day." She opened the door. "Makes me laugh though. I always told her Nona just followed the recipe on the back of the chocolate chip package." The chuckle escaped again. She reached for Darcy's elbow. "But she didn't." She pointed a crooked finger to the last piece of paper. "And the secret is right there."

Darcy searched the old woman's face and then scanned the piece of paper, trying to understand two things. One, the malicious cookie recipe intent, and, "Why are you giving this to me?"

Ms. Viola fell quiet for a minute and let go of Darcy's elbow. She lifted her chin. "Let me see, what were your words? Oh yeah…I care."

Nothing could have prepared Darcy for that. She shifted the load in her arms. "Really?"

"Yes, I do. But don't go getting all mushy on me," Ms. Viola said. "Besides, there's no telling when this old battery is going to wear out. I need to pass the secret on to someone, and you're it." Ms. Viola shuffled Darcy through the door. "Thank you for coming by," Ms. Viola said. "You're a good girl."

Darcy stood outside the closed apartment door for a few long moments.

The woman never ceases to amaze you, does she?

After depositing the afghans in the back of her SUV, she headed back up to her apartment, replaying the last hour. Ms. Viola had said Darcy was a good girl *and* she cared. *And, all in one visit...*a little much to take in from the apartment manager she used to refer to as the Wicked Witch of the West. And then there was the crack about her battery giving out, which reminded Darcy of the little white nitro tablets.

She secured the two recipes safely away in a kitchen drawer, grabbed a bottle of water, pulled the to-do list over, and drew a line through Ms. Viola's name. She wrote another W-O-W out to the side. The only uneventful item on her list had been changing out her clothes, which used to be a big W-O-W all by itself.

***

Wednesday morning, Darcy sat in the waiting room of her OB-GYN's office, thumbing through a back issue of *Parent's Magazine.* She and Miranda had used the same doctor since...well, since grownup women needed gynos, as Izzy referred to them. She had cleared her morning schedule, promising Miranda she'd go with her if the doctor could squeeze her in. Darcy glanced at her watch. Almost an hour had passed since the nurse had called Miranda's name. She hoped they'd have time to grab a quick lunch before heading out to Katy this afternoon. Having exchanged emails with the Warm Up America lady, she planned to drop the afghans off sometime between appointments.

Darcy reached into her Kate Spade knock-off messenger bag and pulled out her iPhone. Gucci had upgraded to iPhones almost a year ago...until then, she had dressed up her Android in a sparkly cover to make it look cool. She clicked on the map icon and plugged in the address of the afghan Katy lady. Next, she checked her emails and breathed a sigh of relief seeing the confirmation from the Houston Chronicle. She had made the Sunday classified deadline for Ms. Viola's ad. Good...one less thing.

"Darcy?"

Darcy raised her eyes and lifted her hand in a wave. "Over here," she said, and dropped the phone into a side pocket of the Kate Spade knock off. Tricia had been Dr. Holt's primary nurse forever, and felt more like a surrogate mom to both her and Miranda. Darcy fondly remembered Tricia holding her hand during her first "grown-up well-woman" visit with Dr. Holt.

156

"Miranda wants to see you."

Grabbing her bag, she followed the nurse down the hallway.

Tricia stopped in front of one of the exam rooms. "She's in there."

She tried to read Tricia's face, an uneasy feeling starting to churn inside.

Surely not. People have babies all the time, right?

Darcy agreed with her alter ego; however, her stomach wasn't buying it. She poked her head into the room and saw Miranda lying on the table, one hand behind her head, the other holding a Kleenex and extended out to Darcy. Miranda's eyes glistened with fresh tears.

Oh God, it's bad. Miranda never cries.

The doctor entered data on a laptop, but looked up when Darcy entered. "My goodness; I haven't seen you girls together since you were…well, I guess not girls anymore." Dr. Holt, a woman in her mid-fifties, had soft blonde hair, paled by streaks of gray, curling almost to her shoulders. The gentle smile she often wore was in place, easing Darcy's fears a bit.

"Boop." Miranda swiped her eyes with the Kleenex. "C'mere, c'mere, c'mere."

Darcy edged her way across the small room and grabbed Miranda's hand. "What's wrong?"

"Nothing's wrong." Her voice sounded shaky. "You've gotta see this. They've even got surround sound in here." Miranda shifted her head over toward Dr. Holt. "Okay doc, let's do it."

Dr. Holt flipped a switch on the nearby machine and slid the hand-held device over Miranda's bare stomach. The doctor rotated a knob on the machine, filling the room with a loud and high-tempo *swoosh-swoosh, swoosh-swoosh, swoosh-swoosh.*

"What is that?" Darcy asked. The sound resembled a dishwasher on wash cycle.

"It's real! It's alive!" Miranda crushed Darcy's hand. "That's the heartbeat. Can you believe it? I have something inside of me with a heartbeat!"

The dishwasher sound pounded in Darcy's ears. No words seemed to be coming out her mouth, so she just squeezed Miranda's hand back.

"But that's not the best part." Miranda's raspy voice was easily heard above the roar from the surround sound. "We've got movies. Let 'er roll, doc."

Dr. Holt flipped another switch and the blank monitor screen transformed into a black and white snowy image of something Darcy had no way of describing, except maybe an underwater scene from a really, really old movie. In the middle of the ocean shot swirled a small squiggly capsule shaped like a kidney bean, and inside the squiggly kidney bean...a pulsating tiny dot. She squinted to bring the picture into focus. "What is it?"

"It's my jellybean, Boop." Miranda pulled her hand and Darcy's toward the screen. "See, that's the heart beating."

Darcy fixated on the monitor. "That's a heart?" How could a heart be that miniscule? She broke her gaze away from the screen and shot a look at Dr. Holt. "Is it supposed to be that little?"

"Everything looks fine." Dr. Holt smiled and printed out two copies of the black and white ultrasound. "Here, one for each of you. And I want to see you in three weeks." Dr. Holt handed Miranda a prescription, a sample pack of prenatal horse-pill vitamins, and several pieces of literature. "Darcy, you might want to read over the material I've given Miranda, since you're going to be involved with this."

"I am?" Darcy corrected herself. "I am." The doctor left the two women alone in the small room. Miranda dressed while Darcy sat on a stool, staring at the black and white blurry picture. "Wow. Wow, wow, and wow."

"I know." Miranda smiled. "I'm having a jellybean."

"So...this is a done deal?" Darcy asked. "Finished thinking it through?"

"Done deal." Miranda grabbed her purse. "Let's go eat, I'm starving."

"Since when?"

Miranda shrugged. "I don't know. I guess when I heard the jellybean's little pitter-patter." She rubbed her still flat stomach.

***

The two women sat at a table at California Pizza Kitchen, across the street from the Memorial City Medical Center. Miranda polished off her California Club sandwich and reached across for a piece of Darcy's herbed focaccia bread dipped in olive oil and parmesan cheese. Darcy scanned the list of do's and don'ts from the packet Dr. Holt had given Miranda.

"No alcohol, drugs, or cigarettes. No fish, no caffeine, lots of calcium and iron," Darcy read aloud. "Are you going to be able to do this?"

Miranda pursed her lips and rolled her eyes around the restaurant before zeroing in on Darcy. "Yeah, Boop. I think I can. We're adults…I'm sure we can figure this thing out."

"Miranda, I'm not your husband…or your wife. This is your baby we're talking about. There can't be any of this 'I think I can' bullshit."

"Don't be ridiculous." Miranda licked the parmed olive oil from her fingers. "I know we're not married…but you *will* be a godmother."

"I will?"

Maybe she's thought more about this than we thought.

"Of course," Miranda added. "And if there's going to be a swear jar…you can drop in a quarter now."

Darcy shook her head. "I can't believe this. You're going to be a mom."

"And a damn good one, too."

Both sets of eyebrows shot up, then the women laughed. "Okay, we're even," Miranda said. "We'll start over with the swear jar."

"This may be a bad time to ask, but will you be able to come to Becca's bay house next weekend for my birthday?"

Miranda's crazy smile crossed her face. "I'm not sick Boop…just pregnant. And I think I'm going to start feeling like my old self again."

Darcy finished the rest of her day out in Katy, making her two afternoon appointments with optometrists and dropping off the afghans for Ms. Viola. But her mind was not on selling Gucci eyewear *or* Warm-Up America. Miranda was going to be a mom, and had said she felt she was going to be back to her old self again. Darcy didn't know much about motherhood, but she was pretty sure Miranda's words had to be an oxymoron. Wow. Wow, wow, and wow.

Terry Lee

Chapter 12

Before the ad came out in the Sunday classifieds, Darcy had helped Fletcher with the promised punch-list for the two vacant apartments. She'd also suggested replacing the shredded For Lease sign hanging on the rail of her balcony.

Arriving home Friday afternoon, Darcy spotted Fletcher on a ladder attaching the new banner. She smiled. Pulling an over-sized demo display case from the back of her SUV, she noticed the cooler weather had switched Fletcher to his winter uniform…a long-sleeved camouflaged hoody.

"The sign looks good, Fletcher." At the sound of his name, Fletcher turned and gave Darcy the two-finger peace sign. Thumbs up would have made more sense, but then again, it was Fletcher.

She hauled the heavy Gucci case up the stairs, through the door, and past Stash. Her head swiveled back at the furious blinking of the answering machine.

"You have four new messages."

"Four?" That hadn't happened in a while. She listened to the messages and deleted all but the last one. The first two were from Miranda and short. "Call me!" Her mother had just called to say hi, although she could hear Izzy yelling something in the background.

The last message was from Sam. They had a date the next night, and he had suggested she pick the place. "Anywhere is fine," he had said. Darcy made a quick trip downstairs with Stash, and had just put her Jimmy Choo lizard pumps back in their designer box when someone, or something, banged on the door.

She padded through the living room and shooed Stash back, but not before the second round of banging started. The seriousness of the knocks sounded more Ms. Viola-ish; however, she doubted the elderly woman could even make it up the stairs anymore. Since it was not forceful or repetitive enough to be Lawrence, it could only be one other person.

"What is all that out there?" Miranda said, her voice ragged and her hand pointing down the stairwell. She pushed past Darcy.

"Come in." Darcy pulled Stash away from the human cyclone and closed the door.

By the time she turned around Miranda had her head in the refrigerator. "I need food."

"You've come to the wrong place," Darcy said. "I don't feed myself well."

Miranda shoved the refrigerator door closed and hit pay dirt in the freezer. She pulled out the remains of a half-gallon of ice cream. "G'on, finish what you were doing. I can't talk until I feed this baby."

"And fudge-brownie nut is food?" Darcy headed back to the bedroom to change clothes.

"Dang straight," Miranda said between bites of the dark chocolate ice cream. "That is, until you get something decent in here. Besides, it's dairy, which means calcium. So there."

Tossing her work clothes aside, Darcy pulled out a pair of faded jeans and a soft long sleeved fitted t-shirt. She returned to the kitchen feeling much more comfortable.

"Boop, I have three questions," Miranda said, licking ice cream off a serving spoon.

Darcy couldn't help but smile. Only a week ago she had been worried sick, not having heard from her best friend in weeks. *Then*, she discovered the disarray of Miranda and her apartment. *Then* she found out about the pregnancy and accompanied her for the first time visit to the ob-gyn…for the "ob" part. *Then*, they'd heard the heartbeat of Miranda's jellybean, and Darcy learned she would be a godmother. It had been one hell of a week.

Oops, that could cost you another quarter.

She and Miranda were seriously going to have to curb their language. If not, the jellybean could have his or her college education paid for by the delivery date.

Which, I'd say, gives profanity an upside.

So there Miranda sat, eating fudge brownie nut ice cream and acting like nothing had changed. The mere fact that Miranda showed up at her apartment on a Friday night with nothing better to do pretty much convinced Darcy *everything* had changed and *nothing* would ever be the same. Madonna amazed her.

Miranda bopped her hand down on the bar top in front of Darcy. "Hey Boop, come back from wherever you are."

The whack on the counter snapped Darcy out of replay mode. "What?"

"I said I have three questions." Miranda let out a loud burp. "Sorry. I do that a lot now."

Darcy smiled at Miranda's nonchalantness. "Go for it."

"Okay, first of all…what in the hell is going on around here? There're live things in the flower beds, the garbage stench is gone, and the place actually looks livable."

As usual, Miranda could get away with saying stuff Darcy would find insulting from anyone else. She opened her mouth to deliver a short version of the new and improved Fountain Oaks when Miranda burst forward.

"Second, what are we going to do this weekend? I thought it'd be fun to wallow in junk food, no make-up, watch *Ischtar*, that kinda thing." Miranda polished off the ice cream and shoved the empty container back across the bar.

"What's the third?"

"What's for dinner?"

The first question didn't surprise Darcy, but the second and third did. Miranda had had her own "plans" on weekends since they had started dating, which seemed like a long time ago in a land far, far away.

"The first question can wait. Second, anything we want, except tomorrow night I have a date. And third, the only legitimate food in the house is for the pets. We need to go to the store."

Miranda stood and grabbed her purse. "So, let's plow."

***

Friday night at the grocery store didn't seem as disgustingly pitiful when accompanied by your best friend. They dumped a loaded frozen pizza in the basket, followed by Cheetos, more ice cream, a box of wine (for Darcy), shells and cheese, Twinkies, Ding-Dongs, a large bag of sour cream and onion potato chips, and any other junk food they could spot. Before arriving at the store, a pact had been established. This would be the last "hoo-rah" weekend before the healthy, nutritional, all-for-the-baby diet plan took over.

Darcy threw several reusable grocery bags and the contents of the cart on the counter at the register, prying the Cheetos out of Miranda's grasp long enough for the bag to be scanned.

Before Darcy could dig through her purse for her wallet, Miranda had shoved a debit card to the cashier. "My treat, Boop," she said between yuk-yellow crunchy bites.

Darcy opened her mouth to protest, but Miranda lifted up a stop-sign hand.

"Nope. Won't do any good," Miranda said. "You're in this with me, and I want to buy your junk food this weekend. It's the least I can do."

"Are you suggesting we get married?" Darcy asked, getting a "well okaaay" look from the cashier.

Miranda shrugged her shoulders. "Nah...I thought about it though." Madonna brushed the unnatural orange residue from her hands. "I'll just buy the food," she said, and grabbed one of the filled reusable bags. "What's this about? You going green on me?"

"It's Ms. Viola's idea," Darcy said with a half-smile. "I'm becoming responsible." Miranda raised her eyebrows, tilted her head, and for once didn't say a word.

***

Back at the apartment, Miranda sat cross-legged on the couch waiting for the buzzer to signal the pizza had dropped the frozen part. Darcy returned from the bedroom with two books she had recently purchased at Half-Price Books. She tossed one on the couch.

"*What To Expect When You're Expecting*," Miranda read. "What's this?"

"Homework." Darcy dropped down beside Miranda and pulled the second book onto her lap. "We've got studying to do."

"Is there going to be a test?" Miranda flipped through the pages.

"Final exam is July 11." Darcy headed to the kitchen to quiet the oven buzzer. "But for the time being, don't go past chapter six."

"Why?"

"It gets a little scary after that. Trust me." She pulled the pizza out of the oven, reloaded her wine glass, and poured chilled Canada Dry ginger ale into another. "Hey, does it bother you if I drink wine? I didn't even think about that."

"If I was an alcoholic, maybe." Miranda headed to the kitchen for the pizza while Darcy deposited drinks on the ottoman coffee table. "At first only Sunny D stayed down. Now, as you can see, I've broadened my horizons. But alcohol doesn't even sound good."

Good to know. Making it through Miranda's pregnancy sans boxed wine could be a deal-breaker. Just kidding. No, probably not.

"Let's eat before we study."

"Why?"

"You may have broadened your horizons, but believe me, it's in your best interest to get something besides Cheetos in your stomach before you open that book."

"Sounds scary." Miranda pulled the first pizza wedge to her mouth.

"Just a precaution. According to the book, your baby is going to look more like a little alien with a tail for a while."

Miranda shot Darcy a "yikes" expression and shoved the book away from her. "I feel better calling it a jellybean."

Darcy studied her friend. Miranda didn't *look* pregnant, but she definitely looked different. Just the fact Madonna sat on her couch, on a Friday night, eating frozen pizza and drinking ginger ale broke every exception to the rule in the Four-of-a-Kind girlfriend handbook. She watched Miranda shove more pizza into her mouth and couldn't help but smile. Speaking of an oxymoron…Four-of-a-Kind in no way, shape, or form described the friends she'd had since middle school.

"What?"

Darcy shrugged and picked up a slice. "I don't know. You're certainly not showing yet, but there's something…." She couldn't figure out how to finish the sentence.

"C'mon Boop, you can't leave me hanging like that. What?"

"I don't know…."

"You've said that." Miranda wiped her mouth with a napkin. "Explain. C'mon, use your words."

"Very funny." Darcy took a long swig of wine. "There's just something softer about you. I'm just not used to seeing you in anything that's not tight and sl—"

"Slutty?"

165

"I was going to say slinky." Darcy smiled. "Well, look at what you're wearing...leggings and just a regular old long-sleeved top. On Friday night. It's weird...but in a good way."

Miranda had little trouble finishing off yet another slice of pizza. "Yeah...well, I've been thinking. This whole Madonna thing? Think it's time to retire."

Darcy couldn't imagine that happening, but then again, she'd never imagined Miranda pregnant either.

"Did I tell you I'm spending the night?" Miranda had moved to dessert, returning from the kitchen with a bowl of ice cream...butter pecan. She curled up on one end of the couch. "We've got a lot to talk about."

Darcy thought about going for ice cream, but decided "wine time" hadn't ended. She headed to the kitchen for what she promised herself would be the last glass for the evening.

I wouldn't count on it. This is a special occasion. When was the last time Madonna came for a sleepover? On Friday night?

"So tell me about Captain Kirk. He really doesn't think he's the father?" Darcy propped herself up on the opposite end of the couch and threw an afghan over both of them, just like when they were teenagers.

Miranda rolled her eyes and shrugged. "Not really in the mood to talk about *that* in my fragile state. Did you get rid of the box of crap I gave you?"

"No worries. It sleeps with the fishes."

"Good. So, tell me what's going on around this place. You never answered my question." She pulled the blanket up around her.

Darcy chewed on the inside of her cheek. The Fountain Oaks story had moved from a bad fiction novel to horror, with bits of mystery, some tender moments, and sprinkles of satirical comedy. Using the heel of her hand to rub her forehead, she searched for a Cliff Notes version of life at Fountain Oaks. Not coming up with anything in the least big logical, she just started to talk. "Remember the apartment get-together the week after Becca's wedding?"

Miranda nodded, licking the last of the ice cream from her spoon.

"Well, I wrote a letter to the management company complaining about the landscaping. Then I found out Ms. Viola has a heart problem and is sleeping with Mr. Will. And then—"

"Whoa Boop, back up." Miranda pushed herself up and sat cross-legged on the couch. "Remind me about Mr. Will."

"Norman Thayer."

"The Wicked Witch is shacking up with Norman Thayer?" Miranda let out a throaty laugh. "You've got to be shitting me!"

"Why does everyone say that?" Darcy grabbed for her wine. "How could I be shitting about something like that? Do you know the possible brain damage I've probably suffered since I saw that?"

"You *saw* them having sex?" Miranda's eyebrows stayed lodged in a worried line over her rounded eyes.

"No! Oh God no!" Darcy shivered and pulled the blanket up to shield her eyes from the visual she'd been shoving away for over a month. "He just opened her door one morning and there they were…in their jammies."

Miranda blew out air. "Yeow."

"You're telling me." Darcy decided to hold on to her wine glass…no sense putting it down. "And another thing. The Wicked Witch isn't really a witch at all, at least most of the time. Glenda!*"* Darcy blurted. "*That's* her name. Anyway, she's been nice. She even said she liked me and then said she cared."

Still hard to believe, right?

"You're acting strange. Who the hell is Glenda, and why is the witch being nice? Have you figured any of this out yet?"

"Not really, but after I wrote the letter, things around here started getting better. Hell, we even have two new sets of fancy washer-dryers down in the laundry room." Darcy drained her glass and went to the kitchen, this time returning with the entire box. "You've seen the landscaping. And the place has been painted. Fletcher has been working his ass off."

"Your rent is about to double, I imagine," Miranda said. "This place was what…like government housing cheap anyway, wasn't it?" Once again, Madonna could fling insults all around the room and not piss Darcy off. Miranda knew too much about Darcy's life for her to start acting offended at this point. "And you still haven't told me who Glenda is."

"I just remembered the name of the good witch in *The Wizard of Oz.* You know, the nice, pretty one who's the witch of some other direction?"

Miranda grabbed her iPhone.

"What are you doing?" Darcy asked.

"Checking you out on IMDB. Can't say I've watched *Wizard of Oz* lately, but...yep, there she is. G-l-i-n-d-a. Says here she's the witch of the north." Miranda let out a froggy belly laugh. "Well, what do you know?"

"What?"

"Not everything is ugly in this world. You're starting to find some good in people. You're growing up, Boop." Miranda winked at Darcy. "I'd say my work here is done but...I don't think so." The "I don't think so" tone sounded cute and kind of baby-talkish, very un-Miranda.

"What do you mean?" She couldn't imagine what Miranda had up her sleeve.

"I saw a For Lease sign hanging from your balcony."

She stopped, her glass mid-way between lap and mouth. "Yeah, so?"

"I think I should move over here."

Darcy blinked hard a couple of times, like walking into full-blown sunlight after spending time in a cave. "You? You." Darcy's finger and wine glass pointed in Miranda's direction. "Here. At Fountain Oaks...at the loony bin."

"Yeah, I think so." Miranda set her empty ice cream bowl aside and nestled further down on her end of the couch. Her eyes closed. "Wake me up in thirty minutes. I...just need...a little catnap. That's normal, right?"

The "normal" word again. Studying Miranda's face, the word beautiful came to mind...strikingly beautiful, actually, even when she yawned, like now. The slutty (oops) sultry, slinky persona had slipped away. Something had taken its place, something softer. Darcy took the ice cream bowl, stemmed glasses, and box of wine back to the kitchen. She'd read the first couple of chapters of *What to Expect,* and knew Miranda was out for the count.

After the ten o'clock news, Darcy nudged Miranda. "C'mon, Mom. Time to go to bed."

Miranda lifted her head and looked around, like trying to get a grip on her surroundings. She wrestled to her feet, dragging the blanket off the couch.

"We gotta go shopping tomorrow, Boop."

"What for?" Not that Darcy ever needed an excuse.

"I need a bigger bra." Miranda trudged down the short hallway to Darcy's bedroom.

"Bigger?"

"Yeah, the Supremes are out of control," were the last coherent words Miranda uttered that night.

Darcy refilled the water and food bowls for both animals, made some minor clean-up adjustments to the litter box, took Stash outside for his "business-trip," changed into comfortable pajamas, and slid under the covers. A soft but steady snore came from the lump on the other side of the bed. Two guys could never share a queen-size bed without some gay comment surfacing. Darcy smiled. Girls did that all the time…like a sisterhood. She and Miranda had shared a bed many times since their first sleepover way back in their teens. She laced her fingers behind her head. *Normal*, she thought. A mental-Miranda-list began to form of the *normal-but-not-really-normal* things she struggled to wrap her mind around.

Pregnant

Dressing normal on a Friday night and at Darcy's for a sleepover

Actually wanting to have the baby

Moving from the I'd-die-to-live-there loft in Midtown to Fountain Oaks, home of the weird and weirder

Wanting her, Darcy, aka Betty Boop, to help, be there…there as in at-the-time-of-delivery there

Falling asleep before the end of the ten o'clock news

Needing a bigger bra

One hell of a start for a normal-not-so-normal list. Maybe the whole moving into Fountain Oaks was just the beginning of one of Miranda's pregnancy dreams. But maybe not.

Darcy flipped over on her side, punched the pillow a couple of times, and tried to close her eyes. Didn't work. She stared at the digital clock on her bedside table. Ten thirty-five...on a Friday night. She rolled again onto her back and watched the shadows on the ceiling. A small slit in the mini blinds filtered light from the newly lit courtyard into her bedroom.

The idea of Miranda moving to Fountain Oaks rolled around in her brain. A bizarre thought, but Darcy admitted bizarre had become the new norm these days. Ms. Viola should be pleased. At least one of the vacancies would be filled. She wasn't sure how those two opposing personalities would work out, but who knew? Lawrence would be thrilled at first, remembering how he'd tripped over his own chaps the night of the Halloween party. Then he'd pout when he found out about the pregnancy.

Next weekend...her Tiki Island birthday party with the girls. Everything going on lately had taken the sting out of turning thirty-one. She blew out air. Really, no big deal. With that thought, she slipped out of bed, returned to the couch, and watched a couple of late-night *Friends* reruns.

***

The next morning, Darcy had been up two full hours before Miranda surfaced. She had been extra kind to Stash and taken him for a walk through the neighborhood behind the apartments. When she got back she popped a can of cinnamon rolls in the oven, made a pot of coffee for herself, and poured Miranda a large glass of chocolate milk. If this was going to be the last of their crazy, unhealthy eating for a while, they might as well do it right. She heard movement from the bedroom only moments before Miranda padded her way to plop down on one of the barstools in the kitchen area.

"What's up, Boop?" Miranda's tangled hair had been wadded and clipped on top of her head. She still wore her comfortable leggings and long shirt from the night before.

Darcy pushed the chocolate milk across the countertop. "Your nourishment." She removed the cinnamon rolls from the oven and smeared white gooey icing on top. Moving to Miranda's side of the bar, she pulled the hot pan of killer cinnamon rolls and coffee toward her.

"Did you say you have a date tonight or did I dream that?" Miranda shoved a rather large bite of cinnamon roll into her mouth.

Darcy almost spewed hot liquid across both of them. "Oh my gosh. I completely forgot! Sam!"

"Batman?" Miranda asked.

"You sound like Izzy." Darcy grabbed her cell phone. "His name is Sam."

"Batman, Captain Kirk, Howdy Doody...geez, *that* seems like a long time ago." Miranda rubbed her eyes and yawned.

Darcy texted Sam, naming the place and time for their date. How could she have forgotten about their date? Too much had been happening too fast, and she felt the need for some organization, which also sounded bizarre and should be added to the normal-not-so-normal growing list.

"Shower. I need a shower." Miranda had left the barstool and headed toward the bathroom, dragging her over-night bag behind her.

Darcy used Miranda's shower time to fill in the calendar on her iPhone, make some quick reminder notes, and change into a pair of jeans and a soft hooded long-sleeve tee. Without much thought, she grabbed the first pair of shoes she found in her closet and slipped them on. She stared down. Since when had she carelessly thrown on a pair of shoes, especially when doing something besides taking Stash down for his relief efforts? The crazy list continued.

By the time Miranda emerged from the bathroom, Darcy had thrown on foundation, blush and mascara, and had cleaned the kitchen after their highly caloric breakfast. Miranda's long dark hair hung limp and wet down past her shoulders. She had dressed in a different, however very similar, outfit to the one she had arrived *and* slept in.

"Where did you get all these clothes?" Darcy fed the last cinnamon roll to Stash, sitting patiently at Darcy's feet. "I didn't even know you owned stuff like that. Uh, not that they don't look great," she added.

"Good save, Boop."

"Have you taken your horse pill yet?" Darcy asked.

Miranda shot Darcy a look, pulled her overnight bag up on the counter, and brought out a large prescription bottle. "You're taking this shit seriously, aren't you?"

Darcy handed Miranda a bottle of water from the refrigerator. "I'm assuming the swear jar thing is off till Monday also?"

"Might as well…everything else is. And you might not want to watch this. It's not pretty." Miranda tossed the over-sized vitamin in her mouth, took a swig of water, and tilted her head back. She shivered. "That wasn't too bad. I usually gag a couple of times." She let out a disturbingly loud burp. "Sorry. Yeah, about the wardrobe thing. I had to do something. Fishnet hose and leather miniskirts weren't cutting it." Miranda let out another unladylike belch. "I've been picking up some things at Stein Mart, Target…whatever is close by. I told you, I think the whole Madonna thing is over."

Madonna fit perfectly for Miranda's nickname. She had a style, ease, and personality (especially the personality) that stood alone. Even as middle schoolers, besides being best friends, Darcy had hung around Miranda for a reason…that was where the cool people (especially the guys) hung out. She could just never figure out why Miranda hung out with her. Well…not true, exactly.

Miranda's family life had been far different from Darcy's. While Darcy had two parents who actually operated as parents, Miranda had never met her real father, and her mother, Cheryl, didn't have a flicker of maternal instinct in her body. Cheryl spent most of her time with boyfriends and husbands who never stayed around long, leaving Miranda in the role as surrogate mother to her two younger brothers. Darcy knew for a fact Miranda would have left home way before graduating from high school if not for the responsibility she felt for her little brothers. At least Cheryl's negligence kept Miranda in school, a big plus in Darcy's mind. But it came at a price. Once at Texas State, Miranda made up for lost time after shouldering all that heavy responsibility at such a young age. She turned into a wild-child, and looking for love in all the wrong places, unfortunately, seemed to have become her new motto.

The pregnancy during Miranda's sophomore year, the abortion, and sudden trip abroad came as no real surprise. The surprise came after her return. Miranda starting keeping men at arm's length. Flirt? Always. Sleep around? Surely. But let someone get close enough to have a serious relationship, to break through the shield she used to protect herself from being hurt? Never. Fortunately, Miranda had the good sense to finish college and land a fantastic job with a pharmaceutical company. No big surprise Cheryl offered zero support or enthusiasm when she learned of Miranda's pregnancy. Cheryl had only ever shown concern about one thing and one thing only…Cheryl.

"Go dry your hair," Darcy said. "We've got serious bra-shopping to do."

"See what a good friend you are?" Miranda slid off the barstool. "I'd already forgotten about the Supremes."

Chapter 13

Serious shopping had to take place for Miranda to find a new bra…no knock-off allowed. The two women headed to Dillard's at the Galleria.

"What are all these people doing on the road? It's Saturday for God's sake." Miranda fished around in Darcy's car and found a spare pair of Gucci shades.

Darcy smiled and thought again about how much Miranda's life would change, forever. No more partying till dawn on weekends, to mention one.

After two major (industrial strength) purchases, the two treated themselves to lunch at The Cheesecake Factory. True to their girlfriend weekend agreement, they chose probably the most fattening item on the menu, the macaroni and cheeseburger. The decision to split the burger only came after they decided to each have their own slice of heavenly cheesecake.

"Did you mean what you said last night?" Darcy had been dying to bring up the subject again.

"Which part?" Miranda picked out clumps of fried macaroni and cheese from her sandwich and popped them into her mouth.

"About moving to Fountain Oaks." Darcy washed down French fries with Diet Coke, which served no purpose calorie-wise.

"Wouldn't be so bad, huh?" Miranda took a break from stuffing food in her mouth and leaned back against the leather booth. "Besides, wouldn't hurt to live somewhere more affordable, right? I mean, I'm gonna have formula, diapers, all the shit that comes with having a baby. Play pen?"

"I think they're called Pack 'n Plays now."

"See? I'm ill equipped. I don't know any of this crappola." Miranda dropped her eyes to her lap. "And...I think I'm getting a little scared."

Darcy couldn't remember the last time she'd seen such vulnerability in Miranda. She scooted around the horseshoe-shaped booth. "We'll figure it out." She gave her friend's hand a squeeze. "Hey, it'll almost be like being roommates again. We'll go talk to Ms. Viola when we get back. She'll be thrilled to have one less vacancy to fill."

You hope she'll be thrilled.

Darcy had to agree with her alter ego, remembering their first encounter when Miranda looked like a prostitute after a hard night.

"Can you talk to her for me?"

Darcy's eyebrows pulled together. "Why?"

"Since Madonna has left the building, I'm a little shaky on my own."

There it was again...vulnerability. And all this time Darcy thought *she* had cornered that market. The mood turned somber, so they got their cheesecake to go and headed back to Darcy's.

Miranda settled back on the couch looking more than ready for a nap. "Think I'll read a little of my assignment." She picked up her copy of *What to Expect.*

Yeah, right. Like that's gonna happen.

The voice of reason in Darcy's head won her bet. Within five minutes, Miranda's eyes had closed. Weight gain, horse pill vitamins, Pack 'n Plays, receiving blankets, diapers, giving birth, formula, car seats. A lot to take in—

Don't forget about a new vehicle. That two-seater Beamer of hers won't work with a car seat.

Yeah, that's right. And a new car. The hits just kept on coming. She peeked out the mini blinds and spotted Fletcher in the courtyard. Instead of spending Miranda's naptime deciding what to wear for date night, she leashed Stash and slipped out the front door.

"Can you walk him around a minute?" she asked Fletcher. "I need to tell Ms. Viola something."

"She's gone."

"Where is she?"

"At the hospital." Fletcher reached for the leash. "That man took her." He pointed toward Lawrence's apartment.

Darcy felt air suck out of her lungs like a vacuum. "What? When? What happened?"

"Dunno," Fletcher said, scratching Stash's head. "She wanted you this morning. You weren't home." Fletcher squatted down to Stash's level. "The guy was."

She pressed her thumbs into her eyes, trying to squelch the anxiety running laps inside her. "Oh no…." The one time Ms. Viola needed her. "Mr. Will, did he go too? What hospital?"

Fletcher shrugged, obviously tripped into overload by the panic-laden questions.

"What do I do? What do I do?" Her eyes on the ground, she paced in a circle around Fletcher and Stash.

"There," Fletcher said.

Darcy looked up, spotted Lawrence rounding the corner from the carport, and took off in a sprint. "What happened? Is she okay? Where is she?"

Lawrence placed his hands on her shaking shoulders. "Calm down. I think she's going to be okay," he said. "They'll probably keep her overnight. She had another one of those attacks you told me about. Only this time the pain didn't go away." His eyes, though serious, held a look of bewilderment. "She must have been feeling really bad to allow me, of all people, to take her to the hospital."

"Where's Mr. Will?"

"One of his daughters came to the hospital and took him home for the night," Lawrence said. "He seemed a little confused."

"Family? Does she have family we should call?" Darcy scoured her brain for mention of family. The bitch of a sister?

No way.

Tons of pictures hung on Ms. Viola's wall, none she'd ever bothered to ask about. "A nephew!" She drummed her chin with shaky fingers. "She said she has a nephew."

"She wants to see you."

"What? Me? Are you sure?"

"Ah, let me think. Yes." Lawrence answered. "Her specific instructions were 'find Missy for me.'"

"Fletcher," Darcy yelled. "Watch Stash for a while?" Fletcher nodded.

Darcy took off for the stairs. "What hospital?"

"Memorial City."

175

"Don't come knocking on my door. Miranda's asleep on the couch. I'll find you when I get back."

"Oh?"

Darcy felt sure the "I'll find you" part flew straight over Lawrence's head once he heard Miranda was on the premises.

Wait till he finds out she's knocked up.

Within thirty minutes Darcy had pulled into Parking Garage 5 of Memorial City Hospital and taken the elevator up to the second floor.

"I'm looking for Viola Middleton," she told the receptionist. After not being able to locate a room number, the receptionist phoned down to Emergency. "She's just now been assigned a room. I'll let you—"

"It's about time you got here."

Darcy swung around in time to see an attendant fighting to maneuver an IV pole and Ms. Viola's hospital bed down the hallway.

"Young man, stop this thing. Now!"

Darcy's heart immediately went out to the attendant. No telling what hoops he'd already had to jump through. She ran over, grabbed Ms. Viola's hand, and shot a "Yikes, yeah I know" look at the attendant.

"Where have you been?" Ms. Viola demanded.

"Just calm down. Let's get you to your room first." Ms. Viola wasn't her grandmother, yet she felt a surprisingly strong and growing attachment toward the elderly woman.

"Oh, pu-lease." Ms. Viola sounded more disgusted than usual.

The attendant wheeled the bed into, thank goodness, a private room in a section of the hospital reserved for people being held for observation. After securing the wheel locks, he pulled an oxygen hose from its station on the wall and attempted to secure the clip around Ms. Viola's head.

She swatted his hand away. "I'm not going to wear that."

He shot a pleading glance at Darcy, who moved to take the oxygen clip from him. "Thank you," she said. She would have added a few more words like "she's really not so mean" or "be glad you get to leave," but he had gone. Probably left the building, heading out I-10 West, on foot. She swerved back toward the hospital bed. "You *are* going to wear this."

"I will not!"

"You *will* wear this or I'm leaving…right now."

Ms. Viola narrowed her eyes, then the strangest thing happened. She smiled. "Very good, Missy."

Darcy placed the oxygen hose around Ms. Viola's head, secured the nose clip, then sat on the bed. "What happened?"

"Augh," Ms. Viola blew out. "I forgot to have my diuretics refilled."

"How long have you been without them?"

Ms. Viola shrugged. "Couple of weeks, three maybe."

"And you're supposed to take it every day?"

"Don't start," Ms. Viola said. "Isn't there some place you need to be?"

An objection and what could certainly be the beginning of an argument formed on Darcy's lips. "Ahhh, will you excuse me real quick?" Before Ms. Viola could respond, she slipped out of the room and sent Sam a text. *So sorry. Have to cancel tonight. At hospital with apartment manager.*

With your apartment manager?

Darcy agreed it sounded pretty lame. She re-entered the hospital room.

"I thought you'd taken me seriously."

"Just had to send a quick text." Darcy smirked. "Besides, I'm learning how to handle your bark."

"I see that." Ms. Viola patted the bed. "Come sit."

Darcy pulled up a chair. "Go on. Tell me about this morning."

"I woke up and I couldn't breathe," Ms. Viola said. "Scared the hell outta Will. Told him to get you. Next thing I know his little fishing buddy is taking us to the hospital."

"Lawrence said you were in a lot of pain."

"Yeah, pain that you weren't home and we had to squeeze into that Ford Carnival thing."

"It's a Ford Fiesta. Why didn't you just call 911?"

"Thought I'd save a thousand bucks. You know those rides aren't cheap."

"But they could have gotten oxygen to you a lot faster."

"Well, whatever," Ms. Viola said. "Guess I'll have to give the twerp a reduction on his rent next month."

"That twerp probably saved your life. And besides, you said you'd try to be nice to him."

Ms. Viola rubbed her forehead with her non-IV arm. "Yeah, I did, didn't I?"

"You have a nephew, right? Should I call him?"

"He's been called." Ms. Viola yawned. "Should be here shortly."

"Are you comfortable?"

"The hell with comfort, there's no such thing at my age." Ms. Viola adjusted the oxygen nose clip. "How's Will?"

"I think one of his daughters came and got him for the night." Darcy paused. "Lawrence said he seemed a little confused."

"That's just great." Ms. Viola puffed. "He's going to be miserable over there. His daughters think—"

"So, why me?" Darcy interrupted. "You told Mr. Will you wanted me."

Ms. Viola eyed Darcy, then patted her arm. "Missy, we've got a lot to talk about. There are things I need for you to—"

"Aunt V!" Both women turned at the sound of someone busting through the door. "Are you okay?"

Darcy stood at the sight of a man close to her age and way more attractive.

The nephew?

"I thought your father was coming." Ms. Viola pushed herself up on the pillows. "Darcy, this is Lucas, my nephew. My great nephew, actually."

The two exchanged handshakes.

"Are you okay? Dad's on his way back from Bolivar."

"I am now that I have this diuretic pumping into me. They're keeping me overnight just so they can run up my bill." Although the words sounded bitter, the old woman's face had softened at the sight of her nephew, great or not. "What's he doing in Bolivar?"

Lucas threw out an imaginary fishing line and reeled it in. "Fishing."

"Do your aunt a favor and give Darcy your number and your dad's," Ms. Viola said. "She lives at Fountain Oaks."

Darcy handed her iPhone to Lucas to plug in the numbers. "Do you want me to stay with you tonight?" she asked Ms. Viola.

"No, I'll be fine." While Lucas busied himself loading Darcy's phone with the required phone numbers, Ms. Viola motioned for Darcy to move closer. "I guess now isn't a good time to, you know…talk." She tilted her head toward Lucas. "But promise?"

Darcy nodded and grabbed her purse. "I guess I'll let you two visit."

Lucas returned the phone. "I put our numbers under Aunt V's name. You know…easy to find."

"Sure, thanks." She turned once more to the old woman. "Do you need a ride home tomorrow?"

"We'll get her home," Lucas answered, "but thanks."

"I think she was talking to me." Ms. Viola smiled at her nephew, then turned to Darcy. "If they don't show up, I'll call you." She winked. "And see if Fletcher has put up the Christmas lights, will you? Looks damn dreary around there."

Darcy took her time getting home instead of traveling at the break-neck speed she'd driven getting to the hospital.

Look at that. Good for Fletcher.

Pulling up to Fountain Oaks, multi-colored lights lined the eaves of the two buildings, and several of the large newly planted shrubs also sported lights. In the center of the courtyard Fletcher had secured a tall, vertical PVC pipe, from which strands of lights had been angled out and anchored, forming a sort of geometric Christmas tree.

She entered her apartment to find Stash, Miranda, and Lawrence. She knew he wouldn't be able to stay away.

"Welcome!" Lawrence stood and moved to the kitchen to pour Darcy some wine. "Looks like we have something to celebrate." He handed the glass to Darcy.

"And that would be?" Darcy asked, thinking even Lawrence wouldn't actually toast Ms. Viola being rushed to the hospital.

"Miranda has been quite entertaining."

"I bet she has." Darcy peered in Miranda's direction. "So, what have the two of you been talking about?"

"Mostly this." Lawrence picked up *What to Expect* from the ottoman coffee table.

"Oh." Darcy took a sip of her wine.

"She's going to be a mommy!" Lawrence's cheesy smile looked more like he'd just received a flu shot. "Isn't that great?"

"And you're sure it's Miranda and not me?"

You sound offended you're not the one knocked up.

"I think he called it deductive reasoning." Miranda dug her hand into a bag of Cheetos.

"Well, there you go." Darcy lifted her glass. "Cheers."

Two glasses of wine and a can of Canada Dry ginger ale came together for the toast.

"So, how is our Ms. Viola?" Lawrence asked.

"Gritty as usual, but she seems to be okay." Darcy took another sip from her glass. "Thought she was going to have a poor attendant on toast for a while."

"Some things never change, do they?" Lawrence slipped on his professional face. "Although, I must admit I conducted myself rather confidently today in the midst of the emergency. Quite proud of that."

"I bet." Darcy grabbed some Cheetos. "Especially since you didn't have me to hide behind."

Lawrence's professional face slipped into a pout. "You are cruel at times, do you know that?"

"Only when poked with a stick." Darcy's eyebrows did their dance.

Lawrence folded his arms across his narrow chest. "You sound more like Ms. Viola every day."

The Cheetos chomping slowed.

Ouch, that hurt. Shit. Is that what Ms. Viola sees too? That you're just like her? Ah man, this story just keeps getting worse. Remember, you are a kind person, you do good deeds...like take care of strays.

She raised her eyes and bit the inside of her cheek. "Okay, okay...I'm sorry. Actually, it was really good you were here this morning. Miranda and I were out buying her some new...uh, things." No need to go into detail about the mammoth purchases for The Supremes.

"I accept your apology." Lawrence drained his glass. "By the way, did you see our cone-shaped Christmas tree in the courtyard?"

"Yes. And Fletcher did all the decorating today?" Fountain Oaks had been transformed into a half-festive complex.

The confident smile reappeared on Lawrence's face. "I helped."

Darcy raised her eyebrows and struggled to stop "you sound like a Shake n' Bake commercial" from escaping through her tight lips. Tacky. Not trusting herself, she settled for a nod.

"Well, actually, I untangled the cords," Lawrence said. "I don't do ladders. Looks rather nice, though, doesn't it?"

"That reminds me." Darcy padded to the bedroom and returned with a slender Christmas tree box. "Guess this needs to go up if everyone else is decorating." In less than ten minutes the three-foot tree had been de-boxed, branches straightened, and placed on the small table in front of the window. She plugged in the pre-lit tree. "There, all done."

The three stared at the stark and what could be considered Charlie Brown Christmas tree. Darcy mentally crossed her fingers and hoped Lawrence wouldn't break out in a rendition of Deck the Halls. She gazed toward her neighbor and best-friend slash soon-to-be-neighbor. She didn't know about the two of them, but it became clear Christmas would be a much bigger and more important deal next year after the birth.

Wonder if the jellybean is pink or blue?

Her fingers pulled *What to Expect* into her lap, flipped to the index and then to page 217. Twenty weeks. Still a ways to go…and a lot to do.

***

"I appreciate you coming down here Lucas," Viola said to her nephew. "If it wasn't for you and your family I'd have no family at all."

"Now, Aunt V, you know that's not true."

"It is as far as I'm concerned. And besides, they could care less. The feeling is completely mutual." Viola lifted her nose. "It's a wonder your dad turned out so well, considering the la-de-dah insanity he grew up in."

"Yeah, Dad said he always felt more comfortable hanging out with Uncle Mike at your house."

At the mention of Michael's name, the familiar knife twisted through her heart. Her hand automatically reached for the dog tags she usually kept close by. Coming up empty, she offered Lucas a forced smile. "Your dad was like my second son." Her eyes turned toward the window. "Yeah, like my second son."

"I'm sorry, Aunt V. I shouldn't have—"

"Do I have a living will?"

"Ah…I'll check, but I'm sure that's been covered with all your other—"

"And what about one of those DNA things?" Viola turned back to her nephew.

"DNR."

"Whatever. Make sure that's all in order." She rubbed her hands together. "Now. Be a good boy and go get your favorite aunt a two-piece dinner from KFC. The one with a side and a biscuit. I'll take mashed potatoes."

"I doubt that's what you should—"

"Don't make me get out of this bed, Lucas."

Her nephew breathed out defeat and pulled his cell phone from his pocket. "I'll get Dad to pick it up on his way in." He paused. "Aunt V, are you—?"

"Dark meat."

***

Sunday morning Darcy and Miranda sat cross-legged on the couch, polished off the box of Ding Dongs, caught the end of a *Sex in the City* episode, then switched to *The Perfect Storm* on AMC.

"I love old movies." Darcy refilled her coffee cup.

"Especially those with George Clooney?"

"It helps." On her return to the couch, Darcy grabbed the phone after the first ring.

"Are you coming today?"

Izzy? Ms. Viola?

She now had two grumpy old women in her life.

Better to err on the side of caution with the blood relative. "Izzy?"

"Of course, it's me," Izzy huffed. "Well? Yes or no?"

"I probably won't make it today." Darcy needed to get Miranda off on the right foot for the week, food wise. Plus, she wanted to be available in case Ms. Viola needed her.

"You got a life going on we don't know about?" Izzy asked. "We haven't seen you in weeks."

"It's just been a busy time." Actually, she felt sort of proud of herself for not going to Mommy and Daddy's every Sunday.

"Your mother will be disappointed," Izzy said.

Total BS, Izzy just wants scoop.

Besides, she'd just as soon not have to tell her grandmother she'd cancelled a date last night due to her apartment manager being rushed to the hospital. "I'll see everyone Wednesday night for my birthday, Izzy. Love you, bye." She turned to Miranda. "Drama queen." In the kitchen, about to dispose of the Ding Dong box, Darcy halted. "Hey you, on the couch. C'mere."

Miranda shuffled to the kitchen, where Darcy held an empty Canada Dry can she had pulled from the trash.

"These don't go in the trash." She pointed to a white kitchen garbage bag hanging from the pantry door. "They go there." She handed the empty Canada Dry to her friend.

"Geez. Yes, Ma," Miranda said, dropping the can in the hanging garbage bag. "Hey, you know, once I move over here I can go with you sometimes to see the fam." Miranda stuffed her bag with the few unopened ginger ale cans, her copy of *What to Expect,* and the healthy grocery list Darcy had put together for her.

"Sure you're up for that?"

"Yeah, it'll give me a chance to work on my people skills." Miranda pulled out a compact and applied lip-gloss. "It's my family tree that's full of nuts. Your parents are great. And Izzy liked me at some point, didn't she?"

Probably at birth.

Darcy only smiled, guessing Miranda's reference to people skills was directed to people other than men. "Now, we're clear on the do's and don'ts? This baby needs your full attention."

"You really *are* being a mother." Miranda zipped her overnight bag. "You might just get a new nickname. Hey, you picking me up Friday morning?"

"Nine o'clock." Darcy peeked out the front window for any sign of life at Ms. Viola's, something she'd probably be doing a lot that day. "Any problem getting off work?"

"Nah, I kinda used your story and told them I had mono. They've cut me some slack on my hours."

"We had a lot of fun this weekend, but there are still things we need to discuss."

"Like what?"

"Oh, I don't know…the father, you moving in here, fitting a car seat in your Beamer."

Miranda popped a wad of gum in her mouth. "Awww, look at you, taking care of me."

"Letting your company know about the preg—"

"Okay, I get the picture." Miranda hoisted her bag onto her shoulder. "I'm outta here." She blew Darcy an air-kiss and left.

***

"She's back." Fletcher delivered the message to Darcy, camouflage attire and water hose in tack. "She wants to see you."

Fifteen minutes later Darcy had been introduced to Tim, Ms. Viola's nephew and transportation home from the hospital.

Easy to see where Lucas gets his handsome-ness.

"You sure you'll be okay here, Aunt V?" Tim said. "You're more than welcome to stay with us for a while."

Ms. Viola winced. "Timothy, I appreciate the offer but I'm fine. Just went too long without my diuretics. Now, go home to that sweet wife of yours."

After Tim left, Darcy turned to Ms. Viola. "You sure you're okay?"

The elderly woman rearranged herself in her recliner. "Don't baby me, Missy."

Darcy folded her arms across her chest. "It's really hard to let people care about you, isn't it?"

She pointed toward the other recliner. "Sit down."

Darcy sat.

"I told you once I didn't want you to make the same mistakes I did. Remember that?"

She nodded.

"And yet you never asked what those mistakes were."

Feeling like she sat on a hot seat, she switched gears. "What about those pictures on the wall? I've never asked you about them either."

Mimicking Darcy, Ms. Viola also crossed her arms. A stand-off. After a moment, the old woman blew out air. "Okay, let's start over. Thank you for coming to the hospital yesterday…and also being here today." She paused. "Your turn."

Like making a chess move, Darcy reviewed her options. "I've got a tenant for one of the apartments. You remember my friend Miranda?"

"The human predator?"

Yep, she remembers Miranda.

"Oh, c'mon. She's changing her lifestyle and thought this would be a good place to live. She makes good money, so paying rent on time won't be an issue. And...she's pregnant."

"Well, I didn't see that coming," Ms. Viola said. "If you think it'll work, I trust your judgment." The old woman snickered and shook her head. "A baby...and she's the mother. She does know you can't keep it in the attic and only bring it out once a year to decorate, doesn't she?"

It would have been nice if Darcy had been able to come up with a reply or better yet a defense, but she was still digesting the scenario herself.

"I've got a question that's been bugging me," Ms. Viola said. "You obviously have a decent salary...you wear designer clothes and shoes I'd once have died to own." She drummed her chin with her fingers. "So, what I can't figure out is, why Fountain Oaks? Why here?"

Just like that, she'd been brought front and center with her most questionable major flaw in life...the one she had recently started to revisit. After being dumped in high school by a guy she referred to as "letter jacket guy," she'd convinced herself she needed to improve her image, which started the whole teenage fairytale dream of living happily ever after, hopefully to include a Prince Charming. Her mind's eye reverted to the letter jacket still hanging in the back of her closet. Her stomach knotted.

A waste of good closet space, if you ask me.

From that teenage heartbreak, her focus had been on two words. Designer and label. Recently, those same two words, imprinted on her brain for all those years, had been scrambled to spell something totally different...teenage and fairytale. Which led to yet two more words...immature and shallow.

She spent the next hour trying to explain the farce of a life she'd been living, omitting the letter jacket guy, which made the entire story sound that much more ridiculous. She paused only long enough to make the two of them a cup of tea. Ms. Viola had sat quietly and never interrupted until Darcy finished the gutspilling.

"And that's why I'm living here." Her eyes dropped to her lap. "I've never really told anyone all that before," realizing "all" by no means meant *all*. She surrounded herself with people who only had a couple of the puzzle pieces, and knew full well she held the letter jacket missing piece. Even Miranda hadn't been privy to this detail of her life.

"Well, there you have it." Ms. Viola broke the silence after Darcy ended her monologue. "I was right. You do remind me of myself when I was younger. I just hadn't connected all the dots."

Feeling the old woman's eyes burning a hole through her, Darcy sat up and grabbed her cup.

"If that *is* all the dots," Ms. Viola added.

She gulped her hot tea, scalding the roof of her mouth. "Uh-huh." How could relief, regret, disappointment, and embarrassment rumble through her all at the same time? "So…you wanted Prince Charming too?"

"Oh, hell yes. Doesn't every woman? Only I got all the fancy stuff when my fourth stepfather entered the picture. The marriage came with the full package. Big fancy house in West University, all the clothes and shoes…everything." Ms. Viola set her cup of tea on the table beside the cedar box. "But I ended up hating all of it. Bunch of rubbish."

"So how did *you* end up here?"

Ms. Viola swatted the question away. "Agh…maybe later. Come help me up. You asked about the pictures on the wall. I'll give you a quick tour."

Darcy assisted the woman out of the recliner and offered her arm for support.

Ms. Viola stopped in front of a black and white photo mounted in a brushed silver frame. "This is my wedding day. March 10, 1945." She moved a step and Darcy stared at the next picture in an oval frame of an older woman and a young girl. A portion of the picture to the other side of the old woman had been ripped out.

"That's me and my grandmother. I called her Nona." A soft smile eased onto Ms. Viola's face. "Oh, how I loved that woman. She was exactly what every grandmother should be. And this one—"

"Wait." Darcy stood her ground, keeping Ms. Viola in place. "Did you tear someone out of this picture?" She pointed to the missing part of the photo.

Pursing her lips, Ms. Viola seemed to roll the issue around in her mouth before she spoke. "My sister used to be there. I got tired of looking at her." The woman paused and darted her eyes at Darcy. "We don't like her."

The use of the collective word "we" kept Darcy from inquiring any further at the moment.

Ms. Viola stood in front of the next photo, her hand moving from her heart to her throat. "This is…Timothy." The photo showed two young men in military uniforms.

"Who's the other guy?" Darcy asked.

Ms. Viola shrugged. "Just a friend." She continued to the end of the row. "And here's the last picture before we enter the pet cemetery."

A man in a double-breasted suit, a cigarette in one hand, extended the other to a little boy who looked to be around two years old.

"This is an Easter picture of Robert, my husband…." Ms. Viola paused. "And…uh, Timothy." She grabbed Darcy's hand. "Now for my animals."

The woman introduced Darcy to all four of her previous dogs. Each pet picture had a little plaque mounted at the bottom of the frame citing the date of birth, date of death, and presidential name. Abe, Teddy, Woodrow, and Calvin.

Viola patted Darcy's arm. "Let's go sit back down."

"Do you have the prescriptions you need?" Darcy asked. "I'll be around this week after work if you need me, except for Wednesday night. Oh, and I'll be in Galveston for a three-day weekend." Life was getting a tad complicated with apartment rentals, Miranda's pregnancy, Ms. Viola…. "But still call if you need me."

"Ah…Galveston." Ms. Viola leaned back in the recliner and scanned upward like a video clip played across the ceiling. "Those were good days." Bitter-sweetness spread across her face. "If I'm still around…think we could make a day trip down there? I'd love to see it again."

"Uh…sure," Darcy said. "What do you mean if you're still around? Do you feel like you're dying?"

"How the hell should I know?" the old Ms. Viola barked. "I've never done it before."

Darcy narrowed her eyes. "Now, don't start that."

"I know." The woman rubbed her eyes. "Being a bitch is just so easy some times." She breathed out. "So what takes you to Galveston?"

So many really significant things had happened recently that fretting about her oh-my-God-I'm-turning-thirty-one drama seemed laughable. "My birthday is this Wednesday. I'm going to dinner with my family that night, and then Friday morning me and three of my girlfriends are heading to Tiki Island for a birthday weekend."

Before Ms. Viola could answer, someone knocked on the door.

Darcy rose. "I'll get it." She opened the door to a disheveled Mr. Will.

"Is she home? Can I come back?"

"Will, get in here," Ms. Viola ordered from the recliner.

Mr. Will plopped down in the adjacent recliner and pulled his fishing hat from his head. "You all better? Can I come back now?"

"How in the hell did you get here?" the woman asked.

Darcy, still standing at the open door, wondered the same thing.

"I took a cab." Mr. Will wiped his forehead with a handkerchief. "It was horrible over there."

"Does your daughter know you left?"

"No."

"Oh, good grief." Ms. Viola shook her head. "Darcy, hand me the phone." Ms. Viola made a quick call to Will's daughter, assuring her he had arrived safely and there was no need to worry.

Darcy wondered how long that story would fly. You could knock either one of them down with the flick of a finger. "I'll bring dinner over tonight." She didn't cook lasagna, but Stouffer's did. "And when can I tell Miranda she can move in?"

"Come by before you leave next weekend, and I'll have the lease ready. You can take it with you. The end of the month should be fine."

***

"She's leaving out a dot."

"Huh?" Mr. Will lifted his face out of the newspaper and pushed his eyeglasses up on his nose.

"Nothing," Ms. Viola said, realizing she'd left out a few of her own. "Just talking to myself."

***

188

Darcy spent the remainder of the day organizing her thoughts and making a new to-do list. Purchasing the lasagna at the store, she picked up a Sunday Chronicle and found the ad she'd placed in the classifieds. Good, one less thing.

After heating and delivering the Stouffer's dinner and a bag of Sister Schubert's rolls across the courtyard, Darcy sat on her couch with her glass of comfort wine. She replayed the afternoon with Ms. Viola, stumbling headfirst onto the highly flawed childhood and fairytale conversation. A fork in her personal road of life appeared before her. After biting the inside of her lip for a long moment, she picked up her cell phone, punched in Sam's number, and set up a lunch date for Wednesday. He didn't need to know it was her birthday, but what the heck…might as well make it a good one.

Chapter 14

Sam and Darcy sat at a rustic table at Texadelphia on Westheimer, another one of her favorite lunch spots. Actually, the entire place was rustic, which appealed to Darcy's more down-to-earth side. They both chose the "Texican" sandwich, which came with grilled onions and mozzarella cheese, and was topped with plenty of jalapenos. Darcy chose chicken, Sam, beef. A side of queso to pour on top of the sandwiches had them choosing fried pickles instead of chips and queso as an appetizer.

"Man, I'm glad you picked this place," Sam said before shoving waffle fries into his mouth.

"I thought after 13 Celsius you'd be way above all this." Darcy downed the last of her ice tea and nodded to the waiter standing nearby for a refill.

"Are you kidding? I was trying to impress you. I don't know about you, but dating these days is a bitch." Sam leaned across the table and formed a tee-pee with his fingers. "Have you ever tried Internet dating?"

Darcy scratched her nose. Honest, or an in-the-know answer? "Uh…I've actually gone to some of the sites, but haven't quite gotten past the whole profile thing. I guess you have?"

"I've tried a couple of times." He wiped queso from his mouth with a napkin. "It's…well, it's like playing fantasy football. Nothing's real. It sucks."

"My friend, Miranda, has been pestering me for ages to give it a shot." She picked up a waffle fry and pointed it in Sam's direction. "You know Miranda…that's where I met you. At her Halloween party."

"Oh yeah," Sam said. "Catwoman."

And you brought Miranda's name up why?

She studied her lunch date. First impressions could be deceiving. On date number one he'd seemed a little too sure of himself, but not today. She'd been right about his height though…at least 6'4". His ears and nose seemed a little large for his head—*like mine aren't*—but he had a nice smile…and a sense of humor. And he liked Texadelphia. And he'd carried Lawrence to her car. The first time he ever saw her she had spent hours trying to be a Paris Hilton clone. The second time she'd tried to impress him with her hotsy-totsy outfit and designer shoes she couldn't wait to shed as soon as she hit the apartment.

"One of my good friends." Sam air-quoted good. "An Internet-dating guru, got me invited to the Halloween party. And *that's* a perfect example of what I'm talking about. These people hook up on the Internet." He paused for a swig of iced tea. "Get a group of them together and you end up with a room full of people who've probably lied about their careers, their age, weight, and who knows what else." Sam picked up half his sandwich. "Total BS. Who needs that?"

Her Wednesday lunch date turned out way better than she expected, especially in lieu of the fact she had to meet up with the tribe that evening at Christie's. She'd been able to halfway explain having to cancel their date on Saturday, and felt relatively okay he believed her…which was good, because as ridiculous as it sounded, it was true.

"Would you like to go out again sometime?" Sam asked.

Darcy dropped her hands to her lap. "Yes."

"With me?"

"Oh…yes."

"How about this weekend?"

Rats. She had to turn him down, and ended up spilling the beans about her birthday and the weekend ahead. They did, however, decide on getting together the Friday night before Christmas, just a little over a week away. She reached for the bill and he beat her to it.

"I'd like to buy your birthday lunch," he said.

"Oh," she said, and smiled.

And manners, too. Remember that in case you have to come up with something good for Izzy.

***

192

The annual shebang at Christie's was pretty non-descript, thank goodness. She'd had enough recent disturbances in her life to last a while. Izzy had her ritual martini, and everyone ordered shrimp dinners—with the exception of her shell-fish-allergic soon-to-be-sister-in-law, who opted for the Greek salad with chicken to avoid any complications. Actually, Darcy kind of wondered how someone who looked like they'd been carved out of cream cheese would fare with a blow-fish allergic reaction. Mean. She'd have to rethink that. A lot of her thoughts these days seemed to be falling under the "rethink" category.

Andie wore appropriate clothing for a change, nothing neon or overtly pierced, but acted totally bored the entire evening, evident by the constant texting between her and whoever.

Alex and Anna announced their wedding date…June 23. Darcy's throat had tightened. She'd surely be asked to fill a bridesmaid position. Hopefully Miranda would go full term, or either she'd have to explain possibly missing the ordeal due to a prior labor coach agreement. Oh well, she had months to agonize over that one.

Her parents gave her a Visa gift card, as did Alex and Anna. Everyone knew the drill…all except Izzy, who produced a pair of glittery Santa Claus dangle earrings.

"Remember I said I got you something at the craft show? They look just like you." From the smile on Izzy's face, she couldn't tell if her grandmother had sincere or snarky up her Kleenexed sleeve. Her mother coughing into her napkin did little to help alleviate the situation.

Not too bad of an evening, or day, for that matter. And with all the talk at the table, plus Izzy's martini, there hadn't been one word mentioned about, well…the dating scene, which Darcy always considered a huge plus.

***

By 9:00 Friday morning, Darcy and Miranda were working their way through Midtown traffic, with one quick stop at the VA Hospital before heading out I-45 South. The animal kingdom would be looked after by her sister. Hopefully Andie would remember…otherwise she'd probably have to have the carpet ripped out, along with her sister's hide. She'd stopped by Ms. Viola's the night before to pick up Miranda's lease, and had been handed a double batch of the woman's super-special chocolate chip cookies.

"What's this?" Darcy had asked.

Ms. Viola had shrugged her reply. "I'd normally say 'what does it look like' but I'm working on my attitude. It's for your girls' weekend."

Arriving in the Medical Center at the VA Hospital, Darcy quickly delivered the remaining afghans to the front desk, asking if they could be delivered to a volunteer. She'd held on to them long enough to get in trouble if quizzed by Ms. Viola.

"So," Darcy said when they passed Baybrook Mall, one of her "road to Galveston" markers. "I'm guessing we tell Becca and Lisa?"

"Might as well, Boop, since I'll be the only one drinking ginger ale." Miranda half-laughed. "You think they'll be shocked?"

"I'd say that's definitely a possibility. I read in the book last night you probably shouldn't get in the hot tub…maybe just dangle your feet in or something."

"Yeah, I read that too. Belly stays out of the hot tub."

Darcy stole her eyes from the road to shoot Miranda a quick glance.

"Yes, I read, Boop. I'm gonna be a good student."

Don't you hope so?

"I think we should have the Captain Kirk talk now. You know, get it over with."

Miranda let out a loud burp, as if defining how she felt about the baby-daddy. "He's a jerk."

"Do you still talk to him?"

"Nah, he's moved on. Hit the dusty trail. Got the hell out of Dodge…what a player."

"Is he going to pay child support?" Darcy's grip tightened on the steering wheel. She could have been in this same situation years ago, and she sensed Miranda felt way more pain than she let on.

"I don't want anything from him." Miranda almost spit out the words. "With any luck this little jellybean won't have any of his asshole father in him. Or her."

"Are you sure that's the way you want it? I mean, you could take him to court."

Miranda leaned back against the headrest. "Hey, I've been meaning to ask. Do you like *Jersey Shore* or the Kardashians?

Snooki or Kim? I can't decide. And when the hell did Oprah go off the air?"

Darcy got the message. "That's two quarters for the swear jar."

"Asshole counts?"

"It counts."

They rode in silence for quite a while. The Bayou Vista exit produced the first sign of gulf water, which meant they were only minutes away from Tiki Island. Darcy smiled. As a little girl she'd referred to the ocean as "the big water," and seeing the inlet immediately snatched her back to that feeling of wonder. She took exit 4, veered past the Valero on the corner, and barreled down Tiki Island Drive.

"Hey Boop, don't forget about Barney."

Darcy slammed on the brakes, dropping her speed below thirty miles per hour. "Glad you reminded me."

Barney Fife, the security cop on the island, received his nickname from, who else, Miranda. And sure enough, ahead they could see a patrol car wedged between two sego palms off to the right side of the road. Miranda waved when they crept by. Darcy felt relieved that's all she did. In Miranda's earlier and if possible, wilder years, offering a universal finger sign or even mooning would not have been out of the question. Who knew, after all the years of going to their friend's Tiki Island home, the badge and single bullet in the pocket could have been passed off to several different guys. But the main objective, the speed trap down the wide open Tiki Island Drive, remained the same.

Friday turned out to be a clear, cool day on Tiki Island. The bay house perched perfectly at the end of a canal, with a huge upstairs deck on the backside extending out over the water. The downstairs looked like any Caribbean Island bar, outfitted with an actual thatched hut bar area, palm tree umbrellas, tables and bar stools, love seats, a neon Corona sign, and a flat screen TV. A swimming pool and Jacuzzi sat off to the side. Ceiling fans helped move the breeze along in the summer; outside stand-alone heaters accommodated people during the handful of winter months. Jet skis and a fishing boat hung from their respective slings, and a couple of kayaks were mounted to the side of the fish-cleaning area. Many fun times had been had there.

Too early in the day to sit by the pool due to the chilly breeze, Miranda, already munching on a couple of Ms. Viola's cookies, went ahead and spilled the news about the jellybean. Brooding wasn't Miranda's style. The most sulking Darcy could ever remember from her best friend was the day she'd found her in her apartment swimming in empty Sunny D bottles. Since then she'd snapped back to her snarky self in record time.

After the initial shock—c-o-m-e o-n, girls like Miranda were supposed to know better; at least that's what Izzy would say—the questions started. Miranda handled most of them with not quite a flippant attitude, but close. The nurturing-mommy-excitement had yet to fully kick in. Darcy wondered how and when that boulder would actually drop into place. *What To Expect* stated the full realization sometimes didn't hit until the first time movement was felt, which according to Darcy's calculations probably wouldn't happen for another month or so. And even then, knowing Miranda, the front-and-center-smack-in-the-face-reality could possibly take longer.

As expected, Miranda, in her PJ's and a few chocolate chip cookies in hand, had found a pillow and conked out in one of the bedrooms before ten o'clock. And, also as expected, the *real* discussion started.

"I didn't see that coming. Did you?"

"When she said she had something to tell us, I was thinking more like a DUI, or a being busted for pot."

"How did you find out?"

"Does her mother know?"

"How is she going to do this? I mean, we *are* talking about Miranda."

"I think we need to hunt this creep down."

"I'll give her a baby shower."

"No, let's all do it."

"Do *your* parents know what you're doing?"

"Is she really going to move to your apartments?"

"I can't believe this happened."

"Miranda…a mommy."

"I've got tons of stuff she can use." Lisa crossed her fingers. "Hopefully I won't be using the baby things again."

"I can submit the petition for child support." Becca pulled out her iPhone and made a note.

Darcy nodded. "I know. It's been a strange two weeks." She went into more details about tracking Miranda down at her apartment and banging on the door till she opened up. "And I couldn't believe the shape she was in…or her loft." Darcy took a sip of her wine. "It scared the shit out of me. I mean, I'm the one who usually freaks out over things, but her place looked like a makeshift cave for a homeless person living on nothing but crackers and Sunny D."

"Well, I'm proud of you," Becca said.

"Me too," Lisa added. "Just look at you, taking charge like you did. Getting her to the doctor? I'm impressed."

"Yeah, I'm kind of shocked about that too," Darcy said. "I don't think Miranda is as tough as she wants us, or anybody for that matter, to believe. And things have really started to change around Fountain Oaks." Not that she felt ready to have them do a drive-by. "Looks a whole lot better. And I've even done the walk-through on Miranda's apartment. But Becca, you're gonna have to hold up on the child support issue."

"Why?" Becca reached for her wine glass. "She doesn't have to do this on her own."

"I talked to her about that on the way down here." Darcy scratched the side of her head. "She doesn't want the help. Actually, she doesn't want anything from him."

"She may regret that," Lisa said. "I don't think she has a clue how much it costs to raise a baby."

"All I'm saying," Darcy said, "is now isn't the time. If you think back to her childhood and all the daddys Cheryl brought home." She air-quoted daddys. "I doubt she has a very high opinion of men."

"Miranda?" Lisa rearranged herself on the overstuffed couch. "Men is *all* she's in to."

"Yeah, but she usually keeps the upper hand in all her encounters." Darcy gathered the wine glasses and scooted to the kitchen for refills and the remainder of the cookies. "Maybe it's that she's never really had a good male role model. You know, a strong father figure." Darcy surprised herself with the male role model bit.

Me too.

197

After kicking around Darcy's profound words, Becca spoke. "I think you're right."

"I do too." Lisa accepted her refilled wine glass.

***

Saturday morning, after Darcy retrieved plastic bottles and aluminum cans from the trash and gave the women her spiel on recycling, the four drove over the causeway into Galveston and cruised down the seawall to decide on their lunch stop. Today, the Seawall...tomorrow before heading back, someplace down on The Strand.

"Oh look." Miranda pointed off to the left. "The Poop Deck! Man, does that ever bring back memories."

Darcy rolled her eyes, and she could bet that Becca and Lisa did the same at Miranda's reference to the popular biker hangout with more than one skull and crossbones flag waving in the salty breeze.

"Remember that time I—?"

"Yes," the other three piped in.

"We had to come get you after you hooked up with that dude on the beach who wouldn't bring you back to the bay house," Becca said.

"Nah, not that time," Miranda said. "I was thinking about when that guy, oh what was his name...?"

"Make up one," Lisa said. "Let's call him Rocko. Now, what happened with Rocko?"

"I was this close to getting a tattoo." Miranda used her thumb and index finger to measure less than an inch. "A real one too, not like the kind we got in Vegas."

"Oh, I remember him." Becca smiled at Miranda in the backseat. "He actually *did* bring you back to the bay house. Those were the days we almost gave my parents coronaries."

Miranda rocked back against the seat, chewing gum and gazing out the window. "Yeah, he was one of the good ones."

"What about there?" Darcy pointed to one of the Seawall's most popular restaurants.

"Fine with me," Miranda said, "but just a warning. I can't stomach seafood. Makes me want to puke. I'll find some kind of chicken something. Just please, no oysters on the half-shell today."

Darcy's thoughts immediately swerved back to Anna, and the way she'd secretly mocked her brother's fiancée about having a seafood allergy. Guess that wouldn't be happening anymore.

The hostess ushered them to their table. A waiter, dressed in the traditional black slacks, white collared button-down shirt, and black tie, introduced himself as Jess and handed each woman a menu. He then proceeded to recite the specials of the day.

"I'll have the chicken BLT," Miranda said to the waiter. "The bacon will give me heartburn, but what else is new." She handed over her menu. "And a Perrier with lemon."

After the other three ordered, Lisa, the seasoned mother of the group, started in with the pregnancy questions. "So, anything besides seafood make you want to puke?"

Miranda grimaced. "Raw meat. I can't even go near any of that stuff in the grocery store." She buttered a piece of warm bread. "And green beans. Go figure that one."

"I hated brussel sprouts when I was pregnant," Lisa said.

"I hate brussel sprouts, period." Becca also helped herself to some bread.

"What I've been craving is Whataburger chicken strips with cream gravy." Miranda buttered her second piece of bread. "And I could live on ice cream, but Ms. Nutritionist here…." She nodded to Darcy. "Has me on a healthy diet. Only once a week on the chicken strips and gravy, but I still get a small bowl of ice cream at night." She batted her eyelashes at Darcy. "Isn't that sweet of her?"

"So what about breastfeeding?" Lisa started. "Are you going to do that?"

"Now that'll make me puke." Miranda brushed breadcrumbs off her hands and stuck out her chest. "Have you seen these things? They've taken on a life of their own."

The other three laughed.

"I'm serious." Miranda's eyes widened. "When I lay on my back at night they head out in opposite directions, like they need their own pillow or something. I don't think babies come with mouths that big." She paused. "Do they?"

Darcy choked on her water and Becca gave her a couple of swift pats between the shoulder blades, while Lisa found words between gulps of laughter. "Believe me, it's possible. Don't worry, they'll teach you about all that. Just had to ask."

"My BFF here gives me reading assignments." She pulled *What to Expect* from her oversized satchel purse. "She tells me what I can read...says it gets scary if I get too far ahead of myself."

Lisa finished off half of her shrimp po-boy and looked at Darcy. "I am so impressed with you!"

"Oh stop." Darcy felt a flush move up her face. "I'm not doing anything. She's the one having the baby."

"Don't sell yourself short, Boop," Miranda said. "I'd still be wallowing around in cracker dust and drinking my weight in Sunny D if it wasn't for you."

"I'm with her, Darcy." Becca nodded toward Miranda. "You've really stepped up to the plate."

Later that evening, Darcy wrapped a blanket around her shoulders and wandered out on the deck after everyone had gone to sleep. The cool, salty night breeze brushed across her face and through her hair. She pulled the blanket tighter and leaned against the deck rail. Although on the bay instead of the beach, the water in the canal always seemed to have movement. Flickers from the half-moon rippled little sparkles in the water.

"Why here? Why Fountain Oaks?"

"So, you wanted Prince Charming too?"

"Oh, hell yes."

"I'm proud of you."

"Me too."

"Don't sell yourself short, Boop."

"You've really stepped up to the plate."

Her thoughts turned back to the letter jacket. "Agh."

***

Sunday morning Darcy and Miranda took a walk around Tiki Island. Walking also appeared on Miranda's "do-what's-right-for-the-baby" regimen, compliments of Darcy.

"So, who's this guy you're seeing?" Miranda asked.

"You've met him, but you probably don't remember." Darcy stopped to pull her right leg back, stretching out her thigh muscle. "He was the token Batman at your party. His name is Sam."

"I do remember a Batman." Miranda did some side stretches. "Never saw the face without the mask. What's he like?"

"Not bad. He went all out on our first date and took me to 13 Celsius, then to Osaka's." Darcy stretched out the other thigh. "Must have dropped some bucks that night."

"Did I invite him to the party?" Miranda asked.

"He said some buddy of his is an Internet-dating guru and got him invited."

"Oh yeah? Well, he ought to pick better friends." Miranda puffed. "Does he hang out a lot with this 'guru'?" She air quoted guru.

"I don't think so. Why?"

"Let's just say you could add 'asshole' to the Internet-dating guru title."

Darcy halted. "Captain Kirk?"

"Yep, in the creepy flesh."

"You get a pass on the swear jar this time."

The four women lunched at a restaurant a couple of blocks off the actual Strand but directly on the water, adjacent to the docked Disney Carnival cruise ship. Miranda held her nose until they entered the restaurant due to the nearby fish markets and shrimp boats. They were seated next to a window with a full view of the cabin cruisers, cigarette boats, sailboats, and all the other sea-worthy vehicles traveling down the waterway to the Intercoastal Canal.

Lisa eyed Miranda. "You okay?"

"Yeah," Miranda said, then shivered. "The smell just makes me want to gag." She unpinched her nose. "Glad it's better in here." She decided on the chicken Romano while the other three avoided the tempting oysters on the half shell, but found suitable seafood alternatives.

The talk of Miranda over the weekend sort of trumped the birthday, which Darcy found totally acceptable. She did end up with more gift cards, although these were from Banana Republic, The Gap, and Macy's. The Fountain Oaks lease had been signed, and Miranda would move into the downstairs apartment adjacent to Lawrence on December 30. Miranda had no problem subletting her loft, saying she'd found a decent guy from her Rolodex to finish out her lease.

A guy? Woo-hoo, big surprise.

She arrived back home, checked to make sure her apartment hadn't been hit by a wrecking crew, and then returned the signed lease to Ms. Viola. During her absence, lights had been strung around the doorframe, and a small decorated tree could be seen through the mini blinds.

After she knocked Mr. Will answered, his finger to his lips. "She's sleeping."

Darcy handed him the lease. "How's she feeling?"

Mr. Will shrugged. "Not too bad. Her nephew and his wife came for a visit today. Put up a tree." The old man took a step back, pulling the door with him. "Wanna see?"

"No, no." Darcy stood her ground. "I don't want to disturb her if she's resting."

"Wait here." Mr. Will disappeared behind the door and returned with a folded sheet of paper. "If you came by, she wanted me to give you this."

Darcy took the paper and nodded. "Uh, does Ike need walking or anything? I've got some time."

Mr. Will's boney finger pointed toward the courtyard. "Fletcher's got him out somewhere. Wanted to know if the damn dog could spend the night." The old man snorted. "A canine sleepover."

In the past, Darcy would have retorted with an equal if not more sarcastic remark. Tonight, however, she thought how fortunate Ike and Fletcher were to have each other.

Surprised, but not sure why, she found Lawrence sitting outside her front door, a small gift bag in his lap. She shoved the note in her pocket.

"Happy Birthday." He held up the present. "I'm know, I'm late. Did you have fun on your girls' weekend? How's Miranda?"

Darcy opened the door and held Stash's collar till Lawrence had entered. He headed to the kitchen and held up a wine glass. "Shall I?"

"Why not?" She plopped onto the couch, itching to read the note in her pocket.

"Open your present."

She pulled the ribbon from the gift bag and extracted a corkscrew.

"I noticed you didn't have one." Lawrence set two filled glasses on the ottoman coffee table.

"Aw, gee, thanks." *That's because I drink wine from a box, you moron*, she would have said. However, like Ms. Viola, she had been working on her attitude and kept her trap shut.

"I have a favor to ask," Lawrence said.

Only after he'd pulled a handkerchief from his back pocket did Darcy notice the thin bead of sweat on his upper lip. "What's wrong? Are you ill?"

"Quite frankly, I do feel ill." He blotted his lip area and forehead. "But I know it's just nerves." He inhaled sharply. "You see, my parents have invited me over for lunch on Christmas Eve. Not dinner, mind you…lunch."

Darcy's mental radar reverted to high alert status.

"Will you go with me?"

Before Darcy could open her mouth, Lawrence moved beside her on the couch and locked his fingers like a little kid saying a night-night prayer. "I'm begging you. I know I've been a nuisance, but if you have an ounce of compassion for me at all you'll at least consider it."

She took a sip of her wine and crossed one knee over the other. "Sure, why not."

"At least consider—" Lawrence's eyes rounded. "You will? Did you just say 'sure, why not'?"

"Yeah, I'll go." She tilted her head. "I'm going to my parents' house that night, but lunch ought to work." She ushered Lawrence through the front door and with his mouth still O-shaped, she felt the timing to be perfect. "And by the way, Miranda is moving into the apartment next to yours a week from Friday." She closed the door, her eyebrows doing their mischievous dance, reasoning mischievous sounded better than sarcasm, and her last tidbit of Miranda moving in could cause the O-shape to last for a while.

She pulled the piece of paper from her pocket and read the decrepit scrawl. "Hmm, that's weird." Using an "I Love My Pets" magnet, she secured Ms. Viola's message to the refrigerator.

Chapter 15

The following week progressed without much commotion except for Lawrence checking daily to make sure they were still on for lunch at the Ousted's on Christmas Eve. Actually, she looked forward to the event out of mere curiosity. Who were these people? Lorelai's parents? She'd watched *Gilmore Girls* for years and spent many hours daydreaming of being Lorelai. Except in *her* fantasy, her parents, though filthy rich, would be much nicer and Luke, her beautiful hunk of a boyfriend, would have a more profitable career than running the local diner.

In her mind, she pictured Mr. and Mrs. Ousted to be Richard and Emily Gilmore, living in digs closely resembling *Downton Abby*. Although she knew, as humongous as some of the estates were in River Oaks, even the wealthiest didn't live the aristocratic life of Lord Grantham and his lot. She knew this because she'd recently made the switch from reality shows to something with more substance…*Downton Abby*. Before that, she had no idea what or who could be called an aristocrat…or a lord, for that matter.

Ms. Viola had rebounded somewhat, now back on her daily diuretic medication, and two things had been agreed upon between her and Miranda. They would touch base once a day, and the swear jar would be shelved until the birth of JB, Miranda's nickname for her jellybean. She'd talked to Sam twice during the week, and each time the conversation had become more relaxed. He'd told her he had Friday night already planned, and it would not require wearing anything dressy.

"Just something comfortable," he had said. She even agreed to him picking her up at her apartment. A first e-v-e-r. What had happened to all the pretentiousness she'd hauled around all these years of living in a shambles of an apartment complex merely for an

Uptown zip code? Nothing had changed, yet everything seemed different.

An honest to God cold front blew in Thursday night, dropping the temperature early Friday morning into the mid-thirties. Now it *really* felt like Christmas. Cutting her workday short, Darcy sped home, showered, and dressed in an Ann Taylor Loft Ombre stripe cotton sweater she'd snagged at Marshalls, jean leggings, and her Frye Lindsay Plate knee boots. She pulled on the DKNY trench coat she'd bought before the sun came up Black Friday a year ago and stood in front of the mirror. She bit the inside of her mouth and narrowed her eyes. Something didn't feel right. She dug through her closet until she found a pair of Style&co. Ryder boots she'd bought on clearance from Macy's. She may have paid thirty-five dollars for them, and up until now they had been part of her low-end menagerie of shoes she kept handy for appearances at her parents' house. She slipped the high-dollar fancy riding boots back into their designer box and pulled on the oh-how-tacky-because-they're-cheap boots. She returned to the mirror and tilted her chin upward. Shrugging out of the designer coat, she retrieved the faux leather bomber jacket she'd tagged at Target several years ago. There. Much better.

The evening with Sam was the best date she'd had in…well, probably ever. After he picked her up, they headed to the Canyon Café for a leisurely dinner before walking the levels of the eloquently decorated Galleria and admiring the ginormous and utterly breath-taking Christmas tree sitting in the middle of the ice skating rink. Everything held a sense of excitement for what was to come, freshness…happiness.

Christmas can ring magic, if you let it. She loved her alter ego when she came up with something truly refreshing.

Sam grabbed her hand when they left the glitter of the multi-story mall and headed toward the nearby infamous Williams Water Wall. She'd lived in the Galleria area for several years and had always known of the Water Wall…had even caught a glimpse of it when she'd inched from red light to red light in the congested area. But tonight was the first time she'd ever really seen, really appreciated the beauty of the towering sky-high water structure.

Stopping inside the concave arch of the waterfall, Sam raised his eyes. "Do you know how tall it is?"

The icy mist hitting her face from the cascading waters sent a shiver through her. "Not a clue."

"Sixty-four feet, to represent the sixty-four floors of the Williams Tower…which of course, used to be the Transco Tower. Eleven thousand gallons of water per minute spill over that wall."

"How do you know all that?"

"Because I'm a total nerd when it comes to architecture," he said. "And I checked my stats on the plaque over there." He squeezed her hand. "Are you impressed?"

"That you're a nerd or that you can read?" poured out of her mouth, matching the rate of the water falling over the wall.

Sam pulled back like he'd caught a whiff of bad cheese.

Where the hell did that idiotic remark come from? It's like when you try so hard to say the right thing you always screw up…like that time you swore in church.

"Gee, I didn't mean that." She mentally rolled her eyes.

"Do the Hallmark people know about you, because you're a natural."

Darcy scrunched up her nose. "You might as well know this. I can be a real smartass sometimes; but you and the rest of the world ought to appreciate the fact that I'm working on it."

"Glad to hear that."

She couldn't tell from his tone whether he was sincere or contemplating slowing down to thirty miles an hour before pushing her out at her place on his way home. She hated it when words spewed from her mouth the exact moment she realized she needed to reel them back in. What was wrong with her? Sam was a nice guy…a really nice guy. Okay, so she wasn't crazy about the sweater vest he wore tonight, but thought it looked pretty stylish with the untucked button down he wore underneath.

Do you hear yourself? And you think Lawrence is a moron? I'd hand you a shovel for that hole you're digging, but it'd probably just slow you down. Quick, do or say something before you start pumping him for his credit score, you snob.

Darcy moved to stand in front of him. They were so close the tips of their shoes touched. She grabbed the lapels of his jacket, reached up, and placed a soft kiss on his lips. "I really am sorry."

He eyed her, a hint of his own mischief lurking. "Okay, but when you get home, you need to find a new therapist, because the one you have isn't working." He kissed her back, as quick and gentle as hers had been. "Want some coffee? I'm freezing."

Good save. And learn from your own mistakes, bone-head.

They ended up with warm specialty Christmas drinks from Starbucks at the corner of Post Oak and Westheimer, across the street from the Galleria.

Darcy ran her finger around the edge of her red holiday-themed cup. "What does your family do for Christmas?" She paused. "Or, maybe I should start with…tell me about your family? Do they live here?"

"Yeah, most of us. My parents and my younger brother." Sam used his stir stick to draw designs in the whipped cream of his peppermint mocha. "My older brother lives in Denver. He and his family will be flying in tomorrow."

"Three boys. No girls?"

"Nope, just a lot of testosterone in the house growing up."

"My three sons."

"Something like that." Sam finished his coffee. "I'm driving out to my parents' house in The Woodlands tomorrow after they fly in. Want to come?"

"Uh, well…thanks, but I can't." Darcy dropped her eyes to her lap. "I, uh, sorta have plans. I promised someone I'd have lunch with him and his parents. It's kind of important."

Sam nodded. "You've…got a date."

"What?" Her eyes bulged, thinking this was the point in the horror movie where the entire audience screamed "don't go in there." "Oh God, no. It's Lawrence!"

He shrugged. "Who's Lawrence?"

"Lawrence, the wimpy Howdy Doody you carried to my car the night I met you. He's my neighbor."

Relief, or what Darcy chose to call it, smoothed over Sam's face. "Ah, yes. The little guy with the furry chaps."

The night had been saved, at least she felt it had, by the way-longer-and-more-sensual exchanged kiss at the end of the evening. A nice date. And if she didn't blow it, maybe there'd be more.

***

"We're late. We're late. Can't you drive any faster? Oh, run that red light. No one's coming." Lawrence's hands grasped the side of the passenger seat in Darcy's SUV.

"You sound like the white rabbit in *Alice in Wonderland*," Darcy said. "I rarely say this to people who aren't me, but you've *got* to calm down."

"You don't understand." Lawrence gripped the seat tighter when Darcy rounded a corner. "Lunch is at noon. *Precisely* at noon."

"So, say we get there at five or ten after; we don't get to eat?"

"Oh, we'll get fed...eventually." Lawrence checked his watch for the umpteenth time. "But there will be a delay, and no doubt we will be assured it is because of our tardiness. Not to mention the lecture on punctuality."

Darcy glanced at the digital clock on the dash, picking up on Lawrence's anxiety while she barreled down San Felipe. "Just tell me where to turn."

Lawrence shot an arm out to the left. "Here!"

"Well, crap." Darcy missed the left turn lane, flew through the intersection, and maneuvered a three-point turn, which had them turning right on River Oaks Blvd.

"Go straight."

Darcy had slowed her speed to a reasonable crawl just to gawk at the mansions on either side of the wide boulevard. Nearing the end of this magnificent yellow-brick road, she hit her brakes. She'd been wrong. The Ousted's *did* live in a *Downton Abby* castle.

"Holy shit. Is that it?"

"Fortunately, no. Take a left. That's the River Oaks Country Club. My parent's house is much smaller." Lawrence extended his neck to peer down the road, as if no longer sure of the neighborhood where he'd grown up.

She followed directions, the reasonable crawl now down to a bare idle. A senior jogger could make better time than her SUV.

"Here." Lawrence's pointed finger shook. "Turn in."

Darcy followed the shaky finger and inched up the pebbled circle driveway. She shut off the engine and peered up through the windshield. "Not *much* smaller. Where's the moat and the drawbridge?"

Lawrence checked his watch. "You're a saint. We're even two minutes early. How can I ever thank you?"

"Don't spend our last two minutes thanking me. I'm hungry and I don't want to beg for food. Get out!"

Mrs. Emily Gilmore Ousted opened the door herself.

"Hello, Lawrence." She extended her hand to Darcy. "I'm Frances Ousted, Lawrence's mother. Won't you come in?"

Darcy accepted the limp hand. "I'm Darcy. Thank you for having me."

"Hello, Mother." Lawrence moved to place an obligatory kiss on the highly made-up offered cheek.

So far, Mrs. Ousted had nailed the Emily Gilmore routine, even down to the linen slacks, two-piece sweater set, and single strand pearl necklace. They were ushered through a mile-high museum foyer with imported marble tiled floor, large enough to land a private plane in, to a formal living room off to the right. Darcy didn't know as much as she often pretended to, but she knew for a fact she was in way over her head.

The walls were painted a dark charcoal trimmed with gleaming white triple crowned molding. The room itself had been filled with austere and extremely intimidating black and white furnishings. In the corner stood a Christmas tree equal in height to the ten-foot ceiling and adorned with every sort of white frosted or feathered decoration possible; doves, poinsettias, bows, snowflakes, angels, bells, icy white branches...each one strategically placed for balance around the tree. There were no lights and no presents.

Do you think she actually watches Gilmore Girls?

Darcy could just picture Emily Gilmore strolling through Nordstrom's and spotting this exact tree in a display. "I'll take that one," Emily would say.

"Your father will be joining us shortly." Mrs. Ousted lowered herself into a white leather chair. "Do sit."

The statement, obviously meant for Lawrence, could well have been delivered to anyone...or no one. Mrs. Ousted made zero eye contact with either of them. Lawrence and Darcy sat side by side on the edge of the matching white leather couch.

"I see you've redecorated since I've been away." Lawrence slid back on the couch, obviously trying for a relaxed pose.

"Yes." Mrs. Ousted raised her eyes to Darcy. "And what line of work are you in?"

Darcy felt heat moving from her backside all the way to her face, like she had been sitting on a heating pad, which made her feel more than uncomfortable. This woman had totally and purposely dissed her own son. What a bitch for a mother. "I sell eyewear for Gucci," she said. "Most of Houston is my area."

"I believe Lawrence said you were neighbors," Mrs. Ousted said.

"Yes." Darcy felt her mental radar come to high status.

"So you find that place suitable?"

Ba-zinga. There it was. The slap and dis had spread to her spot on the couch. She suddenly had a flash of what a crappy childhood Lawrence had. Who did this woman think she was anyway? She moved to the edge of the couch like a mother lion ready to protect her cub from approaching danger. "Yes, and as a matter of fact—"

"And where *is* Dad?" Lawrence said, and nonchalantly touched Darcy's elbow to quiet her.

"He had a meeting at the club," Mrs. Ousted said.

"Someone mention my name?"

Darcy and Lawrence stood at the sound of the male voice.

"Hello Dad." Lawrence offered his hand. Mr. Ousted, a handsome and extremely tall man, shook Lawrence's hand. "Oh hell, come here." Totally catching Lawrence off guard, the father pulled his son in for a rousing hug. "How have you been, son?" Mr. Ousted, dressed in the traditional Ousted khaki slacks, a button-down shirt open at the collar, and a stylish yet casual sport coat, pulled Lawrence back as if to get a closer look at his MIA son.

Lawrence's arms were pinned to his side and his face looked as if he'd just been hit by a stun gun. "I'm...good, Dad. Thanks for asking."

"And you must be his neighbor." Mr. Ousted once again extended his hand. "William Ousted. Welcome."

Darcy accepted and returned the large, warm handshake. "Darcy Daniels. I'm happy to meet you."

More so than Mommy Dearest perched over there on her icy white throne.

"C'mon, let's eat." Mr. Ousted glanced at his wife. "We're ready, aren't we?"

"Yes, I suppose so." Mrs. Ousted left her seat and led the group to the dining room.

If not for Lawrence's dad, lunch would have been as much fun as learning you'd maxed out your only credit card in the pre-dawn hours of Black Friday. The conversation, although light and borderline superficial, carried them through dessert.

"Excuse me." Mrs. Ousted rose. "I'll see that we have coffee in by the tree."

Ah yes, it was Christmas Eve, an event obviously easy to overlook in this cold, dark house. Darcy referred to it as a house because it damn sure didn't feel like a home.

Once Lawrence's mother left the room, Mr. Ousted leaned his elbows on the table. "You'll have to excuse your mother. I think her medications need some tweaking," he said, and then winked. "Let's move to the living room."

Lawrence and Darcy smiled, mostly from shock, but also from a total lack of a response.

After coffee, next to the unlit and almost scary Christmas tree, Lawrence's dad rose. "I have to admit I have a little last minute shopping to take care of."

"Yes, well, we must be going," Lawrence immediately came to his feet.

"I'll see you to the door." Mrs. Ousted wasted no time moving toward the foyer.

"It was a pleasure to meet you Darcy," Mr. Ousted said. "I see Lawrence has made a good friend." From the inside of his sport coat he produced an envelope and handed it to Lawrence. "This is from me."

Lawrence pocketed the envelope. "Thanks Dad."

Mrs. Ousted stood at the door holding two small packages. Darcy recognized the Neiman Marcus signature wrapping.

"These are for each of you. We appreciate you dropping by," Mrs. Ousted said. "Do have a Merry Christmas."

"Thank you, Mother." Lawrence moved in for the exit cheek kiss.

Sitting in the SUV, Darcy could hardly find words...but she managed a few. "Are you shitting me? We appreciate you dropping by?"

"Isn't she lovely?" Lawrence stared at the mansion through the windshield. "She makes you proud, doesn't she? Whoever came up with the chant 'sticks and stones may break my bones, but words can never hurt me' must have been an idiot."

"That's some serious weirdness. I'm surprised she didn't drown you at birth." Darcy shook her head. "I had no idea people like that really existed."

And you've been holding out for all that, Ms. High and Mighty?

"If you look in the society page in the Sunday paper you'll probably see Frances Ousted at some charity event in all her finery." He paused. "You know the ironic part?"

Darcy sat still, not wanting to disturb Lawrence's train of thought.

"It's usually for a children's charity." A disturbed laugh escaped his throat. "As if she likes children. What a farce."

The silence filled the inside of the SUV like a deployed smoke bomb.

"Have you ever heard of people divorcing their parents?"

Darcy shook her head.

Lawrence studied the well-manicured topiary bordering the flowerbed next to the circle drive. "It's a psychology term for grown children who are better off without having a relationship with their parents."

He looked over at her, his brown eyes watery. "I'm done, at least with my mother." He rubbed the side of his neck. "I'll never do anything to please her," he said. "And I'm tired of trying. I'm thirty-six years old and still trying to get my mother to like me."

Darcy ran her hands around the steering wheel. "I think your dad's crack about her medication was his way of saying it's not your fault."

"Yes, I caught that."

"Honestly, I don't know how he puts up with her. She's evil," Darcy said.

"I do." He glanced once more up at his old house. "It's her money. I always heard stories about my mother being the sort of heiress who paid for a multi-million dollar house in cash. Much the same way a normal person buys a blender or a microwave." He paused. "Let's get out of here."

***

Darcy insisted Lawrence come to her parents' for Christmas Eve. "Nothing fancy," she explained on the way to the Daniel's house, such an understatement after their lunch at the Ousted's. "On Christmas Eve we eat chili from Roznovsky's and Gloria's famous

213

tamales. She's a friend of Izzy's. Then after we're completed stuffed, we always watch *Christmas Vacation*."

"No traditional stringing of berries and popping popcorn in the fireplace? No *It's a Wonderful Life*? *Miracle on 34th Street*? *A Christmas Carol*? Drinking wassail?" Lawrence was on a roll.

She laughed, happy to see he still had a sense of humor after the hammering he'd taken from his mother. "What Norman Rockwell painting did you step out of?"

"The one I always dreamed of. You know, where the little kiddies gather around the tree after hanging up stockings, all their hopes of Santa Claus coming, putting cookies and milk out. Listening to a l-o-v-i-n-g parent read *Twas the Night Before Christmas*."

There was no mistaking the emphasis he put on loving.

Opting for a lighter tone, Darcy said, "Nah, we're pretty much new age. We stick with either Chevy Chase's *Christmas Vacation* or *The Christmas Story*. Then after the heartburn medicine kicks in, we usually toast with a little Amaretto over ice."

Lawrence went silent, probably sinking into his own thoughts. A long moment later, he spoke. "Sounds nice." His voice had dropped so low, she almost missed the two-word sentence. "Have you opened the gift from my mother?"

"Not yet, thought I'd wait till tomorrow. Have you?"

"Don't need to. I know what it is."

Darcy's eyebrows arched in a question mark.

"It's a Lenox porcelain dated ornament."

"That's a beautiful gift," Darcy said. "I love those."

"Yes, it is beautiful." Lawrence watched the passing landscape out the window. "And would actually mean something if she didn't hand them out like left-over party favors. Anyone who comes to the house during Christmas gets one."

Darcy winced. The depth of his unhappiness careened through her head like the cracking of billiard balls in a smoky pool hall. She shot him a glance. "Oh, I forgot. If you come back tomorrow, we do this really weird sort of gift exchange on Christmas Day."

Lawrence's eyebrows pulled together. "How weird?"

"My dad came up with the idea about five years ago." While she pulled off the freeway and onto Highway 6, she explained how everyone bought themselves gifts, wrapped them, and reversed the names on the tags.

"I don't understand."

"You'll catch on." Darcy said. "I buy a gift for myself and the tag reads 'to: Darcy, from: Izzy.' Then Izzy opens the present to see what she gave me. See?"

Lawrence pondered the scenario. "I think that's an ingenious idea. Has he thought about a patent?"

"I doubt it." Darcy pulled in front of her parents' house. "He just got tired of getting gifts he didn't really like. One year he bought an entire outfit and handed out little wrapped boxes with notes inside saying what part of the outfit each person gave him. Izzy ended up giving him the boxer shorts he had on. Thought we were going to have to tie on gloves and put both of them in a ring. My dad's a grade A pot stirrer where Izzy's concerned." She shook her head and thought of the words she often used to describe her family: ridiculous, clingy, weird, dysfunctional, meddling, over-protective. She always felt feelings toward her family would be more rewarding if they didn't always have the overtones of a circus sideshow, kind of like *Married With Children*. But man, between Lawrence and Miranda, her family came off looking more like the Huxtables.

***

Darcy informed her family Miranda would be joining them on Christmas Day.

Izzy turned to Andrea and said, "Your sister is bringing over a piranha," before turning to Darcy. "Is she in heat?"

"Not anymore. A bun in the oven took care of that," Darcy said.

Izzy clamped her hands on her hips. "And a husband?"

"No husband."

"So she's having a baby out of wedlock."

"Wow Izzy, I haven't heard that term in a while. Think you can shelf it for tomorrow? She's had a hard time—"

"You'll come too, won't you Lawrence?" Nina's skill of dividing and conquering a potential verbal combat zone kicked in.

"Well, that's very kind," Lawrence said. "If I won't be a bother."

"Of course not." Nina walked them to the door. "The more, the crazier." She paused and wrung her hands before turning back to Lawrence, replacing the smile that had slipped off. "And as you can see, for our family that's a good thing." She shot Darcy a meaningful look. "I'll talk to Izzy about Miranda."

Before heading back the next day, Darcy grabbed Ms. Viola's note from the refrigerator and paid a quick visit with a foil-wrapped plate in her hand.

"What is this?" Ms. Viola asked, sitting in her blue leather recliner.

"I made these for you." Darcy held her breath and mentally crossed her fingers, watching Ms. Viola take a bite from one of the chocolate chip cookies on the plate.

Ms. Viola took what Darcy considered to be an hour-long-moment assessing the texture and taste of the cookie. The wrinkled old woman motioned to the nearby ottoman. "Come sit."

After Darcy eased onto the matching leather footstool and crossed her arms around her knees, Ms. Viola patted Darcy's hands and offered a soft smile. "Very good, Missy. Very good."

"Really?" Darcy returned the smile. Whew, what a relief. She had wanted to give Ms. Viola some little something for Christmas, and finally decided trying to perfect the sacred chocolate chip recipe might do the trick. And here it presented itself again...one of Ms. Viola's lessons about the joy of giving, like on Thanksgiving Day at the GRB. It really did feel good. She pulled the piece of paper from her pocket and held it in front of Ms. Viola. "About this."

"Can you do it?" Ms. Viola asked.

"I'm a little confused." Darcy glanced over the message again. "You want me to take you to two places, but it'll be an overnight trip?"

"That's right." Ms. Viola ran her hands down the front of her gown. "If you don't have the vacation time I'll reimburse your pay."

"No, that won't be a problem. When do you want to go?"

"As soon as it starts to warm up. My treat, you drive."

"I can do that." She figured that wouldn't be until maybe the middle of March, which would give her time to schedule it with Vanessa. The devil-boss had been strangely nicer than usual these days. "Before I go, would you mind if I give you a hug?" Darcy asked.

"Is it something you feel strongly about?" The words sounded gruff and standoffish; however, the glint of a smile behind those faded blue eyes spoke otherwise.

Darcy leaned forward to hug the pencil-thin body, and for a brief moment, she felt Ms. Viola's arms tighten around her.

"Now, be off." Ms. Viola pushed back from Darcy. "I know you have better things to do than hang around here." She zeroed in on Darcy's face, nodded toward the plate of cookies, and mouthed the word "thank you."

***

"Your boyfriend didn't come?" Izzy met the trio at the front door.

"No, his white horse is in the shop." Darcy turned so Lawrence and Miranda could see her eye roll. The additional guests joining the Daniels for Christmas certainly changed the crazy dynamics of the day. Alex and Anna showed up a little after noon, which signaled the crazy gift-opening scene. Presents were labeled "legitimate" and "illegitimate," which couldn't have been worse timing with Miranda's situation and Izzy nearby. Every time the word illegitimate came up, Izzy raised one thin eyebrow and gave Darcy an "I-told-you-so" glare. Darcy and Nina joined forces in volleying back a warning be-nice expression to Izzy.

However, Izzy did win the prize for the best "illegitimate gift." She handed Stephen a carefully wrapped package. "Open this and see what a lovely gift you bought me this year." Stephen ripped off the paper to an oversized bottle of Crown Royal, his all-time favorite adult beverage, and begrudgingly had to hand it over to Izzy.

Ba-zinga. Let the games begin.

"Isn't there a violent cartoon you can go watch or something?" Stephen said through a pasted on smile.

Nina immediately jumped to her feet and scrambled for another present. "Who's next?"

Even on short notice, both Lawrence and Miranda received several gifts, which surprised them. Darcy noted, with much relief, the gifts weren't just party favors...another plus in the Daniels' column.

Dinner progressed nicely until Nina forgot herself and asked Miranda, "Are your parents upset you're not spending Christmas with them?"

Before Darcy could change the subject, Miranda came out with a true Miranda response. "My mother is, so much so she flew off to Vegas. A couple of dads could care less."

"Your mother was married more than once?" Izzy asked.

Darcy could feel food back up in her throat.

"Yeah, but at least she kept trying."

Good grief. Change the subject moron.

Darcy jumped to her feet. "Can we open some more wine? Miranda, ginger Ale? Izzy, will you help me?" She caught her grandmother's attention and nodded toward the kitchen.

Darcy grabbed another bottle of chardonnay from the refrigerator. "Will you behave? I know Mom slipped with her question, but you didn't have to use it as a launch pad for your own agenda. You have a slew of questions lined up. I know your mind, Izzy. I'm right, aren't I?"

"How is it possible there's anyone left in the country who doesn't know you wear white only between Easter and Labor Day?"

The remark caused Darcy to glance back into the dining room at Miranda's attire. She wore white leggings and a red, green, and white diagonal striped long sweater with red suede flats.

"She's festive."

Izzy flipped the switch on the coffee pot and unwrapped the pies sitting on the counter. "You seem to pick the most interesting friends."

"Oh pu-lease." Darcy uncorked the bottle of wine. "I thought our family was weird, but those two out there? Those *interesting* friends of mine? They're both going through a really hard time right now, and could use just a little bit of kindness."

Izzy pulled back. "Take me to Vegas and I'll keep quiet. Besides, I gave them a gift."

"You did, and I really appreciate that." She put an arm around her rotund grandmother. "C'mon Izzy, you can do it."

"I know I can do it." She paused. "It's just not as much fun."

Darcy smiled. "I know. That's where I get it from." She picked up the wine bottle and headed out of the kitchen. "But I'm working on it. Sometimes it's okay to be nice."

"Too much of nice and I could forget how to use sarcasm. So what about Vegas?" Izzy followed Darcy back to the dining room.

Sam called just as dinner came to an end and the table was being cleared. Darcy stepped out back to take his call. When she returned she froze when she saw Miranda talking to Izzy. She slipped to the side so she could eavesdrop on their conversation.

"Can I ask you a question?" Miranda crossed her arms, making the Supremes look like they were about to break out of their over-sized compartmental bra.

Izzy caught sight of Darcy and cleared her throat. "Of course, dear, ask away."

"Why did you buy me such a nice gift? I love stuff from Bath & Body Works, but I didn't think you even liked me."

Darcy held her breath waiting for Izzy's reply.

Before she spoke, Izzy glanced again at Darcy. "I don't know where you get such nonsense. Of course I like you. And I'm told kindness is a natural virtue, don't you agree?"

Miranda shrugged, then nodded. "Yeah. Sure. A natural virtue. I like that."

Darcy bent her neck around to see if Izzy had any of her fingers crossed. Whew, none that she could see.

Terry Lee

Chapter 16

"Did you read chapter seven like I told you to?" They sat in the OB waiting room for Miranda's name to be called.

"Sorta. I got kinda tired and just started looking at the pictures."

"I can't do this for you." Darcy put on her Mother Mary look. "If you want to understand what's going on inside there," she nodded toward Miranda's belly, "you better find time to read. And here, I found this at Half-Price Books." Darcy handed over *The Girlfriends Guide to Pregnancy*.

"Another one?" Miranda rubbed her hand over her itty-bitty baby bump. "I gotta tell ya, if this jellybean looks anything like the picture I saw last night, we're in big trouble."

"Why?"

"Because its dang head is as big as the whole body. And his eyes are so far apart they're not even looking in the same direction."

Darcy rolled her eyes. "That's why you read instead of looking at the pictures." She shook her head. "What am I going to do with you?"

Tricia, Dr. Holt's nurse, called Miranda's name. "Keep me, I hope."

***

"Well, let's see." Dr. Holt felt around Miranda's belly. "Everything seems to be fine. Do you have any questions?"

Miranda shot Darcy a "You wanna take this one?" look.

"I've been trying to get her to read up each month so she knows what's happening, but she's fallen a little behind." Darcy crossed her arms like "I don't know what I'm going to do with her."

Dr. Holt rolled her stool close to Miranda. "So, what's up?"

Miranda looked uncomfortable, a very un-Miranda state of being. "I saw this picture and it kinda scared me."

"How so?" Dr. Holt asked.

"I know it's still little and all that, but what if it doesn't turn out to be a normal-looking baby? I mean, Darcy told me it sorta looked like an alien at this stage. I didn't believe her till I saw the dang picture myself."

Miranda's uncomfortable look switched to flat-out fear, which sent Darcy into her protective mode. She reached for Miranda's hand and found it icy.

"I think that's probably what Darcy had in mind when she suggested you read up on the fetal development. This little baby is growing very fast right now." Dr. Holt pushed back and pointed to a forty-week developmental chart on the wall. "Here you are." Her finger landed on the twelve-week photo, then moved to the fifteenth week. "The next time you come, your baby will look more like this."

Miranda tilted her head. "Aww, that looks better."

"It's normal to be scared, especially since this is your first pregnancy."

Darcy turned to meet Miranda's "do not say a word" glare.

"There are a thousand emotional transitions we go through in our lifetime, and most come without a road map. The books help, but life, especially a pregnancy, can still be scary." Dr. Holt moved to the laptop on the counter. "Any complaints? How have you been feeling?"

"Good, I guess." Miranda rubbed her nose with the back of her hand. "Except for the belching, farting, and having to pee every five minutes, I feel fine."

"Are you exercising?" Dr. Holt made a notation on the laptop.

"I did a couple of weeks ago," Miranda said. "But I'm betting that's all about to change real soon."

"How so?" Dr. Holt asked.

"Because I'm moving into Mother Mary's apartment complex in three days." Miranda nodded toward Darcy. "And walking is on the agenda, I'm bettin'. Right?"

"Right," Darcy said.

"Well, good." Dr. Holt stood. "See you in three weeks." She smiled at Darcy. "Keep up the good work."

Darcy and Miranda waited for an elevator to take them to the lobby.

"Dr. Holt doesn't know about your first pregnancy, does she?"

"That one didn't count." The door opened to two men already in the elevator, one in a suit, the other in scrubs. The women stepped in, and just as the door closed Miranda let go with an, "I'm glad I had all that sex before I became a nun."

Darcy closed her eyes, mentally clicked her heels, and wished she was anywhere besides in an elevator on the twenty-third floor of the Memorial City Medical Tower. One of the men coughed...Darcy wasn't sure which one, and did not dare glance at anything except the descending digital numbers on the panel. It was going to be a long, l-o-n-g six months. She figured if she could keep her best friend *off* cigarettes, alcohol, and marijuana, and *on* the prenatal horse-pill vitamins, she'd have Miranda batting over five hundred...which wasn't bad for Miranda.

Friday. Moving day. Darcy was surprised at how organized Miranda was in handling the move. She had hired packers and sold most of her furniture to the guy subletting her loft, except for what she calculated would fit into the smaller apartment at Fountain Oaks. By noon the move had been completed. Darcy had taken the day off, and after a quick lunch at Roznovsky's, the two spent the rest of the day unpacking boxes.

"I can't decide what to do with some of these clothes." Miranda had filled the closets in both bedrooms to overflowing. "I don't see me wearing a lot of this stuff anymore."

"What about after the baby?" Until today, Darcy had no idea of the extent of the black, leather, spandex, and blingy bits of clothing Miranda owned. Even after helping Miranda stuff the closets she still had trouble wrapping her mind around everything she'd just hung up. "You ought to have your own designer label."

"Nah, I think I'm done with the slutty clothes." Miranda packed a dozen assorted pair of hosiery in a plastic storage container. "I do plan on being skinny again, but the last thing this baby needs is to have a mother like I did. I mean, who needs that shit?"

She couldn't argue with that. Actually, Darcy admired Miranda for her words. At least she'd given some thought to the role-modeling-mother part of this whole thing, which would make Darcy's job oh so much easier.

"When was the last time you talked to her?" Darcy had moved to the kitchen and started unpacking dishes. Knowing Cheryl hadn't been happy about being a grandma, she wondered if they even still talked.

"We talked at Christmas." Miranda rounded the corner to the kitchen sipping on her Sonic iced green tea. "As I said, she was in Vegas. That's how much she missed me." She lightly slapped her cheek. "Aren't we surprised?"

"How about your brothers?" Hands on hips, Darcy studied the layout of the kitchen and decided to set it up identically to hers. "You haven't said anything about them in ages."

"Ethan is still up in Alaska working on some pipeline thing." She watched Darcy fill her cabinets with the contents of the kitchen boxes. "Dale drives a semi cross-country." She bit the inside of her lip. "Yeah, they got the hell out of Dodge as soon as they could. We talk though. They may be grown, but they're still my little brothers."

"Either one of them married? Have a girlfriend?"

"Humph, with the background we've had?" Miranda slurped the end of her iced tea. "They didn't walk away, they hi-tailed their asses out of Texas, as far away from Houston and Mama Cheryl as they could get. Neither one of them has a clue what a decent relationship...."

Miranda's words drifted off like a swift wind extinguishing a candle flame.

Darcy pulled her head out of one of the boxes. "What?"

"I was going to say neither one of them have a clue what a decent relationship looks like." She dropped her eyes. "But neither do I." She swiped a tear from her face. "Are you finished yet?"

"Are you crying?"

"Are you my mother?" She laughed. "Like she'd care."

Darcy studied Miranda for a moment, thinking how no one really knows what goes on in another's family. For years, all she ever wanted was Miranda's looks, *money*, and dating status, Becca's IQ, family *money* and law degree, and although Lisa didn't come from a lot of money, she had plenty of down-to-earth stability and nurturing techniques. Then she thought of Lawrence. He'd had everything growing up, and yet he and Miranda ran a close race for shittiest home life. They could have their own reality show. The Kardashians didn't have anything on her two friends. Next her thoughts turned to the letter jacket in the back of her closet. What she thought she wanted…needed…to be happy all started with that damn jacket. Wow.

None of the usual handful of suspects had beat down the door asking her to a New Year's Eve party, and Sam had headed to Vail with his buddies. She wasn't really in a position to start an inquisition on the list for the ski trip, but….

"Is Captain Kirk going?" she had asked Sam.

"Who?"

"You know, your Enterprise friend from Miranda's party."

"Derrick?"

"I never thought of him having a real name, but yeah, I guess that's who I'm talking about."

"Sure," Sam had said. "He's part of the group who always goes. Why?"

Even over the phone Darcy had shrugged. "Just…asking." She hadn't even met Derrick and had no desire to. She wondered how much Sam knew about his "friend."

New Year's Eve, Darcy, Miranda, and Lawrence played Scrabble, ate pizza, and watched a *Big Bang Theory* marathon on TBS. Miranda and Lawrence had voted for *Friends,* but Darcy put her foot down. "No! I've seen every episode ever made. I want something different."

"Whew." Lawrence turned to Miranda. "Where did she obtain that tone?"

"About the time she morphed into Nurse Ratchet." Miranda opened the bag from Party City and handed out party hats and whistles. "I've got some Silly String in here in case things get out of hand."

During episodes of Sheldon, Leonard, and Penny, they'd play a round of Scrabble. The established rules were…Lawrence could never use a dictionary, Darcy was allowed a peek every other turn, and Miranda had free rein. Not that Darcy's IQ ranked higher than Miranda's, but over the years she'd gathered way more *Jeopardy* episodes under her belt.

By the time 2012 rang in, all three were asleep on the couch like tumbled dominos. Darcy woke Miranda only to direct her to bed. She returned to the living room, shut off the TV, and covered Lawrence, who had curled into an almost fetal position, with a blanket.

Looks just like a sleeping baby, doesn't he?

Before turning in she stood at the double window and peered down into the now inviting courtyard. Twenty twelve would most definitely merit several journal entries….if she kept a journal.

***

"Well, I won't need these this year." Miranda pulled out a pair of blingy Miss Me jeans, part of her rodeo committee attire. The end of February always signaled the start of the most prestigious event in Houston, the Livestock Show and Rodeo. Several weeks prior, trail rides from every direction worked their way to Memorial Park the Friday night before the big parade Saturday morning, which traditionally kick-started the three-week rodeo.

"You by-passing the rodeo scene this year?" Darcy lay across Miranda's bed and flipped through the mostly un-touched copy of *What to Expect.*

"Yeah, no can do. Having humongous boobs is one thing at the rodeo, but adding a baby bump…ah, no." Miranda plopped down next to Darcy. "I can't get into anything but leggings anymore."

"It's about time. You're half-way through your entire pregnancy." Darcy knew if the roles had been reversed, she'd have ballooned out before the third month. "Just put something on. We need to get going."

"You ought to see me naked." Miranda pulled a sweatshirt over her head. "It's freaky."

Winter had been almost non-existent that year. While other parts of the country had suffered through more extreme cold, people in Houston pretty much got along with sweatshirts and lightweight jackets. Although late in February, spring lurked nearby, sending hoards of people to Memorial Park on Saturday mornings; that was, except this Saturday. Due to the trail riders and the consequential crowds, their walking route had been diverted to Afton Oaks, the neighborhood behind the apartment complex. Darcy loved Afton Oaks, filled with rambling ranch houses with immaculately manicured lawns and huge oak trees on near half-acre lots. After thirty minutes of walking, they had maneuvered through the subdivision and popped out on Richmond Avenue to head back to Fountain Oaks. That particular stretch of Richmond Avenue housed a couple of strip centers, a few fast food stops, a convenience store, and Bayou City Seafood, another one of Darcy's favorite restaurants.

"I need to stop." Miranda braced her arm against a street light pole near the convenience store. She slugged down several mouthfuls of water and then pointed her Ozarka bottle off to the right. "Hey, isn't that…what's his name from high school?"

Darcy lifted her Gucci sunglasses, her eyes following the direction of the water bottle. Seconds later she slammed the shades back in place, her heart banging somewhere up around her throat. "Let's go." She grabbed the sleeve of Miranda's sweatshirt.

"Didn't you used to—?"

"Come on!" This time Darcy jerked Miranda's arm and speed-walked past the convenience store.

Miranda freed her sleeve from Darcy's grasp. "What the hell? Woman with a baby here."

"Sorry. I'll explain later." Darcy maintained her pace, her mind spinning. Miranda had spotted letter jacket guy getting into his truck at the convenience store.

Back at Fountain Oaks, and fearful too much free-air time might ignite discussion of her peculiar behavior, Darcy suggested they head to Babies "R" Us to start a registry. Since the color of the jellybean wouldn't be revealed until next week, they decided to look at some of the basic necessities. What seemed like a good idea at the time turned out to be a daunting task.

"This is ridiculous." Miranda flipped through the twelve-page printout of "suggestions" provided by the store, all neatly categorized by row and bin number. "All this for just one baby? What did people do before Babies "R" Us?"

Darcy had to agree. Her eyes blurred, partly due to the overwhelming page entries, but also from the jolt she'd received earlier on their walk. "Let's just get your name and due date in the system. How about that?"

With that menial task accomplished, Darcy folded the printout and stuffed it into her recently purchased Nicole Miller satchel bag.

She'd never given Nicole Miller much thought, or JC Penney, for that matter. But a couple of weeks ago she had arrived in the area early for Miranda's OB check-up and found herself browsing through the store at Memorial City Mall. She rarely paid homage to JC Penney; not that there was anything wrong with the store, she'd just always set her sights more high-dollar. To her surprise, she found several fantastic handbags at about a quarter of the price she usually forked over for a designer knock-off. She liked the Nicole Miller bag so much she almost bought two, but resisted the urge and settled on the orange leather satchel she'd spotted right away.

Arriving back at Fountain Oaks, Miranda had to maneuver her BMW around a U-Haul truck in the parking lot. "I'm off for a shower and a nap." Darcy, not ready to deal with the conversation she needed to have with herself, walked across the courtyard to Ms. Viola's.

"I'm assuming we have a new tenant?" Darcy pushed her shades up onto her head.

Ms. Viola had emptied the contents of the sideboard onto the Ikea kitchen table. Stacks of pictures and old newspapers cluttered the tabletop. "You assume right. A young man who we'll probably never see. Works during the day, goes to school at night. Seems normal enough though."

"Then he probably won't fit in around here." Darcy sat in one of the kitchen chairs and draped an arm along the back, laughing at her own joke. "What's his name?"

Ms. Viola pointed in the direction of her recliner without raising her head. "Scott something. The lease is over there."

Darcy glanced over toward the living room and saw the open cabinet doors under the flat screen TV. "What's going on here?"

"It's time I start going through all this mess." Ms. Viola studied a yellowed newspaper clipping and then tossed it into the small trashcan beside her. "People do that when they get to be my age."

"Spring clean?"

Ms. Viola peered over her glasses. "I guess you could call it that." She returned to a stack of pictures. "Would you mind checking on Scott sometime later on and see if he needs anything?"

"Sure, I'll be—"

"And I think we need to start looking at dates for our little trip." Ms. Viola stopped her sorting and dropped her hands into her lap. "I was thinking about going in a couple of weeks. Maybe the sixth and seventh?"

Darcy calculated ahead and figured she'd have enough time to schedule a couple of days off. "I think that'll work. Can you tell me where we're going?"

"Galveston. I want to see the water."

"And we're still staying overnight?"

"That's the plan."

Back in her own apartment, Darcy marched directly to her closet, pushed clothes aside until she found the letter jacket, and laid it across her bed. The stupid old thing and all its attached baggage had hung in her closet for almost fifteen years. Crossing her arms, she scratched her neck. Last she had heard, he lived in Austin. Was he back in Houston? What were her feelings? Excited? Angry? He was the first guy she'd ever loved. He had been a year older, and when she was a junior, he'd taken her to homecoming. She'd had a crush on him since forever and could not believe they were actually dating...at least, that's what she called it.

Acting horribly irresponsibly that homecoming night, she'd said yes when she knew she shouldn't. She didn't know he didn't love her. He didn't know she was a virgin. Sad story, although it could have been worse. Being late the following month had sent her into panic mode. And when she mentioned it to letter jacket guy, he looked at her like she'd grown horns. By the time she got her period, letter jacket guy had moved on. As stated...sad story, at least for Darcy.

**

Viola had the rest of the day to herself. Will's daughter had picked him up, saying she'd have him back after dinner. After making herself a cup of tea, she slid a DVD into the Blu-ray player, grabbed the remote, and then lowered herself into her soft blue recliner, sitting in silence for a moment, her eyes closed. Why had she lived this long? Maybe there was a reason...maybe not. Who knew? She figured she'd find out soon enough.

As she reached for the dog tags in the always present and nearby cedar box, her hand brushed over a small pamphlet Timothy had left on his last visit. Picking it up, she read the title. *Thoughts On Aging Gracefully.* She rolled her eyes and tossed it across the room. He tries, she thought, and what would she have done over the years without him and his sweet family? But damn, she was not aging gracefully and she had no one to blame but herself. It wasn't like she'd made an effort to stay healthy. Being a cynical dried-up bitch for as long as she could remember, she only allowed certain people into her inner circle. She liked to help people...on her terms. She did what she could, but shied away from all that feeling shit. Then, along came Darcy Daniels, who'd somehow chipped away at her hard

229

exterior to the soft part of her heart. Hell, she'd just about blasted the damn thing wide open. Feelings…they didn't always feel good. The very reason she'd shut them down years ago…much easier not having to deal with that sort of rubbish. But she'd found Darcy different; either different, or more like herself than she cared to admit.

Ms. Viola took a sip of her herbal tea and pushed play on the remote, mentally fastening her seat belt. She hadn't watched these old movies in years. The eight-millimeter reels had been converted to VHS back in the early '80s. In the late '90s she'd had the VHS tape put on DVD.

For the next hour and a half she watched home movies of Michael as a child, and how happy they all were. She watched Robert teaching him to swing, and taking the training wheels off his bike for the first time. Then she watched Michael wave back to her the first time he stepped onto a school bus, losing his first tooth, swim lessons, birthday parties, little league baseball games. The next segment showed Michael receiving merit badges at Boy Scout ceremonies, their family vacations, high school baseball games, prom, and then graduation. The DVD ended a short while later, as did Michael's life.

With painful clarity she recalled the night he and Timothy announced they had enlisted in the Army. They were so proud to be eighteen and make that decision for themselves. Both had relatively low draft numbers, which meant there was a good possibility they would be called anyway…but to enlist? She and Robert had been crushed, but kept their tears in-check until the two young men left the house for a celebration. There was no celebration for her and Robert that night, or any night after. Vietnam was a nightmare. As are most wars, she thought.

Viola rubbed her eyes. In many ways the pain moved through her as gruelingly fresh as it had all those years ago. The dog tags in her hand felt like a leaded paperweight. Yeah, there was a damn good reason she'd cut out the feelings portion of her heart a long time ago. They hurt.

***

"So, what's that guy's name we saw today? Didn't you two used to date?" Miranda and Darcy stood side by side folding clothes at the table in the laundry room.

Darcy focused on her folding and shrugged. "Yeah, sorta." Lucky for her Miranda's dating calendar had been so full she had little recollection of Darcy's. Even today, four and a half months pregnant, Miranda turned down several dates a week.

"Bad memories, huh?" Miranda snorted. "I've had my share of those." She stacked her clean clothes in the laundry basket and turned. "And what about that guy you've been seeing? I know absolutely nothing about him. C'mon. Give me some dirt."

"Sam?" She'd gone out with him quite a bit since Christmas, but that had all changed a couple of weeks ago. He was a great guy, but he hadn't called lately and she knew why. Seeing letter jacket guy that day only clouded the issue. "There isn't any dirt. He's clean…almost too clean."

"That's not possible." Miranda hoisted her laundry basket onto her hip. "If he's an adult, there's dirt somewhere."

Almost too clean? So you're looking for someone who treats you bad? Is that what you're looking for, bone-head? Just keep it up. Hook up again with letter jacket guy. See where that gets you.

"Call him."

"I can't." Darcy followed Miranda out of the laundry room, the February crispness hitting her in the face.

"Of course you can. We're not exactly in the Brady Bunch era, you know." Miranda stopped at her apartment. "Girls get to call guys. Read the handbook."

"Get back to me after you've read chapter nine."

"Smart-ass."

"Slut."

Back in her apartment, Darcy tossed the laundry basket to the side and crawled up on her bed. She crossed her legs, chewed on her thumbnail, and thought about her last date with Sam.

***

They had met up with some of Sam's friends at Dave and Busters, played a couple games of pool, and had had a few beers when Derrick, aka Captain Kirk, descended with a new Miranda. The night had suddenly turned dark. Darcy could not keep the venom out of her eyes, and Sam had no clue of the evil thoughts running through her mind. He did, however, pick up that something had changed with her mood and asked if she wanted to leave. Darcy sprinted out to Sam's car in record time.

"Wow." Sam slipped into the driver's seat and turned the key in the ignition. "Was it something I said?"

"Can you just take me home?"

"Not until you tell me what's wrong."

Darcy felt bile in her throat. Mentally she knew it was insane to judge all men by Captain Kirk's behavior, especially Sam.

"I don't want to talk about it."

"Uh…well, we'll just sit here then." Sam switched off the ignition. "Let me know when you're done."

She turned to face him, her eyes cold. "That f-r-i-e-n-d in there, Derrick? He got Miranda pregnant."

Now that sounds childish.

"What do you mean *he* got Miranda pregnant?"

See what I mean?

"Okay, so he didn't actually do it alone."

"Thank God," Sam said. "I was going to have to check my facts on Wikipedia."

"This isn't funny."

Sam downshifted to a more empathic gear. "I'm sorry for the wise-crack. I see this is really bothering you."

"He knows Miranda's pregnant, and he doesn't want anything to do with it…her or the baby."

"What? You're kidding me, right?"

Darcy crossed her arms. "Nope."

"What a jerk." He slid his arm around Darcy's shoulder. She flinched.

"Wait. Are you mad at me?"

"Can you take me home now?"

Neither spoke until Sam had pulled into the Fountain Oaks parking lot.

"Look." Sam turned toward Darcy. "I like you. You know that. I knew it the first time I saw you in that Paris Hilton get-up at the Halloween party. I liked you even more when I saw how uncomfortable you were. You were one of the few real people there. Everyone else looked like they were in a Zombie movie directed by Ralph Lauren."

Darcy stared straight ahead, her arms clamped around her.

"What's the plan, Darcy? What do you want?"

"I want not to want you."

232

Oh, that's so Oprah.

"Wow, are you trying to make me cry? Because that's not really the answer I was expecting." Sam sat back in his seat and ran his fingers through his hair. "This isn't complicated. It's not a soap opera."

She knew she owed him some sort of explanation. "I don't trust guys."

Do ya think?

"Would you feel better if I told you I was gay? Would that let you off the hook?"

"See? You're being an asshole." She opened the door and stepped out.

"Yeah, maybe I am. But I'm not Derrick, and I'm the only asshole around here who gives a shit about you. When you finish with your pity party and decide what you want, give me a call."

Darcy slammed the door.

Guess you showed him.

She heard the tire screeching of an angry driver leaving the parking lot. He didn't deserve that, but for some asinine reason, she couldn't separate Sam from Derrick or most of the creeps she had known.

Terry Lee

Chapter 17

Everything seemed to be status quo for the trip with Ms. Viola. Lawrence had befriended Scott, the new tenant, which kept him thankfully occupied. Fletcher had spent the last week working the beds around the property, preparing them for a round of assorted spring flowering plants. Even Izzy had stopped bugging her as often. Apparently she'd discovered Words With Friends on her phone, and reality television.

Look out reality TV.

Darcy had checked to see if letter jacket guy was on Facebook. He wasn't.

Take that as a plus on your side.

Early on, she had "friended" Sam, and at first they'd frequently commented on each other's page. There hadn't been any "comments" lately on Sam's end, although she found herself checking his homepage almost daily to see what he'd been up to. Was he dating someone else?

Can you blame him?

Maybe he had already been seeing someone before her.

And you never even thought to ask, did you? Remember Miranda saying she wouldn't have a clue what a decent relationship looks like? Well, look in the mirror, bonehead. We're gonna need a bigger boat.

"Where to first, Galveston?" Darcy had packed the SUV with both overnight bags and helped Ms. Viola with her seatbelt.

"Memorial Oaks."

Darcy's eyebrows pulled together to almost form a straight line. "The cemetery?"

"That's right. You know where it is?"

"Uh, yeah." Darcy merged onto 610 Loop and headed to I-10 West. She would never have guessed a cemetery to be on the day's agenda.

Ten minutes later she pulled into one of the most pristine cemeteries in the city of Houston. The flush headstones with the exception of a few well-placed statues and benches provided a tranquil, aesthetically pleasing view across the acres of pine and oak trees. Memorial Oaks resembled a quiet, well-trimmed forest floor in the middle of the busy city. Although already behind in rainfall for the year, they'd had just enough small showers to bring out the different green shades of new growth.

Ms. Viola pointed to the right. "Turn here."

As soon as Darcy made the turn Ms. Viola continued with her directions. She raised her hand over toward the left. "See that thing over there? That's where we need to stop."

Darcy pulled to the curb adjacent to a large stone replica of an open book set back away from the street. Narrowing her vision, she spotted "Middleton" on a bench not far from the curb. She helped Ms. Viola out of the SUV and onto the bench bearing the woman's name.

"Your husband is here?"

She nodded at the marker in front of them. "Right there."

Darcy circled around to see the inscription more clearly and caught sight of another Middleton marker to the left. She raised her eyes to the older woman. "Who's Michael?"

Ms. Viola's head tilted upward. "Do you hear the birds? And just look at that sky."

Feeling some pivotal moment approaching, Darcy remained still.

"And it's so quiet." Ms. Viola's gaze dropped to meet Darcy. "Except for the traffic from I-10, it's almost completely...peaceful." The old woman opened her clenched hand, exposing the dog tags.

Air locked in Darcy's lungs.

"Michael was my son. He was killed in Vietnam."

Darcy froze in open-mouthed shock. Quickly regaining her composure, she snapped it shut. "I thought...." Ms. Viola looked like a strong wind could shatter her into a thousand pieces. Darcy moved to where the old woman sat, but halted when a vibrant yellow butterfly flitted overhead and landed on Ms. Viola's arm.

"Look." Darcy pointed to the butterfly.

Ms. Viola's gaze lowered to the sleeve of her jacket. A long moment passed. The butterfly, gently opening and closing its wings, seemed perfectly content on her arm. "Would…you give me a minute? I need to talk to Robert."

"Sure, of course." Darcy left Ms. Viola and walked toward the large stone open book, then headed to the right before turning to make a spacious semi-circle around the Middleton gravesite. She noticed Ms. Viola had moved to the foot marker of her husband's grave and could hear the raspy voice. Darcy kept an eye on Ms. Viola, fearful the woman may need assistance at any time. Ten minutes later, Darcy had been waved back.

"We can go now."

Approaching the gravesite, Darcy noticed the butterfly performing wing exercises on Michael's marker. "I think that butterfly likes the Middletons."

"Hmm."

Once again, she helped Ms. Viola into the SUV.

"To Galveston?"

"Yes."

Silence filled the SUV like a smoke bomb in a walk-in closet and remained painfully obvious till the Houston skyline could barely be detected from Darcy's rearview mirror.

Viola finally broke the impasse, causing Darcy to jump. "So tell me about your beau. I assume you have one."

Beau? Haven't heard that term in a while. Right up there with Euell Gibbons.

"I'm not sure whether I have one or not."

"You're not sure? Either you do or you don't. Which is it?"

"He hasn't called in a couple of weeks."

"Do you like him?"

A short pause before Darcy answered. "Yes."

"Are your fingers broke?"

"No, it's just—"

"Yeah, I know…it's complicated, right? You ever get tired of hearing that crap? Tell me about him."

Darcy blew out air, then relayed the story of Sam, beginning with the Batman attire at Miranda's party, including him carrying

Lawrence to her car, and ending with the fact he'd made it pretty clear he liked her.

"He sounds absolutely horrible." The sarcasm dripped from Ms. Viola's words. "Are you *trying* to find something wrong with him?"

Darcy opened her mouth, but was silenced by Ms. Viola's raised hand.

"Don't answer that question, just think about it. And take the 61st Street exit."

She'd been so caught up reliving the short saga of life with Sam, Darcy somehow failed to notice they had already crossed the causeway into Galveston.

"Then take a left at the Seawall."

Turning onto Seawall Boulevard, Darcy barely had time to admire the unusual green of the water so close to shore before more directions were fired.

"Take a left here."

"Here?"

And the hits just keep on coming.

Darcy turned into the grand circle drive of the San Luis Resort, possibly the most prestigious hotel on the island. Ms. Viola seemed to catch a second wind when she slipped a ten-dollar bill to the valet attendant, who removed their overnight bags onto a brass-railed dolly.

"Reservations for Viola Middleton." The old woman slammed an Am-Ex Platinum card down on the check-in counter.

Platinum?

Ten minutes later the two were ushered into a suite on the concierge level of the massive resort. Darcy hadn't felt this speechless since she realized Ms. Viola and Mr. Will were....

Yuck, reverse, reverse...full throttle reverse on that thought.

The suite caused another round of speechlessness. A plush couch and two matching chairs filled the large sitting area. They each had their own private bedroom and bath. It would have been difficult to not notice the huge flat screen television mounted on one wall, and a sofa table off toward the balcony sporting an elegant, fresh flower arrangement, an assortment of fruit, chocolates, assorted cheeses, crackers, a bottle of chilled champagne, and two crystal flutes containing vibrant red strawberries.

Waiting until the bellhop closed the door, Darcy turned to Ms. Viola. "Are you serious?"

"Not often, but yes." Ms. Viola's eyes shone with a hint of a smile. "Is there a problem?"

Darcy checked out her sleeping quarters, and found a remote control on the marbled countertop in the bathroom. For lights? Jacuzzi? She pushed the power button and jumped back when the local Houston anchorman appeared in the large mirror over the sink.

Geez, Louise! It's like the magic mirror in Snow White!

She returned to the main living area.

"There's a TV in the bathroom mirror."

"Really?" Ms. Viola shuffled over to one of the cushioned chairs. "Let's have some champagne."

A couple of hours later, after a dinner delivered by room service, Darcy had been directed to settle Ms. Viola onto one of the balcony chairs. She tucked a blanket tightly around the frail shell of a woman, providing shelter from the still cool spring breeze. Darcy sat in the adjacent chair, also wrapped in a blanket.

"I know I said I never had children." The woman stared straight out across to the horizon. The sky had switched to purplish-blue.

Silence at this point seemed as necessary to Darcy as always having boxed wine on hand.

"Now you know that was a lie." Ms. Viola sighed and raised her fist to her chest. "It hurts too much to talk about him. That was such an awful time. And then Robert died of a heart attack four months later."

Four months? How awful.

"I'm...so sorry."

"Yeah, me too." Ms. Viola dropped her fist to her lap. "But what are you gonna do."

"I heard you talking back at the cemetery." Darcy stepped with caution into the conversation. "Do you talk to both of them?" She caught Ms. Viola brushing a possible tear from her face.

"I talk to Robert. Actually I cuss at him most of the time."

"You're angry at him?"

"Damn straight. Have been for years."

"What did he do?"

"He died. He left me with all this grief. I always thought he took the easy way out." Ms. Viola paused. "But that's not true. His heart

239

just couldn't live without Michael." She turned toward Darcy. "And mine wouldn't let me die."

A couple walked along the seawall, hand in hand. Darcy watched till they were out of sight before she spoke. "You talk to your husband, but not your son."

The first stars appeared in the evening sky before Ms. Viola responded. "Michael's gone. I lost him a long time ago."

"So...the pictures on your wall." Once again, she tiptoed. "The little boy in the picture with your husband was—"

"Michael."

"And the one with Timothy and some other guy in the military uniforms?"

"Michael."

Darcy sat back, attempting to categorize the new information. "If your husband talks to you, why wouldn't Michael?"

Ms. Viola's puckered her lips and shook her head. "I told you I lost Michael a long time ago."

Another round of silence prevailed until Darcy gathered her nerve to delve a bit. "Are there any other truths you want to tell me?"

The old woman shook her head. "Highly over-rated commodity if you ask me." She rearranged herself in the balcony chair. "Any particular truth you're after?"

Darcy shrugged. "Doesn't matter. Pick one."

Ms. Viola puffed her cheeks out like her mouth had filled with marbles. "Okay, I can think of a couple. First, back when I could still drive I spent quite a few hours a week visiting with vets at the VA hospital. Guess it made me feel closer to Michael, or something like that."

Darcy thought back to the number of people she'd noticed in wheelchairs clustered around the entrance of the VA when she delivered the afghans. "And the second?"

The old woman turned to Darcy and pulled the blanket tighter around her. "The real reason I volunteered all those years is because it was easier than having to look at the way I had screwed up my own life. Volunteering made me feel good, like I was finally doing something worthwhile. And besides, I had to do something to straighten out my karma."

Darcy counted to ten v-e-r-y slowly. "Anything else?"

"I didn't plan on living this long." The woman hunched down in her chair, almost completely covered by the blanket.

"Are you cold? Do you want to go inside?"

"I want a margarita. When Robert and I used to stay here at the San Luis, we'd sit on the beach down there." Ms. Viola pointed a shaky finger to the beach across the street. "He'd walk back over here and get us margaritas. Make yourself useful. Go call room service."

Fifteen minutes later the two women sipped their frozen drinks, both trying to ignore the cool night air.

"You know why I recycle?"

Darcy wondered if that was a trick question. "Because…you're conscientious?"

"Let me rephrase the question. "Do you know why *you* should recycle?"

"Because…I need to be conscientious?"

Ms. Viola shot her an "oh pu-lease" glare. "You know that 'save the planet' campaign?" The woman didn't wait for a reply. "It's a bunch of horse shit. The planet is going to survive, you can bet your money on that. Whether it'll be inhabitable is another issue. I can't think of anything worse than Lucas or Clayton's grandkids, or your grandkids for that matter, thinking back on us with disgust. I don't want them to wonder what kind of thoughtless generation we were, not having concern for anyone besides ourselves. Of course, I never had grandchildren, but people I care about do…or will. Which brings me back to another topic."

Okay, no more tequila.

The effects had obviously turned Ms. Viola into an antiquated Chatty Cathy.

"Remember that day when I asked why you lived at Fountain Oaks?"

Why had she agreed to the margaritas? It was always good to know which direction the tornado was coming from. The obvious answer to the casual observer would be across the street from the Gulf waters. However, Darcy had a premonition this particular twister sat next to her, laden with tequila fumes. "Uh-huh."

"Since we're talking about truths…."

Crap.

"You left some dots out, didn't you?"

241

Note: always travel with your own box of wine. You're gonna need more alcohol.

She took several deep breaths and spent the next thirty minutes filling Ms. Viola in on her pregnancy scare and how belittled she'd felt by letter jacket guy, a story she'd never shared with anyone until now.

"Ah, the missing dots." Ms. Viola attempted to stand, which brought Darcy to her feet. "We can go in now."

Both had changed into their PJ's and met back in the living area. Once settled on the comfortable couch, Ms. Viola continued. "So, you didn't feel good enough back then, and convinced yourself that all the designer shit would do the trick."

How ridiculous it all sounded. "Yeah, I guess so."

"And you never once stopped to re-evaluate."

"Not really." Which didn't say much for Darcy's depth perception. "I guess it finally played itself out. That stuff doesn't seem as important anymore. I mean, don't get me wrong, I still like nice things, it's just—"

"You don't need them now." A smile pulled at one edge of Ms. Viola's mouth. "You've grown up, Missy. I don't think you really want Prince Charming to come rescue you on a white horse. That's not the kind of guy you want, is it? Maybe it's time to update your fairy tale."

***

The next day back at Fountain Oaks, Ms. Viola left Darcy with one last bit of wisdom. "Remember when you said what's his name hadn't called?"

Oh, uh...Sam?

Darcy nodded.

"That's a swinging door, Missy."

Miranda, Sam, and now Ms. Viola had all told her the same thing. Call.

***

At the last OB checkup, they had found out Miranda would be having a pink jellybean, which meant final decisions could be made for decorating and accessorizing the nursery. The baby shower would be held in May.

The Saturday after the Galveston trip, Darcy and Miranda finished the registry at Babies "R" Us and moved on to Target. Darcy grabbed a cart. "We need to start thinking of names."

"I'm thinking about getting a pet." Miranda scratched her growing bump. "And I need to get some cocoa butter. My skin itches. I think that book said I need it so my skin won't explode or something. What do you think about a hamster?"

"I think you're nuts." Darcy steered the cart toward the lotion and self-care isles.

"Hey, guess what?" Miranda opened a can of mixed nuts she'd earlier thrown in the cart. "My lease is up on the Beamer next month, and I'm actually going to get something more reasonable. Ya know, for the jellybean and all."

Darcy picked up a tub of cocoa butter and added it to the growing pile in the shopping cart. "That's great. What did you decide on?"

"I thought about getting one of those cute little Lexus SUVs."

Darcy and the shopping cart came to a grinding halt, which sent Miranda nearly plowing into her backside. "A Lexus?"

"Yeah, what do you think?" Miranda recapped the can of nuts and reached for a bottle of water near the checkout stand.

There had been a time—not so long ago actually—that this news might have been the straw that completely broke the proverbial camel's back…a real deal-breaker. But not today. "I think that's great," she said, and meant it.

Work had kept her busy, and she was back to only receiving messages on her answering machine from Izzy, her mother, and Miranda. She hoped Sam would make the move and call, but deep down she knew she'd screwed up. On her last visit to see Ms. Viola, she'd noticed a marked decline. The old woman seemed to rarely leave her recliner. Darcy also now knew the cedar box on the table next to Ms. Viola's chair was home for Michael's dog tags.

On Wednesday morning, two weeks after the Galveston trip, there was a knock at the door just as she finished with her makeup. Pulling Stash aside, she peered through the peephole and quickly opened the door.

"I'm sorry to disturb you so early."

"Come in." Darcy backed up and allowed Lucas, Ms. Viola's nephew, to enter the apartment.

"Aunt V was taken to the hospital during the night." Lucas looked like he'd slept in his clothes.

"Is she back at Memorial City?" Darcy grabbed her iPhone off the ottoman and dropped it into her Nicole Miller satchel.

"Darcy...."

She could be as dense as molasses sometimes, and although the look on Lucas's face spoke volumes, she clung to the molasses. "She's in ICU, right?"

"She...died."

Darcy backed up until she felt the couch against the back of her legs. "Died?" She felt the words kick her in the stomach, knocking all the air from her lungs.

"I wanted to come tell you in person." Lucas ran a hand over his face. "The two of you seemed to have gotten close. I've told Mr. Will and Fletcher." He paused. "Fletcher doesn't seem to be handling it too well."

Her eyes studied the carpet in front of her. "I'll check on him. Should I tell the others?"

"If you don't mind. I need to get back to help my dad." Lucas moved to the door. "I'll keep you posted about the service."

The service.

"Right. Thanks."

After the door closed, she felt a tear escape the pools gathered in her eyes. She snatched a Kleenex from her purse and fell back against the cushions of the couch. Stash, sensing whatever it is dogs sense, lay at her feet. A half hour passed before she felt strong enough to stand. She called Vanessa, cancelled her appointments for the day, and headed out to find Fletcher.

When he didn't answer her knock, she opened the door a bit. "Fletcher? It's Darcy. Are you in here?" If she hadn't been on high alert status for any movement or sound she might easily have missed the faint "Yeah."

Fletcher sat on a worn but somewhat clean couch with a can of Vienna sausages and an opened bag of pork rinds in his lap. Darcy's mind immediately zapped back to the soiree in the courtyard last fall. The only item missing from what he had brought to the table was a loaf of white bread. Fletcher's water hose lay on the carpet in front of him. She sat on the couch and put an arm around his camouflage-clad shoulders.

"It'll be okay. We'll get through this together." They sat side by side, head to head.

"First my mom, my plant, and now Ms. Viola." A sob erupted. "All my friends."

Her grip tightened around the shuddering camouflaged heap, realizing the extent of his lonely existence. "Would it help if I brought Stash over to stay for a while?"

Fletcher's body started rocking back and forth, pulling Darcy with him like a glider. "Yeah," he said in the faintest whisper.

***

On Saturday, Lucas appeared at her door once again. This time he held a cardboard file box.

"We've been going through some of Aunt V's things, and this had your name on it."

"Come in."

Lucas sat the box on the couch and took a seat beside it.

"Can…I get you anything? Coffee? Water?"

"No, thanks, I'm fine." He shifted on the couch. "She left specific instructions about her service. Aren't we surprised?" Despite his obvious sadness, he let out a mild chuckle.

Darcy smiled and sat on the couch, the ominous box between them. She waited for him to speak.

"The service is set for two weeks from today, and it'll be held down at League City. As Aunt V said, it'll be a three hour cruise."

"We'll be on a boat?"

"Yes…and a rather large one." Lucas stood. "Can you let the tenants know? She left word she'd like them all to attend."

"I…uh, sure. Anything else?"

"Not at the moment." Lucas stopped at the door. "But I'll let you know if anything comes up. Otherwise, we'll all meet at noon in the lobby of the South Shore Harbor Hotel. Are you familiar with the place?"

Darcy nodded.

After Lucas left, she lifted the lid off the box. A folded piece of paper lay on top of several items wrapped in tissue paper. Pushing the note aside, she opened the first package and lifted out a soft pastel crocheted baby blanket and a children's picture book with a beautiful butterfly on the cover, obviously gifts for Miranda's little jellybean.

245

Wow. She never ceases to amaze you, does she?

Next she unwrapped a shadow box. The label at the top read, "The Life Cycle of the Butterfly—Michael Middleton." A Monarch butterfly had been mounted in the center, with small captions and pictures spread around explaining the life stages from egg to caterpillar to chrysalis to adult. Beneath the shadow box she found an extensive folded and laminated quick reference guide for butterflies of the Southeast Texas Coast. Next she opened a manila envelope containing a stack of Ms. Viola's super-secret recipe cards. The contents of the last manila envelope held a Hurricane Preparedness Guide. A half-smile tugged at a corner of her mouth despite the sting of tears behind her eyes that splashed down her face. She picked up the folded piece of paper and squinted at Ms. Viola's shaky penmanship.

> *You asked if I ever talked to Michael. I thought I'd lost him a long time ago. I was wrong. He's been here all the time. I found the shadow box he had made for a merit badge in Scouts. In my grief, I had completely blocked out his obsession with butterflies. He was there that day at the cemetery. He landed on my sleeve. He's always been there. As I'm sure you have figured out, the blanket and book are for Miranda's baby. I'll refrain from any further comments. Take good care of my recipes–do not let my sister EVER know you have them or I WILL haunt you. And I won't be some fancy pants butterfly either...think scary. Of all the things I wanted to teach you, I never got around to the item in the last envelope, which is self-explanatory. If you're reading this then you can assume all the Crisco I've ingested over the years has finally kicked in. My message to you is this: I won't be far, so if you need me, just holler. And as for the mistakes in my life you never asked about...well, that list is long, and now I'm too tired. But remember this—don't overlook the butterflies in your life like I did. Let go of grudges and choose happiness instead of bitterness. Butterflies are free and designer labels are just*

that...labels. Take care of yourself. That dream you've held on to for so long doesn't seem to be working worth a shit. Have you updated your fairytale yet? The only failure in life is failing to try (don't go quoting me...some other genius came up with that one). But don't fail at least to try. And if that means making a phone call...make the damn call.

There, I feel better–Viola

With Ms. Viola's letter in one hand and the laminated Hurricane Preparedness Guide in the other...she cried.

Two Saturdays later, Darcy, Miranda, and Fletcher drove down to League City in Miranda's recently leased Lexus SUV, with Lawrence and the newest tenant, Scott, following close behind. Mr. Will's daughter had informed Darcy she would be bringing her dad to the service. They entered the already crowded South Shore Harbor lobby. She made her way around to Ms. Viola's family.

"Who are all these people?" she asked Lucas. "I don't recognize any of them."

He smiled. "Surprising, isn't it? She was something else. There are people here from the VA, Meals on Wheels, the Thanksgiving Day Feast committee, and everyone else we were ordered to contact."

"Wow."

"For such a cranky old broad, she made an impression on a lot of people."

I'd say that's a highly understated remark.

"That she did."

A few minutes later, the crowd was led outside and down the dock to a magnificent one-hundred foot yacht. Once on the boat and directed inside, Darcy noticed an altar with several sprays of flowers along the massive windows lining the front of the cabin. At least twenty rows of chairs had been arranged to accommodate the people in attendance. After all had been seated, the yacht eased away from the dock and slowly made its way past the Kemah Boardwalk and out to sea.

"Once the service is completed," said a yacht employee, "I'd like to ask everyone to move to the upper deck so we can set up tables and chairs for the meal."

"I had no idea you could have a funeral on a boat," Miranda whispered.

"Me either."

But wow, what a way to go.

The service was short and the upper deck provided an open bar and appetizers while music played softly in the background. Stepping to the outside deck, a pleasant breeze hit Darcy's cheek.

"I rather like this." Lawrence had moved to her side. "Want one?" He held two shrimp *en brochettes* on toothpicks. "Who *are* all these people?"

"Her friends." Darcy took one of the bacon-wrapped shrimp.

"Her friends who obviously knew a different side of her."

"She did have a different side." Darcy finished off the delectable shrimp.

"Remember how she used to scare me?"

Before she could respond, a staff member appeared at their side with a basket filled with deep red rose petals. Darcy noticed everyone had moved to the outside deck and all held handfuls of the same colored petals. The massive engines stopped, bringing the yacht to an almost standstill, which must have been the signal for Timothy, Lucas, and Clayton to descend to the lower level.

A piano rendition of "Unchained Melody" began to play and the group moved to the right side of the yacht. Darcy reached the rail just in time to see Timothy lower what looked to be a pillow-like box into the water, followed by rose petals he and his two sons cast out. The yacht slowly circled Ms. Viola's floating remains, and the group above cascaded the water with their own rose petals.

Darcy had never witnessed such a serene and pleasant service for someone who had died. The tears she shed that day seemed to be soothed by the gentle rhythm of the yacht, the surrounding water, and the warmth of the sun on her face.

I won't be far, so if you need me, just holler.... She heard Ms. Viola's words as clearly as if the old woman stood beside her, which brought a bitter-sweet smile to her lips.

Edging closer to Lucas once he had returned to the upper level, she asked, "What are you going to do with Michael's dog tags?"

He glanced around then leaned in. "We got them inside the pillow." He held a finger to his lips. "Not supposed to dispose anything that isn't biodegradable, but we couldn't help it. That's where they needed to be."

She nodded. "I couldn't agree more."

"Hey, would you mind being the temporary liaison between me and the tenants until the estate is settled? I told Dad I'd ask you."

"I…uh, sure." Darcy pushed her Gucci shades up on her forehead. "But…I mean…what about the owners? I just assumed they'd be taking over now."

Confusion clearly masked Lucas's face. "What owners? Aunt V is the only owner I know of. Did you think there were others?"

"She's F.O.A.M.?"

Are you shitting me?

"Fountain Oaks Apartment Manager."

"But…she…." Rational words no longer formed in Darcy's head.

"Seriously. You didn't know?"

Darcy could only shake her head thinking about the old woman's wardrobe of overalls and assorted tennis shoes. Her obvious confusion bordering on disbelief brought a laugh from Lucas.

"Sorry." He attempted to regain his composure. "But, that's just like her, isn't it?"

Terry Lee

Chapter 18

April rolled into May and Darcy collected rent from all the tenants, smiling at the acronym, F.O.A.M, in the "pay to the order of" line on the checks. No wonder Ms. Viola had tossed her complaint letter aside. Miranda's stomach continued to grow, as did her apprehension about the birth. Darcy's thoughts aligned more with the what-happens-when- the-baby-comes-home part. Ms. Viola's words replayed often in her head: "She does know you can't keep it in the attic and only bring it out once a year to decorate, doesn't she?"

At her last OB appointment, Miranda had the glucose screening, which luckily showed no signs of gestational diabetes. Several symptoms popped up that were customary for any woman closing in on her due date: constant oversensitivity, lower-back pain, being easily distracted, and an overall sense of restlessness.

"Do you want to go over to the couch with me?" Miranda asked her swelling belly after she and Darcy had assembled the baby bed in the nursery.

"Are you tired?" Darcy asked. "Your ankles look a little swollen. Here, put them up." She helped Miranda prop her feet on the coffee table. "Is that better?"

"I'm a planet," Miranda said just as her phone buzzed. She looked at the caller ID and tossed the phone aside.

"Is that your mom?" Darcy asked. "She's the only one besides Captain Kirk you don't talk to."

"It's a guy."

"Really." Darcy scratched her head. "I don't know how I feel about you dating in your condition."

"I'm wearing a fat suit I can't take off. I'm scary looking…thing-from-the-swamp scary." Miranda worked to rearrange her position on the couch. "I'm not dating. I guess he didn't get the bootie block."

Darcy's eyebrows did a wonder-what-that's-like dance. "You want anything to drink?"

"I'll have a double vodka martini, hold the olive."

Hilarious, isn't she?

"Ginger ale?"

"I'm about done with ginger ale. What else do I have in there?"

"Water." Darcy brought two Ozarkas from the kitchen and an opened bottle of white wine. "What's this?"

"You weren't supposed to see that."

"Obviously. Have you been drinking?" The hair on the back of Darcy's neck prickled thinking of her never ending attempts to keep Miranda healthy.

"I bought it a couple of weeks ago and had an itty bitty glass." Miranda tried to cross her legs but failed. "But it didn't taste right and gave me heartburn that radiated to my knees."

"Good." She put the bottle of wine next to her keys and purse to take up to her apartment.

"Hey, look at this!" Miranda had pulled her top up to expose her belly and pointed to her convex navel. "I've got a snooze button."

Seriously?

"Stop that." Darcy plopped onto the couch next to Miranda and turned to the notes icon on her phone. "I've made a list of things we need to talk about."

"Okay Boop, but first I need to ask you a little favor." Miranda's once svelte frame spread across the couch like a beached baby whale.

"What?"

"I'm going to need for you to raise this baby." She turned toward Darcy, her eyes rounded and watery. "I have no motherly instincts; isn't that obvious by now?"

"We've been through this before." Darcy took a slug of water. "Remember, all new moms feel this way. It's perfectly normal."

"And you believe that?"

"Yes."

"Swear?"

Darcy put an arm around her best friend. "I've never known you to be in a situation you haven't been able to handle. You're going to be a great mom. And besides, we'll figure this out together."

"Aw, man." Miranda's water-works flared up again.

Handing her a Kleenex, Darcy turned back to her list. "Okay. The shower is next weekend. And I think it's time we talk about a birthing plan."

"I say when it's time for the jellybean to pop out we head to the hospital." Miranda scratched her belly. "Oh, and I want all the drugs they have."

"Spoken like a real trooper." Darcy rubbed her chin. "So, when you go into labor, wherever you are, you call me, right?"

"Yeah, I pretty much had that one figured out."

"We'll call the doctor and…what about Cheryl?"

"What about her?"

"Do you want her there? You know, when the baby is born?"

Miranda's eyes dropped to the swell of her stomach. She shook her head.

"O-kay." Darcy tapped in *no* next to Cheryl's name on the list.

"Birthing classes start the first of June. We visit the hospital, nursery, learn what to expect, that sort of thing." She turned to find Miranda staring at her. "What?"

"I don't think you realize how good you've had it."

"What do you mean?"

"Like going to your house for Christmas." Miranda's eyes misted. "I've never experienced anything like that. You know, a real family."

Darcy had recently re-evaluated, as Ms. Viola had said, feelings about her family and her life in general. She'd spent more time than anyone should finding fault with…everything.

Do ya think?

She didn't have the right car or an upscale apartment. She needed designer shoes, expensive clothes. Her paycheck was never adequate. She wanted Miranda's looks, Becca's IQ and credit score, and Lisa's stability. In her own family, she'd been jealous of Alex for his looks and his smarts, Izzy absolutely drove her nuts most of the time, and Andie…well, the only envy she had toward her little sister revolved around her living rent-free and being irresponsible.

She'd always thought of her family as dysfunctional, and had only recently realized dysfunctional had become the new norm.

And then, Ms. Viola. And Lawrence. And Fletcher. And even Miranda sitting beside her, who Darcy had thought had the perfect life.

"Yeah, I guess I have been—"

"A whiny bitch?"

Finishing her water, she nodded and let go of a Miranda belch.

"Good one."

Darcy stood and pulled on Miranda's arm. "Let's go do something fun."

"I don't wanna. I can't drink. I can't dance…I can barely walk."

"Oh please. You're almost thirty-one weeks, not fifty. It's not too hot…let's go for a walk through the neighborhood; it'll do you good."

"And then?"

"I don't know, I'll think of something."

***

The following weekend Darcy's apartment was transformed into a Cinderella-pink baby land for the shower. Several of Miranda's work friends showed up, as well as a handful of female friends from Midtown, her now old neighborhood. Cheryl had been on the invite list at Darcy's urging, but as Miranda predicted…no RSVP and no Mama Cheryl. Miranda had insisted Nina and Izzy be invited, saying they were family to her now.

Darcy agreed but had to remind Izzy about being on good behavior.

"I don't know what you're talking about," Izzy had said. "No one but you thinks I don't know how to mind my manners."

Is she for real?

"I know you have manners," Darcy had started. "I just want you to use them. The good ones."

Even over the phone she had felt Izzy cross her arms in a huff. "Have you had a date lately?"

"See? That's what I mean."

"What?"

"You know that's a sore subject with me, but you just can't help twisting the knife." She had briefly filled her mom and Izzy in on the fact she and Sam were no longer dating, which obviously had been a mistake by the long grandmother- interrogation that followed.

"I was just asking," Izzy said. "You know, Marge told me about those dating websites where they can match you up with someone. Maybe you and I could both sign up and get a discount."

"Not for me, Izzy. But I think you should do that." Darcy knew good and well Izzy considered computers to be a nuisance and should be destroyed…right up there with mosquitos.

***

Miranda received the bedding set she had registered for from Nina and Izzy. Darcy, Lisa, and Becca had gone in together on the extensive (and expensive) travel system. The little pink jellybean raked in a ton of onesies, bibs, receiving blankets, a Diaper Genie, and a bouncy seat. Miranda's company purchased a Pack 'n Play and had it delivered in time for the shower.

"Have you thought of names?" Lisa asked.

The question caught Darcy's attention. She'd come up with a mile-long list of popular girl names, none which seemed to interest Miranda.

"Well…." Miranda rubbed a hand over her basketball-size belly. "I think I'll name her Sadie."

Not bad…was Sadie on your list?

"I like that," Darcy said, more than surprised Miranda had given thought to the topic.

"Yeah, I read somewhere Sadie means princess." She shot Darcy a sly grin. "Jelly Bean Princess?"

A lot had changed, but then again, some things stayed the same…like Miranda and nicknames.

Two gifts remained unopened. Darcy handed Miranda a wrapped box. "This is from the tenants. They wanted to get you something. Even Sister Alice chipped in."

"You mean she's for real?" Miranda's eyes rounded. "I thought she was just an aberration."

Darcy pulled back, suddenly reminded of all the Scrabble games when she and Lawrence had allotted Miranda full thesaurus time. "Aberration? Where did you learn that word?"

The Catwoman sleazy smile reappeared briefly. "And you thought I couldn't read." She opened the box to find a baby monitor. "Oh, wow. Gee, I can't believe it. Now, how thoughtful is that?"

"There's another one." She handed over the decorated bag containing Ms. Viola's gift.

"Aw, man. This is too much." Miranda's water-faucet emotions immediately switched to full-blast. "I can't believe everyone is being so nice to me...even Ms. Viola."

Tears also blurred Darcy's vision. At least ten times a day her thoughts turned to the crusty old woman who had wormed a path into her heart. She and Miranda exchanged a boo-hoo hug, which brought a round of tearful "awwww's" from the group. A knock on the door broke apart their soppy reunion. They locked eyes. Cheryl? Darcy peered through the peephole, and with a puzzled brow shook her head at Miranda and slipped out the door.

"I'm sorry to bother you." Lucas held an envelope in his hand. "I didn't know you were having a party."

"It's just...um...a baby shower."

Why is he here?

"Is something wrong?"

"No, no...not at all." Lucas shifted his weight. "I just wanted...you know what? I'll come back another time."

"No wait...what is it?"

He ran a hand through his hair. "Aunt V's will has been probated. The hearing was yesterday."

"O-kay...."

"There's more formal documentation, but this was included in her will." He handed over the envelope.

Her fingers suddenly felt like all thumbs, and shaking ones at that. She opened the envelope and read Ms. Viola's decrepit scrawl.

> *I want Fletcher to have Ike. They will keep
> each other company. And besides what I've
> set aside for Timothy and the boys, I want
> Darcy Daniels to have it all, to include my
> black skillet and flat screen TV.*

She raised her eyes to Lucas. "What's 'all'?"

A smile edged up on Lucas's mouth. "You now own Fountain Oaks, and quite a bit more."

Darcy fell back against the door, her mouth locked in an O shape. Lucas grabbed her shoulders to make sure she didn't end up on the floor.

"My aunt was quite wealthy. From what she got from Uncle Robert and the VA after Michael's death, plus her share of her mother's inheritance…well, let's just say she invested wisely." He stepped back once Darcy found her footing. "Actually, she owned several other apartment complexes, but sold all but this one. Which means…you are now quite a wealthy lady."

She never knew how long she stood in the hallway. Obviously, long enough for Nina to open the door and usher her back into the apartment.

***

Shortly after the baby shower Miranda suggested they return the bedding set she and Darcy had picked out.

"Why?" Darcy asked, walking the isles of Babies "R" Us.

"I dunno. Doesn't seem to fit anymore."

"So, which one do you want?"

Miranda stopped and pointed. "That one."

She immediately felt the sting of tears. "Really?"

"Yeah. It seems right. Kinda makes up for calling her the Wicked Witch of the West, don'tcha think?"

Darcy swiped the dampness from her face and placed the new butterfly-themed bedding set in the cart. "I think she'd like that."

"And these too." Miranda held up a package of large matching butterfly wall decals.

***

She now had more money than she'd ever dreamed possible, which ran contrary to her selling most of her designer shoes on Craigslist. She kept a few of her favorites, but ironically, fashion and labels rarely interested her anymore. With the settlement behind her, she moved into Ms. Viola's downstairs managerial apartment, and as her first executive order of business had a gazebo installed in the courtyard. After hounding the Arboretum employees at Memorial Park for information on the best plants to attract butterflies, she had Fletcher plant multiple variations of milkweed around the gazebo.

Two main events were penciled in on Darcy's calendar for June: birthing classes and Alex and Anna's wedding. She and Miranda attended several scheduled sessions to visit the nursery, discuss types of anesthesia and possible complications—including a C-section delivery—and to participate in a hands-on class on how to bathe and diaper a baby.

"What if I don't like any of those choices for anesthesia?" Miranda asked on their way back to Fountain Oaks. "I mean, can't they just put me to sleep and let me know when it's over?"

"No," Darcy had almost screamed, which caused Miranda to jump. "You're the mother. You signed up for this, remember?"

Geez, chill out. I'm the voice of reason and I'm ordering you to calm down!

The closer the delivery date, the more reticent Miranda became, which short-circuited Darcy's nerves. For several days they didn't even speak, which Darcy rectified, realizing they weren't in fourth grade and couldn't avoid each other by riding their bikes home in different directions.

On the wedding end, preparations were in full swing, and she attended several bridal showers for her soon-to-be sister-in-law. She'd officially dropped the allergic-to-seafood part when referring to Anna after making the declaration to work on not being a whiny bitch. She'd even been pleasantly surprised at Anna's choice for the bridesmaid's dresses. At least the A-line knee-length halter dress could be worn again. And if she hadn't screwed things up so royally with Sam she would have had a date for the event. She considered her small business card list of other possible dates, but decided to fly solo.

Miranda, although still three weeks away from her due date, had not been feeling well and had been put on bed rest. Dr. Holt said Miranda had lost some amniotic fluid, and wanted to see her in a week to assess the situation. Darcy checked on Miranda before leaving for the church and found the soon to be mom flipping through magazines and watching taped recordings of *The Biggest Loser*.

Emotions got the best of Darcy when she walked down the aisle toward the front of the church where her handsome and very happy brother stood. Her eyes glistened when she stood in line with the other attendants and watched Anna make her way to the altar. Darcy glanced out at the crowd. Nina looked a mess, blotting her eyes constantly. Izzy had positioned herself on the edge of her seat so as not to miss any gossip-worthy activities. Luckily Andie, although looking totally bored, wasn't chomping on a wad of gum. Her dad, not looking much more attentive than Andie, put his arm around his sobbing wife. Darcy had to wonder if she'd ever be standing at an altar. A golf-ball lump formed in her throat.

Don't even think about waterworks…your mascara isn't waterproof.

After an excruciating hour of picture taking, the wedding party was transported to the Marriott Westchase Hotel for the reception, where Darcy received her first glass of well-deserved wine. Finding her place card, she moved to the groom's family table and found Izzy drinking a martini.

"Is that vodka?" Darcy asked.

"Tanqueray; what's it to you?"

"No need to get testy." Darcy pulled her phone out of her beaded purse to switch it off silence. "I was just…holy shit!" She jumped to her feet.

"For heaven's sake." Izzy took another sip of her martini. "Pipe down…I don't want your mother to see what I'm drinking."

"I've…gotta…oh shit. I don't have my car here."

"What's blown your dress up?"

"Something's wrong." She glanced at the numerous missed calls from Miranda, and the last one showing Lawrence had called and left a voicemail.

"I've gotta go Izzy. I'll explain later." Darcy paused long enough in the lobby to listen to Lawrence's message before she jumped into one of the waiting cabs outside the hotel.

"Memorial City Hospital."

She sat in the back of the cab and tried unsuccessfully to calm the banging of her heart around her rib cage.

What could be wrong? She was fine when you left her this afternoon.

Luckily the trip to the hospital took less than ten minutes. Tossing more than enough money toward the driver, she stopped only long enough for the elevator to reach the third floor and for her to find the labor room she needed.

"What happened?" she nearly screamed, bursting through the door.

"It's the jellybean, Boop. She's not happy." Miranda's long dark hair had been wadded up and clipped away from her face, which was marked with pain and fear.

"Thank God you're here." Lawrence held a cup and plastic spoon, a bead of sweat lining his upper lip. "The doctor is on her way and I must say these ice chips aren't helping one bit."

Dr. Holt entered the room with two nurses. "Darcy, you two wait outside while I see what's going on."

Out in the hallway Lawrence chewed the cuticle away from his finger. "Why is it you're the one they call, but I'm the one who gets them to the hospital?"

Darcy batted his hand down. "What happened?"

"She called saying her back was killing her and she had a strange feeling...well, in her female area." He removed a handkerchief from his back pocket and wiped his forehead. "I'm ill prepared for this, Darcy. And I certainly didn't want to have to...you know...so I brought her here."

"You did the right thing." For the first time she realized she stood in the hallway of Memorial City Hospital wearing a cocktail dress.

It's just going to have to do. Deal with it.

Dr. Holt stepped into the hallway. "She's lost more amniotic fluid and the baby is in distress. We've got to get her to the OR." The doctor paused long enough to notice Darcy's attire. "Do you have any other clothes?"

"Ah...no." Darcy smoothed down the skirt part of her A-line cocktail dress. "Just came from a wedding."

"It'll have to do."

Didn't I just say that?

Dr. Holt headed down the hall. "The nurse will show you where to change into your scrubs."

"You're not...." Lawrence's hand flew to his mouth. "Are you? You're going to be in there?"

Not exactly how Darcy had planned this whole scenario. She'd figured her role would be more along the lines of coaching with a "push, breath," or maybe a "you can do it"...not actually in the operating room for an emergency C-section.

No time to be a wimp; remember you're not in fourth grade anymore.

"Yeah, I guess I am." She threw her arms around Lawrence. "Wait for me."

"That I can do."

The epidural eased Miranda's physical pain, although the death grip on Darcy's hand did little to hide her fear. A framed curtain protected Darcy and the top half of Miranda from seeing what was taking place on the other side. Darcy made sure her head stayed tucked way down on the gurney next to Miranda. Only when Dr. Holt announced she was making the incision did Darcy feel blackness close in around her. Thankfully, a nurse added cool towels to Miranda's forehead and the back of Darcy's neck. Within minutes the ear-piercing squeal from the jellybean taking her first breath filled the sterilized room, causing both women to burst into tears.

A nurse handed Darcy a handful of Kleenex to wipe their faces just as another nurse placed a swaddled baby girl Sadie next to Miranda.

"Oh...she's so...tiny," Miranda said. "Does she have everything? You know...toes and fingers?"

"She's perfect," the nurse said before taking the minutes-old newborn away.

"Where's she taking her?"

Darcy hugged Miranda. "They're going to clean her up a little, make sure she's okay and get her weight."

See, aren't you glad you did all that reading prep?

"Okay, but be careful," Miranda yelled to the nurse. "She's really small." Her eyes swept across Darcy's face. "I have a daughter."

She would never have believed the transformation if she hadn't witnessed it herself. From the moment Miranda spoke those four powerful words, *I have a daughter*, Darcy no longer held on to any doubts about her best friend stepping into the role of...mother.

"She's beautiful." Such a simple statement, but nothing came close to expressing the magnitude of witnessing the birth of a real human being. On her scrubs the nurse wrote with a Sharpie "It's a girl!-6 lbs. 9 ozs.-19 inches" before escorting Darcy and the little bundle to the labor and delivery waiting room while another nurse wheeled Miranda to recovery.

Lawrence, slumped in one of the stiff waiting room chairs and once again chewing away on his cuticles, stared blankly at an Astros game on the television.

"Hey you. Come look."

His eyes broke away from the hypnotic motion on the screen and squinted for a long moment before realizing he had been summoned. He jumped to his feet. "Oh my God. I didn't recognize you."

"I have someone for you to meet." Darcy pushed the blanket from the infant's face for Lawrence's first glimpse.

"She's…it's…." He pulled the handkerchief once again from his pocket, only this time to wipe his eyes. "She's…so…perfect."

Darcy couldn't have said it better.

"What's her name?"

"Sadie Viola."

***

The 4th of July, Ms. Viola's birthday, fell on a Wednesday, which felt odd having a holiday in the middle of the week. Darcy had planned a small get-together, or soiree to coin Lawrence's term, for the tenants later that afternoon in the courtyard. She sat across from Miranda and Sadie Viola in the gazebo. A colorful yellow and orange butterfly flitted around the inside of the gazebo before landing next to Darcy.

"Do you think that's…Ms. Viola?" Miranda's eyes softened, watching the butterfly exercise its wings.

Darcy shook her head and pointed to one of the milkweed plants. "I'm betting more on that wasp over there." How her life had changed….

"She is pretty, isn't she?" Miranda rearranged the swaddled baby on her lap. "I mean, I see newborn babies all the time and I think, ugh. But seriously, she's pretty, right?"

The child is only ten days old, and how many times have we had this conversation?

"Yes, Mommy, she's pretty. In fact, she's beautiful." Darcy folded her arms, taking in the sight once again of Miranda in the mother role. "You feeling okay?"

"Yeah, except for these things." Miranda tugged on one of her bra straps, fighting to maintain the weight of her inflatable boobs.

262

"And I thought the Supremes were out of line. These straps give out and we're gonna have to announce a flood warning."

"So, you're saying Sadie isn't going to go hungry?"

"Not in this lifetime."

"Have you heard any more from Mama Cheryl?"

"Nah, not after the hospital incident. Just as well."

Cheryl had made a grand appearance at the hospital after Sadie's birth in skin-tight capris, a blouse exposing more than enough cleavage to cause attention, and orange cross-strapped cork platform sandals. A bouquet of flowers and an oversized stuffed teddy bear, obviously purchased at the gift shop downstairs, hung off one arm.

"Oh, isn't it cute." Cheryl deposited the purchases on the window sill and stood beside the hospital bed, arms tightly folded across her chest.

"It's a she. Do you want to hold her?" Miranda asked.

Cheryl immediately took a step back. "Oh, I can't stay. I've got…someone waiting for me downstairs."

"Of course you do." Miranda's eyes glistened, her hand gently rubbing Sadie's head.

Darcy bit her lip, totally floored by Cheryl's lack of affection toward Miranda or her first grandchild.

"I just wanted to come by and say hey."

"Hey." Miranda's voice was flat.

Cheryl eased backward toward the door. "Oh, and excuse my manners. Hi, Darcy. How in the hell are ya?"

"Mom." Miranda blotted her eyes with a Kleenex.

Cheryl came to a halt before stepping out of the room. "Yeah?"

"I just want to say…." A tear escaped down Miranda's cheek. She swiped at it with a bare hand. "I want you to know…you did the best you could. I know you tried, in your own way."

A moment of stone-cold fear, or possibly shame, shot over Cheryl's face before her lips pulled tight in a straight line across her mouth. She nodded and left the room.

Darcy crawled up on the hospital bed and lay next to Miranda and Sadie Viola for the next hour while Miranda cried long overdue tears.

***

"So…you planning any fireworks for today?" Miranda asked.

"I, uh…." Darcy shrugged. "Hadn't really thought about it. Why?"

Miranda nodded to someone crossing the courtyard toward the gazebo.

Darcy leaned her head around the lattice and shaded her eyes from the bright sun. Her heart pounded somewhere up around her throat.

Miranda scooted out of the gazebo. "I think…uh…Sadie and I will go…maybe read her little butterfly book."

Darcy pulled herself back in and tried to calm the racing of blood through her veins.

"You called?" Sam slid into Miranda's spot in the gazebo. He had lost a little weight since the last time she'd seen him, but still had the same gentle smile.

She took a deep breath and then blew out. "I called."

Epilogue

One Year Later

Darcy had taken a leave of absence from selling eyewear, which pissed off Vanessa Hargrove, boss extraordinaire from hell, but had given Darcy the needed time to research more updated options for Fountain Oaks. High efficiency appliances replaced the antiquated energy suckers, and she had solar windows installed in all the apartments. The A/C units were upgraded as well as the entire ventilation system, which eliminated mold issues. Formica countertops had been switched out for marble, and hardwood floors took the place of the old musty carpeting. She'd even had a rainwater collection system installed to harvest water for the landscaping. And beside the carport, recycle bins for plastic, aluminum, and paper had been added next to the dumpster. Tired of waiting for season three of *Downton Abby*, which wouldn't air until January, 2013, she'd started a quarterly newsletter for the tenants, with articles and postings on different species of butterflies, news from her visits to the VA Hospital, and opportunities for future community involvement.

A few additional items now accompanied the gazebo in the courtyard. The first had been a pond with a power efficient fountain. Her rationale? Fountain Oaks needed a fountain.

Duh.

And second, she had purchased several trees. She realized it would take years before they could provide any significant shade, but she didn't care. So many trees in the area had recently been lost with the drought, new trees needed to be planted. The cycle of life, Ms. Viola would say.

Fletcher remained at Fountain Oaks and now held the title of head grounds keeper-maintenance man. Two part-time employees worked under him to maintain the property. He still wore camouflage attire and carried a water hose over his shoulder, but his position as grounds keeper seemed to have moved him out of his comfort zone of speaking to the ground and avoiding eye contact. Stash often accompanied him and Ike around the property.

Mr. Will's dementia progressed dramatically after Ms. Viola's death, and Darcy had assisted his daughters in finding a wonderful specialized facility. She visited him often. His apartment had been leased to a young newly married couple, each working their way up the corporate ladder.

After "divorcing" his parents, Lawrence had found new strength in becoming his own person. For the last six months he'd been seeing more and more of Scott and seemed genuinely happy. She suspected they would move in together before long, which meant she'd have another apartment to fill.

Sister Mary Alice, the Nun Hun, as Miranda had tagged her, continued to be an anomaly. Darcy received a rental check in her mail slot the first of every month, but the woman was rarely seen.

Miranda and Sadie Viola had settled into something of a normal existence. And the shocker? Miranda and Lucas, Ms. Viola's nephew, had started dating.

Did you see that one coming? I didn't....

Darcy and Sam married in a simple yet elegant ceremony at the gazebo in the courtyard. The attendees had been few: the Fountain Oaks tenants, family, and close friends, with the exception of Izzy's beauty shop cohorts. The couple purchased a ranch house in Afton Oaks, the neighborhood behind the apartment complex.

Izzy and Darcy's dad continued to exchange barbs, with referee Nina in attendance. With Izzy no longer Darcy's personal dating headhunter, she had more time for her new obsession. She'd become a reality show junkie. While thumbing her nose at *Honey Boo Boo* or anything with the name Jersey or Kardashian, *Celebrity Rehab* and *Mob Wives* came in first and second on her own rating score card. Alex and Anna were to become first time parents within the next six months, while her sister, Andie, still lived at home and continued her career at Houston Community College.

Darcy decided to maintain the annual community volunteer event at the GRB on Thanksgiving in honor of Ms. Viola. She also continued to hold annual soirees in the courtyard for the tenants. She and Lawrence had been appointed godparents, and the swear jar contents had been converted to a college savings account for Sadie Viola.

The letter jacket and its baggage had found a new home shortly after Ms. Viola's service…the dumpster. Darcy had finally rid herself of letter jacket guy, and realized, after all this time, that she, too, could dish out nicknames.

Terry Lee

About the Author

As a native Houstonian, a rarity these days, I hold two licensures in the state of Texas: one in chemical dependency counseling, the other in massage therapy. In 2004, I trained to be a volunteer for Houston Hospice, a life-changing training session I believe would benefit all. Hospice, contrary to popular belief, is not about dying. Hospice is about helping you *live* until you die.

Although writing has been a part of my genetic lineage, the writing bug didn't officially bite until 2007. From that point on, my true life passion sprouted and came into full bloom. I'm an observer by nature…ask any close friend or family member. I've studied lines and movie dialogues for years, which can often become annoying to said above friends and family (I can see them nodding in agreement).

I'm married to a wonderful man and have grandchildren I adore. As a hobby, I crochet baby/security blankets (quite obsessively) for the Linus Project. Crocheting keeps my hands busy at night while I study movies and sit-coms for story ideas. I have always said I will learn to knit when I grow up. So far, that hasn't happened.

Please visit me at my blog: terryleeauthor.blogspot.com or my website www.terry-lee.net. Welcome to my world!

www.ingramcontent.com/pod-product-compliance
Lightning Source LLC
Chambersburg PA
CBHW070904180626
46817CB00003B/909